Mistress

of

Silverthorn

ALSO BY JOANNA CHALLIS

Eye of the Serpent

The Secret of the Phoenix

The Pendragon Legacy

Murder on the Cliffs

Peril at Somner House

Villa of Death

MISTRESS OF SILVERTHORN. Copyright © 2012 by Joanna Challis. All rights reserved. Printed in the United States of America. CreateSpace, an Amazon Company.

ISBN 978 1480 189676

First Edition: October 2012

*M*istress

of

Silverthorn

A MYSTERY OF GOTHIC SUSPENSE

JOANNA CHALLIS

PROLOGUE

Spanish Coast, August 7, 1884

It is amazing to think one person's behavior can dramatically alter your life.

I have never looked back until now, many years later, and shudder at the thought of my life taking any other direction than the one it has.

There comes a time, I believe, when these sentiments arise—whether we wish it or not. I prefer to think of it as an exploration—a chance to lay Madeline's ghost to rest, whom, even I am reluctant to admit, occasionally still haunts me.

Perhaps by setting it all down, from the very beginning, I will be able to let go of the past and in doing so, rise like a phoenix from the restless ashes of my memory.

CHAPTER ONE

On the eve of my ninth birthday, Madeline came to live with us.

I remember the day clearly.

My Uncle, the good Rector Morgan, struggled to conceal his horror when a letter arrived two weeks ago. He never expected another orphan child would be placed into his care.

I felt pity for her, my poor cousin, Madeline, who'd recently lost both her parents in a tragic sea journey. I was in a similar situation—a penniless orphan, fortunate to have my Uncle, the good Rector Morgan, accept me into his home at the Rectory.

I will never forget the day I first met Uncle Clive and Aunt Mary. I was only five, but some things from childhood are never forgotten. I was very frightened when I saw a great, dark shadow looming over me from the doorway.

Yes, the illustrious Rector Morgan, a large-girthed man with a permanently grim face. I often watched him practicing his sermons and the power evident in his physical voice caused me to liken him to God himself, for Uncle Clive was indeed a god in those early years.

For Madeline, things would be different. Things would always be different for Madeline.

I never knew I had a cousin until last week, when Aunt Mary took me into her confidence, sitting me down in the small Drawing Room devoid of color. She always summoned me to the Drawing Room when something important was to be discussed. Uncle Clive had no time for children and the poor kitten, me, who'd been thrown at his door, rather annoyed him. I tried to keep out of his sight as often as possible.

Aunt Mary, unquestionably kind towards all, appeared somewhat of an angel compared to her autocratic husband. Although in awe of him, she carried out her duties in love and compliance. I never once heard her complain.

Small and fine-boned, she sat down, her delicate hand resting on the lace at her neck. "'Dear Mary,'" she read out the letter in her soft, angelic voice. "'I'm afraid I have tragic news to impart. Our dear brother, Charles, and his wife, Miriam, never reached their destination. The office has confirmed their ship went down off the coast of Africa. As you know, they left behind their only daughter, Madeline, in their missionary pursuits. Dear Mary, Lord Vere refuses to accept the child into our house, however, will set up the necessary funds if you agree to do so. I am sure the good Rector will find this arrangement agreeable...yours etc, B.'"

I knew who 'B' was. One could never forget a prominent character, particularly in this household. 'B' or Beatrice was Aunt Mary's younger sister and having secured Lord Vere as her husband, held the title of Lady Vere. I'd never seen the elusive Lady Beatrice, but I knew Aunt Mary often wrote letters to her.

"So I have a cousin..." I murmured.

"Yes, my dear, you do," Aunt Mary smiled. "I have spoken with your Uncle and he has agreed. Madeline will arrive the day after tomorrow."

"How old is she?" I asked, for that was more important to me than any other details at the time.

Aunt Mary glanced at me sympathetically. "Madeline is fifteen years of age. She will share your room, Laura. I want you to make it ready for her...ask Ruby to help you. Jake will move in the spare bed later today."

I nodded and although was very excited about my new cousin's arrival, did not show it. One did not display emotions in this household.

Two days later, Madeline arrived.

I will never forget my first sight of her. She stood outside with Uncle Clive and Aunt Mary. The relative who brought Madeline from London promptly departed with the hired coach, leaving the girl clutching an old, worn carpetbag. The sun came out at that moment and touched the lights in her tawny hair.

I gasped, for she was the most beautiful thing I had ever seen. I peeked through the lace curtains in the Drawing Room, watching her smile, a lovely smile, which made me warm to her instantly. I could not see what color her eyes were but it didn't matter. I decided I liked her immediately and would not mind sharing my room with her.

Uncle Clive caught me staring and beckoned me in his stoical manner. I crept out in an obedient, silent manner as Uncle Clive insisted I learn. 'Women must learn in silence with all submission...' was one of his favorite sayings and I knew better than to encourage his disfavor.

"Laura," he introduced with all pomp and severity, "this is your cousin, Madeline."

I could not help feeling a little jealousy over the beauty of this newcomer, who brought such a smile to Aunt Mary's face. I knew I was plain in comparison, although, Ruby, our maid, assured me I would be handsome one day. I found it difficult to believe, examining Madeline's porcelain skin, emerald green eyes and striking tawny hair. But as soon as she smiled and held out her hands, I accepted her.

I always wanted a sister.

Madeline soon found Rectory life tedious.

Usually, one did not laugh over these dreary matters but Madeline ignored the rules with a reckless abandonment. She continued to act according to her instincts and wouldn't allow anyone to tell her different.

The leniency shown to her by Uncle Clive and Aunt Mary constantly irritated me. I couldn't believe it. How could they ignore Madeline's willful disobedience? Whenever I committed a social sin in the past, Uncle Clive never forgot it. Madeline, however, possessed the uncanny ability to charm the good Rector Morgan. She charmed everybody, including me.

"Poor little Laura!" she would laugh, "you always get in trouble, don't you? I must teach you to be more careful." Her green eyes sparkled mischievously and I could never quite tell what she was thinking.

"But how do you get away it?"

She shrugged, tossing her glorious tawny hair in the mirror. She examined her face and smiled.

She knew she was beautiful. Even at fifteen, I heard the women at church exclaim over her figure and her beauty. Aunt Mary beamed and now presented Madeline before she presented me. In fact, nobody seemed to take any notice of me since Madeline had arrived.

Except Ruby.

Ruby, our one and only housemaid. The Rectory could only afford to engage three servants. Our household consisted of Ruby, the housemaid, Jake—the butler, gardener, coachman and whatever else needed to be done and lastly, our cook, Jeanette.

Ruby always took an interest in me when nobody else did. She was also the only one who seemed impervious to Madeline's charm. "Beauty is a sin..." she used to say to me. "What counts is what's inside, Miss Laura."

I wish I had taken more notice of what Ruby told me, instead of moaning over my hurt pride.

"She's an old crow, that Ruby," Madeline said to me one night. "But she's your *friend,* isn't she, Laura?" She laughed and turned back to the mirror to examine her face.

I suppose it was her beauty which attracted people for even I was caught up in it, failing to see her true personality. If Madeline looked like me, I was sure I would have despised her. But one failed to note the inside flaws when one possessed such beauty on the outside. I didn't know the real Madeline then. I only came to understand Madeline many years later.

She was cruel to me at times, in those first few days. I didn't take much notice of it, happy to bathe in the glory of her shadow. I think she enjoyed having me in the background—someone to boss, someone to talk to, someone to share secrets. She often took me into her confidence, which is why I probably grew to like her.

Aunt Mary was at her wits end. Uncle Clive expected her, in his pompous manner, to preside over our education. The Rectory could not afford to engage the services of a governess.

Poor Aunt Mary! She had so many important duties to perform and I knew she didn't have the time or the stamina to tutor two lively girls.

Too frightened to ask assistance from her husband, Aunt Mary took matters into her own hands.

It was a bold effort on her part and I admired her. I knew what she decided to do and, as Madeline was still new to the Rectory, she pestered me to confess the secret. I liked having a hold over her. I knew so much more than she did, about life at the Rectory, about everyone who lived in this little town.

"Where is she going?" Madeline demanded, as we collected flowers outside.

I shrugged. "You'll find out soon enough. Patience is a virtue, remember."

Madeline expressed surprise at my new independence. Her green eyes danced intuitively.

To her chagrin, I kept silent until the end of the day. We were awaiting Aunt Mary's return when I decided to relieve her. "She has gone to the Big House to ask if we can use their governess."

"The Big House!" Madeline cried.

I sighed. This new information would no doubt lead into her favorite subject: the aristocracy of our small village—the Rohan family who lived in a fourteenth century manor across the lake. Madeline could never know enough about them.

I disliked the Rohan family altogether. Lord Rohan, a middle-aged rogue man showing signs of his debauchery, never came to church; Lady Rohan, the picture of respectability, constantly reminded everybody she was the daughter of an Earl and thus too far above us; Their son and heir, Adam, spent most of his time in London, and, their daughter, Elizabeth, was a pretentious snob.

As we were talking of the Big House, Aunt Mary's coach came into view. Even from a distance, I could see she was unusually excited.

We went out to meet her.

"I have good news," she gushed, stepping down from the coach.

"What happened, Aunt Mary? Do tell us! Come, sit down."

We went into the Drawing Room. I ordered tea while Madeline impatiently waited for the news.

Aunt Mary winked at us. "I cannot believe our good fortune. I have spent the entire day with Lady Rohan, going over details for our Winter Fair in a few weeks time. As you know, I am too busy to be able to tutor you both and explained my situation to Lady Rohan."

"And she has asked us to go to Rohan House," I finished for her.

Aunt Mary and Madeline looked at me in surprise, for I seldom interrupted.

"Yes, you are right, Laura, and I need not stress the privilege of this offer. You must both be on your best behavior. Laura, you will wear your normal day dress," she said, looking over me quickly before turning her attention to Madeline, "...and yes, Madeline, we shall have to have a day dress made up for you too..."

I was about to say that I needed a new dress more than she did, however, something prevailed upon me to be silent. Aunt Mary evidently thought Madeline's appearance more important than mine. I turned away angrily, for I felt Madeline had usurped my place in little more than three weeks.

Aunt Mary left us and Madeline turned to me with a glowing face.

"Oh, Laura, this is going to be wonderful! It's hard enough living at the Rectory at night, lest all day! Come, let us go to our room." She snatched my hand and pulled me into our private sanctuary.

I did not share her confidence. I did not like the inhabitants of Rohan House and if we went there, I would see Elizabeth Rohan every day.

I couldn't imagine a more dreadful prospect.

CHAPTER TWO

One year later, our lives seemed to be dominated by Rohan House and its occupants and our life at the Rectory dimmer in comparison. We talked incessantly about Rohan House and the celestial beings inhabiting the mansion.

Madeline was sixteen, her figure fuller and her beauty growing. I remembered the first day we went to Rohan House and how Lord Rohan found it difficult to stray from her. Of course, I was too young then to realize the importance of his attention.

Miss Elizabeth Rohan resented my presence immediately. She was plain and possessed no desire to be with me, the plain girl from the Rectory, in the schoolroom all day. Interestingly, she didn't seem to mind Madeline's invasion and I caught her ogling my cousin many times, no doubt bewildered by her beauty as we all were.

I should have hated this time in my life save for our governess, Miss Theresa Banks, who made up for the lack of attention I received. I imagined she was in her early twenties at the time. She wore her brown hair in a knot on the top of her head. Her nose was pointed, a little too long, and her skin was unfashionably olive, however, her sharp brown eyes missed nothing.

She must have looked severe but I thought her perfect. She encouraged me from the beginning and although she treated us as equals, I became her favorite pupil. Of course, she could never show it. Her employment with Rohan House remained contingent on pleasing Elizabeth Rohan.

Elizabeth often played upon the fact. "Don't forget, Miss Banks," she would say in her haughty way, "that *we* have employed *you*."

Madeline laughed at Elizabeth and I could safely say that she was the only person who could laugh at Elizabeth Rohan and get away with it.

I learned much from Theresa Banks and I believe I made up for what was lacking in Elizabeth and Madeline. Both showed no desire for learning. Constantly inattentive and fidgety, they enjoyed poking fun at Miss Banks. I ignored them and continued to excel in my studies, often taking extra work home to the Rectory.

"La! I don't know how you can do that!" Madeline sniffed contemptuously when Jake came to collect us. "You're an incorrigible bookworm!"

"Better an incorrigible bookworm than an incorrigible featherhead," I retorted to which Madeline laughed. She often said she enjoyed my sharp tongue.

Madeline quickly became the favorite of our small community. Scores of young men would hound her at church and seek out Rector Morgan, hoping for an introduction. As always, I watched from a darkened corner. I couldn't understand why Madeline enjoyed being the center of attention. I found their small talk insipid and their smiles empty.

I treasured my friendship with Miss Banks.

On Saturdays we would go into the village to buy ice cream and travel up to an old Roman ruin on Rohan land. There we would spend the time reading, imagining faraway places and exotic adventures. I cherished these times. The ruin was the most romantic location and the gentle hills framing it made it an ideal place to dream. We would stay there until the sun set, bathing the blue heather into a sea of purple.

Madeline laughed at our Saturday excursions. "How could you read on your day off when we have to do it all week? La, I can't fathom it."

"No, I don't suppose you can," I said, genuinely amused at the thought of Madeline reading for enjoyment.

Every Saturday she did something different. Elizabeth would invite her to Rohan House for the weekend at times. The Rohans would have visitors from London and I knew Madeline enjoyed the extra time at Rohan House.

I questioned her about it.

"It's the most exciting life, Laura! We're missing out..." she sighed, "oh, what I would give..."

"For what?" I asked.

She looked at me, her arched eyebrows rising in unison. "To be rich, of course. I will be, one day, you know."

"I don't doubt you," I said, not thinking much of the comment. However, I saw Madeline's chances of rising into society as dim as a poor man's candle. They would never take a penniless girl and she had much better hopes of forming a marriage alliance with a respectable gentleman visiting the Rectory.

Madeline scoffed at the idea. She wanted the best or nothing at all. She already possessed an advantage over me, being sponsored by Lady Beatrice.

Lady Beatrice often wrote to her young protégé and Madeline seemed anxious to keep up the correspondence. Her spelling was dreadful and she begged me to help her. "Your hand is beautiful, Laura, and you are so intelligent...I'm sure you could write a dozen letters in one day if it pleased you." She smiled at me and I knew that flattery was her way of getting what she wanted out of me.

So, I helped her. I wrote all the letters to Lady Beatrice, impressing her with my knowledge and perception of the world. Lady Beatrice would never know she was growing fond of me, not Madeline. In fact, Madeline soon tired with Lady Beatrice's letters and neglected to read my responses. I was angry and threatened to tell Lady Beatrice the truth.

I repeated the warning whenever Madeline vexed me. She would listen to me then, for she did not want her allowance to stop. She said she needed the money for gowns to compete with Elizabeth Rohan and her wealthy friends from London.

I could see her obsession becoming a habit and Madeline grew more frustrated as time went on with Rectory life. On Sundays, we would attend church and help Aunt Mary with charity visits in the afternoon. Aunt Mary went to Rohan House every Wednesday to discuss community affairs with Lady Rohan. We never saw her for we were in the schoolroom and I pitied poor Aunt Mary living a life only to please her betters.

Uncle Clive was also good in the art of striving to please his betters. He often went to Rohan House to encourage Lord Rohan to attend church on Sunday and update his lordship with village trivia. Uncle Clive flattered Lord Rohan to such an extent that when I once accidentally overheard, I felt sickened. I hated to see our class kneel to our so-called betters and I knew Miss Banks thought the same as I. We shared many opinions, thoughts, hopes, aspirations and I began to dread the day our schooling would stop and we would have to part. Already, our lives were conditional on pleasing the Rohans.

I could sincerely say I enjoyed helping Aunt Mary with the poor and the needy and this helped me to realize my plight was minimal in comparison. In fact, I felt guilty for having such feelings, witnessing poor struggling families, whose main aim was to bring food to the table. We knocked on the door of one house and when no answer came, Aunt Mary suggested we leave.

I tried the door and it opened. It was a small, shabby hut with a dirt floor. In one corner sat a woman dressed in rags, her hair disheveled and caked with dust. In her arms, she nursed a sickly babe, no more than two months old. She turned her face away in shame when she saw us. I went over to her and took the babe from her arms. She looked up at me in awe, her eyes full of unshed tears.

I learned why later.

The woman's name was Felicity Chalmers and she was, as Lady Rohan termed, 'a loose woman.' I overheard a conversation when Lady Rohan arrived at the Rectory to have an urgent word with Aunt Mary.

It was a Saturday afternoon and as the rain continued, Miss Banks and I decided to postpone our journey to the old ruin. Madeline went to Rohan House and I decided to stay at home and read a book. I loved dark, somber days...it gave one time to ponder on things.

I was innocently on my way to the kitchen for a snack when Lady Rohan landed on the doorstep.

I could sense her anxiety. She snapped at Jake and demanded to be taken to the Rector's wife at once. By her tone, I imagined Lord Rohan on his deathbed. She invaded the Drawing Room where Aunt Mary sat embroidering cushions.

"...I have heard a most disagreeable rumor," she began and I saw Aunt Mary put down her sewing in surprise.

"What is it, Lady Rohan?"

Lady Rohan sat poised for battle. "I heard you visited the hovel of Felicity Chalmers."

Aunt Mary searched her memory. "Hovel? I remember seeing a young woman with a sickly babe in a poor establishment..."

"Yes," Lady Rohan sniffed, "I dismissed her from Rohan House a year ago. As an immoral woman, she deserves no help."

I thought of Felicity. She looked like a helpless kitten to me, afraid to face the world and ask for help. I thought it snobbery on Lady Rohan's part. Surely all the poor were deserving? However, I learned later, there was more to Lady Rohan's interference.

Madeline smiled knowingly when I told her about Felicity and implied she knew the reason behind Lady Rohan's outrage.

"What do you mean?" I asked. "The poor woman has suffered cruelly and needs attention...especially for the poor child..."

"Yes, especially for the poor child," Madeline mimicked me, "that is the reason, you silly goose."

"I don't understand you."

"Oh, really, you're not such an innocent! Whose child do you think it is?"

I raised a brow in surprise. "How should I know? It could be anybody's."

"Least of all the man who owns the county."

"You mean Lord Rohan?"

She nodded. "He has a taste for outside women, you know. Surely you've realized that?" She turned away and looked out the window, a secret smile on her face.

I grew up very quickly in Madeline's company. I was surprised by how much she knew and whenever I questioned her about it, she simply shrugged.

She would never say.

I took delight in my outings to the old ruin with Miss Banks.

Madeline no longer laughed at our adventures and asked me questions about the place. I was astonished. I asked her did she perhaps have a secret appreciation for Roman architecture? She neglected to answer and I went no further.

I suppose I should have realized then. My youth and innocence concealed the obvious signs.

I remember the first day...I returned from shopping with Miss Banks and feeling ill, decided to go to bed.

An hour later, Madeline woke me with her noisy intrusion into our bedchamber. She pulled off her bonnet and tossed her long, fiery hair over her shoulder. Her cheeks were flushed and her green eyes bright with excitement.

"What has happened?" I asked, groaning with my headache.

"I have been to see your ruin today..." she smiled, "it is beautiful. I wish I had discovered it sooner."

"Who accompanied you?"

She turned away and shrugged. "Oh...some friends."

I knew by her vagueness that she would tell me no more.

A week later, she brought home an exquisite bracelet.

She did not show me at first. I was angry, for since she was invited to Rohan House most weekends, it left me to help Aunt Mary with her charity visits. The extra load of work cut into my own personal time.

I didn't think it fair and voiced my concerns to Uncle Clive and Aunt Mary.

"I think Madeline recognizes the privilege of having such esteemed friends and is eager to retain them. Whereas you..." Uncle Clive waved a finger in my direction, "should follow her example instead of running about with your governess and keeping your nose in books. Intelligence is not for women and men rarely enjoy the acquaintance of women sporting knowledge. I advise you, young Laura, to heed my advice."

Aunt Mary nodded in acquiescence. A flicker of rebellion crossed her face but quickly faded away. I guessed she did not think Uncle Clive's advice valuable and I smiled at her for I planned to ignore it anyway. Uncle Clive posed no impression upon me, except perhaps tyrannical authority...and my forced appreciation for his kindness in taking me in as a poor relation.

Madeline grew impatient with my complaints about Uncle Clive and his dominance over Aunt Mary. "Faugh! If you had a diversion, you would think nothing of it. Believe me, you need it, living in this droll country."

"You would much prefer it in London?" I asked a little sarcastically.

Madeline nodded, adjusting her hat. "I will one day, you know." She smiled and turning around, flashed a beautiful diamond bracelet under the light. "Do you like it?"

I stared at her in astonishment. "Where did get such a thing?"

She laughed. "That...my dear Laura is what pays to have *wealthy* connections."

"You should stay in your own class," I advised seriously. "We don't belong in their world. You'll find out one day these so called 'friends' will turn on you."

She laughed. "You are becoming philosophical...I daresay you sounds like mousy Miss Banks sermonizing."

"I *like* Miss Banks," I retorted. "Teresa is my friend."

She made a face. "No need for offence. I meant well. Little mousy-haired Miss Banks is quite nice, really."

"Yes, really," I said. "At least she is more worthy a friend than Elizabeth Rohan."

Madeline sighed. "Elizabeth is tiresome at times...but it's her connections that I find interesting. You know, she is off to London this weekend."

It was my turn to make a face. "What are you going to do? Don't tell me you are going to offer your services to the poor?"

She laughed. "You know me well, Laura, and of course not. I am invited out."

"Do you have Aunt Mary's permission?"

"Oh yes...she could not refuse. I am invited to dine at Rohan House Sunday next. The prodigal son is returning."

This was news to me. "You mean Adam is coming home?"

She nodded. "Elizabeth showed me one of his letters. He enjoyed the Grand Tour of Europe immensely and is now ready to come home and assume his responsibilities. Lord Rohan is very pleased with his son and wishes to reward him."

There was an undertone in her voice, but I chose to ignore it. Who could know what empty thought consumed Madeline?

So, Adam Rohan was coming home.

I hid my elation. I thought of Adam as my particular friend. He had taken a sincere interest in me as a child and never neglected to say hello to me at church. In secret, I harbored a romantic fondness for him. At the tender age of twelve, his fair good looks reminded me the Vikings of old—something regal, primitive and god-like.

I couldn't wait to see him.

Lady Rohan and Elizabeth went to London to accompany Adam home and Madeline and I went to Rohan House. She said she had been asked by Lord Rohan to help with the reconstruction of the Library. Madeline dragged me along, bribing me with, "you can see your mousy Miss Banks."

It was Saturday and as I didn't wish to cloud my day with the dissolute Lord Rohan, I went upstairs to visit Miss Banks. I told Madeline I wanted to leave in two hours. I could not imagine why she would be asked to help Lord Rohan when he could easily have enlisted the aid of his servants. "It's a surprise for Adam," Madeline told me.

One hour with Miss Banks passed quickly and I said I would go down to fetch Madeline. She was tired and needed to rest.

It was very quiet downstairs. I remember thinking the lack of servants about as being odd. I walked down the corridor to the Library door. It was closed. Without knocking, I entered, only to draw back in horror.

Madeline was there...lying on the floor...doing *that* with Lord Rohan! His forehead shone with perspiration, his eyes intent on his activity. He did not see me.

I felt sickened with fear. Madeline saw me and waved me away.

I ran...I did not know where I was going but I needed to get away. My cheeks felt hot with horrified embarrassment.

Madeline found me twenty minutes later, fully restored to her usual self. Her appearance was immaculate. She said nothing but clasped my hand and led me to the carriage.

I think the journey home was the longest journey I have ever taken. Madeline chatted on aimlessly about nothing. I wondered how she could return to being normal after doing *that* with Lord Rohan. I shuddered in horror. I had never liked the man and suddenly recalled his interest in Madeline on our first day at Rohan House. Suddenly, everything fell into place.

Back at the Rectory, we went straight to our room.

I closed the door.

Madeline seated herself on the chair in front of the mirror and watched me. "Well, I am awaiting your judgment."

"How could you?" I spat out. "How could you—do *that* with that man? He is monstrous but your behavior is worse. You will be punished, you know."

She laughed and I believed, at that moment, I had confronted the devil. "I will do as I please. I've always done. I rely on myself, Laura, and no one else. I never told anyone this before—but I hated my parents. They didn't look after me—they forced me to fend for myself. It taught me self-reliance..."

"Did it also teach you to be immoral?"

Madeline smiled. "Oh, you really are Miss Prim, aren't you? `Tis a shame. But you're young, you'll learn—"

"I'd never do *that*!"

Madeline looked at me with pity. She thought of me a child, a grown-up child in some areas but a tiresome moralist in others.

"How long have you been with Lord Rohan?" I asked quietly, wondering what Uncle Clive and Aunt Mary would think of Madeline's reckless behavior. They believed her to be the epitome of goodness and she certainly played the part. How deceived they were!

"Oh...awhile now. He's rewarded me well. Don't look at me like that! La, but you are an innocent, Laura Morgan. I haven't been a virgin for a long time, you know, and I don't think I was born to be one."

"No, you were born to create trouble," I said to which she hugged me. She confided in me later that she loved it when I reprimanded her.

I suppose she bemused me. We shared a room for nearly two years and regarded each other as sisters. It was not really a friendship but a kinship, a chance relationship in which two orphans clung to each other because there was no one else.

I think I ceased being a child at that point.

Adam returned in the fall and we received an invitation to dine at Rohan House.

I was excited at the chance of seeing him again and wondered whether he would remember me. I secretly hoped he still carried a special fondness for me.

Madeline was put out by our invitation to Rohan House. She regarded her private invitation by Elizabeth as a singular achievement and believed we were encroaching on her territory.

I wondered what Adam looked like now. I had not seen him for four years. I think Madeline noticed my anticipation and laughed. She was amused at the thought of me being excited to dine at Rohan House.

The question of appearance was very important on this occasion and Aunt Mary managed to procure enough funds out of Uncle Clive to order new dresses for each of us.

A dressmaker was hired from the village, the same one used by Lady Rohan. She was a middle-aged French woman, extremely skilled with the needle.

She picked out a beautiful cream silk for Madeline, cut low at the front and complimented by pale mauve gauze and matching flowers in her hair. I was envious, for I knew Madeline would look spectacular in her new dress and I could never look as good.

At twelve and a half, I retained the awkwardness intrinsic to this period of life. My features were undergoing changes and I despaired that I might never be beautiful. It was usually Ruby's vocation to cheer me over such ill tidings, however, this time, Aunt Mary did by saying: "Ah, Laura, you will turn out exactly like your mother."

"What did my mother look like?"

Aunt Mary smiled. "Bess! Ah, she was handsome...but she was plain, like you, until a certain age. I would not despair child...I know it must be difficult having such a beautiful cousin but I am quite sure you will turn out handsome although..."

"Not beautiful?" I nodded sadly. It was a harsh fact of reality. One looked like one looked. Not everyone could be beautiful like Madeline.

Madeline examined herself in the mirror while the dressmaker took her measurements. Her face glowed and her green eyes sparkled with excitement.

I wondered if she thought of Lord Rohan and turned away in disgust. For some time I thought of confessing to Uncle Clive what I had witnessed in the Rohan Library. However, I was sure Madeline and Lord Rohan would deny it and no one would believe me over them. I would never be believed so I remained silent on the subject.

The time passed quickly and finally, the day arrived.

Uncle Clive waited outside. I could sense an urge of expectancy even in him as we climbed into the carriage. I watched him look us over with approval. The longer examination went on Madeline as expected.

"You are in very good looks this evening, my dear."

"*Both* girls are in looks this evening," Aunt Mary corrected.

We arrived and the Butler admitted us into the Blue Salon, where the Rohans received their guests before dinner. I was particularly nervous on seeing Lord Rohan and wondered how I would survive the evening...until I saw Adam.

He stood casually by the fireplace, looking every inch the god-like Viking I imagined him to be. He possessed a worldly air about him I found captivating. I felt a little weak as we were presented to him. He winked at me in recognition.

My heart fluttered.

And then he saw Madeline.

"This is my cousin, Madeline," I said. "She came to live with us at the Rectory."

Adam seemed to forget all about me. He raised her hand to his lips and kissed it and his eyes remained focused on her the entire evening.

Madeline seemed to enjoy Adam's attention too and I watched her flirt with him during the course of dinner and later in the Music Room. I felt sick when I realized she would always have that magnetism over men. They would never look at me with her at my side.

The night passed painfully slow and I never felt worse in my life.

I suppose I shouldn't have been surprised when I discovered them together at the ruin.

Madeline would never change her ways and I still remember the picture of her that night, dressed in cream and looking so innocent.

It was early Saturday afternoon. Miss Banks and I had cancelled our rendezvous to go to the old ruin for she felt ill. I read to her for a while and when she fell asleep, I left Rohan House.

I didn't want to go home. As long as Madeline and I stayed away from the Rectory, the better we liked it. This was my day off and I decided to go to the ruin anyway. I hoped, perhaps a little vainly, to meet Adam there by chance. He had mentioned last night his intention to go riding after luncheon.

Elizabeth glanced at him in disbelief. "There will be a storm...you have not seen the change in the weather these last few days."

"I love storms," Madeline replied and I thought how very like her. Yes, she loved stormy times.

Before I went to Rohan House, I asked what she might do today, since Elizabeth had an appointment with her dressmaker.

She shrugged. "I thought I might go to the village and buy a new bonnet..." She lifted up her old one and examined it critically. "I want a new color...red perhaps."

I made my way happily up to the old ruin, hoping to be fortunate enough to meet Adam on horseback. I was a little disappointed on approaching the ruin for I could not see him. Then my heart skipped a beat.

I saw his horse tethered to a nearby tree.

I couldn't stop smiling and was in the process of turning the corner when I saw them.

This time they did not see me. They were so involved with each other. I think the scene will be permanently imprinted in my mind...naked bodies entwined in perfect accord. The look in their eyes shocked me the most. They were completely enraptured with what they were doing, their pleasure evident in their murmurs and pants.

I ran away, tears streaming down my face. My dreams had been shattered in the space of a few seconds and I didn't think I could ever recover.

I did not want to see her triumphantly happy little face. Was she the reward Lord Rohan wished to give to his son? The little prostitute who lived at the Rectory? I wondered what gift Adam would give Madeline. Some trinket for her services? Or perhaps a bonnet? Was the sake of virtue and chastity all worth a mere few pounds?

I was right. When she returned, she sported her new red bonnet but this time, I remained silent. I felt hurt and betrayed by her actions. If she'd taken more notice of me, perhaps she would have realized my childish fancy for her lover.

I took no notice of her after that...and her activities. I think she continued to see Adam for a long time after.

Madeline confidently thought no one knew of her true behavior. She would behave as normal, going to church on Sunday, helping the poor...and it was at these times I hated her. Who would have believed evil lurked behind such an angelic face?

I felt relieved to confess to Ruby during these moments of despondency. Whenever I was upset, I would knock on her door and she would sit me down on her little bed and comfort me. She hated what Madeline did to me.

Madeline continued to resent my knowing about her. I would sometimes say a magic word such as 'library' and she would close her mouth. I hated how she manipulated people, particularly members of the opposite sex.

Ruby would glint and say, "One day they'll know, me pet. One day. Evil, that one is...I can see it in 'er."

Then things would return to normal and Madeline would wield her charm over me to turn me back to her side. "You know, young Laura, a word of advice. I could show you a side to life you've never discovered before."

"I have no wish to be evil," I said.

She laughed and twisted around in the mirror. "Oh, evil am I?" Her green eyes glinted dangerously. "Yes, perhaps I am to a certain degree."

"And cruel," I added.

She smiled. "You mean to those poor, simpering fools? Yes, I admit that too."

"And deceiving."

To this she looked up sharply and examined me. "Believe me, Laura, you are the only one who knows me in this world."

"I cannot understand you now," I replied. "Or your questionable behavior."

She shrugged and changed the subject.

As time passed, I knew things would soon change.

Madeline turned eighteen, Elizabeth seventeen, and I thirteen. Elizabeth's rich relatives—the Hatfields of Bath—invited her to visit before the London season. Elizabeth was elated at the prospect and teased Madeline about it.

Madeline grew to resent Elizabeth. I sensed her mood beneath her false smile and knew she must be furious. She would love to go to London.

But I reminded her even if she went to London, she would not be invited to all the famous houses and clubs privy to the nobility. She would have little chance of forming a marriage alliance when she lacked both dowry and connections.

Madeline wasn't interested in matrimony, as she often expressed to Uncle Clive. She wanted to go to London for a change, an adventure, and as the Rohans departed for Bath, she became more insistent about the idea.

With the coming out of Elizabeth, my poor Miss Banks began looking for a new post. I promised to keep in touch and hated to part with her.

"Remember Laura, keep up with your studies," she said to me in farewell. "And promise to write."

I hugged her. "I will."

Madeline was fretting. I resumed my studies and helped Aunt Mary with her charity work. My correspondence with Lady Beatrice ceased, for she had neglected to write for some time. I was relieved...for I felt deceitful in attempting to write in Madeline's voice.

Therefore, when the invitation came, I couldn't conceal my disappointment.

Madeline was to go to London.

She was called into the Drawing Room.

It was half an hour later when Aunt Mary requested my presence in the Drawing Room. Uncle Clive stood solemnly by the hearth, warming his hands, while Aunt Mary sat on the sofa with a letter in her hand.

I thought how prominent those memories were of Aunt Mary on the sofa with a letter in hand. On each occasion, they seemed to change my life in some way or another.

I wondered how Madeline's going to London would affect me. My place remained at the Rectory for I did not have a wealthy benefactress like Madeline. I lacked breeding and beauty. Who would want me? I would not grace the famous houses and besides, I must continue my studies.

Uncle Clive spoke. "Laura...we have received word from your Aunt Mary's esteemed sister, Lady Beatrice."

He uttered the title eloquently and I was disgusted by his reverence for the nobility. I had been a prime witness to the fact that the nobles were not noble at all.

"...Lady Beatrice resides in London this time of the year." He glanced at Aunt Mary. "We are surprised by this bizarre invitation for both of you to join her there."

"What?" I could not stop the astonished gasp. Uncle Clive never failed to remind me of my duty. 'Children are to be seen and not heard,' he usually replied to my interruptions.

However, this time, he ignored the rule. "For some time now, we have been thinking about your futures...especially yours, Madeline. Unfortunately, your tuition at Rohan House has ceased. Normally, we would insist Laura continue her studies but she appears seemingly intelligent and, therefore, requires no more education."

He continued with his proverbs and plans for the future but I could only see stars. I had never received a compliment from the good Rector Morgan. *Seemingly intelligent*. I could see Madeline seething underneath, for she wasn't used to me being praised.

Later, she laughed about it. "I daresay they now realize your worth, Laura Morgan."

It was only a few minutes later when she requested I take out the letters to Lady Beatrice.

"I've lost them," I said slowly. It was time to teach her a lesson. I hadn't lost them at all in the sense, only misplaced them.

I would not allow her to take the credit for *my* letters.

She flicked her glorious hair. "No matter...I will survive."

"Yes, I daresay you will."

CHAPTER THREE

London was gay and alive in the summer of 1873 and I remember this time as one of the happiest of my childhood.

At thirteen and a half years of age, my body began to develop into womanhood, altering my features in the process. Although I found the transition extremely trying, I was pleased to see some improvement.

Uncle Clive remarked upon it when we stood outside the Rectory to say our farewells. "Young Laura is beginning to look like my brother's wife, Bess, isn't she, my dear?"

Aunt Mary admitted she'd seen Bess only on two occasions, both unfortunate (of which she did not elaborate), and I felt a pang of loneliness for I did not recall what my father, mother or brother looked like. I was only five when I came to live at the Rectory.

Lady Beatrice's handsome coach gleamed on the road. Inside sat our traveling companion, Mrs Courtney.

Mrs Courtney, hired only for the journey (we hoped), was a middle-aged widow and the very epitome of respectability.

I could see our journey being quiet and decorous. There would be no un-called for excitableness or cause for criticism on our behavior. Madeline likened Mrs Courtney to Ruby and rolled her eyes whenever she went on one of her 'respectable' speeches. Mrs Courtney possessed a list of instructions from Lady Beatrice and related the entirety of them in her dry, monotonous tone.

Lady Beatrice and her husband owned a private house in Kensington, a three-story mansion with a courtyard. As Lady Vere, all doors were open, all confidences shared, and all invitations given.

I remembered Lady Beatrice once wrote of her husband as a 'dedicated gambler who took pleasure in little else.'

The thought of meeting a dedicated gambler made me smile. I wondered how Uncle Clive agreed to our visiting the home of a dedicated gambler. However, he could hardly refuse a noble, could he?

When we arrived at Vere Court, my first impression was of elegance. The streets and character of the great city left a deep impression upon me. I fell in love with London immediately and felt guilty for betraying the gentle country of my childhood.

I felt I knew Lady Vere through our correspondence. As we stood in the Indigo Drawing Room, I studied her sharp, beak-like features and recognized the character in the letters.

Lady Beatrice rose from her ornate sofa and embraced us. "Girls! How happy I am you have arrived!"

Mrs Courtney was soon dispatched and another young maid entered the room. She curtsied prettily, her white cap bobbing around her face.

"Daisy will show you to your room," Lady Beatrice smoothed her exquisite green skirt. "Wash away your travel stains and return to me here. We have much to discuss."

Daisy glanced at us shyly and I warmed to her. I saw her gaze linger on Madeline and the blankness come into her face. I had seen it many times. It was the recognition of beauty. I looked sideways at Madeline; her face was glowing as she looked around at the luxury before her. Yes, indeed, she was beautiful.

We walked up two flights of stairs before Daisy opened two large doors to reveal a small, but exquisitely furnished, antechamber.

"Isn't this lovely!" Madeline gushed.

I followed them into the next room and gasped. I never imagined we would enjoy such luxury. Two, ornately carved, four-poster beds dominated the room matching the tapestry-covered armchairs by the fireplace.

Daisy opened the door to our toilette chamber and dressing room. "There's hot water ready, Miss," she bobbed, leaving us to become adjusted to our new surroundings.

I removed my bonnet. Madeline did likewise, jumping on the bed near the window, which she claimed as hers. At another time, I might have been annoyed with her. She never considered anyone's feelings but her own.

I was too preoccupied with the room to care. To two orphans, Vere Court resembled a royal palace.

We decided to leave the unpacking for later and changed into fresh, muslin dresses. The small clock on the mantle-piece chimed two.

Madeline yawned. "I hope the interview will be a short one."

Lady Beatrice smiled when we entered the Salon. Despite her very good taste in clothes, I wondered why Lord Vere decided to marry such an odd bride. How did a penniless and plain girl manage to attract a peer of the realm?

I should have known Beatrice's eccentric nature charmed everyone around her. She determined to enjoy life at any price and became a fitting companion for her dedicated gambler. After fifteen years of marriage, I found it peculiar to see no children about, however, I remembered Lord Vere did not care for children. Nor was he concerned with providing an heir for, as we learned later, Lord Vere already possessed one in his nephew.

Lady Beatrice's hair shone a rich auburn in the pale light and her blue eyes widened. "I am happy to see you have arrived safely," she began, her lips twitching humorously. "I hope Mrs Courtney was not too boring?"

I was unprepared for this frankness, despite my years of correspondence. Madeline sat tongue-tied beside me.

"She made the journey interesting," I said finally.

Lady Beatrice laughed. "Very diplomatic of you, my dear. You are young Laura, are you not? Yes, you are beginning to resemble dear Bess. I saw her only once, you know. It was at her wedding...she was not conventionally beautiful, but very handsome. She too had been plain when young."

I would not allow her candor to upset me. I knew I would never be beautiful like Madeline.

Lady Beatrice slowly examined Madeline. "Ah, this is my little protégé...Lud, I declare I've never seen such beauty...you'll be a success here for a certainty. How old are you, my dear?"

"Almost nineteen, m'am," Madeline answered perfectly.

Lady Beatrice clicked her tongue. "I was nineteen when I caught Lord Vere...let us hope you share my good fortune. I daresay you are like me child, and do not want to spend the rest of your life in a Rectory...yes, I know this from your letters. You are very intelligent and I daresay, after my own heart. We will see what manner of entertainment you will be permitted to enjoy...as for you," she turned to me, "you are only twelve, are you not?"

"Thirteen," I corrected, concealing my anger for giving Madeline the credit for my brilliant letters. However, I consoled myself, one day Lady Beatrice would know the truth. One day Lady Beatrice would remember something and Madeline, although clever, would not be able to answer her.

"Thirteen...an awkward age, is it not? I'm afraid you will not be permitted to join the season. You are too young, although your eyes look very sharp to me. You seem very fond of your cousin?"

I turned to Madeline whose green eyes betrayed a glimmer of amusement. "Naturally. We consider ourselves sisters."

"And all the good for it," Lady Beatrice approved. "Two orphans should stick together...especially in these times when true friends are so rare...anyway, enough of my tilly-tally. Lord Vere and I have decided that you, Laura, will attend a finishing school here in London. It is only a small class and no expense spared on Lord Vere's part." She leaned over conspiratorially. "Lord Vere was very successful at the gaming room the other night. He won a fortune and being in such a good mood, donated the money to me to provide for you girls. Half the money will pay for Laura's finishing school while the other half will purchase the necessary items needed for my little beauty here." She smiled at Madeline and I wondered how much she really knew of 'her little beauty'.

One day Lady Beatrice would find out her little protégé was not so white and pure.

I was grateful to Lord and Lady Vere for supplying me with such a brilliant education, all, I thought cynically, brought about by a chance turn of the card.

I wondered why so many people would risk fortunes and heirlooms for the thrill of the sport. I despised people who carelessly threw money away, especially when it could have been donated to charity...to help the poor and the needy.

I will never forget my first day at the finishing school. Well-bred English girls usually attended popular finishing schools in Europe; however, I found London a wonderful place to learn.

I quickly realized how sheltered my life at the Rectory appeared against the busy shades of London. Nobility from all parts of the country flocked to the city for the season, establishing the delightful madness known as the *haute ton*.

Madeline took no pleasure in listening to my ramblings; consequently, most of the time we spent talking was about her day.

Six weeks had passed since we arrived in London and already Madeline was the most talked about girl in the city. Her beauty made many mamas want to scratch her eyes out and I could imagine Madeline smiling to herself as she walked past. Her new clothes emphasized her beauty and gave her new confidence. As she made friends, she traveled in all the popular circles and delighted in preying upon those plain ladies with large dowries who constantly snubbed her.

Vere Court soon became the marbled steps of the old Roman senate. More and more of the privileged class called to see Madeline. I would sometimes watch them alight from their fancy carriages. Madeline told me everything about them: she seemed to have all the latest scandals at the tip of her fingers. I enjoyed listening to the gossip. It was a treat after the stuffy classes of Madame Grenville.

Madame Grenville's academy for girls was situated in a fine old building overlooking Hyde Park. Each day Romey would drive me. I considered myself fortunate, for some girls at Madame Grenville's had to board. Most of the boarders came from France, Germany, Scotland and the north and south of England. The remainders, like me, were residents of London.

The academy, famous for its exclusivity, was relatively small. I wondered what methods Lady Beatrice employed to have me accepted here. Because my tutelage was paid in advance, I did not have to put on pretences. The girls soon discovered I was a penniless orphan with weak connections and did not bother to include me in their friendships. I imagine they talked about me when I left but I did not care. I was enjoying my own freedom, however, I still missed the companionship of my dear Miss Banks.

I wrote to her. She was now stationed in the midlands as a schoolteacher for the underprivileged. Most of these children, she informed me, used to work with their parents in the mines. Until the Education Act a couple of years ago introduced compulsory State Elementary schools for children of these ages.

I could relate to Miss Bank's situation and her pupils for if my family had lived, I would have worked in the mines alongside them. I thought it funny, the chances of fate, which brought me to the Rectory and Madeline...and now, here, living in comparative luxury in London.

I expected the dream to end at any moment.

Lord Vere must return late to the house, for we hardly ever saw him. Occasionally, we met once or twice at luncheon. I found him charming and eccentric, a perfect match for Lady Beatrice who didn't appear to miss his nightly pursuits.

As a gamester, Lord Vere's good fortune could turn at any moment; therefore, our present situation was constantly suspended on a thin thread. Lady Beatrice understood this as well as I.

I could scarcely believe how fast time traveled past. Aunt Mary wrote us monthly, informing us of life at the Rectory. The Rohans, having returned from Bath recently, planned to be in London later in the year. Lord Rohan constantly complained of a frail heart and was not expected to live out the year.

I showed the letter to Madeline. "Your old father for a lover is not in good health...perhaps you should send your regards?"

"At least I have lovers," she snapped at me, glancing at her reflection in the mirror. "I tell you...if you would but try—"

"I will never be like you," I said. "To be frank, I can never imagine myself in that position."

"No," Madeline laughed. "I can't imagine it either."

She sat at the dresser, removing her jewelry and accessories for the day. Having dispensed with the routine, she would examine her face in the gilded mirror and look for any imperfections.

I thought her excessively vain and told her so, to which she usually shrugged. However, if I caught her on a bad day, she accused me of being jealous.

Jealous.

Yes, I suppose I was to a certain degree. Living with someone as beautiful as Madeline could be difficult. Sometimes, I would cry to myself late at night, with no Ruby to comfort me. And when I recovered, I would dismiss my foolishness.

I wondered about Madeline, if she engaged any secret lovers during this time. I knew she received *carte blanche* offers from wealthy men, for she told me of them with a smile of triumph.

Indeed, her very reputation as the toast of London forced her to be extremely careful in her behavior and choice of associates. As I watched her during the weeks, I concluded, with relief, she intended to remain the pure, untouched virgin she was supposed to be.

Lady Beatrice wanted to snare Madeline a husband. She targeted men whom she thought would be willing to marry a beautiful, albeit penniless, wife. She cautiously sifted through Madeline's invitations each day and wrote out acceptances and pretty refusals.

Lady Beatrice also charged Madeline with strict rules as to whom she should see and whom she shouldn't. She particularly emphasized the need to refuse the advances of certain men Lady Beatrice termed 'men of the world...and not interested in matrimony.'

Therefore, Madeline entered the great marriage market and came under instant scrutiny. Those jealous of the attention she received from the 'desirables' promoted her lack of connections and dowry. Madeline told me of these silly games and how she combated them. She enjoyed the challenge and took great pride in manipulating others for her gain.

Of course, there were those who snubbed the Veres and their beautiful charge by refusing invitations. At these functions, the desirables would be gathered together, in one big large society gathering with the purpose of establishing forth-coming marriages. I learnt much of the rules and regulations through Madeline's debut and was grateful I would never have to endure such humiliation.

I enjoyed my days in London immensely. I considered it my fortune to be too young to join society. I would not benefit from a debut—failing to possess one of the three essentials—breeding, fortune and beauty. I told myself I would never be auctioned like cattle for any man.

Madeline did not seem to mind. She enjoyed any attention and especially the stories concocted by her enemies to slander her reputation.

She would sit at night while I brushed her hair and tell me of their silly games. She laughed at them all; she was too clever.

She managed to gather a flock of 'eligibles' at our door; however, Lady Beatrice knew the majority would never be permitted to marry a penniless girl. "No," she said to Madeline one evening, "we must find the right fish...like my Lord Vere."

We often heard stories of penniless young girls securing wealthy, titled men through their beauty. I thought Madeline possessed a good chance of doing the same, if she remained pure. I wondered how long it would last.

Six months later, the incident began.

It was a Friday afternoon. Following the unexpected cancellation of my classes, Lady Beatrice gave us permission to take out the gig, accompanied, of course, by Romey.

"It's going to rain," I protested.

"Nonsense," Madeline laughed. "Don't you have a sense of adventure?"

It is called common sense, I wanted to say, however I conceded, knowing I would never hear the end of it.

We drove out, regardless of the ominous clouds hanging above us.

The storm broke suddenly. Our fashionable and completely unpractical gig stopped in the middle of the road, deserted by our faithless Romey. Madeline and I clung to each other, huddling under her parasol.

I imagined how ridiculous we must have looked sitting in the gig, trying to avoid the pounding rain under a lacy parasol.

"This is common sense," I led her to shelter in the market place, where, I assumed, we would find the faithless Romey.

Relieved to be out of the rain, we didn't seem to mind our soaking dresses. Madeline removed her bonnet and smoothened out her damp curls.

A sheepish Romey returned to us, uttering apologies. "Pardon me, but ye might like to `ave a bit of a look at what's to offer hereabouts—" he pointed to the market place down the lane.

I would have been quite happy to wait with Romey but Madeline saw the opportunity and seized it. "Come on, I have a little money. Perhaps we can find some ribbons to buy. I need a new blue one."

"You have plenty," I groaned in complaint.

"Yes, but I need a particular shade...I gave it to Sir Humphrey as a favor. Look here..." By now, she had talked me down to the market lane and there was no point in trying to turn back. I could see what little harm it would do to her reputation for I was with her, her little 'priggish school-mouse' sister, as she often called me.

It must have been while she was examining the ribbons when a passing vagabond snatched her purse. I heard her alarmed cry and we stepped out to see the thief running down the lane. A swift punch from a young man stopped him. His dark eyes appraised Madeline and he grinned.

I instantly recognized him as a gypsy, as he twisted the gold earring in his left ear. Between his strong fingers, he held Madeline's pathetic little string purse.

I watched Madeline's face glow with interest. I suppose it was foolish but the storm that day could have symbolized a premonition as to what this meeting would mean in the future. I often look back and am amazed at how trivial an incident can later turn into one of significance.

"Yours, I believe," the gypsy said, handling Madeline her purse.

I saw her green eyes widen when he failed to be stunned by her beauty. She found it a challenge when somebody did not love her instantly.

"Oh wait, please," Madeline begged in a sweet voice. "You must allow me to thank-you. I only wish there were more heroes on the streets like you. Not many, you know, would bother to save a lady's purse." She offered her perfect, little white hand.

The gypsy smirked, betraying white teeth in a very dark face. He didn't make much of an impression upon me but I could see why others found him irresistible. Two strong brows framed liquid black eyes, a thin, Adonis nose and a sensual mouth. I thought his manner quite forward, likely because of his dissolute life, which would explain why he dared to address Madeline as an equal.

Madeline was smitten. I glanced sideways at her face, her green eyes greedily feasting on the gypsy. I should have foreseen the outcome of what this look meant but Romey caught my attention. A sudden break in the weather brought the gig around to collect us. I tapped Madeline on the shoulder, disrupting her interlude with the gypsy.

"I am summoned," she laughed.

"Let's hope to meet again," the gypsy murmured, having the impertinence to kiss Madeline's hand.

I scolded her on the way home.

"Faugh!" she cried. "He behaved most gentlemanly, much more than those insipid men who have their sweaty paws all over me when we dance," she shuddered and continued, "I don't know why you're upset about it. It was all quite innocent, you know. His name is Lucian...and he's a very devil, I daresay."

"I daresay he has many others to keep him busy," I said.

Madeline turned to watch the scenery. A passing gig carrying one of her faithful admirers failed to catch her attention. I knew then the gypsy had made a deep impression upon her.

Two months went by before I heard of Lucian again.

By this time, Madeline had a serious suitor. Having danced with her once at a ball, he became infatuated and constantly sent flowers and chocolates to the house. Lady Beatrice's eyes shone with impending triumph, since she believed this gentleman to be 'the one.'

Madeline sneered when I teased her about it. "He's an old man. I cannot imagine his hands on me...although he's rich, you know, and titled. I will be mistress of Silverthorn if I marry him."

"Well, that must compensate for something," I said cynically. "It may be wise to keep him on a string."

"Yes," she agreed. "A very loose string. I have no desire to be married to an old man who suffers with a gouty foot!"

The gentleman, Lord Thomas Braithfield, looked healthy for his sixty years. He owned a vast estate west of York called Silverthorn, as well as a townhouse in London and a box at Ascot. Being a widower, his serious pursuit of the beautiful young charge of Lord Vere became the talk of the town.

On Lady Beatrice's advice, Madeline permitted Lord Braithfield to call on her. The arrangement appealed to Lord Braithfield for he did not desire to run with the popular crowd. He told Lord Vere plainly that he wanted a young wife to bear him a son. As long as she was healthy and willing, he didn't mind a dowerless bride.

I learned these details through a combination of luck and intuition.

Lady Beatrice preached caution, allowing Madeline time to adjust to Lord Braithfield's advances before he declared his intention of marriage. However, Madeline was too busy to become fully aware of Lord Braithfield's intent.

I should have recognized something was different about her. She lived in a dream world and even neglected her nightly ritual of examining her face in the mirror. I approached her with my fears one afternoon.

"Nothing's wrong," she smiled, stretching like a cat, "I've never felt so happy in my life."

"Have you seen Lord Braithfield today?"

An instant scowl appeared on her beautiful face. "That old man? Even he couldn't lessen my euphoria today. I feel like a queen!"

You are definitely not like our Queen, I mused. Queen Victoria, proud to be the 'grim widow of Windsor,' since her husband's death was rarely seen in public.

I thought Madeline's behavior very odd, however, I was too preoccupied with my studies to worry unduly about it.

Five weeks later, it happened.

I noticed the first sign when I awoke early on a Sunday morning. Her bedclothes were thrown aside and I wondered where she could be for she loved to sleep in until noon on Sundays.

I went into our toilette and found her kneeling on the floor, vomiting. Shocked, I closed the door and knelt down with her, patting her back. She looked at me in fright and I realized I had never seen Madeline ill. I dampened a towel and wiped her forehead. "Are you all right?"

She raised her extraordinary green eyes to my face, taking in every detail of my honest concern. "T—thank-you for helping me, Laura."

Her voice trembled and she gazed up at me with large, troubled eyes. I thought it amusing that I, a simple fourteen year-old schoolgirl, could comfort the toast of London so easily. As her confessor, I knew enough about her to condemn her, however, she was like a sister to me. "Shall I call for the doctor?"

"No!" Madeline seized my hand. "No, please, I shall be all right."

"Madeline, you cannot fool me," I said stubbornly as she threw herself onto her bed and wept uncontrollably.

"Have you quarreled with Lady Beatrice? Have you heard some vicious rumor about you that's incorrect?"

She dumbly shook her head.

I tried my last question. "Are you in love?"

She sat up and dried her cheeks, tossing her fiery hair over her shoulder. "I wish I was...with the right person!"

"What do you mean? You're making no sense."

"No, I never make any sense, do I? I'm not sensible like you, Laura. I've always acted impetuously but now I'm really in trouble and I don't know what to do..."

"You need a solution?"

"Yes...a solution. Can't you guess why I'm ill?"

I looked at her, poised regally in her bed. She looked like an enchantress and I felt unworthy to be in her presence. "Whose child is it? It's not...Lord Braithfield's, is it?"

"No...well, yes, it's going to be—"

"What do you mean?"

"I'm going to marry Lord Braithfield...as soon as possible. There can be no harm in it...he would never suspect, he's such a doddering old fool. And I suppose this time I'm to pay for my own foolishness. I knew I'd have to render an account one day and I know he'll marry me if I said yes. You all thought I knew nothing of it, didn't you? I will accept his proposal now. It will provide me with an escape...as I cannot possibly go on living with the Veres like this. Lord Braithfield wants an heir so I shall give him his heir."

I stared at her, shocked by her ruthless plan. "Won't Lady Beatrice suspect your sudden change of heart?"

"Not if I mention I'm in a hurry to be a rich and titled lady. If I can't have a young, rich and handsome fish why not an old and doddering one? He's sure to die soon...and then I'll be permanently settled. He has the most magnificent mansion in Yorkshire called Silverthorn...and once I'm settled, I'll send for you. I'll be like old times...but we'll be rich, as we've always wanted."

"As you've always wanted," I corrected her.

She knew I didn't agree with the plan, however, I could see no way of stopping it without ruining her. I told her I would have no part in trying to foster her bastard off to Lord Braithfield and it would be on her own conscious.

She laughed. "I have already made far too many *faux pas* for God to forgive...what harm can one more do? I'm certain to pay for my mistake being confined in the country playing mama!"

"Whose child are you carrying?"

Madeline smiled. "It's Lucian's, the gypsy."

"The gypsy! How on earth did you manage...no, I don't want to hear the gruesome details."

"Hardly gruesome. This is the best time I've had with a man, Laura, and if you take my advice, go to a gypsy camp. They know women and are experienced enough to deliver. In fact, I am quite in love with Lucian...he'll be heartbroken when he hears I've married Lord Braithfield."

"Does he know you're pregnant?"

"Oh yes...he said he was going to get me with child from the beginning. He said he's never made love to a beautiful white socialite before. I took precautions of course but they don't work with gypsies."

Her secret smile told me all I wanted to know. "How will he feel when he hears you've betrayed him?"

She shrugged. "He wants me to run away with him...but I could never endure life in those gypsy camps—" she screwed up her nose, "the stench and the foul language..."

"Yet, you seemed not to have minded for him to..." I faltered.

Madeline laughed. "You're an innocent, Laura Morgan. Why, you're blushing!" She made a face. "To be truth, I cannot wait until you become a woman...and you know what I mean. Then we might be able to compare notes."

"Don't you have any decency? You should have stayed a virgin until you wed."

"That's exactly what I'm going to be...a pure, white virgin when I marry Lord Braithfield and you are not going to tilly-tally on me, do you hear?"

Her urgent voice warned me. I thought of the few attempts in the past, when I tried to expose her crimes—without success. I should confide to Lady Beatrice, however, something held me back. The same feeling overwhelmed me during the Rohan affair.

I could not betray her confidence.

CHAPTER FOUR

She succeeded as she always did and married Lord Braithfield a month later.

She stood at the altar, dressed in white organza, a breath-taking bride, carrying the virginal air required of a well-bred young lady. In her hands, she held a bouquet of orange blossom.

The *ton* showed up in large numbers to witness the occasion, mourning the loss of their brightest star, though very few were prepared to ask her hand in marriage. I felt relieved, for I knew she'd received countless and no doubt, tempting, *carte blanche* offers.

I was her only bridesmaid, dressed in a simple pink gown Lady Beatrice had hastily ordered. I remember the anticipation of the day, wondering what would eventuate. I must have looked guilty for I could never hold a secret and Lady Beatrice questioned me after the ceremony. I told her I would be quite destitute without Madeline. Lady Beatrice seemed satisfied with my response and dismissed the subject.

Lord Braithfield was embarrassingly attentive towards his lovely, young bride. Madeline kissed me on the cheek when they said their farewells and handed me her bouquet. She showed no remorse in duping her new husband and I experienced a terrible premonition when they drove away in their elaborate carriage. One day her actions would come back to haunt her.

However, she'd escaped retribution in the past, I thought pensively, as we drove home. She married Lord Braithfield because she needed a husband and because she liked to disappoint certain members of the *ton.* Her plan, after her lengthy honeymoon in Europe, would be to return to London, triumphant, as the new Lady Braithfield. Every door would be opened to her and she would once again become the *toast.* I suppose I envied her and her cunning, the way she succeeded despite the odds.

The society page was full of the wedding the next day and I wondered whether Madeline's gypsy lover learned of it.

I wouldn't know, until much later, how fatally that very thought eventuated into reality.

I sensed there would be a change in my life and I expected it any moment.

Madeline had been gone for five months. I felt she'd cheated me somehow for she neglected to send word. It was torture to live alone in our bedroom and go to my dullish classes without Madeline to be there when I returned.

Lady Beatrice noted my depression and called me into her boudoir one morning. She sat up in bed, sipping her hot chocolate.

"I can see you're unhappy, child. No doubt this is due to Madeline leaving us?" She didn't wait for my nod and continued: "Lord Vere has also experienced an unfortunate turn at the cards...I'm afraid we won't be able to fund your tutelage at Madame Grenville's for much longer..."

I remained silent.

"...so I have decided to send you back to Mary and the Rectory. It's the only solution I can offer. Mary writes she is under duress coping with the affairs of the village and looks forward to your going home. How do you feel about this?"

"I would like to go home," I said, knowing I could not imagine living here without Madeline. The rectory seemed, oddly enough, like a blessed refuge.

"I daresay some color in your cheeks does you good, gel," Lady Beatrice examined me critically, "and your looks are changing. Perhaps Mary could send you back when you fully flower." She smiled to herself. "I do like a challenge...and my success is almost guaranteed."

I laughed, for I liked Lady Beatrice and her blunt tongue.

"Yes," she winked, "come back in a couple of years...we'll see what we can arrange."

Lady Beatrice, interestingly, found out long ago that I had written Madeline's letters. Sensing something amiss, she sent Aunt Mary a letter or two and discovered she'd grown fond of me and not Madeline.

Beauty did not buy everything, I thought with satisfaction.

I still received no news of Madeline. Many months had passed and she must be nearing the time of her confinement.

I was back at the Rectory, dealing with the usual affairs. It's amazing how different one sees things when one grows older. I was nearly fifteen, quite a lady, and was passing through the dramatic change. My nondescript brown hair had lightened to a kind of honey-blonde color and my pale, watery eyes had deepened into a sky blue. To my utmost delight, my freckles faded, leaving my skin slightly brown but smooth and even. My nose remained small and straight, and my lashes dark and long. I wished Madeline could see me now for she had always known me as an ugly duckling.

I would never be beautiful but I was turning out exactly like Bess, my mother. Aunt Mary had always promised this change and although I didn't place too emphasis on personal appearance, I was happy that I could no longer be termed plain or unattractive.

I resumed my old duties with new confidence. An unfortunate incident occurred whilst I was away. I learned of it in coming home. We could no longer afford to keep Jeanette the cook. Jake and Ruby remained, both finding it extremely difficult to cope with their extra duties.

I asked why.

"The Rohans are experiencing some financial strain," Aunt Mary explained. "Two weeks ago old Lord Rohan died, leaving a fortune of debts behind for young Adam. There is no money...Lord Adam is gone off to London to find a rich wife...Miss Elizabeth was called back from her finishing school in France...Lady Rohan is suffering from nerves and is constantly having attacks of the vapors...they've had to lay off half their staff."

"Let's pray he finds a buxom purse," I said, examining my travel stained clothes.

It did not take me long to settle into my old way of life. The little room Madeline and I shared seemed oddly uninhabitable now. The place lacked Madeline's lively vitality and I knew I'd have to get on with my life without her.

I didn't expect it to be easy, especially when Madeline remained our favorite topic of conversation. Uncle Clive persistently reminded me of Madeline's good fortune. He glowed with pride and hastened to tell every living soul about his niece's advantageous match.

Aunt Mary shared his sentiments. "I knew she wouldn't be so beautiful for nothing but I never imagined she'd become a titled lady. Lady Braithfield—how fine that sounds."

If only you knew the whole story, I thought to myself, wondering if Uncle Clive and Aunt Mary would ever know Madeline's true character.

Only one person in the village shared my knowledge of her—Adam Rohan.

We had become friends again. He had a constant struggle on his hands and I suppose I felt a little sorry for him. We never spoke of Madeline, but I sensed he still thought of her from time to time and wondered if he those memories included his sojourn with her at the old ruin. He couldn't have guessed I knew about these carnal activities, for he addressed me in a respectable manner.

"You're fifteen now, Laura...and becoming quite the young lady. I hope you don't mind returning to the country again after your time in London?"

"No," I replied. "It is peaceful here..." I thought back to those last days in London when I had taken Madeline's concerns on my shoulders and experienced difficulty in sleeping.

"Yes, peaceful," Adam echoed and I took my leave for Lady Rohan caught us talking and gave me a stinging glare. She didn't like me and resented me speaking to her son when I was only 'that girl from the Rectory.'

Elizabeth Rohan, following her mother's example, snubbed me when she arrived home with her fancy Parisian clothes and haughty French air. She simply dismissed all those years we spent in the schoolroom together and barely addressed a single word to me. Only a polite nod sufficed in church. However, she lowered herself to congratulate Aunt Mary on Madeline's 'grand success', as she termed it. "Fancy Madeline," Elizabeth mused, "Lady Braithfield! I declare I am quite *piqued*...she'll be mistress of Silverthorn—but then, you know Madeline."

I received a letter from Miss Banks. It had been addressed to the Vere residence in London and Lady Beatrice had forwarded it on.

I was happy to hear of Theresa's progress with the miner's children. She said things were improving in the industry to the benefit of the workers. However, some mines continued to employ young children, completely ignoring the law. Terribly mistreated and underpaid, many of these children became ill by their exposure to the deadly gases and died.

I kept her letter close to my heart. I suppose I felt a bond with these underprivileged children, for if my family hadn't passed away, I should be working alongside them in the mine.

A week later, a letter from Madeline arrived.

As soon as I received it, I ripped it open, eager to hear her news.

Silverthorn
May 20, 1874

Dear Laura,

> Well, I am now a mother...and have a two-month-old daughter, whom I have named Laura after you. Lord Braithfield is much disappointed, as he was hoping for a son...but does not suspect, yet, even though the baby was premature. As soon as we returned home from our honeymoon, I informed him of my pregnancy. Poor old fool could hardly believe his good fortune. He became so besotted with the whole idea; he left me alone to rest and became afraid to touch me, lest he jinx his chance of a healthy son.

> Silverthorn is a splendid place, worthy of what they say about it. My husband has a nephew, a horrid man...his name is Justin and he hates me...ever since we came back. I can't blame him really. Justin was to be Thomas' heir...I know he suspected when I gave birth prematurely, even though I planned it so well. I went for a walk and did a dramatic fall right about the due time and it brought on the labor.

> Justin is of course, pleased the child is a girl. Silverthorn is entailed but I will bear a son...just to spite him.

There is another nephew by the name of Vincent. He is a Braithfield and not at all like Justin. He was so attentive to me during my pregnancy and simply dotes on little Laura! He also dislikes Justin and warns me, quote, 'his cousin will go to any lengths to achieve what he wants.'

Well, that's enough of me. How are you coping in that dreary old Rectory?

What did I expect of her? I thought perhaps she might tell me something of the house but Madeline had always been more interested in people than in places.

I sat on my bed and re-read the letter. I felt my cheeks glowing when I skimmed over the part about Justin Braithfield. He is obviously put out, I thought to myself, by Lord Braithfield snapping up a young, penniless bride.

The cousin Vincent sounded personable and I felt relieved Madeline had some young company to keep her occupied. I thought of little Laura, whom she had named after me and smiled. I imagined what my little namesake looked like—small with a pink round face and charming little features. Or perhaps she was born with a black tuff of hair, owning to her gypsy parentage?

I pictured Madeline, mistress of Silverthorn, snapping commands, ordering extravagant clothes, and dazzling local society with her beauty. And beside her, Lord Braithfield, still embarrassingly tickled over his young bride...and in the background this cynical Justin, disliking his ill fortune. He had been cheated out of a great estate and title by a Rectory girl! How humiliating! I could foresee there would be trouble and prayed Madeline kept free of any compromising situation that would give voice to Justin's objection.

I hurriedly replied to her letter, scolding her because she neglected to tell me about the house. A few weeks later, her letter arrived.

Dear Laura,

There are no words to describe the beauty and charm of Silverthorn. It is a place where dreams are made. Rohan House does not even rate on the scales compared to Silverthorn—I can't wait to show it to you.

It's all mine, Laura. You can't imagine how that makes me feel.

The place, even with its quaint little town and insipid society, agrees with me and I have no desire of returning to London yet.

There is an old fable that Silverthorn is protected by the ghost of Lady Eleanor, who, the day before her wedding, fell from the topmost tower. It was a terrible accident and months later, her sister, Cecily, married Eleanor's groom and it is said that Eleanor still haunts the tower, where she saw her bridegroom with her sister. Sometimes, they say she can be heard weeping but I think that is nonsense. It is only the wind...roving over the moors.

Thomas, as expected, dotes on his little daughter. He has become the proud Papa and I watch on silently, knowing the truth and the irony of it. You are the only one who will ever share my secret, Laura. I know I do not deserve you but I believe some inexplicable force binds us.

Yours truly,

Madeline.

So preoccupied with my letter, I neglected to remember dinner. Ruby pounded on my door in a fluster. "Miss Laura! They're expectin' ye...quickly!"

I scurried to my feet and raced in a most unladylike manner to the Dining Room. Before I entered, I straightened a few wisps of my hair for Uncle Clive always stressed the importance of a neat appearance.

As expected, I was scolded for being late.

"A letter from Madeline?" Uncle Clive laid down his fork. "This is interesting indeed. What does she say?"

"She is a mother," I blurted out.

"A mother!" Aunt Mary cried. "But how...it is so soon. I understand Lord Braithfield was anxious to produce an heir..."

"She has done her duty," Uncle Clive bluntly pointed out.

I didn't feel like contradicting him so I mentioned nothing of the estate being entailed on the male line. "She gave birth to a daughter two months ago," I told them. "Madeline has named her Laura after me."

"How lovely," Aunt Mary gushed. "We could not have hoped for better fortune for dear Madeline."

"Let's hope it comes our way this time," Uncle Clive said gruffly, disappearing into the library.

"Don't mind him," Aunt Mary smiled, "...he's a little tired tonight. Come, eat your dinner and tell me more."

So, I told her as much as I could without divulging any confidence. Aunt Mary, after listening to me with rapt attention, asked if the child had been born with any defects.

"Laura is perfectly healthy...which is lucky," I added quickly, "when one considers the labor was brought on by Madeline's unexpected fall..."

"A fall?"

"Yes...she was walking in the gardens and tripped or something. It brought on the birth pains and little Laura was born later in the night. Thank heavens the baby is all right!"

"And Madeline," Aunt Mary seconded quietly. "It all seems so strange, doesn't it, Laura? Us here, talking about Madeline when she was only with us a short while ago...so much can happen so quickly. It won't be long before you will leave us too."

"What do you mean?"

"You know very well what I mean..." her eyes glinted mischievously. "Lord Adam. He has designs on you."

I felt the color run into my face. "We're only friends," I replied firmly. "You know he must marry an heiress to raise the family's fortunes."

She sighed. "I suppose you are right. His mother and his sister will ensure he marries well to keep them in their finery. Goodness! Can there be more to life than prestige and invitations to grand houses?"

She described Madeline's new life without knowing it. I couldn't help but feel a little jealous. She now lived in a beautiful old house while I seemed condemned to Rectory life. She ignored my pleas for an invitation to Silverthorn—saying it was much too early for family to visit.

I knew my discontent grew out of intense examination of her letters. I longed for a different life, new faces.

And it appeared highly probable, if Madeline continued to ignore my requests, I would be forced to either marry or look for a post of my own.

In either case, I welcomed change.

A year passed before I received another letter.

The winter months passed slowly and the Rohans, eager to escape the boredom, returned to London to look for the much-needed heiress.

Having been one of the worst winters of my experience, many fell ill, including my Ruby. I spent my days caring for her and relieving Aunt Mary by taking charge of the household duties.

I found I missed Adam Rohan's company and began to wonder if I had imagined his frequent visits to the Rectory. I was certain Lady Rohan herded him to London in the hope it would cool our friendship. I overheard her remark before they left, "that plain Rectory girl...she will never do as well as her cousin. Madeline, Lady Braithfield now, possessed the beauty to secure her advantageous match. This one will be lucky to marry the village idiot!"

I still had no word from Madeline. Her last letter was so precious to me, I knew it by heart. Silverthorn became like a fantasy world for me—somewhere I could go to escape the realities of life.

I was cleaning the Drawing Room when Ruby handed me the post. I thanked her with a warm smile, sorting through the cards and invitations, pausing on one letter addressed to me. I thought it must be from Miss Banks and set it down without even looking at the envelope. Miss Banks was always speedy with her reply.

After dinner, I checked on Ruby before retiring to my room, eager to learn Theresa's news. I picked it up and my heart skipped a beat when I recognized the messy handwriting.

Silverthorn

December 25th, 1876

Dear Laura,

What an unusual time to write to you, I know what you're thinking. I am neglecting the pleasantries for I thought of you today and realized how much I missed you.

I wonder how you are doing in that dreary old Rectory...marriage is the only answer for you, dear Laura. It will give you the impendence you crave.

I must tell you I am more than happy with my lot. As I said, marriage allows a certain amount of freedom...I won't shock your sensibilities by saying anything more. I can see you still quite angry with me for betraying poor Thomas. What a pity he isn't like his charming nephew Vincent.

The society here is limited. Our closest neighbors live five miles away in a quaint manor house called Ashton Grove. There is one young man, Brett Ashton, whom I have singled out for you. He has two sisters, Tabitha and Eliza. Then there is Mr Weston and his sister, Olivia. Olivia has the cool, blonde beauty of an angel but her claws are sharp. She has set her cap at Justin, probably hoping, as he does, I will not bear a son to disinherit him.

Justin is becoming increasingly suspicious of me. I daresay he watches me like a hawk! He disturbs me for I am certain he wishes me ill.

I believe Thomas knows Justin is only waiting for an opportunity to prove me false...he covets Silverthorn like a relentless ghost. Why can't he be like Vincent?

I wish you were here...you would know what to do. I do miss your sharp reprimands and your funny little ways. I will ask you to come to Silverthorn soon...when the time is right.

Yours truly,
Madeline.

I thought it selfish of her to ignore my questions, especially about little Laura. I sent her letters frequently, knowing I would never receive a proper reply.

An invitation to Silverthorn! I wondered if it would ever eventuate. Why did she keep me in the dark? What was more natural than one's cousin being allowed to visit? Perhaps she felt uncomfortable about Justin's disapproval of her. I frowned. Madeline needed protection...and guidance. She was too prone to do something foolish. However, how could I possibly help her when she refused to let me come?

She even failed to send her regards to Uncle Clive and Aunt Mary! But that was Madeline; she liked to ignore convention and follow her own code of behavior.

I was particularly disappointed when she failed to answer my heart-wrenched letter about Adam Rohan. I questioned my feelings for him, asking her for advice. I could never love him but he had a charisma about him I found irresistible. If he strove to become a reformed rake for my good opinion, as he said to me, should I encourage the relationship to the next level?

I knew the answer.

I was almost seventeen, a poor girl from the Rectory and he needed an heiress. His family would surely oppose the match and Adam wouldn't be happy living in squalor.

I suddenly felt much older than my years.

The option of taking a post increasingly appealed to me as time went on. Adam Rohan finally found his prospective bride or his mama and sister found her for him. She was at Rohan House now and I knew little about her. Aunt Mary heard from Mrs Jennings that the young lady was as plump in figure as she was in purse.

Poor Aunt Mary couldn't hide her disappointment. She hoped I would marry Adam and defeat the odds, like Madeline.

Two days later, I saw Adam. It was a Sunday afternoon and I left Aunt Mary with Mrs Jennings in the church, eager to get away. It was such a lovely day and the gentle beauty of the countryside beckoned me to it, scented with the intoxicating sweetness of blooming roses.

The Rohans took the front pew in Church, Adam's prospective pride, Miss Josie Farrah, seated between Lady Rohan and Miss Elizabeth. After prayer and song, Elizabeth whispered to Josie before both girls turned to look at me and promptly smiled in unison.

I turned away only to face Adam. "Good morning, my Lord, it is a fine day, is it not?" I said without a hint of feeling in my voice.

"Yes...it is," he replied, his blue eyes shifting from me to Elizabeth.

"Your sister seems anxious to catch your attention," I remarked casually, "and I must go. I have an errand to do with Aunt Mary—"

"Laura, I need to see you, to explain—"

"There is nothing to explain, my lord."

"I will find you," he called out softly as I hastily walked away. I could feel Lady Rohan's eyes boring into the back of me.

Fortunately, charity visits with Aunt Mary occupied my mind for the next hour or two. Aunt Mary noticed my pallor and sent me out for a walk.

I decided to pick some flowers in the field beyond the graveyard. The roses would cheer the dull Rectory. I was as eager to escape it as Lady Rohan and Elizabeth, for Uncle Clive's new clerk, Mr Brody, continually pestered me with his suit. No more than twenty with thin, sweaty palms, sandy hair and old-fashioned spectacles, Edwin Brody was the direct opposite of Adam Rohan.

Determined to be free of him and all the ills of my life, I collected my roses, startled when a hand thrust one before me. I looked up sharply, knowing it was Adam.

He held my hand firmly. "Laura...perhaps you know what I want to say to you. You know my feelings...I have made that quite clear. I can only hope you feel the same..." He turned away with a reluctant sigh. "My family has already made known their wishes. They want me to court Josie...I suppose you know that. They consider you unsuitable but I like you, I always have...and now I believe I love you—"

He turned my face to his before he seized me. My basket dropped to the ground as he leaned forward to kiss me.

I pulled away, furious. "How dare you try to seduce me! I am not like my cousin, my Lord. Perhaps you thought so...and hoped I would meet you at the ruin like she." I know I should never have mentioned such a thing and scolded myself afterwards. My anger drove me to commit the *faux pas* and I now looked up at his handsome, shocked face.

"I regret I disappointed you," Adam turned on his heel.

His name remained on my lips. I expected a proposal of marriage and all Adam Rohan proposed was a *carte blanche.* I would be happy to see him wed to Miss Farrah.

Why did every man have to obey the rules of society? Why didn't they have the courage to marry a girl for love instead of monetary gain? I believed Adam Rohan loved me in his own way but not enough to marry me. He needed an heiress and I needed to get away, to escape the inevitable marriage with Mr Brody.

Six months later, the wedding between Lord Rohan and Miss Josie Farrah took place in our small village church. Uncle Clive performed the service, beaming at the new Lady Rohan and no doubt, her moneybags.

Adam had done his duty.

And I felt it was the end of an episode.

CHAPTER FIVE

I was in London when I received Madeline's last letter.

Lord Vere, coming home late one night from White's, found himself at the mercy of a notorious highway and subsequently died from the encounter. On hearing the news, Aunt Mary sent me to London.

Anxious to escape, I readily accepted and made the necessary travel arrangements. A year had passed since Adam Rohan's wedding and the dowager Lady Rohan had recently contracted influenza. Adam, now handsomely flush with his bride's dowry, sent his mother off to Bath to take the waters. Miss Elizabeth Rohan, enjoying the freedom only money can buy, flittered between Rohan House, Bath and London. Growing older each season, she was desperate to find a husband. Oddly enough, she seemed to take her frustration out on me. 'That horrid Rectory girl,' she would say, 'she is nothing compared with her cousin. Why, she looks positively spinsterly in those plain, muslin dresses. Some might mistake her for a common farm girl!'

She would mention such to Josie, the new Lady Rohan, purposely within my earshot. Poor meek Josie followed her new sister-in-law's suit. She agreed to anything Elizabeth suggested.

Sadly, Adam seemed to dominate her also. Each Rohan possessed a natural tendency to officiate a dictatorship and I felt pity for Josie, a rich merchant's daughter who would never fit into their world. Adam appeared to despise her, although he performed the perfunctory duties required by a husband. To deepen my disapproval of him, he simply ignored his adoring wife and continued to pursue me, which is how I became the gossip of the village. I incurred everyone's disapproval and several nasty stories found their way to Aunt Mary's sensitive ears.

I was furious Adam let it happen and told him so on many occasions. He appeared to enjoy my reproof and begged for forgiveness. I replied there was nothing to forgive and advised him to find happiness in his own marriage and not without.

The pressure from Adam continued day after day. The respectable set of our small town began to avoid me. This seemed to amuse Adam and I secretly knew he did it on purpose to force me into a *carte blanche*.

Lady Beatrice's distraught letter reached us in September. Aunt Mary summoned me to the Drawing Room. "Dear child," she began solicitously, "there has been some dreadful news..."

She explained about Lord Vere.

"I think you should go—I understand you are having difficulties." She frowned, unsure of how to address the subject. "Your Uncle is most displeased by the gossip about you. He claims you have ensnared Lord Rohan on purpose."

I nearly laughed. I, the plain girl from the Rectory?

"And, of course, there is Mr Brody and his feelings to consider."

I nodded solemnly and went to pack. Mr Brody was the second reason why I was anxious to go to London. Aunt Mary sensed my distaste for him and my leaving seemed be the only answer to the problem. It had been an annoying predicament for the last six months and one I never wanted to repeat. In fact, as I left the Drawing Room, he awaited me on the other side of the door.

"Miss Morgan, I wish an earnest word with you."

Edwin Brody stood there, Uncle Clive's protégé, his beady eyes fixed greedily on my face.

"I'm sorry, Mr Brody, but I must beg to retire. I am leaving for London in the morning and have to pack."

He moved in my path, straightening a wisp of sandy hair. "Miss Morgan, I beg of you to hear me out. The good Rector has given me permission to speak with you...alone. What I have to say is a matter of utmost importance that concerns my future happiness and yours, I think."

I wanted to laugh. He honestly thought I desired his proposal of marriage. I began my quick refusal when Uncle Clive appeared in the hall.

"Laura, I want you to go into my study with Mr Brody. He has something particular to say to you."

Temporarily defeated, I lowered my head and walked into the study. The cold and musky smell did nothing to soften my resolve and I wondered what kind of man would propose to a lady in a Rector's study. One couldn't expect a garden proposal from Edwin Brody but one would think the Drawing room would have been more appropriate—

"Miss Laura, may I call you Laura? Over the last few months, I have keenly observed your person. I believe you are a sensible young lady, cognizant of the great honor now bestowed upon you. I consider you a suitable candidate for the vacant position as my wife." He adjusted his spectacles, looking solemnly out of the window. "My reasons for marrying are as follows: Firstly, I believe the desired state enhances my future succession here as Rector. Secondly, I wish to keep faith with the good Rector by considering his niece first, and thirdly, I think it would greatly enhance my happiness to have you by my side, day after day."

And night after night, I finished for him with a cringe. I experienced a terrible desire to laugh and quickly regained my composure.

"I know you will recognize the great advantages in considering my proposal," Edwin went on. "I know a young lady requires time—"

I stood up quietly. "My Brody, I feel you mistake my silence for acceptance. Though I thank you for the great honor you have bestowed upon me with your proposal, I have no desire to wed you or any other man for that matter."

He waved a hand, smiling. "No need to be coy with me, Miss Laura. I know some ladies like to play games...and I am sure you will come to the correct decision, indeed the only decision, when you return from London."

Fortunately, that was the end of the insalubrious episode. Mr Brody refused to listen to another word, asking instead, for my answer when I returned from London.

I thought over the problem during my journey. Uncle Clive made it quite clear that he wished me to marry Edwin Brody. My being Edwin's wife would also secure his own future. He desired me to have a comfortable future, he said, and a respectable position in the community.

Slave to Lord and Lady Rohan, I corrected silently, and tried to picture myself as Mrs Brody, the Rector's wife.

I shuddered before the feeling came to me. An odd sensation that came and went, a feeling of destiny, I suppose.

I knew I did not belong in the Rectory and I could no longer wait for an invitation to Silverthorn. Once my sojourn in London ceased, I would be forced to look for a post as a governess.

I handled all the arrangements for the funeral of Lord Vere. Lord Vere's nephew arrived to collect his inheritance.

Lady Beatrice needn't have feared. Her late husband's nephew was a generous man and despite his wife's disapproval, settled an amount upon her, three thousand pounds, and provided for her future by allowing her to stay in his own villa in Brighton for the term of her life.

I was more than happy to assist Lady Beatrice, who had so generously arranged my education, and in that regard, would help me to procure a post.

"I disagree, dear," Lady Beatrice touched my arm one morning. "I want you to come to Brighton with me. You need not play fiddle to some rich man's progeny."

I thanked her for her kind offer and explained why I must go out into the world. I longed for an adventure, for a change, anything to take me away from the Rectory and Mr Edwin Brody.

I had applied for two positions when Madeline's letter arrived, gleaming ominously in the morning sunlight on a table in the front parlor. Daisy told me the postmark came from my village and I delayed in opening it, thinking it would be from Mr Brody, or worse, Uncle Clive, ordering me home.

I tossed and turned in my bed that night. Each time I thought I was drifting off to sleep, I saw the letter before me, beckoning me to open it. With a grunt of annoyance, I slid out of bed and lit a candle. On closer examination of the postmark, I noted it was misdirected and trembled in excitement.

Silverthorn!

I eagerly ripped open the seal to see Madeline's messy scrawl, written on the crisp Silverthorn paper.

Silverthorn

October 30, 1878,

My dear Laura,

I know I have neglected you...
La, but I am to blame to forget what a friend and a sister you've been to me in the past.

I am in trouble and I don't know what to do. I've considered running away but I am not the type, am I? Remember Adam and Rohan House? And how you had a secret fancy for Adam and never told me? Fie on you, for if you did, I might have not done what I did.

But you have always helped me...and I know we regard ourselves as sisters.

You must help me...I am desperate. They will kill me, you know. I can feel it. My time is not far away...you are the only one I can turn to...can trust. I know I have made terrible mistakes in the past and I am sorry for it...please help me..."

I put down the letter, ignorant of the dwindling flame. *They will kill me* chanted over and over in my mind. It would be cruel of her to jest in such a fashion. No, it must be true. She was frightened out of her wits and begged for my immediate assistance.

I went to a drawer in my dresser and removed the bundle of letters tied with a blue ribbon. My mind raced forward as I flicked through them, looking for any kind of clue.

I found a letter dated two years ago. *His cousin Justin will go to any length to achieve what he wants.* A year later: *Justin has become even more suspicious of me...he is just waiting for an opportunity...he covets the title..."*

He covets the title. The letters dropped from my hands and fluttered down to the floor. I did not even notice, so absorbed in my thoughts. *They will kill me, you know...please help me, Laura.* The desperate plea stung my ears with its potency.

I could not forsake her when she remained in danger.

Justin Braithfield wanted to be rid of her.

I knew what I must do.

I thought it prudent not to mention the contents of Madeline's letter to Lady Beatrice or Aunt Mary. I had to consider all aspects in deciding how to respond to her plea, including Madeline's tendency to exaggerate.

As usual, she neglected to give any detail about her 'desperate' situation, apart from feeling some kind of animosity from her husband's nephew, Justin Braithfield.

What could I possibly do? Did she expect me to rush up to Yorkshire and land unexpectedly on her doorstep without a proper invitation?

I spent the next two hours in my room, trying to work out a solution. Lady Beatrice sent up a note inquiring after me when I failed to remember our lunch engagement. I pleaded a headache and begged her apologies. A few moments later, Daisy brought in a tray of cucumber sandwiches.

The food stared at me for half an hour before I was tempted. Chiding myself for foolishness, I sipped the still warm tea and finished the tray of sandwiches.

Suitably refreshed, I had a plan scribbled out twenty minutes later. I would write Uncle Clive and Aunt Mary, informing them of my decision to find a post. I planned to travel north to visit Miss Banks. She was a sensible friend and teacher who could assist me to find a post in a household. In doing this, I would have to write Mr Brody a letter, explaining my reasons for refusing his suit and thank him for his generous offer.

I decided to send no word to Madeline until I was in a position to help her.

The letters were finished by the time the gong sounded for our evening meal. The empty dining room was a stark reminder of Lady Beatrice's new status as a dependent widow.

She laughed at my solemn reflection. "Lud! How you frighten me with that face! Do not pity me, child. I may not be a London hostess but I can aspire to other professions in my move to Brighton—the gossiping widow, perhaps?"

"I think you will enjoy life by the sea," I said with a cheer I didn't feel. "It will be quiet...but peaceful. It is nice to have peace in one's life."

"My dear Laura, you are correct, as usual." She glanced at me quickly. "And you have changed into quite a handsome young woman. Are you going to accept this Mr Brody? Lud, the very name sounds droll. I hope you have enough sense not to..." she saw my nod and approved. "I admire your courage, my girl. Since you deny me the privilege of your company in Brighton, I can only assume you have decided to return to the Rectory. Clive is certain to be offish with you...he thought he had planned it all out so perfectly—with you as Brody's wife, he could retire at the Rectory and live on your good will." She laughed at idea before sighing, "poor Mary."

I smiled. I liked Beatrice. However, I chose my answer with care. "No, I won't be returning to the Rectory. I have decided to seek a post up north where I have a connection in my old governess, Miss Theresa Banks."

"Very sensible, my dear," Beatrice replied. "And what of your funds?"

I blushed, for I did not have any. I had been thinking of this very aspect when I came down to dinner.

Lady Beatrice confirmed my situation. "You have none, I see, and you hate to borrow. Therefore, I will make of it as a present—no, no, I have been thinking of a way to thank you for your kindness and what gift can better something practical?"

"I cannot allow you to do that, Lady Beatrice," I protested.

"Nonsense! I will do as I please. I've always done so, and nobody can gainsay me, especially now as I am the grieving widow. You would not wish to upset me by refusing, would you?"

"Of course not."

"Good. I will provide all your travel fees and a little extra for your comfort...now, now, don't deny me the pleasure. You should be more shrewd, girl, and accept opportunities. More like your cousin, Madeline. Now, she would not be one to throw away an opportunity, would she?"

"No," I replied.

Lady Beatrice winked conspiratorially. "...By the by, you received a letter from her, did you not? Well, out with it, girl. What does she have to say? Is she enjoying motherhood and her new status as Mistress of Silverthorn?"

"I have heard a little about the place..."

"Place?" Lady Beatrice echoed in disgust. "My dear child, Silverthorn is the pearl of the north. Have you never seen a picture of it?"

I shook my head.

"Well, I don't doubt you will see it in due time. What a success for a penniless orphan! It is the basis for a fairy-story, is it not?"

I stayed with Lady Beatrice until the house closed.

She needed assistance in selling the furniture and packing the few belongings her husband's nephew graciously allowed her to keep. During this time, she continually expressed her gratitude and I continually protested against her desire to pay me for my services.

"It is not for your services, girl," she confirmed matter of factly, "it is because I *like* you...and quite frankly m'dear, I don't take a liking to everyone." She studied me closely. "I know you feel inferior to your cousin but it takes more than beauty to win me over. Of course, I've never seen such a beauty. But I always thought that one would be trouble, it is in her nature. She is an adventuress."

Years later, I thought over those words and how true they proved to be. However, at this time I gloated over my victory. Lady Beatrice favored me over Madeline. I knew it was childish and completely unworthy of me, but I didn't care. In a small way, I had triumphed over Madeline when I never thought I could.

But now she was in danger and she needed me.

I arranged my ticket at the station in the early part of the week. Lady Beatrice assured me I had done all I could do and there was no reason to delay my departure.

I received a curt reply from Uncle Clive, who grudgingly wished me well in my endeavors, not failing to express his displeasure in my turning my nose up at a perfect, comfortable future with his esteemed protégé, Mr Brody. He also declared I knew little of the life I intended to enter and would eventually regret my decision.

As I read his neat writing, I knew there would be no place for me at the Rectory if Mr Brody decided to marry. Suddenly, my own future appeared as uncertain as Madeline's.

Victoria Station thrived with activity the following day and I couldn't dispel a feeling of apprehension as I left the quiet, assured life behind me.

I sat on board waiting for the nine o'clock train to depart, relieved my traveling companions were two elderly ladies who desired nothing more than to sleep on the forthcoming journey.

I needed time to think.

What would I call myself? I thought about it for a while and settled on Miss Anne Woodville. It was a decent name with no connection to Laura Morgan. I soon questioned my own decision. As Lady Braithfield's cousin, why shouldn't I visit her with my own name? Would it seem so odd if I turned up on her doorstep uninvited?

I had to be sure of the reception at Silverthorn before I made such an announcement. Madeline's words rose, unbidden, to warn me: *they will kill me, you know...my time is not far away.*

Perhaps I would place myself in jeopardy by acknowledging my relationship to her. It seemed unlikely but something held me back from declaring my true name. I chided myself for my foolishness but the inkling would not go away.

The journey passed quickly and uneventfully. We arrived at Liverpool and I set about arranging transport. The railroads, which were a marvelous invention, did not travel through every town and I had no choice but to utilize the old stagecoach method. For the first time in my life, I relied upon my own independence. I enjoyed the sensation, if a little daunting, and hoped I would find work as easy as traveling alone. I wanted to pay back Lady Beatrice, despite her kind generosity.

The next day, I reached the town where Miss Banks resided. The township wasn't large, owing its existence to the industrial activity on its outskirts. As the winter had begun, my fingers stiffened inside my gloves, making it difficult to drag my trunk between transports. I was told to wait at a certain point and a wagon would come along, transporting workers and their families in and out of the industrial site. Exhausted and soiled with travel stains, I thankfully sat down upon my trunk to wait.

The wagon came soon enough and I remember feeling surprise at the number of people loaded onto the one wagon. They were mainly miners and they studied me curiously through the journey, wondering why I lowered myself to travel with them and not in a hired coach. I found a seat beside a young man of no more than fifteen. He graciously allowed me to enter and proved a lively companion until we reached our destination. At the end, I thanked him for his friendship and it wasn't until he left his seat I noticed the condition of his swollen, infected feet. I was moved with pity.

The newly erected school of the district stood to the left of me, in the middle of a dusty field. Erected quickly to comply with the Education Act, (which decreed that children between the ages of five and ten must attend elementary education), it looked more like an abandoned tavern than a center for learning. Having no wish to disturb Miss Banks in the middle of a lesson, I quietly knocked on the tiny wooden door, hoping my letter had reached her in time.

A moment later, the door opened and I met the sunny face of Theresa Banks. She seemed taller and browner than I remembered.

"My dear Laura, how much you've grown! Yes, I did receive your letter...no, no, you can stay here as long as you like...no, no, it is no burden. Come in."

We managed to pull my trunk inside and collapsed upon it, laughing.

I felt her keen brown eyes study me closely. "Why, you've grown into quite a swan, my girl. Between friends, being handsome or being plain does not matter but I am happy for you that your looks have changed. And speaking of looks, have you heard from your cousin Madeline?"

My answer went into the late hours of the night. We were both too excited to sleep, eager to catch up on each other's news. Although Theresa's letters were detailed, I wanted to hear everything about her new life and her pupils. Her world suddenly became a reality to me and I fell under its spell.

"The pokey room is a bother!" Theresa apologized with a grin.

When I replied I would prefer this room and its company to Windsor Castle and Queen Victoria, she laughed: "Flatterer! I can't quite believe you are the girl I once knew...you look like someone else. You're welcome to stay here as long as you wish, but I know you have an important path to follow. What are you going to do? You realize Madeline has a tendency to exaggerate."

"Yes, I know," I yawned. We were both lying in bed, neither of us wanting to go to sleep. "But it is unlike her to feel threatened or frightened. Something isn't right..."

Theresa blew out the floundering candle. "She was always a little too conniving for my liking. She liked to queen it, even among her betters! Do you remember the way she manipulated Elizabeth Rohan?"

I laughed. Yes, I remembered. Since Madeline left, the worthy Miss Rohan had completely dismissed my existence.

I was even more determined to make something of my life, if only it proved Elizabeth Rohan wrong.

I awoke to the sound of chirping birds.

Theresa's bed was vacant. I sighed, dragging out my small pocket watch. Ten o'clock! I hadn't slept so late since our early days in London.

I found Theresa in her small sitting parlor, dressed immaculately as usual, her neat brown hair combed into a knot on the top of her head. "There's a fresh pot of tea here," she smiled.

"I have decided to go to Silverthorn," I announced, seating myself on the small wooden chair.

Theresa removed her spectacles before pouring the tea. "Oh...are you going to announce yourself?"

"I don't know...something is holding me back. It has been torturing me for days—I can't say what it is...but I know something's wrong. I can feel it."

"You shouldn't delay your arrival then," Theresa said. "There's a coach going to Yorkshire this afternoon. Shall we book you on it?"

I hesitated. "It seems dreadfully rude of me..."

"Nonsense. You came here for a purpose. When you find all is well, you must come back. At least your journey up there will not be in vain. You'll have a chance to see your cousin, even if you do arrive without a gold-edged invitation."

I left that afternoon.

Theresa accompanied me to the coach. I promised I would return as soon as I'd seen Madeline.

My future remained uncertain but I had to be convinced of Madeline's well being. Perhaps she would invite me to live there as a poor relation. I was sure I could be of some use, perhaps as a nurse to her daughter Laura, my little namesake.

I found a seat beside a young woman named Lucy. She said she was traveling back to her husband after visiting her family.

"I've never had the money to see me family, if it weren't for my Jim," she grinned. "He owns a pub, he does, and he's real good to me...I've been blessed to get such a good man and born him two youngin's. Where ye be going, missus?"

"I am going to visit a...friend."

"Oh...where's ye friend live?"

I could see no harm in telling her. "Her name is Madeline. We—er...went to school together. She married a Yorkshire gentleman."

"Which one, missus? I knows all the noble folk in Yorksh're."

"Lord Thomas Braithfield of Silverthorn."

Lucy's eyes widened, her face paling considerably.

"What's the matter?"

"Ye don't know, do ye missus? Ye know nothing!"

"Know what?"

Lucy shook her head. "Me sister, Dora, used to work at Silverthorn, missus. She'd just be sent pack'ng—new master didn't like her. Mrs Gardner's her name and she used to be lady's maid. Used to tend the mistress, she did. I've been gone this month but before I left, I went to see her. She tells me all the gossip of the place...anyways, last time...there was quite a fuss, ye know, over it all. She was so young...so beautiful...and a mother an'all..."

My throat constricted and the old fear attacked me. "What is it, Lucy? Tell me what's happened."

"Lady Bra'thfield...she's dead."

CHAPTER SIX

The news of my cousin's death left me deeply shaken.

I could scarcely believe my ears...no, it could not be. Not Madeline! I sat rigid, my face transfixed and expressionless. How did she die? Had she been ill all these months and failed to inform me? Perhaps that is why she did not reply to my letters. I felt suddenly ill as I tried to glean more information out of my informant without betraying myself.

Lucy shook her head sadly. "Me sister says it were a big shame...so tragic...an' it happen'd all too quick...at the great spring ball too."

It happened all too quickly. Was not that the way of sudden illness or a murder disguised as an unforeseen accident? My mind raced ahead...Madeline had been fraught with worry in her last letter. I recalled what she had struggled to write in a shaky, almost illegible, hand: *"Justin will go to any lengths to achieve his aim..."*

Any lengths? Would he consider murder an option?

"An'...if that weren't `nough to cope with—the ol' lord dies just before her...ha, what a mess it all is, missus. Must come as a great shock to ye."

Those few words of idle gossip dawned on me. Lord Thomas dead? And his young wife followed him to the grave. I said nothing in return and pleaded a headache. Lucy seemed to understand and kept silent for a time.

I knew I could not turn back now. Madeline and her husband had been murdered and if my suspicious were correct, Justin Braithfield stood alone to benefit from their deaths.

As if adding to my conclusions on the subject, Lucy yawned: "An' now the new lord is at Silverthorn. Me sister's never liked him, Lord Justin he be, and he `ever likes her—that's why he sent her pack'ng."

My mind envisaged what this Justin Braithfield looked like: a middle-aged man with shrewd black eyes and a black heart. He always wanted Silverthorn. He resented Madeline from the beginning—this young new wife threatening his rightful inheritance! Yes, he'd murdered them.

In this frame of mind, I set out to Silverthorn with all speed.

York was a charming town, very old and full of historical importance. I had never traveled in my life, (save for the journeys to London), so this was a great endeavor on my part. I pushed all thought of Madeline out of mind and concentrated upon my next action.

Lucy told me how to get to Silverthorn, which was roughly five and a half miles north of town. "The stage runs out that way twice a day, so ye might be lucky. If not, you'll 'ave to find lodging's for th' night."

I thanked her.

She shrugged. "Sorry I had to be th' bearer of bad news, missus. Hope all goes well for ye."

Once alone, I collapsed wearily on my trunk. Numbed, I absently watched the activity on the dusty street. I simply could not believe Madeline was dead.

Lucy was right. I missed the stage by a mere ten minutes. Suppressing the need to cry, I dragged my trunk into a nearby inn, *The Flying Eagle.*

I was grateful to be out of the cold. The inn was very old, as evidenced by the creaking floorboards beneath my feet, but warmth and cheer filled the rooms. I studiously avoided the curious men at the bar, lowering my hat over my face.

The clerk on the counter showed surprise at my request. "It'll be noisy, missus. It's locals night..."

"It's all right," I assured him and handed over the money.

He shrugged, ordering someone to help me with my trunk. I took the key and followed the man upstairs. It wasn't until I was in my small, but clean, room when my stomach reminded me I hadn't eaten or many hours. I removed my gloves and leaving my hat on, went downstairs.

Luckily, the young clerk was still there and I asked him if I could be placed in a quiet corner.

He led me to a private table and promptly removed the 'reserved' tag. I sat down gratefully, smoothening the crinkled folds of my dusty, traveling gown. Aunt Mary would be shocked by my appearance and Uncle Clive would be furious by my being un-chaperoned in an inn.

"Good evening."

The amused voice startled me. I turned around to see a tall man leaning casually against an obliging post, his dark eyes fixed intently on my person. His handsome face retained an air of hauteur, which, combined with his patrician nose, would suggest his status as a member of the *haute ton.*

Conspicuously dressed, he took in my travel-stained apparel and disheveled hair, barely concealed beneath my hat. "Can I help you, sir?" The words left my lips before I knew it.

He smiled. "Yes, I believe you can. You are sitting at my table."

I felt the color rush to my face. "Oh...I'm terribly sorry. The clerk assured me I could dine here...you see, I did not care to be in there—" I gestured, "and they do not send meals to rooms." I didn't know why I was explaining myself to a complete stranger. Perhaps because I did not care to be judged and found wanting.

The young clerk returned and, having realized his mistake, stuttered a chain of apologies.

"It's perfectly all right," the man assured him. "I will join the young lady, if she has no objections."

What could I possibly say? The man put me immediately on guard. To avoid his penetrating gaze, I studied the menu, though my thoughts remained on him. He looked to be in his early thirties, a dignified rake, clearly at ease with himself and this unusual situation. Did he often make a habit of dining with unknown ladies at this inn?

"What is your name?"

I blinked at the manner of his question. Should I tell him who I was?

He laughed. "Are you afraid to tell me? You do have a name, don't you?"

"Yes," I said quickly. "My name is Miss Woodville." Before I could ask his name, the clerk returned to take our orders. I selected the local stew and to my surprise, my dinner companion ordered the same.

"You feel awkward dining with me, don't you?" the man said, his lips twisting into a half-grin. "Your respectability is of prime concern to you. Let me guess who you are. A paid companion? A poor relation? Or perhaps a play actress in disguise?"

I felt the heat rise to my face. "I am not any of the above."

"Miss Woodville, tell me what a respectable young woman would be doing in an inn, un-chaperoned, and dining with a gentlemen stranger?"

"I would say she was very hungry and had no choice about the matter." I rose out of my chair. "I have evidently engendered your displeasure sitting at your table uninvited...I apologize for the inconvenience."

He barred my way with his hand. "Sit down, Miss Woodville! Two strangers dining alone can be perfectly respectable...ah, our food has arrived!"

The alluring aroma of food forced me to occupy my seat once more. I intended to eat as quickly as possible and leave. When the man offered me a glass of wine, I politely refused. Uncle Clive had enforced the importance of intoxicating liquor one too many times.

Having made a pact to remain as strangers, we talked a little about the town and its history. Though I enjoyed the information, I felt nothing but relief when I finished. "Thank you for your kindness, sir, in allowing me sit at your table," I rose out of my chair, preparing for a quick escape.

He stood up and took my hand. "It was a pleasure, Miss Woodville."

An odd, fleeting sensation passed through me when his fingers touched mine. I turned away from his mocking blue eyes.

"Do not pay the clerk, for the bill has been paid," he said, releasing my hand.

"Thank-you," I stammered, "I do not even know your name..."

He returned to the table. "It is unlikely we will meet again. Good night, Miss Woodville."

I went upstairs in a daze. I had never felt so ill at ease with any gentleman. It didn't really matter.

I would never see him again. Those words brought a sense of loss to me I did not understand. Frustrated, I pushed aside all thoughts of the gentleman stranger and retired to my room.

The stage left at ten o'clock the next morning.

After a good night's rest in a comfortable bed, I felt more than ready to face the world. My curiosity and astonishment over Madeline's death fortunately suppressed any outward display of grief. I could not betray my identity.

The crisp morning added to the beauty of the moors. I watched as the mist caressed the gentle land, lending an aura of mystery to it. The sight haunted me and would for years to come. I felt an affinity with the place I couldn't explain nor comprehend.

The town nearest to Silverthorn existed mainly because of the patronage of that grand estate. As we approached, I studied the quaint red-roofed huts, two-story terrace houses, inns and shops with interest. They all stood in the shadow of a tall, looming monstrosity. I knew at once it must be one of the wool mills owned by the Braithfields.

"Ye look'ng for lodgings, missus?" a scratchy voice said behind me. I turned to find an old woman, dressed in a much-worn gray dress soiled with work.

I nodded and she gestured towards the opposite side of the street, eyeing me curiously as I lifted my trunk and followed her advice. I felt suddenly foolish and wondered whether I should turn around and forget this whole charade. But I could not. I had to do it for Madeline. She had pleaded for my help, beckoned me to Silverthorn, and now I could not desert her. Not until I discovered the truth.

A kindly old gentleman ran the two-story accommodation block. He directed me to his fair-haired daughter, who sat at a small delicately carved table, counting cash.

The sturdy girl greeted me with a sunny smile. "What can I do for ye, missus? Me name's May."

"I wish to procure a room, please," I replied, rubbing my hands together for warmth.

May smiled, smoothening a wisp of her curly hair. "Certainly missus." She glanced speculatively at me. "Sorry if I seems staring-like, but no' many young ladies travel up this way without a place to go. Are ye seek'ng work, missus?"

I could see no harm in telling her the truth. "Yes. I would consider any suitable employment."

"Ah missus, then ye're in luck! There's a place at Silverthorn for the tak'ng—they want a governess for milord's children. Ye'd best get in quick though for there's many a lass look'ng for a comfortable post." She noted my travel-stained appearance. "Why don't ye rest up a bit and apply to the place and I'll send Peter `round with ye note."

"Where is Silverthorn exactly?"

May smiled. "Ha, tucked away like a gem is Silverthorn, missus. It's on the moors, to the west, right in between the mills. Clever of them to place it so, I reckon."

"Are the mills still owned and operated by the Braithfield family?"

"Aye, missus. If ye can fill in ye name here..."

As I signed my name as Miss Anne Woodville, I wondered what Uncle Clive and Aunt Mary would think of my expedition. They would scarcely approve of my adopting another identity.

"Ye're lucky to-day, missus," May said as she led me to my room. "We're usually cram full..." she raised her eyes, "so many workers pass'ng through work'ng at the mill." She unlocked the room and briskly stepped in. "It's not big, but it's clean." She pulled back the small curtain at the window and opened a separate door. "Ye can wash and change in here...when ye're ready, send down ye letter and I'll send Peter over to the Manor."

"Thank-you, May," I replied, a little startled by my own luck. Although it was too premature to assume, I never imagined getting inside Silverthorn would be so easy. A governess's post suited me perfectly, as it was my preferred profession.

An hour later, washed and rested, I sat down to write my introductory letter. I thought for a few moments and decided to stretch the truth a little. Biting the end of my writing instrument, I began a draft.

> My Lord Braithfield,
>
> My name is Anne Woodville and I am applying for the position of governess in your household. Although I do not have in my possession any references (I can easily obtain them), I assure you I have had much experience with children of all ages. I have been regarded as a good influence and am familiar with all duties pertaining to the position lying vacant at this time. I look forward to hearing from you soon.
>
> Yours sincerely,
> Miss Woodville.

I made a few minor changes and satisfied, sealed the letter. When I went down to give it to May, my hands trembled. My prospective employer could very well be Madeline's murderer. How did he treat Madeline's daughter, the same as his own children? I clutched the letter to my chest.

I must get inside...I must.

When I came down for breakfast the next morning, a letter was waiting for me. It was marked "Miss Woodville" and the seal, as May was quick to point out, belonged to Silverthorn. I took a moment to study it: two black crows, a peacock and a dagger with the inscription in Latin reading: "The faithful remain." I remembered Madeline's letters, written on the same paper, and felt a renewed chill over her death. What could have happened?

I broke open the seal and took out a single, crisp page.

"Dear Miss Woodville,

Come to Silverthorn at 3.00 tomorrow afternoon for an interview.

Yours etc,
Braithfield.

I could see traces of arrogance in the writing and thought it suited Justin Braithfield admirably. I cringed, knowing I would have to meet him on the morrow and must school my features to betray nothing. I am Anne Woodville, not Laura Morgan, I told myself. Anne Woodville does not have a cousin called Madeline.

I asked May how I might get to Silverthorn.

"It's a nice walk, missus. Does ye good, Yorkshire air. Don't forget to take a wrap. When ye ready, I'll tell ye which way to go."

The crisp, cool air remained my only friend on the long, solitary walk. I watched in awe as the mist hovered over the ground, beckoning my way to Silverthorn. I shrugged off the idiotic fantasy. As Miss Anne Woodville, I needed to be a sensible governess of sound mind. Determined to play out my part, I pulled the wrap closer around my shoulders.

Twenty minutes later, I found the incline May had mentioned and my heart instantly quickened. Rhododendrons in brilliant reds, pinks and yellows suddenly formed a drive. Like something out of a dream, I followed the road, waiting for a glimpse of the famous Manor.

Silverthorn.

I will never forget my first sight of it. Rising out of the mist loomed a gigantic structure built of red brick and stone with elegantly shaped mullioned windows. Ivy clung to the walls, engulfing part of the old stone Tower that struggled to stand independently from the Elizabethan Manor attached to it. The grounds of the Manor consisted of manicured laws and hedges, circular gardens with fountains in the French fashion. Half-castle, half-mansion, it was haunting, like an image out of one's mind or out of a painting, and I wondered for a brief moment if I had conjured it out of nothing.

The wind wiped against my ears, bringing me back to reality. In a few moments, I would have to confront my cousin's murderer, Lord Braithfield.

I found the servant's quarters easily enough and the cook left her kitchen to greet me, a large, rigid-faced woman, who allowed her eyes to travel speculatively over my person. "What can I do for ye, leddy?"

The broad Yorkshire accent was difficult to decipher. "I have a three o'clock appointment with Lord Braithfield," I answered steadily.

"The governess, are ye?"

"I have applied for the position, yes."

"We've had many a leddy come ask'ng for it..." the woman went on without my encouragement. "Tilly, show the young leddy to his lordship's study."

A young, scrawny girl, no more than twelve, left her chopping board and after wiping her hands on her apron, curtsied before me. "Come with me, Miss."

I followed her through a maze of staircases and halls, darkened by the wooden paneling favored by Elizabethan style houses. The furniture was exquisite, what I glimpsed of it. I didn't expect a mill owner to have such lavish taste and style.

"This is milord's study, Miss," Tilly said. "Wait here and I'll tell his lordship ye've arrived."

"Thank-you."

Now alone, I turned around to study the room. Undoubtedly masculine, a large oak desk with curved legs and gilded handles dominated the room, flanked by floor to ceiling bookcases and a fireplace to the left of the door.

The room was evidently well used, judging by the neat stack of papers arranged on the desk under a remarkable ivory shade lamp. Natural light flowed from the large windows into the room, illuminating a box of open cigars whose distinct smell floated through the air. It was a cozy room. I warmed my hands by the fire and studied the portrait of a young man hanging above the fireplace. Dressed in hunting gear, one hand rested on the head of a greyhound and the other held a riding crop. I was drawn to his long and gaunt face, handsome in an arrogant sort of way. The wind caught at his golden hair and his dark blue eyes seemed to penetrate my soul. I shivered, stepping backwards.

"The portrait frightens you?"

I turned gasped at the familiar voice. The man from the inn! "You..." I managed to stammer.

He smiled and closed the door behind him. "It is *my* Miss Woodville...indeed a pleasure."

How could this be Justin Braithfield? There must be some mistake...

"You were expecting the man in the painting? Cousin Vincent fits the picture more of a country lord, doesn't he?" He paused, noting my shocked face. "There is no need for any feelings of embarrassment or awkwardness between us, Miss Woodville. It is to your advantage that we met independently."

I quickly recovered my equilibrium. I could not betray myself, not when I was so close. "I have come about the position, my Lord."

"Yes, so your letter states," he replied lightly, seating himself behind the desk and gesturing for me to sit in the chair opposite.

"It is usually not my policy to interview members of staff. The Housekeeper, Mrs Simmons, does that...but the last governess was disastrous and you would understand my personal interest in the children's welfare?"

"Of course." I noted he did not refer to them as *his* children but the children. I thought of Madeline's little girl and quickly assumed she was included in this group.

"You do not possess any references, Miss Woodville."

I looked up to find him studying my letter. The pale light caught his luxuriant black hair, softening his rigidly handsome face. I caught my breath. I must not allow his physical attraction to cloud my judgment. This was Justin Braithfield, whose lethal, cruel hand had murdered my cousin.

"I can easily obtain them, my Lord," I replied, keeping my voice even. "The vacancy of the position came to me by chance...I did not have sufficient time to gather the necessary credentials...however I do have a letter from a respected, well-educated friend who is now a teacher." I drew the letter from my reticule and passed it over.

I watched Lord Braithfield's face as he scanned the contents. "A flattering estimation, indeed..." He put the letter down and smiled. "I have no doubts about hiring you, Miss Woodville, but are you sure you are up to the challenge? So far, I have had nothing but failures. I trust you will be turn out a success?"

"I will endeavor to be, my Lord."

"Are you certain, Miss Woodville, you are capable of handling the terrors of the nursery? Believe me, it has outwitted the most learned of women."

"I am ready to accept the challenge," I said, setting my mind for the worst.

He smiled. "Then shall we go to the nursery and let the children be the judge."

"Papa!"

I watched my cousin's murderer open his arms and swoop up the young boy. Before I could study this extraordinary behavior, a plump, middle-aged woman with neat black hair, holding a young girl's hand, came to greet me.

"You must be our new governess," she said bluntly. "Name's Mrs Simmons. I am the Housekeeper here. I hope you'll be better than the last one."

I suppressed the urge to seize the young dark-haired girl in her control. I felt a sharp tug of emotion run through me. My namesake, Laura, lifted her little gypsy face in curiosity. The only part she inherited from her mother was her green eyes, Madeline's eyes.

"She seems taken with you," Mrs Simmons observed. "Laura is her name. Turns five next month but hasn't spoken a word since—" she stopped abruptly, glancing towards Lord Braithfield. "The other children belong to my Lord. Miss Cathy, the eldest, is fourteen and as headstrong as they come and Master Brandon will be turning six Saturday next."

I held out my hand to the olive-skinned, golden haired boy. "My name's Anne. What's yours?"

"Brandon Braithfield."

"Well Brandon, now we're acquainted, we're going to have lots of fun together. We can draw pictures and I'll tell you stories and teach you to read and write—"

"And will you walk Winter with me?"

"Who's Winter?"

"My dog."

I nodded gravely. "I should very much like to walk Winter with you."

"You've won one ally, Miss Woodville," Lord Braithfield said behind me. "He bit the last governess on her first day! You have been slightly more fortunate."

I noticed Brandon's sister sitting in the corner, her back to us. She quickly turned away when I walked over, pretending to be engrossed in her book. She had the pink and gold prettiness of a porcelain doll and seemed equally as fragile.

"Cathy, this is your new governess, Miss Anne Woodville."

"I don't want a new governess...I don't *need* a governess!" She burst off the settee, sending her book flying. "I hate them! I hate them all!" Tears rolled down her flushed cheeks as she bolted out of the room, ignoring her father's order to come back and apologize.

"In her absence, you must accept my apology. She is young and headstrong...I am a very busy man, Miss Woodville. I've warned her that if her behavior doesn't improve, she will go to a seminary in London."

"I feel I can win the girl's friendship, my Lord."

"Then I leave you in charge."

CHAPTER SEVEN

Mrs Simmons showed me to my room, summoning a manservant to fetch my belongings. She clearly exerted authority here and I wondered how she got along with Madeline.

"As governess," Mrs Simmons said, "you'll be sleeping in the room next to the nursery. Master Brandon has nightmares and probably will wake you, so be forewarned. You are very young for a governess..."

Her black eyes darted over me perceptively. I thought my limited attractions should pose no threat if she believed I won my post for my looks. "We've never had a governess this young before," she hurried on, "but I suppose it may turn out for the better. Miss Cathy is a difficult girl, willfully rude, who does not behave correctly to her elders."

"I will do my best," I assured her.

I didn't expect my room to be so spacious or luxurious. A warm fire glowed in the corner. I went to the window and examined the view, slightly obscured by the mist and rain.

"Your fire is lit twice daily," Mrs Simmons murmured. "Meals will be sent to your room, unless you prefer to eat with the children."

"Yes I would," I said, removing my gloves and tested out my bed.

"His Lordship expects your duties to begin tomorrow, Miss. I've summoned one of the maids to look after the children today. The children's rooms are opposite yours, as you can see." She paused and asked if I had any questions.

I asked her about the Braithfield family.

"His Lordship is a widower. His cousin, Mr Vincent Braithfield, visits occasionally. He has no wife. Miss Lillian, the old Lord's daughter, lives here in the West Wing. She married an officer who died a year after they wed, leaving her with child. She came to live here at Silverthorn where she produced a stillborn babe. Miss Lillian is not an ordinary sort of girl and she still grieves for her husband and her babe."

I thought she might have mentioned something of Madeline but she didn't. I felt relieved when she finally left me alone.

I needed to prepare myself for tomorrow, for the next few days were important. Lord Braithfield had agreed to a trial of two months and if I proved suitable, I would be allowed to stay.

I wondered why Madeline was not mentioned or the recent death of the old Lord Thomas. Mrs Simmons struck me as a no-nonsense housekeeper who kept strict control of her ship.

I lay on my comfortable bed, suddenly realizing how tired I was. Before I fell into a deep slumber, I remember thinking of Lord Braithfield's face. He was the man at the inn, the one whom I had so shamelessly dined with, and yet he failed to mention any recognition in his letter. Instead, he had opted to make me look a fool.

And, I was ashamed to admit, he succeeded.

The morning began with a storm. I am not usually superstitious but I wondered, as I breakfasted in my room, whether this meant something.

At eight o'clock, I knocked on the children's doors and after a brief pause, entered their rooms. I found Brandon drawing peacefully in bed, his breakfast eaten and a smile of welcome on his face. I poked my head into Cathy's room. A figure wriggled rebelliously under the covers.

"Come and eat your breakfast, Cathy," I implored. "I suspect your new governess will be strict but not today. I believe she desires to watch the storm from the window."

The tentative reply came from a small voice. "W—we won't have to go to the schoolroom straight away?"

"No," I assured her and helped her out of bed. "My name is Anne."

Cathy looked at me squarely. "You're young...and different. Is this your first time as a governess?"

"Yes, and you'll find me very different from the others. I had a governess once and we are the best of friends. It is much better, I believe, to make a friend of one's governess than an enemy."

A few moments later, Cathy joined us.

I hid a smile. Perhaps this was not going to be as difficult as I thought.

The day passed reasonably smoothly.

Mrs Simmons poked her head in on our final lesson. "Miss Woodville. I hope you know what you're doing. Your methods are unconventional, to say the least."

"Lord Braithfield left me in charge, Mrs Simmons, and this is my way. If his Lordship doesn't approve, he will speak to me about it."

Dismissed, she turned from the door in a huff.

We received one other visitor that day. I asked Cathy to read a novel of my selection, *Sense and Sensibility* by Jane Austen. Cathy protested a loathing for books and I promised her she would enjoy the story of the Dashwood girls. Intrigued by the romantic aspect of the story, she deigned to do as I asked and it soon became an hour or so when the interruption came.

"Aunt Lillian is here," Brandon announced.

We both turned to see a small, brown-haired woman whom I judged to be in her mid-thirties. Her plain features were illuminated by her smile, matching the warmth in her dark brown eyes. She held a sleeping Laura in her arms.

I had wondered and fretted over the absence of the child. I considered asking Mrs Simmons but she would be keen to point out my neglect and, no doubt, inform his Lordship of it the moment he returned home.

I watched as Miss Lillian laid the child comfortably on the rug by the fire.

"You must be Anne, the new governess," she said to me, glancing down as Brandon tugged her skirts. She smiled. "Yes, I'll draw you a picture."

We carried on with our reading. Several pages on, I noted Miss Lillian's drawing resembled Silverthorn, in all its intricate detail.

Laura started to stir and I gestured for Cathy to read on in silence. She did so with delight. When Laura settled herself in my lap, I sang a song Ruby taught me long ago and this seemed to settle her. She watched me those large green eyes, so like Madeline's. She'd lost her mother and really was a little gypsy now, I thought ruefully.

Lillian finished her drawing and we all gushed over its beauty. Madeline would have been Lillian's stepmother, I realized suddenly. I should know all this if Madeline had been a little more diligent with her letters.

"You must know the Manor very well, Miss Lillian," I said, admiring her picture. "How long have you been here?"

"All my life. I love Silverthorn. More than *she* ever did."
"Who is she?"
"Oh she probably means Aunt Madeline," Cathy glanced at us from her book. "Laura's mother."
"Oh?" I raised my brows in surprise. "Who is Madeline?"
Lillian hesitated. "It doesn't matter, she's dead. And she never loved Silverthorn as I do...just like Cecily."

Something sparked my memory and I remembered one of Madeline's letters, my favorite one, the one where she described Silverthorn.

Cathy rolled her eyes. "Aunt Lillian will no doubt be now telling you of the famous tale of woe...of poor Lady Eleanor and her wicked sister Cecily, who stole her fiancé by pushing her sister off the Tower before her wedding day. Eleanor is a weakling. She shouldn't have let Cecily get the better of her."

"Cecily was evil," Lillian said, "but she paid dearly for it...by being haunted the rest of her days by the ghost of her sister...who still haunts the Tower."

"Nonsense," Cathy snorted. "There are no such things as ghosts."
"There is too!" Brandon tugged my skirts. "Uncle Vince told me so."
Cathy chuckled. "Oh, you'd believe anything Uncle Vince says."
"Is there really a ghost?" I asked Lillian.

She shrugged. "I don't know...who said anything about a ghost?"

We were to see much of Lillian in those first weeks.

Being informed of her condition by Mrs Simmons, I wanted to help her, but as time wore on, I thought it best to leave her alone.

Her own tragedy in life had caused her to be especially protective of children and she chose retreat from the world when she had enough of them. She was testing me...and I began to resent her constant presence in the schoolroom.

Perhaps she did not consider me a suitable governess?

I had been a month at Silverthorn and when no more requests came for me to report to Lord Justin, I thought my position at Silverthorn secure. Only rarely, after meal times, did Justin visit the schoolroom. Sometimes he would stay and read a book to Brandon.

I had not long put the children to bed, having waited an hour with them for their father's visit. When he didn't appear, Cathy and Brandon went to bed disappointed.

I paused a moment before heading towards my room when a blunt tap sounded at the door. I shivered when the door opened, feeling the draft seep into the room.

"Good evening, Miss Woodville, are the children asleep?"

His half smile captivated me. He moved towards me, confidence in every line of his body, and I detested the quick jump in my heart. "Yes, they waited a long time for your visit."

He nodded solemnly. "Then perhaps now would be a good time to have our chat, Miss Woodville. It will only be brief so you need not be alarmed. Come and sit by the fire."

I watched him stoke the dying fire with remarkable efficiency. "I regret I missed the children, Miss Woodville...I did not expect to be home so late from my dinner engagement."

I recalled a snippet of conversation during the day to which Lillian had informed me of his intention to join a dinner party at the Westons where he would see Miss Weston.

"Who is Miss Weston?" I had asked.

Lillian rolled her eyes. "Miss Olivia Weston has her cap set at Justin. She is the local beauty of the district."

There was a long pause before he continued: "I must commend you, Miss Woodville. I perceive a remarkable change in Cathy. How did you do it?"

"It was very easy, my Lord. She only needed a friend, not a mother."

He raised his brows at my remark, his dark eyes assessing me silently. "I had assumed she needed another mother...I must have a confidential word with you, Miss Woodville. Firstly, I want you to stay. Secondly, because you have won the children's affections so easily, I feel I can trust you with this information."

"Yes, my Lord?"

"There will be an announcement soon of an engagement between myself and Miss Weston." He paused, glancing into the fire, a roguish lock of hair falling on his forehead. "It is Cathy I am concerned with. She has been ill tempered ever since her mother died and I am not sure how she will take the news. She is, of course, acquainted with Miss Weston."

I could not understand the pang of envy I felt and quickly suppressed it. "I assume you want me to break to it to the children, my Lord?" I asked, trying to picture Miss Weston as mistress of Silverthorn. She did pose a threat to me, I thought suddenly, for if she did not favor me, I would be sent packing.

He nodded. "It is not my nature to neglect my duty, Miss Woodville, but I feel they—or Cathy especially, will take it better coming from you."

"I will do my best," I assured him as he walked towards the door. He glanced back at me, his dark eyes studying me curiously before the door closed behind him.

Two weeks later, Lillian told us Miss Weston was coming to Silverthorn.

"They say she is very beautiful," Cathy said, "but I don't think so...there is a coldness in her eyes I don't quite like—"

"Nonsense, Cathy. I'm sure Miss Weston is very amiable. And your father loves her dearly."

Cathy snorted. "I don't want her to come...we don't *need* a new mother!"

I sat beside her and reasoned gently. "Cathy, you are fifteen and a young lady now. Do you want people to treat you like a child?"

"No."

"Then don't behave like one. Think of your father. He deserves to be happy...and if his happiness lies with Miss Weston, you must accept her. Think how happy and pleased he will be if you make an effort to welcome her."

"Why must we have a new mother, Anne?" Brandon tugged at my sleeve. "We have *you*."

There was an awkward pause. Lillian stared at me speculatively. Cathy came to my rescue by proposing we take Winter for a walk.

"What a ridiculous suggestion," Lillian said, glancing out of the window. "It's the middle of winter! You'll all catch a chill, Miss Woodville."

The pronunciation of my title confirmed what I suspected. Miss Lillian did not like me being in control of the children, or if she did, she had an unusual way of showing it. I remembered Mrs Simmons comment: *'Miss Lillian is not an ordinary sort of girl.'*

I fastened a woolen wrap around my shoulders and smiled. "Nonsense. A little fresh air never did anybody harm. Come, children."

Brandon pounced on the idea while Cathy secured his coat and I took Laura by the hand.

I could feel Lillian's eyes boring into my back as we left the room.

The air was delightfully refreshing.

We circled the garden three times, Cathy and Brandon deciding to run around the fountain.

Laura held my hand in perfect silence. She looked up when I pointed out things, confirming her intelligence, however, she refused to utter a single syllable.

I imagined the garden would look lovely in spring and could scarcely wait for it to arrive. How magnificent it must be! I had heard of their famous spring ball: the garden doors would be open...the cool air inviting...the pleasant aroma of roses and—

"Anne! Winter's run away!"

We searched for Brandon's greyhound for a few minutes until the faithful dog came bounding back. I tried to encourage Laura's interest in the hound. I thought I saw a little smile lurking at the corners of her mouth when the hound rolled onto his back and Brandon obliged him with a scratch on his tummy.

We started on our way back when Cathy burst out suddenly: "I like you, Anne. You're the first governess I've liked but I don't want a new mother. I don't want Papa to marry that woman—she'll send us off to boarding school!"

"I'm sure she will do no such thing, Cathy," I replied gently. "By the end of next week, you will feel differently."

"I doubt it," came the subdued reply. "All mothers are the same. Aunt Lillian said so. And I don't like Miss Weston."

Brandon caught up and my tête-à-tête with Cathy ceased. There had been several confidences, however, Cathy neglected to mention anything about her mother or when she died. I knew I would learn more in time and instructed myself to be patient.

It was hard not to pry when so much mystery surrounded Madeline's presence in this household. I must win their trust before I could find answers. Whatever they would be, it would explain why Madeline must not be mentioned, the secrecy, and the mystery of her death.

Was she murdered and why?

These questions tortured me day after day.

"Look! There's Papa with Aunt Lillian!"

I followed Brandon's gaze. From one of the elegantly glazed windows Lord Braithfield and Miss Lillian stared down upon us.

I turned away from their scrutiny. I felt the color rush to my face. What did that man hold over me? *He is my cousin's murderer...*

Annoyed by my foolish fancies, I turned my attention back to the children.

A strange thing occurred the week before Miss Weston's arrival.

I had become used to Lillian's constant presence, watching over us with her large, brown eyes. Mrs Simmons replied to my complaint: "Miss Woodville...you must understand Miss Lillian has had a tragic history. She's lost her little girl; she finds comfort with the children...especially Miss Laura. I can understand the way you feel...you say it makes you nervous, but you will have to put up with it. His Lordship has decided to keep you on...therefore you will be seeing much more of Miss Lillian."

Her presence still made me uneasy, as though I was being judged and found wanting, and I was glad when Miss Lillian suddenly disappeared on the Monday before Miss Weston's arrival.

Miss Olivia Weston, the soon-to-be mistress the house, was expected on Friday. Mrs Simmons and the servants worked tirelessly to prepare for the event and it wasn't until the Tuesday afternoon I discovered the whereabouts of Lillian.

I was looking for Mrs Simmons. Brandon had come to me in the morning, complaining of a sore arm. Unable to straighten it, I feared he might have fractured a bone.

Mrs Simmons, I was told, could be found in the west wing. I hadn't been to that part of the house yet and paused when raised voices echoed in my ears.

"You half-witted imbecile! I said the *blue* china, not the *white*! Take it back. I will not have my orders crossed by disobedient servants."

"Now, now..." I recognized the even voice of Mrs Simmons. She emerged from the room, clearly surprised by my presence. "What are you doing here? Where are the children?"

"I am sorry to disturb you, Mrs Simmons. I can see you are busy but I fear Brandon may have broken his arm. Can you call for a doctor?"

"Simmons! Whom are you talking to in my presence?"

Lillian stood in the doorway, dressed in red velvet, her hair arranged in elaborate curls. Her cheeks were rouged and her lips reddened. "Oh—it's the little governess," she said, airily walking down towards me. "What have you done with my son Brandon?"

"Miss Lillian!" Mrs Simmons begged. "Now, you were doing so well. You don't want a scene to be reported to his Lordship, do you?"

Lillian glanced sourly at Mrs Simmons. "But she's just the governess! She's *inferior* to me."

"Yes, dear, but she's also human. You, as her better, much show kindness—you must set an example for others to follow."

Lillian raised her brows. "Oh, yes, I hadn't thought of that." She spun around to pick up her train and retreated into her room with a regal air.

Mrs Simmons snatched my hand when she left. "Miss Woodville, you will not repeat what you have just witnessed. Silverthorn has many a secret and if word got out about Miss Lillian...she is quite harmless...only a little confused. She's always been that way. The old Lord loved her dearly and cared for her. We must do the same."

I nodded, now understanding the whispers between the housemaids concerning the Braithfield 'madness.'

The doctor arrived an hour later. His hurried arrival coincided with that of his Lordship. I heard the carriage from the schoolroom, where Cathy and I were trying to humor Brandon. Laura lay asleep on a rug by the fire.

The door burst open to reveal his Lordship, the doctor hard on his heels. The doctor looked no more than thirty, an efficient young man with auburn hair who took immediate charge of the situation.

"What happened?" Justin glanced at me.

"He took a fall..." I began to explain.

Cathy interjected: "It wasn't Anne's fault, Papa! I was watching him and when I turned my back for a moment, only a moment, why—there he was—on the ground screaming."

"I see."

The doctor, a Mr Greg Carstares, examined the arm. "There's a slight fracture, here, at the elbow—which I believe is the reason why he doesn't want to straighten it. I'll bind it up but it mustn't be moved for two weeks. After that, I'll come back and check it."

"Thank-you, Carstares."

I showed the doctor out. I liked his personable face and broad accent. "Thank-you, Mr Carstares."

He lingered a moment and took my hand. "It is a pleasure to meet you, Miss Woodville. But I must insist you call me Greg. I often visit Silverthorn...so `tis likely we will meet again."

I smiled, warmed by his instant offer of friendship. When I returned to the schoolroom, I paused in the doorway, observing a touching moment between father and son.

Justin saw me and grinned. "Miss Woodville, you must allow me to apologize-—"

"Don't trouble yourself," I assured him.

"Papa," Brandon pulled at his coat, "can Anne sleep in my bed? I'm scared because my arm hurts."

I ruffled Brandon's golden curly hair, replying that I would be delighted. "But," I warned, "you will have to be very still or you may hurt your arm."

"He wriggles like a snake," Cathy warned. She decided to read him a book and opened the first page. Justin left them, his gaze resting for a moment on the sleeping Laura on the floor. His eyes remained emotionless and I wondered what he was thinking.

The moment quickly passed. He walked towards the door, signaling me to follow. "Miss Woodville...did you inform the children of Miss Weston's visit? She is scheduled to arrive on Friday."

"Yes, my Lord. I believe it went well."

"Good. I don't want any upsets. Miss Weston wishes to remain with us for a while. Oh...one more thing, Miss Woodville. On Friday evening, we are having a quiet family dinner—to introduce Olivia to the children. I have also invited some friends of mine—Mr Ashton and his sisters. I would like you to join us, Miss Woodville."

"Certainly," I replied. "I will bring the children when you require them."

He smiled. "I want you to join our dinner party, Anne."

The shock must have been apparent in my face.

"Do you understand me, Miss Woodville?"

"Yes, but I am surprised by the invitation."

His dark eyes held mine captive. "You will find me somewhat different to the gentry you've known...I do not obey the rules of etiquette."

I promised I would be there, wondering how Miss Weston would respond to my presence.

Whatever my private thoughts, I had to win her friendship.

I was here to discover what happened to Madeline, not to form opinions of my employer's next wife.

Friday came almost too quickly.

The Manor hummed with activity. I awoke to the sounds of Mrs Simmons voice, echoing down the corridor. It was eight o'clock and I was eating breakfast with the children. At a quarter past the hour, I made my way to the window to watch for Lord Braithfield's carriage. Every morning at this time, he would leave for the mill and it interested me to know whether he intended to stay and welcome his bride.

His carriage left at the usual time and I felt a sense of elation I should not. It didn't mean anything.

I was resolved to win Miss Weston's favor, for my sake and the children's, at whatever cost. My pride may receive a blow but I could almost hear Madeline's voice, urging me to stay...

I imagined her quick, light step echoing down the stairwell. I could see her dressed in her finery, a commanding presence, beautiful and resplendent, a perfect hostess. She always had an air about her, a willful determination to achieve whatever her heart's desire.

Oh Madeline! What happened? Please give me a clue.

"Anne?" Cathy pressed my hand. "Are you thinking of home?"

I turned to her and smiled. "Yes...I was thinking of my uncle and aunt," I lied.

"Where do they live?"

An innocent question but I must remain on guard, even with the children. "In the south," I replied. "It is beautiful country. Have you ever traveled down there?"

She shook her head sadly. "No. Once, we were supposed to go to London—when Mama was alive, but we didn't."

I put my arm around her and led her back to the table. One of the maids removed our breakfast plates. Brandon was happily drawing and Laura played with her toys on the floor.

"You've never told me about your mother, Cathy. When did she die?"

Cathy tossed her golden hair. "She never loved us. She only loved herself. She killed herself, I know she did. And I know why. I despise her—the way she used to flaunt—" she stopped suddenly, "she died out on the moors...they say it was a riding accident. It happened two years ago."

I respected this confidence and sensing its abrupt end, began our lessons for the day. Cathy proved to be a bright student when she applied herself and I found it a joy to teach her. I wanted to be her friend; God knows she needed one.

"You've done wonders with Miss Cathy," Mrs Simmons remarked one day. "Miss Cathy was troublesome before you came—and now she is acting like a young lady. I must commend you, Miss Woodville. It's made his Lordship so happy."

Mrs Simmons was an excellent housekeeper. Having survived her initial scrutiny, we became used to each other and at times, she would take tea with me in the afternoon.

She did, however, find my invitation to dine at his Lordship's table odd. "It is unusual...but I suppose his Lordship has his reasons."

"He wants me to be there for the children," I said simply. "I am certain it will only be this one time. Employers don't usually invite staff to dinner, do they?"

Mrs Simmons nodded, pleased with my accurate appraisal of the situation.

I was beginning to learn everyone's first names and his or her various positions and responsibilities. The middle-aged Butler, Maitlan, maintained a cool air of self-importance. Mrs Simmons effectively controlled everything outside of Maitlan's duties. They seemed to keep their positions separate and only came together when it became necessary to do so. The remainder of the household consisted of footmen, coachmen, valets, parlor maids, housemaids, scullery maids, kitchen hands, the cook, the stable master and stable hands, the grounds man and his aide and lastly, there was me, the governess.

From the day I knew my position to be secure, I went hunting for an informant. Mrs Simmons kept a tight rein on gossip but that did not stop the maids from talking when she wasn't about.

I caught two one day, gossiping in the parlor. I gave them an awful fright when they learned of my presence and I assured them I would not tell. This seemed to gain their confidence so I took the opportunity to question them.

"You will think me odd asking this," I began cautiously, "but I scarcely know anything about Silverthorn. I've been here nearly three months...I don't know what to think. I only wish somebody would tell me something so I would have an advantage when a subject comes up that is not supposed to be mentioned. Especially with the children..." I added, "for they, as a younger generation, tend to talk more about things they ought not to."

"Oh aye," piped Hetty in a broad accent. "Me brother Rob's that way, y'know. Spills out all the family secrets...oh, leddy, you've done wonders wi'h Miss Cathy...ye don't know how she used to scream!"

"Tantrums, all the time," Emy confirmed with a nod. "It's good ye've come, leddy. You're no' like the others—ye don't give yeself airs...an' I know of what ye talk'ng about...th' secrets an' all. Been go'ng on for years, I've bin told."

I smiled. "Did you have trouble with the not-to-be mentioned name of Madeline?"

There was a short silence. They turned about, and assured of complete privacy, told what they knew.

"Lady Madeline was th' last mistress here. I'd just come, first day, when she come...I saw 'er stand'ng with his lordship..." Hetty's eyes shone with the memory. "Ah...she was a beauty that one..."

Emy frowned at Hetty's romantic sensibilities. "I'd been here longer and I tell ye it was a black day for th' family."

"Why do you say that?" I asked innocently.

"Old Lord Thomas—on his deathbed he was...an' then he was up sudden-like an' act'ng like a lad again. Crack'ng jokes, pinch'ng our bottoms an' go'ng rid'ng an' hunt'ng like no young man would've."

"They call it the 'madness', Miss," Hetty whispered in awe. "An' it was. He chang'd overnight, he did, an' some say it were th' devil in 'im. An' then he went rac'ng off around th' world—noth'ng to be heard for a year. An' then he comes back to Silverthorn with her!"

"I seen her in th' parlor when Mrs Simmons went to see 'em," Hetty went on, "she was so lovely...th' loveliest look'ng leddy I'd ever see...had everyone agog...an' th' old Lord beam'ng like a lusty lad! Shame it was, that he sprung it sudden-like on th' household. Call'd th' whole family together: Master Justin an' his leddy, Miss Lillian an'," Hetty blushed, "Mr Vincent."

"They weren't happy," Emy shook her head. "An' not to be them fault. Lord Thomas should've giv'n warn'ng. Master Justin had taken over when Lord Thomas bolted an' it was real shame him turn'ng up pud as pie with young wife on his arm!"

"You don't think it was ill of him to be unwelcoming to Lord Braithfield's bride?"

Emy shook her head. "Bad grace, it was, an' I heard Mrs Simmons say it too. But, that was the way and everyone had to live wi'h it."

"But why does nobody mention her name any more? What happened? Was there a great scandal? I know that she is dead."

Emy nodded. "It'd take a lifetime to unravel th' mystery, leddy. Everyone suspects an' thinks things, but nobody knows."

A noise was heard in the distance and Hetty whispered before they scuttled away: "She killed herself...on the night of the spring ball. They found her ly'ng at the bottom of th' Tower."

CHAPTER EIGHT

There was a commotion in the parlor.

Miss Weston had arrived, escorted by her brother, Mr Spencer Weston. Their voices echoed up to the schoolroom and I heard Mrs Simmons's welcoming tone, a masculine laugh, shortly followed by a perfectly clear velvety voice that I assumed must belong to Miss Weston.

"Must we go down now?" Cathy lamented.

Brandon scowled in unison. "Is our new Mama here? I don't want her. I want Anne. Why can't she be our new Mama?"

"Hush, Brandon," Cathy said.

"We're to welcome Miss Weston at dinner," I said. "And Cathy, you promised me you would be on your best behavior. You know I'll be in trouble, may even be sent away, if you do not."

Cathy softened. "Oh, Anne, of course I'll do it for *you*. But I *hate* Olivia Weston and always will. She set her cap at Papa after Mama died...now she has him, she'll take over our home too!"

"Don't be foolish," I murmured. "We must be young ladies about this and put on a good face. No real lady shows her displeasure."

"I *know*," Cathy whined, "but I don't like her. And she doesn't like us, I know that. And she'll take Papa away from us and send us away!"

"Will she do that, Anne?" Brandon asked, worried.

I guided Cathy to a quiet corner in the room. "You must be strong, Cathy. You may not realize, but your attitude affect's Brandon's. You don't want to see your Papa angry, do you?"

Fear swept past her tear-stained blue eyes. "Oh no...I've seen him in a temper before—when Mama was found on the moors and he was *very* angry."

Why wasn't he overwrought with grief? Finding one's beloved spouse in a state of death would be an emotional experience but anger? Why would he be very angry at finding his wife's body? Perhaps he killed his wife and pretended to be angry by her death? The thought perished as quickly as it had been born.

"What was your mother's name?" I asked Cathy.

"Danielle. Papa says I resemble her. She was pretty, I suppose, but I hate her and always will. Brandon is too young to remember...but I remember *everything*." I waited for her to continue but that was all she would say on the subject.

Laura still had not uttered a word. When Doctor Carstares came to check Brandon's arm, I asked him what I might do to get her to speak again. He shook his head sadly. "It's a sad business, Miss Woodville...that Summer. I've been called to Silverthorn on three sad occasions. First—the horrible death of Lord Justin's wife on the moors...and then the close deaths of old Lord Thomas and his beautiful young wife."

"Do you remember her?"

"Lord yes!" His pale eyes shone at the memory. "She was the most beautiful woman I've ever known. Had old Thomas wrapp'd around her little finger, she did." He paused and glanced at me uneasily. "There was a big fuss at the time...a lot of suspicions and all that. I was called here to do a post mortem."

"They say she took her own life."

"That appeared to be the verdict." He looked at the child. "She ceased to speak from that moment onward. I've been told by Mrs Simmons, who brought me here to check on her, that she was always a quiet child—very attached to her mother. It will take time, Miss Woodville—do I have permission to call you by your first name?"

"Certainly," I smiled. "It's Anne."

"Well, Anne, you must gain her confidence. She has had an emotional upset but she'll come round in time."

I watched Madeline's daughter play with her doll. She looked so much like her father, except for her green eyes. I ached for her to talk, to laugh, but I must be patient.

I had no wish to leave the schoolroom that day. Miss Weston would be examining the house.

"I wonder how Aunt Lillian's taking to Miss Weston," Cathy said during the day, "she attached herself to Mrs Simmons, you know."

"Oh, no." I imagined a resplendent and authoritative Lillian gliding down the stairs to welcome Miss Weston. I would have liked to see the meeting but I did not want to be acquainted with Miss Weston until tonight. Natural curiosity overruled, though, and I gave into Cathy's demand.

It was against my better judgment, however, I was as keen to see Miss Weston as Cathy was to see Aunt Lillian playing the mistress of the house.

"It's her favorite game," Cathy whispered as we paused on the landing of the main stairwell. "She always plays it when people are here—anyone who isn't a servant and who is an intruder."

An intruder? Miss Lillian perhaps resented Miss Weston's new status but was it wise to flaunt the role in her face?

Cathy guided me to the old parts of the Manor. I gazed in wonder at everything I saw. The old architecture, the Louis XIV furniture, the tapestries, the creaking floorboards, the family portraits...

"Here are all our ancestors," Cathy said quietly. "I'll tell you about them one day but Aunt Lillian is the one to ask. She knows everything about Silverthorn."

I noticed that a portrait was missing. There was a long line of family portraits dating back to Silverthorn's first owner, James Braithfield, in the Elizabethan era. He restored the medieval Tower and began the Manor house existing today.

I recognized Lord Thomas, Madeline's husband. My heart pounded excitedly as I expected to see Madeline's portrait next.

However, in her place stood a painting of Brandon's greyhound, Winter.

Cathy noticed my disappointment. "They took it down—Aunt Madeline's portrait."

"Why?"

She shrugged. "We're not supposed to talk about her. She was very beautiful, you know. And I always liked her."

"But isn't it her right to be on the family wall?"

Cathy shook her head. "I know she did something bad and that is why she is not there. Papa told me."

Her words stung my heart. So, Lord Justin ordered the removal of my cousin's portrait. Perhaps he felt guilt, being the murderer, having to look into her face every day...

"What's wrong, Anne? You look fierce!"

I schooled my features. "Oh, I'm a little disappointed. Everyone said how beautiful Lady Madeline was and I would have liked to have seen her."

"Oh yes, she was." Cathy paused, her blue eyes shining with mischief. "But I know where the portrait is...I'll show you some day, so you *will* see her."

I could hardly tell her I had lived with Madeline for many years and knew every inch of her face.

I was anxious to see her portrait, though. Maybe the artist captured something in her face that would give me a clue. Hetty and Emy said she'd thrown herself from the Tower.

Suicide.

I could not believe Madeline would take her own life. She loved it too much—the challenge of it...the manipulation of people, the extravagance of the rich and titled...no, the verdict couldn't be right.

"Aunt Lillian is installing Miss Weston in the west wing. I overheard Papa telling her to do so. She's to have the whole wing to herself, except of course Aunt Lillian's rooms." Cathy paused, clicking her tongue. "I don't quite think Aunt Lillian will like that...that is *her* territory. She prefers the old, rambling castle Silverthorn used to be."

I smiled to myself. Whoever had built the various additions to the old castle was to be commended. To achieve a harmony between medieval and Elizabethan was extraordinary. Lillian preferred to live in the old castle, surrounded by ghosts of the past.

I shuddered. Why did I have a strange feeling walking through these parts? It was almost as if something was watching me.

When the feeling threatened to overwhelm me, my common sense brushed it aside. There were no such things as ghosts.

I seized Cathy's hand. "We must go back; we will see Miss Weston at dinner."

Cathy's candid blue eyes studied me. "But I wanted to show you Miss Weston."

"We will see her later."

We decided to go the other way around. I pretended to be delighted with each room but I kept seeing Brandon's dog standing in Madeline's place in the line of family portraits.

As we approached the schoolroom, I saw Mrs Simmons black skirts and inwardly cringed. We'd left Hetty in charge and she was scolding the poor girl.

"Well, Miss Woodville, I wasn't aware tours of the castle to be part of your duties?"

"I wanted her to come, Mrs Simmons," Cathy defended me. "I promised to show her something."

Mrs Simmons looked at me. "You should have asked me to look after the children. Hetty has plenty of other work to do." She spun around to Hetty. "What are you waiting for, girl? Be off with you!"

Hetty scuttled away in fright.

I suggested a quiet spell before everybody changed for dinner. I summoned one of the maids to help me bathe Brandon. Cathy retired to her room to finish an essay I had assigned her.

That evening I sat on my bed observing the clothes hanging neatly in my wardrobe. I possessed one evening gown, a gift from Lady Beatrice. It was in a lovely shade of cornflower blue. Lady Beatrice always said the color became me well.

I laid out my blue gown on my bed, knowing the penalty for servants to dress above their station.

Cathy insisted I wear it.

"I can't possibly—"

"Of course you can! Do you think Papa really cares about class and all that? If you avoid Mrs Simmons...I don't think anyone else will pay too much attention to you. Oh, you must wear it! It's lovely...where did you get it?"

"It was a gift from a friend."

Cathy picked up the dress. "I'll help you dress...you *cannot* refuse me."

Minutes later, she turned me to face the mirror and gushed, "Anne—why—you look beautiful! I never thought you were—you look so plain in those dull gray dresses!"

I smiled. Honesty from children always amused me. With Cathy's help, I removed the pins from my hair, watching it fall loosely around my shoulders.

Cathy let out a small gasp of surprise. "You have nice hair, Anne. Why don't you ever wear it out?"

"It gets in the way," I answered truthfully.

Cathy clasped her hands. "I've an idea! Wait a minute..."

"Oh no," I groaned, but she had gone.

I gazed long and hard in the mirror, a little apprehensive. I even considered changing gowns, though we were expected downstairs in ten minutes. Pushing my fear behind me, I clasped a small pendant around my neck. It was the only piece of jewelry I possessed—a birthday gift from Uncle Clive and Aunt Mary.

Cathy returned with her maid Betsy. Despite my protests, Betsy made quick work of setting my hair.

"You see," Cathy grinned triumphantly, "you can be pretty."

Voices floated from the Drawing Room along with the chink of wine glasses. I had a sudden impulse to run back and change into one of my dull gray dresses but it was too late.

Cathy and Brandon went on ahead. We left Laura in the care of Mrs Simmons.

"Miss Braithfield, Master Brandon and Miss Woodville!" Maitlan announced in his usual pompous way.

Faces turned towards the intrusion of our party. Two women stood in a corner who looked like sisters, accompanied by a young blonde man with glass in hand. Miss Lillian commanded one side of the room, resplendent in crimson with purple feathers, flanked by Lord Justin and another man I didn't recognize. On Justin's right stood a tall, regal lady, exceptionally beautiful with her platinum hair and stylish silver dress. Miss Olivia Weston, I thought.

Justin broke the silence by welcoming his children. Attention was immediately focused on Brandon and his injured arm. I was grateful to be forgotten and paled into the background, or so I thought, when the man standing beside Lord Braithfield stepped in my path.

"I am Miss Woodville, the governess," I said.

He frowned. "I was coming to that conclusion...I never thought Justin would employ someone so young and so pretty. You're bound to make my sister decidedly jealous, Miss Woodville."

I turned to observe Miss Weston and hoped the surprise didn't show on my face. His sister seemed to have inherited all the looks in the family.

"You must understand," he went on jovially, "that old Justin usually employs eighty-year old matrons for governesses. I am pleased with his choice this time."

"And you are..?"

"Demme. Always forgetting my manners. Mr Spencer Weston at your service, Miss Woodville."

I was about to remark on the weather when Lillian saw me and proceeded across the room with all speed. She seized my arm. "Miss Woodville, have you any idea of how ridiculous you look?"

I almost laughed. The purple feathers protruding from her head looked ridiculous but I tried to appear gravely concerned. "I am sorry if my dress disturbs you, Miss Braithfield, but I had no choice. This is my only evening gown."

"A trifle above your class, wouldn't you say?"

"Nonsense," came the retort from the young man standing beside the two sisters. "She looks magnificent."

Lillian flicked open her fan and retreated to a corner.

I tried to keep a wooden face. "Thank-you."

His curly blonde hair and disarming smile reminded me of Adam Rohan. However, he certainly wasn't as dashing, or as worldly, as Adam Rohan.

He kissed my hand. "Pleasure to meet you, Miss Woodville. I am the resident bachelor of the district, except for my good fellow Spencer here, whom you've already met." He bowed eloquently, a vision in his superbly tailored coat. "Brett Ashton of Ashton Grange, *Mademoiselle.*"

"My name is Anne," I smiled, overwhelmed by his absurdity.

"Anne," he tested on his tongue. "Not what I would have called you but here are my two sisters to chide me for my impertinence. May I introduce them to you? The Misses Ashton, Tabitha and Eliza."

As I began a polite conversation with the two ladies, I suddenly remembered Madeline had singled out Brett Ashton as a prospective husband for me. I watched him glide about the room, taking Cathy in hand, a cultured protégé of the *haute ton.* The complete opposite of myself.

Eliza, fair-haired like her brother, with a plain but pleasant, heart-shaped face and sharp brown eyes, studied me closely. "You're the governess!" she whispered unbelievingly. "Where did you ever manage to get such a beautiful dress?"

"The dress was a gift. I know it is a crime to dress above one's station—"

"Nonsense!" Eliza snorted. "I believe the governess plays a very important role in the household. They are not to be treated like mere chattel...they definitely belong to a higher creed."

She intended to put me at ease and instead achieved the opposite. I felt immense relief when Maitlan announced the serving of dinner.

I entered the dining room on the arm of Mr Ashton. Mr Spencer Weston escorted the Ashton girls and Lord Braithfield naturally escorted Miss Weston. Cathy and Brandon followed behind, poking fun at poor Maitlan.

Since I had grown accustomed to having my meals in the schoolroom, I completely forgot the art of small talk. Like a fish out of water, I was happy to be placed beside the jovial Brett Ashton.

Miss Lillian, resplendent in feathers, refused to give up the hostess's chair to Miss Weston. Miss Weston wisely left the unfortunate affair in Justin's control.

He took Lillian by the warm. "Cousin, I warn you. If you are determined to make a scene, I will have no choice but to dismiss you from my table. Understood?"

Lillian glared up at him. She whispered something I did not hear. Justin's mouth set in a grime line as he sauntered to the opposite end of the table.

"I chose to retire," Lillian announced loudly. "I have a headache."

Justin barely acknowledged her departure. He re-seated Miss Weston in the chair Lillian had vacated. Happily installed, Olivia smiled at the company.

"Poor Lillian," Brett murmured in my ear. "She doesn't have a good time of it, does she?"

"A good time of what, Mr Ashton?"

"Oh, soup, lovely...Lillian's a mad old girl...always has been. They say she inherited it from her father—"

Eliza joined the conversation. "Are we talking about Lillian and the famous Braithfield madness?"

Brett smiled. "That's it, Lizzy, always on the ball."

Eliza leaned across her brother. "She has her fair share of the madness, you know...after all that happened."

"I know she lost a child...and a husband," I said, wondering what tomorrow would bring for Lillian's ill-timed performance tonight.

"And her sanity!" Eliza said. "Look at Lord Justin...see how furious he is. He cannot ignore the Lillian problem when Miss Weston is soon to be his bride."

"Has a date been set?"

As if to echo our thoughts, Justin raised his glass in toast. "I wish to make an announcement...and a toast. The wedding date has been settled between Miss Weston and I for Friday next. I raise a toast to the new Lady Braithfield."

There was all the romantic warmth in his smile but not in his eyes. I scolded myself for looking for such signs, for why should it matter to me?

"So soon, Papa?" Cathy's voice floated across the room. "But Miss Weston is only visiting us!"

Justin's eyes immediately connected with mine. I glanced across to Miss Weston, who observed Cathy impatiently.

"I wanted to surprise you with a new mother for Christmas," Justin informed his daughter.

I caught Cathy's eye and warned her to be silent. She seemed to grasp my meaning and hung her head in silence, toying with her food.

"Am I invited?" Brett broke the awkward silence.

"Of course," Olivia returned a radiant smile. "I am determined to have all my friends see me in my glory."

She looked at each of us until her gaze came to rest on me. "Of course governesses are not required at weddings...or indeed at any social functions. It was very good of my lord to include you this evening, Miss Woodville."

My early misgivings proved to be correct. I made a motion to rise when Justin waved me down.

"Miss Woodville will accompany Cathy and Brandon to the church," he informed his bride to be. "I cannot allow my children to run rampant when I am not there to control them."

I felt I couldn't endure any more humiliation. "It's well past the children's bed time," I stood up, monitoring for the children to do the same. Cathy rose immediately in relief; Brandon lingered.

"Surely you're not leaving us so early?"

"I'm afraid it is late, Mr Ashton."

"Well then," Brett smiled. "Until we meet again."

I left the room in immense relief. To my dismay, I could not forget the way Justin looked at me. Were those the eyes of a murderer?

His very presence unnerved me. I mustn't forget what Madeline said: ...*Justin is becoming increasingly suspicious of me. I daresay he watches me like a hawk! He disturbs me for I am certain he wishes me ill.*

Why did mystery follow Madeline wherever she went? Why was her name forbidden in the household? I did not want to appear overly inquisitive talking with the housemaids. And I mustn't forget I was Anne Woodville, not Laura Morgan, Madeline Morgan's cousin.

My own situation remained precariously unstable in Olivia Weston's hands. As the new Lady Braithfield, she would command the household. I wondered what kind of wife she would make Justin. From what I understood from Cathy, there was little love lost between her parents. Had the first marriage ended badly?

I knew I would have to wait for Cathy to enlighten me on the subject. It should not be my concern for a governess had no business in such matters. I thought of Eliza Ashton's remark about governesses and smiled. She was right. They were a very important part of a household.

I was growing fond of my charges, extremely fond, and hated to think how their new stepmother would treat them. In public, Miss Weston appeared perfectly courteous but what would she be like after the wedding? I imagined she desired to send the children abroad, recalling what Madeline had said: *Olivia has the cool, blonde beauty of an angel but her claws are sharp. She has set her cap at Justin, probably hoping, as he does, I will not bear a son to disinherit him.*

Yes, Miss Olivia Weston was determined to become mistress of Silverthorn.

Her luggage arrived continuously. She claimed the west wing and began, with Mrs Simmons help, to prepare her rooms. Miss Lillian, fortunately, shut herself in the Tower to avoid the invasion.

It was purely by chance that I happened to be in the west wing at the time. Mrs Simmons had asked to see me.

I seldom ventured into the west wing. The old part of the house captivated me with its quaint architecture and antique furniture. It possessed a charm the new part could never have—even with its expensive Louis XIV pieces and superb wooden paneling.

The west wing's floorboards creaked beneath my feet. I made my way slowly down the main corridor, overwhelmed by a feeling of the past. Everything appeared exactly as it must have been generations before.

I passed the portrait gallery to the Lillian's rooms in the Tower, assuming this is where Mrs Simmons must be. However, I soon realized she was not talking to Mrs Simmons but to Justin.

"...What do you want to marry her for? She is a cold-hearted bitch—can't you see it in her eyes? I know you do not love her...why *her*, Justin? Can't you pick some nice, little meek thing?"

I heard Justin sigh. "So you can rule over her? I have given you too much freedom..."

"I have every right to be here," Lillian snapped. "I should be the heir, not you, but I am a woman, aren't I? So I must bend my knees to the Weston. At least Danielle showed some human possibilities—"

"You overreach yourself," Justin said in a deadly voice. "If you can't respect my wife, you'll have to leave Silverthorn."

"You would send me away!" Lillian cried. "You can't! This is *my* home! Papa always said—"

"But your Papa brought a new wife to Silverthorn, didn't he, Lil? Do you remember Madeline? Or have your forgotten her so soon?"

I shivered at the passion in Justin's voice. Had he been one of her lovers too?

"I'm sorry, Justin...I didn't mean to upset you. My wind wanders all the time...and sometimes I don't know who I am. I promise I'll try to be good."

My heart pounded when the heavy footsteps came down the stairs, directly in front of me. I glanced around in panic—there was nowhere to hide.

"Miss Woodville."

"My Lord..."

"What are you doing here?"

He was trying to ascertain how much I'd heard. "I have just wandered into the hall," I lied. "Is somebody crying?"

Justin looked relieved. "You are looking for Mrs Simmons?"

I nodded. "I'm afraid I went down the wrong passage."

"Yes, you did. Allow me to escort you."

He offered his arm and I hesitantly accepted. Some time elapsed before he asked: "How are you liking your post here?"

"Very well," I assured him. "I am very fond of the children."

His lips twisted into a faint grin. "I am surprised at the change in Cathy...you have worked wonders."

"She suffers from loneliness, my lord, nothing more."

"Lonely? How can she be lonely?"

"She craves the attention of a very busy father."

"You are very straightforward in your opinions, Miss Woodville. It is the governess in you."

Always the governess, I thought angrily. I missed my dear, practical Ruby who could air my grievances with a few, well chosen words. I wondered if I would ever be free of being in subjection to the nobility. Silverthorn was no different to Rohan House.

We found Mrs Simmons and Miss Weston in the bedroom designated for the mistresses of Silverthorn. The door was slightly ajar and I felt my heart skip a beat for I knew Madeline had once lived in this room.

It was the most beautiful room I'd ever seen and I wondered why she'd made no mention of it in her letters. A large four-poster, draped with the palest pink chiffon, dominated the large room matching the pink and gold drapes hanging from the large windows. Gilded Louis XIV and XV furniture graced the room from the elegant dresser to the white marbled fireplace and the tapestry-covered chair by the fire...I almost pictured Madeline sitting in that chair in her negligee, her glorious curls in wild disarray, a strange smile on her face as she greeted...

"Are you unwell, Miss Woodville?"

I managed to answer shakily. "I am quite well, I assure you."

Justin observed me closely. "You look a little pale."

"Perhaps I need some air."

Olivia emerged from a small antechamber at the sound of voices, Mrs Simmons directly behind her. Dressed in a fetching dark blue velvet, she looked exquisite, a perfect wife for the enigmatic Lord Justin. His handsome features betrayed nothing as she latched onto his arm, steering him away to the opposite side of the room.

A moment later, she turned back to me, her cool blue eyes studying me slowly. "Miss Woodville...are the children ill?"

"No indeed, Miss Weston...Mrs Simmons wanted to see me and I foolishly lost my way."

"How clumsy of you..." she murmured, "but of course—governesses are known to be clumsy." She turned back to Justin with a brilliant smile.

As I expected, Mrs Simmons came to see me in the schoolroom. When she asked for a private word, I directed her to my bedchamber. "What do you have to say, Mrs Simmons?"

"Are you wise, Miss Woodville, in upsetting the new mistress so quickly?"

"Pray do not be alarmed...I am hardly a *femme fatale.*"

Mrs Simmons raised her brows. "They make a handsome couple, wouldn't you agree? Miss Weston is very beautiful...she will grace Silverthorn with her presence."

Wilt Silverthorn with her eyes, I thought.

"...She is almost as beautiful as the last mistress," Mrs Simmons went on slyly. "You seem to have taken an interest in that one..."

"Oh?"

"Hetty and Emy answer to me, Miss Woodville. I keep a strict house and gossiping is strictly forbidden. I would appreciate if you didn't ask them any more of your prying questions."

"I am grieved, Mrs Simmons, if I have upset you. Indeed, Cathy only whetted my appetite in regards to the Lady Madeline."

She looked at me sharply. "Miss Weston has advised me that your presence may no longer be required at Silverthorn. She means to send the children away to school."

This news did not come as a shock to me.

"I suggest you start looking for a new post, Miss Woodville."

Doctor Carstares came to see Brandon that afternoon.

"Anne has been hoping you'd come," Cathy murmured, giving me a smug glance.

Greg smiled. "It has been too long, Miss Woodville..."

I considered his visit unnecessary as Brandon's arm no longer needed to be dressed.

I asked Cathy to continue with her reading. As I glanced up to Greg's friendly face, I wondered why I couldn't settle for someone like him. I didn't want to be a governess all my life, dependent on the goodwill of the nobility. I tried to picture him as a husband, albeit unsuccessfully. I seemed, instead, to have an unfortunate penchant for desiring the wrong kind of men...Adam Rohan and Justin Braithfield.

Reaching for the stars, Ruby would say.

A week later, Justin Braithfield married Miss Olivia Weston.

CHAPTER NINE

They were coming home.

A courier arrived for Mrs Simmons in the morning. After a two-month honeymoon in Italy, Lord and Lady Braithfield were returning to Silverthorn.

I had not expected it would be so soon.

"Three months, he told me," Mrs Simmons echoed my thoughts. "You'd best ready the children, Miss Woodville."

"Are they back to stay?"

Mrs Simmons glanced at me sharply. "Yes...I would say his lordship is anxious to return to his mills."

I heard much about the mills from Greg Carstares.

The last few decades saw many changes in the textile industry. The subject was a source of concern for those in parliament as the gruesome truths of the underprivileged work force were exposed for the first time in history. The landowners who ran the mills set grueling schedules dictated by an overseer who would see men, women and children work up to sometimes fifteen hours a day.

Greg Carstares frequently visited Silverthorn. He called it 'a friendly call' as opposed to a 'business call.'

Cathy teased me about him.

"He is certainly no Mr Darcy but I doubt there's many of those around, wouldn't you agree?"

Miss Austen's novels had given Cathy a new leash on life. She reveled in the stories and displayed a sudden maturity for her fifteen years.

"I'll be sixteen next year..." Cathy said reflectively. "Papa will want to send me to a finishing school, it was Mama's wish, and when I'm gone, you'll have to go too. Oh, there's Brandon, I suppose." Her dark eyes glittered with amusement, much like her father's. "So I'd welcome the good Doctor's visits...he's in love with you, you know."

"Who's in love with Anne?" Brandon echoed.

"Oh, hush, Brandon, you're only a little boy—you don't know what we're talking about."

"I'm not little!"

I was glad the conversation ended there for I did not want Cathy to read into my feelings on the matter.

I had learned little about Madeline in the absence of Lord and Lady Braithfield. The west wing seemed only the more inaccessible and Mrs Simmons watched me like a hawk.

The parlor maids, Hetty and Emy, kept their heads down when I passed them. I felt saddened for it seemed they too were victims of Mrs Simmons dictatorship.

"I wish she didn't have to come back...why couldn't Papa leave her in Italy?" Cathy sighed, laying down her book. "Aunt Lillian is right—Olivia will take over Silverthorn—invite her friends, change the china..."

"She is no longer Olivia but Lady Braithfield, your stepmother," I reminded her. "You must treat her with respect."

"Even if I don't like her? How can I possibly hide what I feel?"

I understood her dilemma. "Do you want my advice?"

She nodded miserably.

"Cultivate a friendship with her—it is in your best interests to do so."

It wasn't the answer she expected. "I never liked my mother, you know...she didn't want to have me...she tried to kill me!"

Tears glistened in her eyes. I sat down beside her and drew her into my arms. "Of course she wanted you...all mothers want their babies."

This was a lie for I remember how Madeline wanted to be rid of Laura. I wondered what misgivings led Cathy's mother to ride recklessly on the day of her death.

"Papa was good to her...he even hired a servant to watch her when she was pregnant with me...so she wouldn't—"

"How old was your mother?"

Cathy shrugged. "Eighteen. That's why she hated Papa—for making her with child so quickly. She told him it ruined her life and her body."

"Who told you that?"

"I found out. I confronted Papa—and he told me the truth. So, you see, it's true—she didn't want me, she didn't want Brandon. If my natural mother can be so unkind, what will a step-mother do for me?"

I suddenly wished, for Cathy's sake, her father had chosen anyone other than Olivia Weston for his second wife. "You must try to like her," I ventured carefully. "Your father would want the two of you to be friends, wouldn't he?"

"He's probably forgotten us by now," Cathy sobbed.

"At least you have a father who loves you," I said quietly. "I don't even remember my parents...they died long ago."

My confession dried Cathy's tears and she returned to her book with resignation. This gave me time to watch Laura play with her dolls, her dark gypsy hair escaping its red ribbon. When she turned to show me her favorite doll, my heart skipped a beat at her dark-lashed green eyes. It might have been Madeline looking at me.

If only Madeline had been more specific with her letters! She neglected to mention all the particulars—a failing she was infamous for—but why didn't she leave me a clue to follow?

They found her lying at the bottom of the Tower. There was a prevailing sense of secrecy surrounding her death and I was anxious to penetrate the barrier. Mrs Simmons could fill in many of the blanks, I was sure, but she made it quite clear I would learn nothing from her.

Why? Who was she trying to protect? Or had she pushed Madeline from the Tower?

Miss Lillian proved to be just as evasive. She visited the schoolroom from time to time. Having mastered her previous behavior, she now dressed in a simple gown of muslin and left her hair undressed, reminding me of a country farmer's wife.

I wondered how the new Lady Braithfield would deal with Miss Lillian.

Poor Lillian. She had a tragic history and clung to Laura. Sometimes I think she believed the child was her own dead baby. I slowly grew accustomed to her presence in the schoolroom again. She behaved like an extra pupil and helped Cathy and Brandon with their work.

Lillian didn't come to the schoolroom this morning and my guess was that she didn't want to face her cousin's new wife.

I couldn't quell a certain anxiety of my own. Miss Lillian couldn't be removed without a good reason—but I was only the governess. I remembered the coolness in Olivia's eyes when she spotted me with Justin. I could see her mind ticking over...planning to be rid of me.

There was a buzz in the hall. As I expected, Mrs Simmons opened the door.

"Miss Woodville...prepare the children. His lordship wishes to see them immediately."

I nodded, gesturing for Cathy to follow me. Brandon was already ahead of us. I caught him before the door, tidied his hair and brushed his coat.

Cathy smiled timidly. "Don't worry, I shall make you proud."

I nodded, touched by her faith in me.

I remember feeling struck anew by Olivia's beauty.

She stood in the parlor, sporting new French fashions and a cultured air that came with her new status as Lady Braithfield and mistress of Silverthorn. She clearly resented her honeymoon being cut short by reasons such as 'the children' and the 'mills.'

Having read the bride, I was at a loss for words for the groom. He did not appear the happy bridegroom I thought he should be. He seemed happy to be reunited with his children though.

Cathy smiled shyly at him and I caught him glancing at her as if it was the first time he noticed her. She had bloomed from the sullen girl I discovered on my arrival into a presentable young lady with neat manners.

"Your step-mother has brought new clothes for you all...haven't you, my dear?"

"Oh yes," Olivia lifted her brow as an afterthought.

Having done my duty, I prepared to leave when Justin called me back.

"Miss Woodville...has our winter proved disagreeable to you? You come from Cornwall, do you not?"

My answer was a little slow in coming. "Yes, my home is in Cornwall."

He smiled. "I'm pleased to discover you haven't run off like your predecessors...we are very pleased to have you at Silverthorn."

"Thank-you, my lord," I replied evenly, feeling Olivia's presence keenly. "I will take the children back to the schoolroom. Will you require them this evening?"

"They usually take their meals with you, don't they?" His dark eyes held mine for a moment. "I wouldn't deprive you of your dinner companions."

"I am able to amuse myself, my Lord."

"Are you?"

I found myself enjoying his mocking smile, realizing I'd missed it.

However, Olivia refused to allow our little *tête-à-tête* to continue. She snatched her husband's hand and whispered something in his ear.

I took my cue and departed with the children.

Lillian's predictions about Olivia proved correct.

Within the next few weeks, the new Lady Braithfield had shaken Silverthorn upside down and re-decorated it to her satisfaction. The china was changed, the cook fired and the furniture and paintings shuffled.

This was to my advantage for Cathy came bursting in, announcing that Olivia had installed the portrait of Madeline in the main hall.

My head swam with delight. What would this portrait show me? Cathy informed me it had been painted three month before her death. "Where did she find it?"

"In Aunt Lillian's room, hiding under a coverlet."

When we reached the landing, I held onto the railing for support.

There it was...Madeline in all her glory. She stood in the midst of a garden scene, dressed in ethereal white, her wide green eyes glittering under the brim of her hat. It was her smile, a haughty, smug twist of her beautifully shaped mouth, that warned me of her current mischief. As the perfect mistress of a grand house, she was ready to take the world to war. I wondered who 'they' were again.

"She's lovely, isn't she?" Cathy prompted. "See her hair...why can't mine curl like that? Betty has to use sugar to get it to curl but Aunt Madeline's did naturally. It looks beautiful against her dress, don't you think? I want a dress like that when I grow up..."

Every girl's dream to grow up to resemble a beauty, I thought, having no such sentiments myself. I was far too practical, as Madeline knew me to be, but I couldn't help feeling melancholy as I gazed up at the handsome portrait.

Did I know this person?

I understood why Olivia placed it in the hall. It was a remarkable painting, even without its chief attraction. I wondered who had removed it from the family gallery and hidden it in the attic.

Its finding in Lillian's rooms could be explained. She was mad—so it was natural for her to do unusual things without practical reasons.

Whoever replaced her picture in the portrait gallery must be her murderer. Who else would be haunted by the sight of her?

"Hello, Papa."

Lord Justin stood on the landing. He did not seem to have heard his daughter's voice because of his preoccupation with the portrait hanging above him.

I couldn't read the expression on his face but his voice betrayed his displeasure. "Who has done this?"

"Olivia," Cathy answered. "Don't you like it, Papa? It's only Aunt Madeline...what is wrong with it? Olivia thought it should be viewed...it is a remarkable piece, she said, of the last mistress of Silverthorn—and painted by Hawthorne, remember!"

There was my answer. *He* must be Madeline's murderer...he had killed her for Silverthorn. Or perhaps he'd been her lover and she threatened to expose him? Only her murderer could not bear to look upon her face.

I felt suddenly ill with the knowledge.

Maitlan lurked in the background. Justin summoned him. "Take the portrait down this instant."

I motioned Cathy to let him pass. She ran up to me, her blue eyes wide. "Why didn't he like it? It looks lovely there."

"I don't know, Cathy," I replied in a small voice.

Madeline would be amused if she knew her portrait caused a rift between the new lord and lady.

"Papa says he doesn't like the portrait...and Olivia doesn't know why," Cathy explained, confessing her eavesdropping. "She demanded he put it back and when he refused, she said he mustn't want to look at his old lover...it was a foolish comment and Papa's very angry."

Could they have been lovers—Madeline and Justin? Madeline hated Justin...or did she? She could have written those things about him to stop me from guessing the truth.

Justin made no explanation to his wife and their arguments could be heard as far as the main hall.

We had almost forgotten the incident when the schoolroom door opened one day and Justin sauntered into the room. He looked harassed and sat down in a chair, glaring into the fire. "Cathy, go to your stepmother..."

Cathy glanced at me in surprise. "Yes, Papa."

"Papa," Brandon sat on the floor below him, his blonde hair a stark difference from his father's. "Why are you and mama fighting?"

Justin's half-hearted smile didn't conceal the anger in his eyes. He ruffled his son's hair and assured him all would be well. "Women, you know."

I wish I could sink through the floor. Instead, the book I held slipped through my hands and dropped to the floor.

Justin immediately looked up, his dark eyes connecting with mine. "Miss Woodville...I apologize—"

"There is no need," I said quickly. "I am aware there are differences between every married couple."

His lips curled in faint amusement. "Are you? When have you been a wife?"

I felt my face grow hot. "I grew up under the protection of my uncle and aunt, my lord...they didn't agree on every subject."

"And did they fight on a thing so trivial as the placing of a portrait?"

He asked the question so I gave him my answer. "I cannot understand your reluctance to accept the position of the portrait...it fits the hall perfectly."

"Yes...I suppose it does."

He did not look like a murderer. Was he her lover then?

"Who was she, my lord?" I asked, watching his face carefully.

He shrugged casually. "She was my late Uncle's wife...a young, common piece he picked up in London. No one of significance."

The portrait of Madeline was hung back in the main hall.

Mrs Simmons' warning of my imminent dismissal led me to seek out Justin during this time.

I loved the house...the familiar creeks in the floorboards, the elusive west wing, the old Tower and my cozy room beside the nursery. It was almost home. I never expected I would become so attached to Silverthorn—as my chief reason for being here was to uncover the mystery behind Madeline's death.

I had no wish to return to the Rectory and wrote to Uncle Clive and Aunt Mary, assuring them of my comfortable situation, shrewdly leaving out all the particulars. Since I remained on trial-basis, I said they could write me via Miss Banks.

Always a reliable correspondent, I sent a letter to Lady Beatrice, thanking her for her generous help.

To Theresa I penned my fears and my discoveries as Laura Morgan. I desperately needed to talk to someone and when I sealed the lengthy epistle, I felt immense relief.

Justin was six days out of seven at one of his mills so I planned to talk with him on Sunday.

Sunday arrived far too quickly.

Olivia was busy preparing a large dinner party. She and Mrs Simmons remained in her chamber the entire morning, leaving me to see Justin without fear of detection.

"Papa's in his study again," Cathy had groaned earlier. "I wish he would take me riding or something...he broods as much as Mr Darcy and he always goes to the study when he arrives home...why Anne?"

To escape, I imagined. He spent the majority of his time at the mills, returning to Silverthorn late in the evening. Due to the late hour of his arrival, he failed to come and kiss the children goodnight.

Cathy understood her father better than she thought. However, it was Brandon who suffered, Brandon who had to accept my miserable excuses.

I managed to keep them busy to lessen the hurt of their father's neglect. I told them they should both try to get Laura to talk as a project. Despite their marvelous attempts, Laura remained silent.

The study door loomed ahead of me. I took a deep breath and knocked.

"Enter."

The autocratic voice unnerved me. I quickly entered the room, closing the door behind me.

I saw a hand holding a book by the fire. I moved forward, my gaze drawn to the handsome portrait above the fireplace. I now knew the man's name—a cousin of the family, Mr Vincent Braithfield. Easily the most dashing of the Braithfield men, I wondered when he should visit Silverthorn.

"The artist interests you? Or is it the man in the picture?"

"Both, I imagine," I smiled, determined to not let his mocking voice disturb me.

Leaving his book open, Justin turned to me, his dark eyes glistening in the glow of the firelight. "Why have you come to see me, Miss Woodville? Are you leaving?"

The question caught me off guard. "Do you wish me to leave, my lord?"

He smiled. "Why should I wish you to leave? I believe you are the sanest person here."

"Thank-you, my lord. It is because I want to stay I have come to see you privately."

He raised a brow in question and I hurried on: "I am led to believe...that my presence is no longer required here."

"Sit down, Miss Woodville."

I nodded, a little too severely, and marched to the chaise lounge he'd gestured towards. The informal setting ill-prepared me for what I wanted to say. "Before you left for your honeymoon, I was advised by Mrs Simmons to start looking for a new post."

The news surprised him. With a flick of his wrist, he closed his book. "It sounds like Mrs Simmons was acting on behalf of my wife...I implore you, Miss Woodville, to ignore whatever she insinuated. I employ the staff here, not Mrs Simmons...and I have heard no complaint about you from my wife. Your position is secure at Silverthorn...you have my word on it."

I stared down at my hands before embarking on my next mission. "My lord...these past months at Silverthorn have enabled me to form a relationship with the children. They are dear to me and I do so hate to see them hurt."

"Hurt, Miss Woodville?"

"Yes, hurt, my lord. Cathy understands a man is busy when he marries...but I know if you let her take riding lessons she would—"

He frowned. "Cathy is well aware of my feelings on that subject, Miss Woodville. My first wife died in a riding accident. Need I say more?"

"No, indeed...but Cathy is determined."

"So is her governess, evidently." He twisted the ring on his finger. "I will consider your suggestion...is there anything else you wish to discuss?"

I wanted to say no but I couldn't let Brandon down. "Your little boy wonders why his father doesn't bid him goodnight. I find I am running out of excuses."

A shadow of irritation passed across his face. "Yes...Brandon is a charming boy...he will turn out exactly like his father."

I followed his gaze to the portrait above the fire and gasped. "You mean...Brandon is..."

His dark eyes hardened. I glanced at the empty decanter sitting beside his chair and cursed myself for my foolishness. He would never have spoken out of turn if he was sober and I should have detected his condition much earlier.

A bitter smile heralded his confession. "Have you any idea, Miss Woodville, what it is like to be a husband—spurned by his own wife? I married Cathy's mother young, I grant you...too young. She accused me of making her fall pregnant," he laughed, "she even blamed her condition on me! She never wanted Cathy...and I had to hire a woman to ensure the baby's safety. She hated me for it...but by the time Cathy was born, I'd given up. Danielle found her solace in her freedom."

He stared into the fire, concentrating of the bright sparks of the slowly burning wood. I kept thinking that I shouldn't be here...that I should go—but how? My legs refused to obey me because I wanted to know.

"She soon made a cuckold out of me," he went on, looking up at the portrait, "with my own cousin. Can you imagine, Miss Woodville, what it is like to look at your son and know he belongs to another?"

I watched his hand grip the decanter and thought I had stayed long enough. I made a bid to rise when he threw the decanter at the portrait. Glass shattered across the floor.

I ran from the room.

From that day forward, I looked upon Brandon differently.

I wondered if anyone else knew. It appeared unlikely, given the circumstances. Even Olivia seemed to believe Brandon was Justin's son, like everyone else.

I was amazed by his fortitude. He would rather give the child the protection of his name than cause a scandal. Others would certainly not tolerate their wife's bastard under their roof.

The fact explained many things. I now understood why there was no likeness between Cathy and Brandon. Cathy with her fair hair and pale skin resembled her mother whilst Brandon's golden hair, olive skin and deep dark-lashed blue eyes resembled his father, Vincent Braithfield.

I was amused to know I had two bastards in my care. Laura with her gypsy heritage and Brandon, the sweet innocent child of a doomed affair between Justin's first wife, Danielle, and the family rogue, Vincent Braithfield.

I thought of the conceited man in the portrait Justin had ruined. He probably seduced Danielle in her vulnerable state and when she fell in love with him, dismissed
her like a common parlor maid.

Learning of her predicament, Vincent probably tried to persuade her to pass the child off as Justin's. Her condition would have lessened the excitement of the affair. Being abandoned by her lover could have spurred her to ride recklessly across the moors that day...

If that were so, why would Justin leave Vincent's portrait in his study? Perhaps it hung there to remind him of the past and his distrust of his cousin. I wondered if the decanter had been thrown at the portrait before. It wouldn't surprise me.

Seeing the picture in my mind raised another question. Why did Justin choose Olivia Weston? Could he not see she was a self-indulgent beauty, determined to get her own way? She'd shown no interest in the children these past weeks and I wondered if she would ever visit the schoolroom.

Cathy didn't seem to mind her stepmother's neglect. She reveled in it and unwisely tried to encourage a rebellion against Olivia with her Aunt Lillian.

Miss Lillian, however, remained neutral on the subject. Justin's threat obviously lingered in her mind. I caught her sometimes looking at Olivia through narrow, expressionless eyes.

I remembered what Mrs Simmons said about her: *she is harmless.* Perhaps with time and a little patience, the Braithfield madness in her would become but a mere memory.

I received a letter from Aunt Mary.

She hoped I was happy in my post and asked many questions I knew I could not answer. Adam's wife, Josie, expected a child next winter and seemed content, though it was known he had an established mistress in town and spent a third of his year there.

Elizabeth Rohan, now flush in funds due to her brother's prudent marriage, was now traveling the continent and due to return to Rohan House before the end of the season.

Still unmarried, I thought with a smile.

The next bit of news interested me. Mr Brody, my lone admirer, had married a farmer's daughter (to Uncle Clive's horror). The girl, Aunt Mary wrote, could neither read nor write but baked very fine cupcakes.

Towards the end of the letter, I noted a change in writing.

My dear Laura, I must prepare you for some bad news. Today the courier came with a letter addressed to you. I opened it by mistake and the contents, as short as they were, filled my soul with profound sorrow...it seems your cousin Madeline is dead.

The note came from a Mrs Gardner, who claimed to be Madeline's personal maid. She said her mistress died rather suddenly and not of her own hand. Why we have had no official notification from Silverthorn is very odd, don't you think? Mrs Gardner also enclosed Madeline's bracelet. I will keep it for you until your return.

   Love, Aunt Mary.

Very odd indeed, I thought.

Madeline's final letter, written shortly before her death, flashed before me. *You must help me...I am desperate. They will kill me, you know. I can feel it. My time is not far away...you are the only one I can turn to...can trust. I know I have made terrible mistakes in the past and I am sorry for it...please help me...*

I had to find this Mrs Gardner. She alone could render the coroner's verdict invalid.

For Madeline's death could be no suicide.

CHAPTER TEN

The key to the silver cabinet was missing.

Olivia's endless attempts to find the key before her dinner party on Friday proved futile.   The key had been last seen hanging in its usual position in Mrs Simmons' bedroom. She always kept her bedroom locked so I couldn't see how anyone managed to steal it.

In the end, Olivia made such a commotion Justin allowed her to buy new silver.

"Papa's not happy," Cathy whispered to me. "He doesn't like spending money...he says it's better spent improving the mill with new machinery to ease the worker's lot."

"Have you been to the mills, Cathy?"

She shook her head. "They've never really interested me before but because you and Mr Carstares talk incessantly about them, I think I'd like to."

"Good, then shall we make a trip of it one day?"

Cathy smiled secretively, her blue eyes sparkling with mischief. "I suppose it's all due to your influence...you'll never guess—Papa has consented to my riding lessons and he wants you go accompany me and Jimmy is to teach us."

I had ridden one or two horses at Rohan House but it seemed a lifetime away. Silverthorn's stables were far finer than Rohan House could boast and I joined Cathy's enthusiasm. "You say Jimmy will show us? Poor Brandon will be disappointed."

She shrugged, non-pulsed. "Oh, he can draw with Laura...why doesn't she talk? Why won't she talk?"

Cathy had long given up on Madeline's little girl. I couldn't really blame her—I had almost come to the same frustrating conclusion. However, I remembered Aunt Mary saying once that persistence would pay off in the end.

And in this case, it eventually did.

To my relief, nothing was said about the scene I'd witnessed in Lord Braithfield's study.

I was furious for not having recognized his drunken state earlier. I almost believed he teased me for enjoyment. How could I have *desired* him to tease me at all?

Mrs Simmons disliked me. She didn't say why she knew I wouldn't be leaving as Olivia intended.

I belonged to the household now.

It was strange but I was becoming very much like Anne Woodville. The only difference was my connection with Madeline, the last mistress of Silverthorn.

I made it a habit to pass the main hall where Madeline's portrait hung in perfect silence. Only alone could I mourn her and recall the old days.

One time, Lillian caught me looking at it. She surprised me when she spoke behind me and I wondered how long she'd seen me standing there.

"...Have you ever seen such beauty?" she whispered. "I'm amazed why Olivia would want to hang it in the hall...a red-haired beauty always outshines a Nordic one, in my opinion. Cecily was Nordic, you know."

I remembered the tale of the two sisters. Cecily had pushed her sister from the Tower in order to marry her bridegroom. "Is the tale really true?"

Lillian grasped my arm. "Come...I will show you."

I followed her, partly out of curiosity, partly because I thought she might start having one of her bad 'turns.'

I had never been in the Tower before and my first impression of it will always stick in my mind. As Lillian preferred the old part of the original keep, the room was draughty and the walls solid and unfriendly. Tapestries covered the bare stone and I missed the warmth of the Elizabethan wooden paneling. Little natural light flowed into the room so candles burned brightly in all corners.

The room was in a state of disrepair. Layers of dust cloaked the few modern sticks of furniture and the four-poster bed in the far corner. The coverlet had been kicked aside and no effort had been made to straighten it. I remembered Mrs Simmons uttering once about Lillian's desire to do her own cleaning. She forbade any of the maids to touch her room and locked it when she left the room, knowing Mrs Simmons well.

Lillian pointed at a small-sized tapestry, very old and worn, near the stone staircase leading up to the turret. "You see," she smiled triumphantly, "this is Eleanor and Cecily...and that is the knight they both wanted to marry."

I followed her gaze to the ingenuous weaving of some poor maiden long ago. Lillian was right—the tall maiden displaying a golden braid beneath her wimple could only be Cecily. She was up at the Tower, looking down beneath her at what I assumed was poor Eleanor. And to the far side of the picture stood a young knight in chain mail.

"This was done centuries ago but the legend is true. Where you are standing was part of the keep *they* lived in and up there," she raised her eyes to the ceiling, "is the Tower you see Cecily standing from. Notice the architecture proves the story true."

The Tower, which was Silverthorn's historical value, stuck out like a lighthouse on a dark night. I imagine the architect who added the Elizabethan wings wanted to demolish the old keep and its Tower.

I asked Lillian.

"There was a fire...which ruined the old castle and left only the Tower standing...and this meager part of the original keep. They say the Tower is the oldest—and the strongest part of the keep for only it survived the times. Even fire could not destroy it."

"You talk like it is magical."

She nodded. "It is. An old wizard enchanted it against ruin."

"Do you really believe that?"

She smiled, her brown eyes dilated. "During the construction in Elizabeth's reign, there was another fire—which ruined the new progress. But the Tower remained unscathed. Doesn't that answer your question?"

"Yes...I suppose it does."

"People said Silverthorn was cursed...and I believe it's true—the ghost of Eleanor looks over us...you can hear her walking down the corridor at night and hear her sigh in the wind across the moors..."

I shuddered. "Have you always lived in this part of the house?"

"No..." she managed in a strangled voice. "Once, I was wed, you know...it was many years ago now."

"What happened?"

"He died," she said simply, "and left me with child...but two days before the birth, I couldn't feel my baby kicking...it died, you see...and I had to give birth knowing my baby was dead."

I could see the pain in her eyes and understood how the tragedy could have grown into the Braithfield madness. Cathy told me Lillian tried to kill herself more than once during that time. "She never got over it..." Cathy murmured. "That's why she clings to Laura so much...she says the baby is hers, not Aunt Madeline's."

The memory gone from her eyes, Lillian turned to face me with an innocent smile, almost like a child. "But I am sad no longer...for I have my little girl. Laura's such a pretty name, isn't it?"

I asked Cathy if she remembered a lady's maid by the name of Mrs Gardner.

"I don't think so...why do you ask?"

I shrugged. "I sat next to a girl in the stagecoach on my way here and she said her sister, Mrs Gardner, was a lady's maid at Silverthorn."

"Oh," Cathy lifted her brows. "Olivia's silver arrives today...I know it cost a fortune—did you hear Papa growling last night?"

I shook my head.

"Well," Cathy elaborated, "he made such a row over it. They found the key, you know... after she placed the order. Papa wanted it cancelled but Olivia refused because some of the pieces were specially made—what do you make of it all?"

"Anne," Brandon tugged my sleeve, saving me a reply, "will you read me a story? I like your stories a lot...and when can we walk Winter again?"

I looked down at the golden child who was only Cathy's half-brother. She must be told one day, I thought, or she will discover the truth on her own. And that would only turn her bitter.

Cathy loved her father. She craved his attention—even the smallest amount. I grieved for her—for he was a very busy man.

Olivia tried to think of the children as non-existent. She would make references to the 'schoolroom' at times and to the 'governess.' She presided over Silverthorn like a peacock on a manicured green lawn. Many of her friends, including her brother, came to see her. They stayed at Silverthorn for weeks, at times, and turned the quiet mansion into a rowdy, uncontrollable nightmare.

Justin allowed his wife this freedom and closed off a part of the house so she could enjoy her company.

"She only married Papa for Silverthorn," Cathy said one day.

"I'm sure that's not true..."

"Oh, yes it is and I wish Papa was here more often so he could see it too!"

"Where is your Papa?"

"At the mill, where else?" She sighed. "Why won't he spend more time with us? He comes home, has a fight with Olivia, eats alone, and never sees us any more...why?"

I had no answers for a father's negligence. "But," I reminded, "he has consented to riding lessons, hasn't he?"

"Yes, I suppose he has," Cathy grumbled.

Brandon interrupted with his book. I accepted his sunny smile with a degree of caution. Why had the information about the heritage of this child been exposed to me?

I watched Olivia very closely with Brandon. It was obvious she didn't know. She avoided Cathy like a plague, however, on the odd occasion, I caught her staring at Madeline's child. Was she perhaps thinking of Madeline—her husband's old lover?

I refused to believe it. Madeline's portrait told me she was up to something around the time of her death. But why would Justin Braithfield, a widower with two children, be of any interest to her?

As the heir to Silverthorn? Did she plan to ensnare him into her silken web, knowing her elderly husband must die one day.

I didn't want to know.

Or did I?

Lillian resented the invasion as much as we did.

"Like hornets!" she rolled her eyes. "Ruining our peace...you never know when a guest starts wandering around and before you know it, they are in your bedchamber searching for a glove!"

"But you shouldn't worry, Aunt Lillian," Cathy chimed in, "for you always lock your room...Mrs Simmons doesn't even have a key for the Tower."

Lillian smiled. "No, you are quite right."

"Will you be attending the party?" I asked Lillian.

She shrugged. "If I feel the urge...I won't know till later, will I?"

Cathy examined her aunt thoughtfully. "If you do go, what will you wear? I know Olivia has been dressing in her chamber for an hour now."

"Yes, I imagine she's putting on some new French thing...she is determined to look the part."

"It is only natural," I said, "for one to want to impress one's guests."

Lillian glanced at me. "Maybe...but it would be nice if we had a say in the matter. I used to have all the say, you know, when Papa was alive. I'd invite company when I felt like it...and I would have peace when I wanted it. Those were the days..."

"Until Aunt Madeline arrived," Cathy provoked slyly, "you never liked her."

"No, I didn't really like her," Lillian replied honestly, "she ensnared my father—an old man—into wedding her. He believed he'd done well in choosing a young, beautiful bride...but it was painfully obvious to me and to my cousins that she only married him for status."

Lillian did not join the guests that evening. She elected to stay with us.

The music and the clatter downstairs filtered into our room. I finally gave in to Cathy's repeated request and we crept down to the landing on the main staircase to spy.

Elegant ladies pranced back and forth, powdering their noses and fixing their jewelry. Cathy exclaimed on the wealth of fashions and jewels while I enjoyed the music. They were playing Mozart. I tapped my fingers against the balustrade, oblivious to everything, until a voice spoke.

"What an amusing sight—a governess who desires to dance and a daughter who cannot resist a peak at the fashions."

"Papa!"

I felt my cheeks grow hot with embarrassment. I watched Cathy curtsy prettily, unable to understand why I felt so ill at ease with him.

"And are you enjoying the music, Miss Woodville?"

"I apologize for the intrusion, my lord...I will take Cathy back to the schoolroom at once."

Cathy looked at me sulkily. "Oh, can't we sit here and watch for a little while? I promise I won't talk to anyone."

"What do you say, Miss Woodville? Does that sound safe enough?"

"We shouldn't leave Miss Lillian with Brandon and Laura..." I began.

"I fear you are determined to be difficult," Justin smiled. "Will I have to order you to stay?"

"You are my employer, my lord, I will do anything you say."

"Really?"

I knew I should not enjoy his attentions and hated myself for blushing. To my relief, Cathy didn't seem to notice and pulled my arm towards a small settee hidden from view. Justin guided us toward it and lighted his cigar.

Olivia soon waltzed into the room. She looked dazzling in a shell pink confection with a silver over-lay, caught up in an attractive bustle. Her hair, pulled loosely on top of her head, sported two diamond stud combs. She looked relieved to have found her husband, however, her smile soon disappeared when she saw us sitting to the side.

I could see the question in her eyes as she dissected the scene. Cathy commented how nice she looked and I remained silent.

"Well..." she finally said, "it is not often one finds the governess hiding under the stairwell...I daresay you took me by surprise, my dear."

"Oh, you'd be amazed by how many governesses hide under the stairwell at a ball," Justin laughed.

"Well," Olivia adjusted her diamond earrings, "society demands girls reach a certain age before attending grown-up parties."

Justin glanced at her. "Yes, that is quite true...but there is no reason why Miss Woodville can't enjoy a little society. She is decently bred, after all. A little society might do her well...she knows the Ashtons, I believe...and the good Doctor."

He paused on the 'good doctor', obviously aware of Mr Carstares' unnecessary visits to Silverthorn.

Olivia's frosty blue eyes traveled slowly down the length of me. "I'm certain she wouldn't possess the appropriate attire to attend such a party, darling."

"...What about that blue dress she wore once?"

Olivia was mortified. She put her hand on her husband's shoulder. "She will feel awkward mixing with our guests, won't you, Miss Woodville? Come, my darling, we are neglecting our guests."

I hated being spoken of as a third party. I looked at Justin and almost detected a hint of rebellion in his eyes. I wondered if I had imagined it for it quickly vanished. He put out his cigar and escorted his wife back into the ballroom.

Cathy nudged me. "Are you going to get changed or not? I told you you look very pretty in that blue dress...that was why Papa couldn't take his eyes off you."

Heat stained my cheeks as I fiercely denied such a comment.

I stood. "We've stayed long enough."

As we were about to move, someone called my name. I turned around to see Brett Ashton smiling at us from inside the ballroom. He looked very handsome in his evening attire and quickly stepped outside to greet us. "Not allowed to join the ball—eh?"

"I can't," Cathy sulked, "but Papa said Anne could; but she won't. 'Parties are not for governesses,' she says."

"Oh, a party is not the same without at least one governess," Brett winked at me. "Won't you do me the honor of permitting me to escort you, *mademoiselle*?"

I was almost tempted—but what did I want with a party? Olivia made it perfectly clear she did not want me to go and I could imagine Mrs Simmons' lecture in the morning.

"I am sorry, Mr Ashton, but I'm afraid I'll have to decline. Another time, perhaps?"

He looked disappointed. "I will accept your refusal...on one condition."

"And what is that?"

"That you will promise to visit us at Ashton Grove."

I smiled in agreement.

I was right.

Mrs Simmons austere glare told a story in itself. I knew she had helped Olivia undress after the party, for Lady Braithfield's new French maid had suddenly fallen ill.

She caught me as I retired to my room the following night.

"Miss Woodville...I would have a word with you, please."

I paused. Why did I suddenly feel like a child—caught with my fingers in the sweet jar? Perhaps life at Silverthorn was not so different from life at the Rectory.

She glanced over me with her sharp black eyes. "The mistress has instructed me to tell you that your presence will not be required at any of her social functions."

"Oh," I said, barely surprised.

"Society being what it is, Miss Woodville, you should learn to appreciate your place in it. 'Tis not a governess's lot to mix with her betters; I hope I don't have to remind you of it again."

"Thank-you, Mrs Simmons," I smiled. "I appreciate your concern for my welfare."

When she left, I locked myself in my room and leaned against the door.

I could not blame Madeline for her ambition to be wealthy and titled. She never would have survived dancing tunes to the likes of Mrs Simmons.

The next day the sun came out.

Cathy lingered at the window. "Soon we can begin my riding lessons...Papa says as soon as the bite of winter is out...he doesn't want me to catch chill."

"A little Yorkshire air won't harm you," Lillian said. "Do you want to turn out like your milk-sop mother? A pink and gold doll, who'd break at the seams?"

I looked sharply at Miss Lillian, remembering the time when she made a fuss in telling Justin I had purposely taken the children outside to their deaths. I could only shake my head—it must be part of the Braithfield madness in her.

Cathy didn't like Lillian's comparison. She sauntered over to the window, more determined to go outside. "See! The mist is clearing...it won't be long."

Brandon shared Cathy's enthusiasm. "I want to walk Winter! Why can't we go out *now*?"

Laura watched the two of them silently.

I asked Miss Lillian what she thought of the child's condition.

She shrugged. "How would I know?"

Her sudden disinterest in Laura confused me. I wondered if she might soon have one of her 'turns' so drew her into her favorite subject, Silverthorn.

"Tell us about Silverthorn's history, Miss Lillian...Cathy, Brandon...come here, your Aunt's going to tell us another story."

Cathy groaned. "As long as it's not about Eleanor and Cecily. I've heard it so many times, it bores me now."

Lillian paled in anger. "I'm going to the Tower!" she announced.

I was glad to see the back of her as I didn't want her to upset the children. Cathy gave me an 'I know' glance and Brandon continued with his sums at my insistence.

The rest of the day passed slowly. I rejoiced to receive a letter from Theresa in the afternoon. She begged me to pry cautiously—for an overly inquisitive governess could be held suspect if anything went wrong. She said I lived in dangerous territory and warned against emotion clouding my thinking.

Wise Theresa—she had guessed my attraction to Justin Braithfield without my mentioning him.

She thought the note from Mrs Gardner bizarre. "Do be careful, my dear Laura. The circumstances surrounding Madeline's death are odd...but the coroner's report says she took her own life. By prying too far, you may open an investigation your employer may not want. And if he is the murderer, take care...for your curiosity might put you in danger."

I knew it all. But how could I stop? I had learned nothing about Madeline and I could not forget her desperate plea for help. Whatever her failings, she did not deserve to be murdered. And I knew she'd never consider taking her own life.

Who had killed her?

All the evidence pointed to Justin and yet I refused to examine it. Why? Because I had heard his drunken confession regarding his first wife and felt pity for him? Because I knew the mills were his prime interest in life instead of Silverthorn?

I wondered where I could find this Mrs Gardner. Could she tell me something about Madeline's last days?

I asked Greg Carstares.

"I know of no Mrs Gardner in the village, Miss Woodville...but there are many folk living in the countryside. I'll ask around for you, if you'd like."

I smiled. "Yes, I'd like that very much. I appreciate your concern for Laura."

"No need, no need...it is a pleasure to visit you, Miss Woodville...and the children of course."

I could feel Cathy watching us with a sly smirk on her face. She had taken it upon herself to see the doctor out every time he visited and I guessed she must have said something to encourage his pursuit of me.

We talked pleasantries down to the hall where I paused to say farewell.

"Oh, pardon me, Miss Woodville...I seem to have lost track of the time—"

"Yes, you seem to be a very busy man."

Justin stood in the doorway, a little surprised, I think, by the sight of us standing there together. Greg's face flushed with embarrassment, which didn't help.

When Carstares left, Justin turned to look at me. "His visits are becoming quite regular...but he does not charge me, I wonder why?"

"He comes only to check on Laura...as a friend."

"Then he would charge me...at a friend's rate."

I avoided his penetrating eyes. "I think he is being noble—following up on a patient. I am told he is the family's doctor—isn't it natural for him to be here?"

"You need not defend Carstares. He has every right to be here, courting my governess, is that is what you wish. When shall I start looking for a new one?"

"Never!" I said, a little too vehemently.

He raised a brow. "Don't you like him, Miss Woodville?"

"Oh, I like him well enough...but not," I lowered my eyes, "...in that way."

"And what way is that?" he persisted, amused.

I looked up. "You are teasing me, my lord."

"Yes...I am," he said softly, some of the amusement fading from his dark eyes.

Maitlan the Butler interrupted with a distinct cough. I turned, saying something about the need to return to the children and hurried up the flight of stairs. Only then could I breathe easily, angry with myself for being so ill at ease with a married man.

I dare not ask why...perhaps because I didn't want to know the answer.

When I retuned to the schoolroom, I found Olivia waiting for me.

"Miss Woodville," she began coolly, "governesses are not permitted houseguests—even a doctor who pretends to come here to see—" she paused and looked at the child, "Laura."

She was dressed exquisitely as usual—in a frost green riding habit, her hair hidden beneath a matching velvet hat. She tapped her riding crop against her hand. "Remember my warning, Miss Woodville."

When she left, Cathy sighed in relief. "Oh, thank heavens you're back! She's been tormenting me with questions—"

"About what?"

"About you and Mr Carstares..."

I closed the door. "What did you say?"

Cathy lifted her chin proudly. "I told her he admires and respects you, which is what he told me anyway, and she laughed."

"Did she?"

Brandon nodded in the corner. "I don't think Mama likes you very much, Anne."

"No, she doesn't," Cathy confirmed. "I wonder why...you're only the governess."

The governess, I thought wryly.

"She's changed since she's come to Silverthorn," Cathy went on, "she'd never dare to be nasty to me like that when Papa's around. But he's never around to see how horrible she is. Aunt Madeline was never like her...she was always nice to me...the few times I saw her."

"Tell me more about Madeline, Cathy."

She stared away dreamily. "I remember when I first met her...she was standing beside Uncle Thomas...gay and lovely. I thought she was the most beautiful thing I'd ever seen. She charmed all of us."

"Even your Papa?"

She nodded. "She liked Papa very much."

I tried not to show my surprise. "Did you see Lady Madeline often?"

She shook her head. "No...but I can't really believe all the wicked things they say about her."

"They?"

Cathy shrugged. "Everybody...they said she married my great-Uncle for money and treated him cruelly. They said she poked fun at Aunt Lillian and flared Mrs Simmons alive. All the women were jealous of her, probably because all the men were in love with her. Ask Mr Ashton...he'll tell you for he was madly in love with her and has never gotten over it."

Brett Ashton, another of Madeline's victims. "Who found her body?"

"Mrs Simmons. They tried to hide the details of her death from the public and the inquest...she's now buried in the family vault."

Vibrantly beautiful Madeline—lying cold in a family vault—surrounded by strangers. Could she have given up on life so easily?

Mrs Gardner's words came to haunt me, mixed with Madeline's cry for help. No, she'd not taken her life. Somebody else had.

But who?

Cathy continued to progress in her studies and became a model pupil. She put so much effort into her work I often gave her the afternoons off, however, she elected to stay in the schoolroom and help me with Brandon and Laura.

She had grown attached to me and believed I resembled one of the heroines out of Miss Austen's novels.

"Society is cruel, isn't it?" she said one afternoon. "Men really only marry for money...never for love. Papa didn't marry Olivia for love."

"It isn't true, Cathy. Your stepmother is very beautiful."

"Beauty is a weapon in the hands of a dangerous woman."

I later thought over her words. Madeline used her beauty like a weapon—so did Olivia. I wondered what it would be like to be beautiful, to be admired and feted, to be wanted.

I examined my face critically in the mirror. My honey-colored hair could be called pretty if dressed loosely. My blue eyes were wide and dark-lashed, my mouth too small and my nose slightly *retroussé*.

Vanity is a sin, Uncle Clive would say. I smiled in resignation as I warmed my hands by the fire. The children had long gone to bed but I was strangely restless.

I decided to go for a walk.

The darkened corridors greeted me, the eerie moonlight filtering through the large mullioned windows. I headed for the west wing.

My heartbeat increased with each step. When I reached the changing point—from the new part to the old—I heard a sound.

Someone had left the shutters open. I shut them, my heart in my mouth. What possessed me to come this far? I had no business here. As if to confirm the thought, a swift breeze doused my candle and I was left in the dark.

I heard a cry.

Or was it the wind?

I imagined Eleanor's ghost...walking along the corridors...looking for peace. The thought terrified me and I ran back to my chamber, knowing I was being watched.

CHAPTER ELEVEN

The Yorkshire winter soon ended.

Cathy was overjoyed to begin her riding lessons and one early morning we went down to the stables to view her new mare.

I breathed in the crisp, spring air. Morning dew covered the manicured lawns like diamonds. The grounds men were busy trimming hedges and planting in readiness for the best months of the year. Young buds already showed promise and I couldn't wait to see Silverthorn in all its colorful glory.

Lillian's Tower remained untouched. *Her* Tower hedges would not be cut; *her* ivy would not be trimmed. Justin continued to indulge her wishes.

"Oh, isn't it lovely!" Cathy sighed. "I don't ever want to go through a horrid winter again." "You would grow tired of it eventually and pray for the cold," I warned.

"Never," she assured me and led me triumphantly to the stables where Jimmy the groom brought out her new mare.

Since Olivia loved to ride, I hoped she would be there for Cathy's benefit. As I expected, she was nowhere to be found. She came less and less to the schoolroom and spent most of her time in London, visiting friends. I knew she often went to Ashton Grove and because of her frequent presence there, I decided to postpone my visit. She wouldn't like her governess calling upon her friends, promoting herself as an equal.

"She doesn't like you because you're intelligent," Cathy blurted out, patting her mare. "I overheard Mrs Simmons saying you were too cluey for your own good and far too young and pretty for a governess. Olivia agreed you should be dismissed for those reasons so you see, my stepmother *is* jealous of you."

"Where is Miss Lillian?" I attempted to change the subject, conscious of Jimmy the groom listening to our conversation.

Cathy smiled knowingly. "Olivia's taken her shopping...it seems like my poor Aunt is her new project. What do you think I should call her?"

Silverthorn bred its own bloodline and Cathy aptly named her white mare *Silver*. She ordered Jimmy to saddle her but Jimmy nodded apologetically. He gestured behind us and we turned to see Justin in his riding attire coming towards us.

Cathy's eyes lit up. "I can't believe it! It's Papa!" She left her mare and kissed him shyly on the cheek. "You left the mills for me?" she said archly, "and here I thought you would put me on old Hyacinth to start with!"

Justin looked stern. "You *are* going on old Hyacinth to start with." He smiled at her cloud of disappointment. "But when you graduate, you may ride—Silver is it?—as much as you like."

Nothing could have made Cathy happier. Her smile was contagious, rounding out her thin, narrow face.

"I believe you can ride, Miss Woodville?"

"A little, my lord."

"Good—when Cathy is ready to ride her mare, you may ride Philippe."

"Philippe?"

"My stallion."

I swallowed. This was a grand privilege indeed—to be given permission to ride Silverthorn's prized stallion. I wondered what Olivia would make of it. A mere governess should not be given such an honor. Having no wish to increase the rift between us, I said: "I would prefer a gentler mare...your stallion may not agree with me."

"But you are very agreeable, Miss Woodville, aren't you?"

He studied me, his handsome face mocking, his stance far too casual. At my bristle, he laughed and assured he wouldn't bite. Once Jimmy led Cathy around the ring, he stood beside me. "I merely wanted to apologize for pouring out my soul in a drunken stupor." He waved away my protest. "No, let me finish. It was unforgivable of me...you had come to discuss your position and I should have been in a better state to receive you."

I lowered my gaze. "I will not divulge a single word—"

"I know." His serious face transformed into a more cynically amused one. "You are the trustworthy type—I knew it when I first saw you"

I wondered what he would say if he learned of my relationship with Madeline—a woman he hated or loved fiercely.

I felt uncomfortable whenever we were together. There was nothing to read in his attentive behavior but I remained uneasy. I thought of Miss Banks and of her treatment at Rohan House. Why did I think Lord Braithfield's treatment of me was different—special?

Determined to forget my foolish fancies, I smiled at Cathy.

When we returned to the house, we saw Olivia and Miss Lillian alight from their coach. The footmen carried in their parcels, Olivia warning them to be careful.

"What did you buy, Aunt Lillian?" Cathy began eagerly.

Olivia caught Lillian's arm before she could reply. "That, my dear, is a surprise...you will see." She dismissed me with a glance and went to meet her husband. "Oh, there you are, darling...I was just about to send a search party out for you. You've no intention of returning to the mill this late, are you?"

"As a matter of fact, I am."

Olivia pouted, twisting her new ruby earrings. "Lillian and I are planning something special. Will you allow us to proceed?"

"How much will it cost me?"

She shrugged. "The cost of a dinner party."

Justin ordered his coach. "All right," he said, giving her a perfunctory kiss, "if it makes you happy."

Olivia's secret consumed the better half of two weeks. Cathy ventured into the west wing to discover what they were doing but Miss Lillian scolded her and sent her running back to me.

"Aunt Lillian said I was as bad as Cecily for trying to pry...and that I reminded her of my mother, the milk-sop."

"Miss Lillian often gets confused. You mustn't take anything she says to heart."

"What they're planning will upset Papa. I know it!"

The following week we found out Olivia's secret. Mrs Simmons informed us that on the night of April 15, Lady Braithfield was hosting a ball.

"A ball!" Cathy cried. "Why can't I go, Mrs Simmons? I'm to be sixteen next year."

"I know, Miss Cathy," Mrs Simmons said. "But it is my lady's wishes. She says you are much too young to attend a masquerade party—where certain young men might make prey of you."

"A masquerade ball..." Cathy breathed in wonder.

"What's a masquerade?" Brandon asked.

"It's a party where grown ups wear masks to hide their faces," I explained, watching his little face twitch in awe.

"He's too young to remember the last masquerade ball," Cathy murmured somberly before she gasped, "oh dear...I just remembered..."

"Remembered what?"

"Papa hates masquerade balls—he forbade the custom when we came to Silverthorn...but perhaps Olivia does not know yet."

"Does not know what?"

Cathy stared at me. "Aunt Madeline died at the last one."

Olivia's preparations for the masquerade ball soon became the talk of the county. Invitations went out across the country and many prestigious people from as far as London sent their acceptances.

Everyone knew about the famous Silverthorn ball, held traditionally in spring, and begged the new Lady Braithfield for invitations as she often journeyed to London.

It is the talk of the clubs and the theatres, she said on her return, determined to make the most of her new position. Her plan was to turn the place into the most famous showpiece of the country—a haven for those seeking relief from a tediously dull London.

Lord Braithfield only interfered once in his wife's preparations. She jokingly mentioned to Brett Ashton one day her intention to restore the gaming tables hiding in the attic. Brett Ashton mistakenly told his sister, Eliza, and Eliza, in turn, promptly visited Lord Braithfield at one of the mills for confirmation.

He returned one night, his dark face set in an angry scowl. Banishing Lillian from his wife's room, he swiftly put an end to Olivia's rash idea and the newly dusted tables were put back in the attic the following morning.

Olivia and Lillian's friendship continued to grow. Lillian's visits to the schoolroom grew less and less. She seemed no longer interested in minding children. She bathed in Olivia's glory and became her 'assistant.' The switch of personality alarmed no one for everyone knew she suffered from the 'Braithfield madness.'

We were kept out of the arrangements. As Olivia did most of her planning in her room or in the morning room, we never crossed paths. Mrs Simmons, however, went to the degree of warning Cathy not to pester Lady Braithfield.

Cathy laughed when she told me of the encounter. "Her warning came too late for Papa says I can go and I know Olivia doesn't want me there!"

"Are you sure your father said you could go?"

She nodded. "On the condition that you accompany me!"

"Me?" I put on my severe governess look. "I am not required at social functions—Mrs Simmons made it perfectly clear."

Cathy waved indifferently. "But I asked Papa—and he said you must accompany me. Those were his words exactly."

"If it is required of me by Lord Braithfield..." I began reluctantly.

Cathy stared me wearily before smiling when a voice said behind her: "Of course I require you to accompany my daughter, Miss Woodville."

I turned around to see Justin leaning casually against the doorframe and I felt my heart skip a beat. His eyes studied me pensively, mockingly. "I personally invite you, Miss Woodville, to the Silverthorn Spring ball."

"I have no wish to upset—"

"I am master here," he returned coolly, "and I will invite whomever I wish to."

"Oh good!" Cathy clapped, breaking the spell. "You see, Anne...I told you so."

That was how I came to be included in Silverthorn's famous spring ball.

As I expected, she came to see me the following morning, Mrs Simmons directly behind her. I wondered how such a gorgeous creature failed to sustain the interest of her husband. Cathy told me, since the gamming table incident, they only spoke to each other out of necessity.

"Since you must be included in the affair," she began icily, "Mrs Simmons suggested you might write up the guest list. I haven't really the time, you know."

Mrs Simmons handed me the box of acceptances. "It is to be finished tomorrow...I will send a maid to watch the children so you may work in silence."

They left me in astonishment. I couldn't understand why Olivia would bestow the great honor on me.

"She has a shocking hand," Cathy explained, leafing through the box. She held out the gold-edged invitations. "She had them printed, you see, because she can't spell. Papa doesn't know, of course. She kept the whole thing hidden from him."

Cathy set about straightening the disorganized acceptances while I penned the list using a special quill reserved for the gilt-edged, hundred year old guest book.

"You have a beautiful hand," Cathy peered over my shoulder as we progressed. "Wherever did you learn to write like that?"

"At the Rectory," I smiled.

"The Rectory?" Cathy questioned before I quickly realized my mistake. "Where is the Rectory?"

"Oh...in Devon," I murmured vaguely.

Cathy shrugged. "I've never been to Devon...is it nice?"

"Ordinary and boring," I said, knowing my reply would end the subject.

A maid came to watch Brandon and Laura. I completed the task in a couple of hours and handed the finished product to Mrs Simmons. She inspected the book with her usual deadpan expression. "Miss Woodville, his lordship has expressed his wish for you to attend...with Miss Cathy. This is highly irregular...I hope you are aware of your good fortune."

"I don't care for parties, Mrs Simmons," I smiled sweetly. "So you may tell Lady Braithfield I shall only stay the hour with Miss Cathy."

Mrs Simmons raised her brow in surprise. "I will tell my lady."

I heard no more of the book. Determined to know if Olivia was pleased with the result, I went to the morning room the next day and hesitated when I heard voices.

Justin stood inside the door, Olivia triumphantly showing him the guest book. "Haven't I a fine hand, darling?"

I was about to retreat when, to my annoyance, Justin noticed me. "Miss Woodville, do come in. Do you know this guest book is a hundred years old?"

"Y-yes," I mumbled, conscious of Olivia's eyes scathing me in silent warning.

"Your name is missing..." He picked up the feather quill and handed it to me. "Would you care to sign in your name? You are a guest too, you know."

"I don't really see the need—" Olivia began.

Justin's look silenced her.

I went over to the open stand and dipped the quill into the near-empty bottle of ink. A feeling of mischief overcame me and instead of fudging my writing, as I intended, I wrote my name in the exact handwriting of the last five pages.

I felt, more than saw, Lord Braithfield scanning the result. He immediately turned to his wife with a questioning brow.

Olivia shrugged innocently. "Miss Woodville helped me a little."

I didn't betray Olivia when asked, however, from that day forward she regarded me with silent contempt. Perhaps she saw something in me—something beauty and wealth could not possess.

The week ended.

Olivia's gown arrived from London with Miss Lillian's 'special' costume. She had been very secretive about it, defensive almost, and Cathy and I concluded we would have to wait for the surprise.

A seamstress was sent to the house to measure Cathy for her gown. After viewing countless colors and fabrics, we settled on a leaf green satin. When it came to style, I had to stress the importance of modesty. Eventually, we decided on a simple, Roman robe design with band of ivy at her waist. The seamstress promised she could fashion the leaves as well as a crown for the young lady's head.

"And now ye, Miss gov'ness," the woman herded me to the mirror. "What shall we do with ye—eh?"

She started pulling at my hairpins when I stopped her. There was only one client, I explained, and she must be mistaken.

The woman obstinately shook her head. "No, no, ye have it wrong, Miss gov'ness. His lordship his self told me it were the two of ye. He says to me, 'Mrs Clark—I want ye to make a dress for Miss Cathy...and my gov'ness.' Ask him yeself if ye don't believe me."

"Mrs Clark is quite correct, Anne," Cathy piped in.

The hairpins were promptly removed, leaving my hair to fall down my back in disarray.

"I didn't know your hair was so beautiful!" Cathy cried. "Why...you're really quite pretty, Anne."

"Thank-you," I smiled.

"I 'ave just the thing for ye, Miss gov'ness," Mrs Clark bumbled away to her design books, pausing on a page. "Here's the one."

I followed her tapping finger to a drawing labeled 'medieval.' The picture surprised me a little for it reminded me of the tapestry Lillian had in her chamber of the two sisters, Eleanor and Cecily. I admired the flattering white costume with long flowing sleeves.

Mrs Clark grinned when Cathy gave her approval. "And—I've something in mind for ye hair, Miss gov'ness."

I couldn't help feeling guilty getting caught up in the excitement of the ball. I must remember Madeline died at the last one and I was here to find her murderer.

Silverthorn became like a hotel. The unused chambers were aired, dusted and new drapes and furniture applied to accommodate the large number of guests staying for the event.

Olivia's brother arrived in the morning—to stay for the ball. I saw him standing in the parlor, gallant Mr Spencer, the complete opposite of his sister.

The large ballroom, now aired, looked almost mystical with its shining chandeliers and gilded mirrors.

"She's spending all our money," Cathy said to me one day.

"Who?"

"Olivia. If it weren't for Papa's management of the mills, we would have been forced to sell Silverthorn a long time ago. I heard Papa once say he inherited nothing but debts."

I found this interesting for I assumed Justin inherited a large fortune on his Uncle's death. Had not Madeline said Lord Thomas was wealthy? Perhaps when she discovered the truth, she began to despise him, for prostituting his title and house to lure a young bride.

"Yes," Cathy went on, "everybody thought Uncle Thomas was rich but he deceived us. Uncle Vincent most of all, I think."

"Uncle Vincent?" I said, glancing towards Brandon.

"He was very angry...he thought there would be a fortune. He caused such an uproar over it that Papa agreed to continue paying his allowance...Uncle Vincent lives in London."

"I see..."

"And that is why Olivia hates Papa now—because she thought he was rich! He has to work very hard, he told me, just to keep Silverthorn."

We didn't speak any more of Silverthorn's depleted funds and I wondered if the lack of money delayed Madeline's sending my invitation to visit her. It would be like her to be ashamed by the knowledge, especially as she'd sold her beauty to achieve wealth and status.

No wonder she took lovers. I had no doubt that she did. I only didn't know whom...and which one played a hand in her death.

Justin continued to surprise me. He had inherited a disaster and saved it from ruin. The more I learned, the more I became confused. Could this really be Madeline's murderer? One who murdered for Silverthorn, only to learn he'd inherited nothing but a very large debt?

Would I ever learn the truth?

"Uncle Vincent! Uncle Vincent is here!"

The man standing in the parlor, surrounded by an attentive Maitlan and a gushing Mrs Simmons, looked exactly like his portrait. Tall and lithe with his golden Apollo hair and disarming smile, Vincent Braithfield charmed everyone, even stone-faced Maitlan.

The very manner of his dress denoted his status in society—his popularity preceded him. I could see why he so easily seduced Justin's first wife.

I don't know why I paused so long, looking down at Brandon's father. He treated Brandon no different from Cathy, as an adored Uncle, and I wondered if his silence on the truth negotiated him out of a difficult situation.

Olivia and Spencer came out of the Drawing Room on hearing the noise, her annoyance reserved for Cathy's squeals. However, her expression instantly transformed when Vincent bowed towards her and smoothly took the blame.

Justin chose to arrive at that moment, waving away the footman standing by to take his coat and hat.

I will never forget the look on his face. He stood there for a moment in perfect silence. Cathy soon recognized his presence and went to greet him but his attention remained focused on Vincent. "Well...you're here again."

There was no welcome in his words.

"My lord," Vincent bowed mockingly, "how I've missed this place!" He looked around him, pausing in faint surprise up at the place where Madeline's portrait hung so briefly. "You should be chided, coz, for not inviting me to your wedding..." he paused and turned to Olivia, "your bride is *ravissant*—were you afraid I might steal her from under your nose?"

Olivia blushed at the suggestion and I wondered if she'd met Vincent in London.

"Indeed, one never knows what you can achieve, cousin," Justin said dryly.

"Devil of truth in that," Vincent grinned, summoning a footman to carry his baggage.

He was installed in the west wing.

I was reading Brandon a story when Justin came to see us in the schoolroom. Cathy stopped playing with Laura and her dolls.

"Hello, Papa! Isn't it nice to have Uncle Vince stay with us?"

I alone could read the hurt in Justin's eyes. As if he read my thoughts, he turned to me. "Miss Woodville, would you care to join us for dinner? Bring the children of course...this is a family event."

"I am not family, my lord."

"I have invited you, Miss Woodville, therefore you are family. Cathy, see that Miss Woodville accompanies you to dinner."

"Yes, Papa," Cathy smiled up at him. "I will not fail."

"Is Uncle Vince going to be there?" Brandon asked innocently.

I saw the brief glint of pain in Justin's eyes before he answered with a curt nod. "The dinner is for Uncle Vincent, so you must be on your best behavior."

"Will Uncle Vincent come riding with Anne and I tomorrow?" Cathy asked.

Justin frowned. "You must allow your Uncle to settle in, Cathy...do not plague him with too many requests."

"Oh, but—"

"And when you do ride, you will ride Hyacinth; do you understand me? I don't want to hear Uncle Vincent encouraged you to ride a horse beyond your control."

"Why don't you come with me, then?" Cathy returned with a hint of anger. "I'd rather *you* take me riding than Uncle Vincent...but you're always busy and I know Uncle Vincent will be there when I need him."

Justin sighed wearily. "Yes, I am always busy and I am sorry for it, Cathy." He smiled a little, perhaps acknowledging for the first time that his daughter had grown up and was no longer a child to be pacified with simple explanations. "I would very much like to take you and Miss Woodville riding. Would tomorrow suit? I promise I'll devote the entire day to you."

"Oh, Papa!"

She ran to her father and hugged him. I'd never seen her so happy...or him. The genuine display of affection left me feeling more alone than ever before.

Having no other alternative, I called Mrs Simmons to watch Laura for the night.

She had caught a chill during the day and refused to speak, even when I examined her. If it weren't for her telling eyes, I would have given up long ago. I explained to Laura that I had to go downstairs for dinner and that Mrs Simmons would look after her for the night.

Suddenly, to my astonishment, she smiled.

My heart started pounding. Would Madeline's child, my namesake, speak? "Laura, Laura...can you hear me?"

"There you are, Miss Woodville," Mrs Simmons interrupted. "I have been searching for you."

I tried to conceal my disappointment in her untimely arrival. "Laura has a cold."

"Well, what are you waiting for? You'd best get dressed...I don't approve—but his lordship has asked you, hasn't he?"

When I reached my room, I was in the state of indecision. The only dress I could possibly wear was my blue one. I stared at it for a while...remembering the comment Justin made at one of Olivia's parties. *What about the one she wore when the Ashtons arrived*?

The memory of his voice made me blush. I quickly slipped on the blue dress and re-pinned my hair. Without the expert hairdressing, I simply looked like a governess in a nice dress.

"Anne?"

Cathy opened the door and entered with Brandon and her maid Betsy hard on her heels. She instructed Betsy to dress my hair. Cathy and Brandon waited on my bed until Betsy had completed the task.

"There is something special about you and that dress..." Cathy murmured thoughtfully. "It becomes you so well..."

When we arrived at the dining room, Olivia and Vincent were already seated, chatting together quite amiably and I again I wondered if they'd met in London. They certainly appeared to have a lot in common with their shared acquaintances and knowledge of London life.

"Well, the little pirates have arrived," Vincent suddenly vacated his seat to greet us. "And how you are, young man?" He ruffled Brandon's hair, so like his own but there was no recognition on his part.

"And what about me?" Cathy interrupted sulkily.

Vincent looked over his niece. "Quite pretty...you remind me of your mother."

Then he noticed me. He seemed a little taken aback by a stranger in the dining room.

"I am Miss Woodville," I said.

"Miss Woodville," he bowed, taking my hand. "Indeed it is a pleasure. And you're...?"

"She's only the governess," Olivia smiled, taking his arm.

I noticed she had taken more than the usual pain with her appearance tonight and looked lovelier than I'd ever seen her.

"The governess," Vincent murmured, kissing my hand. *"Enchanté, mademoiselle."*

Olivia had taken the precaution of seating me down the other end of the table with the children and her husband. Vincent sat on her right and her brother, Mr Spencer, on her left.

Justin entered at that moment with Lillian on his arm. I had never seen Lillian look as pretty. She wore a new lavender gown, her hair dressed in a high coiffure in the current fashion.

Lillian refused to be seated with us and obstinately had the servant set her a place beside her cousin Vincent. The action seemed to annoy Olivia, who remained tight-lipped during the course of the meal as Lillian plagued Vincent with questions about his social life.

I could not read anything in Vincent's perfectly manicured expression. He was charming and attentive to all, especially the ladies.

"A charming group, don't you agree, Miss Woodville?" Justin murmured. "I'm afraid we are at the unpopular end of the table. Does it distress you?"

"Not at all," I replied honestly. "I have not had the opportunity of moving in polite society but what I do see of it, I dislike."

He smiled. "Your opinions are very pert, Miss Woodville. I don't know whether I believe you, Miss Woodville. You don't present the severe governess tonight. In fact," he went on, "you look quite lovely in that blue dress. No wonder Doctor Carstares visits so often."

I was relieved when the servants began to remove the dessert plates. Brandon struggled to stay awake so my excuse to go was sound. To my surprise, Justin rose and picked up Brandon. He accompanied Cathy and I to our rooms and put Brandon to bed. By now, Brandon was wide-awake and implored his father to read him one story. I thought Justin would refuse but he did not.

I don't know how long I stood there, listening to his animated tale, treating Brandon no less than his son.

When he finished, I put out the lights and walked out into the corridor. Justin was standing by the door, watching me with a curious expression.

My heart quickened. *He is a married man and my employer,* I thought to myself. *I shouldn't feel uneasy with him.*

I needn't have worried.

"Goodnight, Miss Woodville," was all he said and I returned promptly to my room.

CHAPTER TWELVE

I couldn't suppress a strange sort of nervous excitement the following morning as I dressed. Lillian had kindly let me borrow a riding habit, a rather dowdy one, but at least it suited the purpose.

I made my way down to the stables with Cathy. Vincent, Olivia, Mr Spencer and Lillian were already seated on their mounts. Olivia, as expected, commanded attention in her velvet blue riding habit edged in white matching the fashionable hat attached to her coiffure. Beside her, Lillian looked quite dull in gray. I immediately sensed some tension between them when Olivia suggested she ride a mule.

Lillian dismounted and retreated to the stables, a victim of Olivia's barbed tongue. Olivia continued to flirt with Vincent while leaning on her brother, who seemed impervious to his sister's faults.

I tried to imagine Madeline in Olivia's stead, as mistress of Silverthorn, a flirtatious beauty, determined to make every man fall in love with her. I still found it difficult to think of her dead—lying in the bottom of a strange, family vault. How could her spirit rest in peace if she'd been murdered?

No, she was deeply troubled...I could feel it. Perhaps that was why I had been lured to Silverthorn—to expose the truth. She knew she could always rely upon me to help her.

Oh, why hadn't she taken notice of my letters?

Lord Thomas's death was a mystery too. Heart attack, some said. Others said he suffered a stroke. I tried to think of the man I knew in London—the middle-aged lord on the hunt for a beautiful, young wife.

Did he suspect—when she gave birth prematurely?

She would have taken a lover eventually. I wondered if she'd had any connection with Vincent Braithfield. He seemed very familiar with Silverthorn and its secrets. And he delighted in flirting with Olivia in his cousin's face. Why?

Justin noticed it too. When he approached the party, I followed his tight-lipped gaze to his wife. When she saw him approach, she merely shrugged. "Justin! I thought you were going to the mill today."

"Well met, cousin," Vincent drawled. "I never expected you would leave those godforsaken mills to gallop with us."

"Those mills you speak of so warmly provide you with your allowance."

Vincent grinned off the sharp retort before whispering something in Olivia's ear. She laughed.

I thought of Madeline on horseback, riding wildly over the moors. So lost in my reminiscing, I was prompted by Jimmy who kindly reminded me it was time to mount.

The horror must have shown on my face for I heard Justin laugh.

"Come on, Miss Woodville...the others are gone."

I peered nervously at the powerful black stallion, the pride of Silverthorn. "You must be Philippe," I whispered, stroking his neck.

"Ye ready, miss?" Jimmy said in his broad accent. "Don't be scared...Philippe likes ye; he won't throw ye off like he did Miss Lillian."

"Miss Lillian!" I cried. "But she is an accomplished horsewoman..."

"Philippe's choosy," Jimmy explained, "but he likes ye, I can tell."

"Thank-you, Jimmy," I smiled, taking the reins and mounted. At once, I was aware of the power beneath me...in my control.

We caught up with the party. I took a moment to appreciate the beauty of the moors. The sun shone through the clouds, bathing the purple heather in a sea of gold.

"What holds your attention, Miss Woodville?"

I turned sharply to see Vincent regarding me thoughtfully. "How does it come about that a governess is invited along with the party?" He lowered his voice. "Have you managed to secure the affections of my so noble cousin?"

"I don't know what you mean, Mr Braithfield."

His long-lashed blue eyes stung me with their beauty. "Don't you think it is highly irregular that a governess is given Silverthorn's finest steed to ride?"

I was relieved when I saw Cathy trotting towards us. "Oh," she sighed irritably, "I *hate* Hyacinth...she is so slow! I wish Papa would trust me with Philippe...do you like him, Anne?"

"Yes."

"Shall we try him out then? I long to gallop! What do you think, Uncle Vince? Can we go now?"

Vincent grinned. "Why not? Let's make a race of it."

"Oh, yes!" Cathy cried. "Papa! We're going to race!"

"Race?" Olivia quizzed with disdain.

"It's Uncle Vince's idea," Cathy said.

Olivia beamed. "Oh...what a splendid idea! Where to?"

"To those sharp rocks up there," Vincent pointed in the distance.

"Let's make a bet of it, shall we?" Spencer suggested after surveying the course. "Fifty guineas?"

"Done," Vincent smiled. "First to the top...I'm in need of some cash."

"Who says you'll win?" Olivia teased. "I'm said to have an excellent seat on horseback."

Cathy rolled her eyes.

I couldn't suppress a certain amount of apprehension as we lined up. I didn't have any more time to think about it. I was aware of nothing but thundering hooves, powerful flanks and the bouncy, unclear view as I struggled to hold on.

When we stopped abruptly, I sighed in relief. I hadn't fallen off...I hadn't disgraced myself in front of the company...

"Anne! *You* won!"

I looked up at Cathy's voice. "Won what?"

"The race! Look, here comes Olivia. She doesn't look pleased. Uncle Vincent and Papa are over there—and Mr Spencer is last!"

I had to turn to Justin to believe the truth.

He smiled. "Congratulations. You have won yourself fifty guineas...compliments of Mr Weston."

Spencer looked mortified. "Beaten by a woman? Good God, how am I ever going to tell them at the club?"

True to his word, Mr Spencer gave me my reward. He said it was bad enough to have been beaten by a woman than to add to his woes by not honoring his obligations.

I accepted the bag of guineas knowing exactly what I would do with it. I would settle the debt I owed to Lady Beatrice first by buying her a gift...and with the remainder pay for my outfit for the ball. I could not accept Justin's charity.

Lillian was exceptionally quiet on the ride home. She had decided to join the party later, determined to ignore Olivia's remark about her riding a mule. She moved her horse closer to mine, a flighty palfrey, and laughed when Philippe neighed in protest.

"That stupid horse never liked me...did you know that Cathy's mother was thrown from his back. Aren't you frightened?"

"A little," I admitted, "but Philippe is an extraordinary animal. He cannot be blamed for a riding accident."

"Yes, magnificent," Lillian mimicked, "but it's only a horse, isn't it? Horses are dispensable."

"I thought you loved horses."

She shrugged. "Sometimes...but now I have something else to love." Her eyes followed Vincent. "He's grand, isn't he? But he'll never look at me. I'm just 'little cousin Lily' to him. See how he flirts with Olivia! I wonder why Justin allows it."

"I hadn't noticed," I lied.

Lillian looked at me through her docile brown eyes. "And have you also not noticed how my cousin pays more than the usual attention to you?"

"I'm sure I don't know what you mean."

"Don't be such a fool. Justin might not be Vincent but he's had his fair share of women, I can tell you. Why, Olivia had set her cap at him for years but now she has him, it has lessened her triumph."

"I don't think we should be discussing such things, Miss Lillian," I said abruptly. "Shall we rejoin the party?"

"Well...if we must," Lillian smiled. "I do like you, Anne. You're a nice person. I like nice people...where are you from again?"

"Cornwall," I replied.

"Cornwall..." she mused. "And are your parents—"

"No, they are dead."

"A long time ago?"

"Yes, a long time ago."

"Oh...I'm sorry...who looked after you then?"

"My Uncle."

"Oh...a wealthy man was he?"

I did not feel comfortable with her line of questioning. My fragile mask must not be lifted, not until I discovered the truth about Madeline. To my relief, Cathy waved for my assistance. "He was a man of the church," I called out to Lillian, pulling away from her to greet my charge.

So secure with my Miss Woodville disguise, I was a little unprepared for Lillian's questioning and hoped she didn't detect any irregularities.

I reminded myself I was Laura Morgan, Madeline's cousin.

I must not let Silverthorn draw me into its silken web of comfort—I was here for a purpose.

On our return to Silverthorn, Mrs Simmons informed me that the seamstress awaited us in the schoolroom. Her dark eyes darted over my borrowed riding habit. "I cannot see why his lordship permits...this attention will only do you harm, girl, can't you see it?"

"Do you suggest I refuse my employer when he wishes me to accompany his daughter?"

She clicked her tongue. "Obstinate girl! Don't forget your place, Miss Woodville."

Cathy raced ahead to the schoolroom and when I entered, held up my dress for me.   "Oh, Anne...it's beautiful...you will look lovely and Doctor—" she stopped abruptly, "and Doctor Carstares...isn't he due to arrive soon to check on Laura?"

"A good man he is, the Doctor," the seamstress, Mrs Clark, winked at me. "Plenty of young lassies after 'im...you'd best get 'im while he's free."

I drew everyone's attention back to the outfits. Mrs Clark insisted we try them on now, to check the fit. I felt a little silly as I slipped into my room. Like Cathy, this was my first ball too and my first ball gown. However, I mustn't forget my place at the ball—a companion for Miss Cathy.

Mrs Clark and Cathy didn't leave me alone to attend to the task. They charged into my room, delighted with the result.   The mirror showed a light woman of medium height, bathed in layers of the softest white with a low neckline and laced bodice. Mrs Clark often commented on what a good figure I had and said it was a pity my governess dresses didn't do me any justice. She offered to alter them for me but I politely refused, knowing Mrs Simmons would think I was out to ensnare the lord of the manor.

"And now for the headpiece," Mrs Clark announced and pulled from her sack a delicate veil attached to a thin coronet.

Cathy shrieked in delight. "You look like a princess, Anne!"

"Cecily or Eleanor?" I asked, thinking of the ladies who haunted the Tower.

"Eleanor...even though she is of tragic sensibilities. I simply can't believe it! I never thought you could be—" her hand closed over her mouth. "Beautiful."

I laughed, assuring her I would take no offence. I thanked Mrs Clark and paid her out of my winnings.

She told me his lordship had already paid for the costumes.

I waited until I heard Justin's carriage arrive.

I could not accept such a gift from him. Vincent and Lillian's remarks earlier this morning disturbed me and I didn't want to be a recipient of harmful gossip.

I found him where I knew he would be—his study. He looked tired and was loosening his necktie when I entered.

"Well, Anne, what have you come to see me about?"

A faint smile hovered on his lips.

"I am here to pay for my gown, my lord. I cannot accept such a gift...so here is the sum." I dumped the bag unceremoniously on his desk.

He raised a brow in surprise. "You defend your independence as fiercely as you ride Philippe to victory...you're certainly not a dull governess, are you?"

"Philippe won the race," I clarified, "I simply hung on."

Justin relaxed in his chair with a low chuckle. Suddenly he didn't seem so intense and I supposed this is how he must have looked in his younger, carefree days. He crossed his arms and continued to study me through amused eyes. "Are you sure you cannot accept my gift?"

I didn't trust myself to look into his eyes. "Y—yes."

"And you refuse to tell me why?"

I nodded.

"You are a stubborn woman, Miss Woodville, but I understand you perfectly. You do know that, don't you?"

I didn't answer.

The hour came upon us.

I loosened my hair in readiness for its first public appearance. Aunt Mary always said a woman's hair was her glory but I knew even she would frown if I left it in such a state. Uncle Clive would never permit me to attend a masquerade ball.

"Fit for the sons and daughters of Satan," he would say.

I'd heard of revelries and unspeakable sins occurring at such frivolous functions. Yes, unspeakable sins like murder.

Why would someone push Madeline from the Tower on the night of the spring ball? Was her murderer masked and unidentifiable? Would her murderer be here tonight—as a token of the anniversary?

I shivered. I knew the murderer would be in this house tonight...

Suppressing such morbid fears, I attached the headpiece to my hair and observed the final effect.

Tonight would be the only night I could describe myself as beautiful.

Cathy came to collect me. She looked lovely in her Grecian outfit with her bouncing ringlets. We attached our masks together, giggling in the hall as we watched the procession downstairs from the balcony.

A sea of masked gentlemen and ladies grouped in the parlor, directed to the ballroom by an officious Maitlan.

Music and laughter flooded our ears as we descended the stairs and I realized one had a certain advantage in being masked. I doubted even Olivia would recognize me with my hair loose.

"I can't tell who any of these people are," Cathy whispered. "Isn't it fun?"

We followed the arriving procession down the corridor and into the ballroom. I suspected this was the kind of society party Adam Rohan frequented in London.

It did not take us long to identify Olivia. She stood beside Vincent, who elected to wear a pilgrim's habit complete with hood, and looked enchanting as a shepherdess with her platinum blonde hair in a simple braid and a golden staff in her hand.

"Look, there's Aunt Lillian!"

I peered through the crowd of pirates, soldiers, warriors, Greek gods and goddesses, Roman centurions and monks to see Lillian in a risqué scarlet robe with her hair flowing in the style of warrior-queen, Boadicea.

Cathy rushed over to her. "So, this is your secret costume, Aunt Lillian! I almost didn't recognize you."

"Yes," Lillian said in a strangled voice, "it certainly isn't attracting the attention I want."

I followed her gaze to Vincent.

"You look lovely, Miss Lillian," I smiled. "I'm certain you'll not want for partners."

She looked at me. "There's only one partner I want."

"Who, Aunt Lillian? I'll secure him for you."

A frail smile appeared on her lips as she looked down at her niece. "That's the problem. He's unavailable...at the moment."

An ugly pirate tapped me on the shoulder. "Mr Ashton," I laughed, "what did you use to blacken your teeth?"

"Deuced waste of time for I can't eat a thing without the stuff coming off! You look a picture, Miss Woodville...who are you meant to be?"

"Eleanor of Aquitaine," I answered, though I thought of the Eleanor who haunted Silverthorn's Tower.

"Well, my lady," Brett bowed, "I intend to carry you off for the first two dances."

"Agreed; where are your sisters?"

He shrugged. "Lost somewhere in the fray. Tab's dressed in a prodigious hoop as Mary of Scots and Eliza is Eve, if you can find her."

Cathy caught my sleeve. "Doctor Carstares is over there and he's not even in costume but he's masked."

"Damnable things these masks," Brett complained when the Doctor approached. "May I present Miss Woodville as Eleanor of Aquitaine and Miss Braithfield as..."

"Cleopatra," Cathy improvised, "turned Roman."

Brett laughed at this, leaving me alone with a startled Greg Carstares. He searched for words to describe me. "Oh, it is you, Miss Woodville. For a moment there...you look quite..."

"Extraordinary."

"Papa!" Cathy smiled. "Where have you been? I've been searching for you *everywhere*!"

Justin lifted his knight's visor. "I see we all look different..."

He commented on Cathy's costume before turning to me. His blue eyes meticulously dissected me.

"Isn't she beautiful?" Cathy prompted. "I'm proud to have such a pretty governess."

"Inappropriate for one's station," Olivia glided to her husband's side. "But I'm sure Miss Woodville will enjoy the once-off opportunity. Come, darling...we should open the dancing."

It must have irked Olivia immensely to see us dancing the entire hour and it did not surprise me when she tapped my shoulder as the hour gonged.

"It is much too late for young girls and governesses," she breathed, her icy blue eyes sparkling with sudden mirth. "Wouldn't you agree, Vince?"

I raised my brows at the familiar use of his name.

Vincent petted Cathy's head. "Yes, I agree this little scamp should go lest someone prey upon her." His gaze moved to me. "But surely Miss Woodville graces your ball, Liv?"

Olivia's smile froze on her face.

"No, we should leave," I said, no longer keen to stay.

"You can stay!" Cathy whispered to me as I led her out of the ballroom. "Papa said you could. Olivia just doesn't want Uncle Vince to dance with you."

We spoke no more of it. I returned her to her room. When asked if I would return to the ball, I shook my head. I was on my way back to my chamber when I realized I had Brett Ashton's scarf attached to my wrist. He had complained of the 'darned thing' while dancing and I had removed it from him.

Breathing a sigh of annoyance, I returned to the lion's den. To my relief, I saw my pirate standing in the middle of the parlor. I followed his gaze up to the portrait of Madeline. "She's lovely, isn't she? Did you know her?"

He turned, the playful light suddenly non-existent in his eyes. "Yes." The answer was torn raggedly from him.

"They say she took her own life. Do you believe it?"

He shook his head. "No; she was murdered."

"Cathy said the inquest—"

"They were *wrong*."

This wasn't the jovial Mr Ashton whom I had danced with two hours earlier. Had he been in love with Madeline? I tried to recall what she'd written about him in her letters. Nothing significant came to mind but I remembered Cathy saying once how Brett was madly in love with Madeline and had never gotten over it.

Why would he say the inquest got it wrong? Did he know something about her murder?

"Is it really true that she died on this date last year?"

He turned slowly to me, his face full of anguish. "She was so lovely, you know. She still held the ball...even though her husband had died the previous month. Some thought it was shocking...but I thought it courageous. Yorkshire is dull enough without Silverthorn's spring ball." He gazed up at the portrait again. "She dressed as a nun that night—in black, out of respect for her husband, but her drab uniform couldn't hide her beauty..."

"What happened?"

"Dashed if I know," he whispered in pain. "Nobody seems to know...I found out she was dead the next morning...but I know she didn't take her life. *Someone* else did."

A noise behind heralded the approach of departing guests.

Brett tensed with the movement before transforming into his usual, jovial self. "You mustn't take any notice of me, Miss Woodville. My sisters tell me I'm a *dramatic.* And I believe them." He glanced up at the portrait again.

I knew then Madeline had scarred his heart in some way. "I must retire...it was nice dancing with you."

He took my hand. "Yes, I liked snatching your hand from Carstares. He is smitten with you, you know. And is in want of a wife, so I hear."

"Governesses are not the marrying kind."

"Perhaps you haven't met the right man yet."

I returned his scarf and had reached the landing when I overheard another set of voices. However, these ones were familiar.

It was Justin and Olivia.

By her protest, I could tell she didn't want to be pulled into the parlor for a private conversation. They stopped directly beneath me.

"I can't believe you," Justin said, "you're behaving like a common trollop!"

"Don't be such a fool," Olivia hissed, "it's only an innocent game— but of course the mill lord never has fun, does he?"

"The mill lord didn't seem so distasteful to you before we married."

"I thought your fortune was enough, but obviously, it isn't."

He must have grabbed her arm for she gasped. "I warn you, stay away from Vincent—"

"I don't know what you mean," Olivia said in an innocent voice.

"Everyone else has noticed."

There was a long pause. "Has Lillian been telling tales? If she has, why do you believe her? She's insane."

"You forget yourself," Justin replied tersely. "You know exactly what I mean. Let this be a warning to you—"

I didn't want to hear any more. Uncle Clive's scolding voice came to my mind, outlining the sinfulness of eavesdropping.

I reached my chamber with relief. I undressed and lay awake, wondering about Madeline's last moments. Today was the anniversary of her death.

I wondered whether the murderer had been at the ball. Why did the inquest fail? I remembered Cathy's words: *They tried to hide it from the public.*

The 'they' could only mean the family. Madeline said Justin hated her. If he'd murdered her, what was his motive?

Silverthorn, of course.

But with the estate entailed away from the female line, there was no need to kill Madeline. Justin, as next male heir, would naturally take his Uncle's place.

So why was Madeline murdered?

"I'm taking you into town," Cathy announced a week later. "Papa says we may ride in with him. We'll visit the mills first—and then I thought we'd visit Ashton Grove."

"What about the children?"

"I arranged their care with Mrs Simmons. Well, what do you say?"

"I don't have a riding habit."

"Oh dear," Cathy mused, "and you shan't fit one of mine...I'll go and ask Aunt Lillian."

I was relieved she went for I did not relish a walk to Lillian's Tower. Miss Lillian spent the entire week locked up in her Tower with the ghost of Eleanor.

Did I really believe Eleanor haunted the Tower?

I would say no until I recalled the night I had walked to the west wing...the wind roving across the moors, carrying Eleanor's soft cry...

Whether true or not, I didn't feel like hearing another one of her ghost stories.

Cathy returned promptly with a riding habit over her arm.

I asked after Miss Lillian.

"She is upset, of course," Cathy whispered. "She always is around this time of year."

"Why?"

"Because her husband and child died. It's the anniversary of their deaths."

"Oh."

That explained Lillian's sudden need for solitude.

She chose a fair time to be detached, I thought, as we walked to the stables. The guests who stayed on after the ball were in a feverish state of activity. Garden parties, picnics, endless dinners and games consumed the better part of the week. Mr Spencer led the party with his sister's approval, successfully gratifying the whims of all.

We passed them. I noticed Olivia remained at Vincent's side, smiling and attentive. However, although he certainly enjoyed her favor, he didn't appear as besotted as she was with him. This became evident when Justin led his wife away, no doubt advising her about her behavior, and Vincent gaily turned his attentions to another woman in the party.

"Papa's angry," Cathy murmured. "Uncle Vince always steals his women."

"Cathy, that is a highly unconventional remark, unworthy of you."

She flushed at my stern reprimand. "But it's true! Mama and Uncle Vince made Papa a laughing-stock in the district."

She told me no more as her father approached. I was ashamed to feel a twinge of disappointment. Silverthorn held many a secret and as each day passed, I was only more determined to discover them all.

We rode into town.

Across the moors and far beyond the inn where I stayed, lay the bustling heart of the industrial town. Smoke filled the air, emanating from large warehouses where all kinds of machinery noises invaded our ears. Everybody seemed to have a purpose, marching down the street-a complete difference from the so-called 'polite' society staying up at the Manor.

"What do you think of our town, Miss Woodville?" Justin asked.

"I've never seen people with such purpose before..."

He smiled. "The merchant world will prevail over the rich and titled, you know."

"Then you must be a walking contradiction, my lord."

"There's an old proverb, Miss Woodville, which says a man can only find contentment with hard work. I don't find gambling at the club to be excessively taxing, do you?"

"Papa is something of a reformed rake," Cathy explained as we dismounted.

"What completed the transformation?"

Justin laughed. "It is my secret. Will you allow me to keep it?"

I felt the color rush to my face under his ardent gaze. Obviously, he still possessed the skills of a society rake.

We left our horses with the groom. Cathy charged off after her father in search of money. I watched the two of them together, trying to recall how strained their relationship was only a few short months ago. Dare I think I had influenced the change?

"Your father is very good to you," I said when she returned, having achieved her purpose.

"Oh, I know and I'm determined to make more of an effort with Olivia—to please him. I see now it only hurts him when I don't try."

We entered a milliner's shop first where Cathy purchased a new bonnet and a pair of gloves before we came to the bookstore.

The old shop inspired me with its layers of dust, hiding the treasures. I thought of Theresa as I selected a few and flicked through the pages. One interested me entitled 'A Lady's Guide.' The cover was crisp and beautiful, as if it had never been opened.

I turned the page, my eye drawn to the handwriting in the top left hand corner. I held it up to the light and recoiled in shock.

For there were the words in bold, black ink: *To Madeline, in remembrance. Love Vince.*

CHAPTER THIRTEEN

"What's wrong, Anne? You look like you've seen a ghost."

We stood outside the shop, waiting for the groom to ready the horses.

"Are you unwell?" Cathy took my hand. "You *are* unwell...we must go home—"

"No, I am well enough to continue. I suppose I've been standing in one place too long."

Cathy frowned at me. "Well, you should have been more active instead of keeping your nose in that book...what is it?"

"Oh, a book on etiquette..."

She made a face. "I hope you aren't planning to incorporate it in my lessons?"

I gave her my stern governess look and she recoiled in horror.

We mounted and rode towards the mills. I tried to savor the atmosphere but those words, black, bold and haunting, stole my vision. Knowing Madeline, I knew they must be lovers. Were they discreet? Did others know?

I could only ask one person for information on the subject—Mrs Gardner, Madeline's personal maid. She would know if her mistress slept in her bed at night or returned late from an assignation with a lover.

"There's the first mill," Cathy announced, pointing ahead. "The others are farther down but we're only going to this one today. I hope we shan't stay long. It is so boring!"

"Boring? I confess I'm quite excited to see how the Braithfield textiles are produced."

Cathy rolled her eyes. "You sound like Papa."

The Braithfields owned three mills. The western one recently had to be rebuilt following a fire. Cathy explained a disgruntled employee started the fire when Lord Thomas was alive. "I don't blame old Jackson," she wrinkled her pretty nose, "Papa says Uncle Thomas' managers were cruel and ruthless...they deserved the consequences."

I raised my brows in wonder as we dismounted. Smoke issued from tall chimneys at the top of the two-story building.

"This is Lester mill," Cathy said.

"How long has it been running?"

She shrugged. "As long as I can remember...look, Papa's over there! He's waiting with Mr Thompson."

I followed Cathy to the landing on the first floor. Justin had discarded his riding coat and the sleeves of his white shirt were rolled up to his elbows. Having never seen him so informally attired, I felt the color rush to my face.

The middle-aged, plump man beside him, Mr Thompson, extended his hand. "Good morn'ng, Miss Braithfield, Miss Woodville. I've heard a bit about ye, Miss Woodville. Not many young leddies like this kind of tour. Are ye sure ye're up to it?"

"Quite sure," I smiled.

"Well—shall we?'"

"I'll take them, Thompson," Justin said.

Mr Thompson concealed his disappointment behind a good-natured grin. "Yes, of course, m'lord. Have a pleasant trip, leddies."

I watched him disappear down a sharp flight of stairs. I put my hands on the balcony and looked over the hundreds of people at work, taking careful note of their ages.

"Lester mill has a bad reputation," Justin said, stretching out his hands to rest on the top rail. "My Uncle showed no interest in the mills. He employed managers to produce results out of child labor and grueling work schedules. Many died or were maimed for various reasons...eventually an employee locked up the manager and burnt down the building. My Uncle was furious...he was ready to hang the man when I persuaded him not to. I asked permission to rebuild Lester and manage them both. To my surprise, he agreed."

I told Cathy not to swing on the balcony.

She glanced at me in rebellion. "But this is *so* boring!"

"This is part of your family history...how can you find it boring?"

"She is horribly spoilt," her father said. "She would perhaps be more interested if she realized this is her main source of income."

The ground level was filled with men and women of all ages. I espied the youngest to be a male of fourteen. Mr Thompson waved at us from inspecting a broken-down machine. "Mr Thompson appears very capable...how long has he been here?"

"How long do you think?"

"Years?"

He grinned. "For once you are wrong, Miss Woodville. I engaged Mr Thompson a year ago. We needed his expertise in managing the workers to have Lester rebuilt and commence operation. Naturally, many things needed to change."

"I can imagine."

To my delight, we were shown the various processes in producing the high quality yarn. New machinery sped up the tedious tasks of spinning and weaving.

Justin removed a sample from a nearby woman. "Here, feel this..."

"I've never seen anything so fine..."

"The recipe is a secret. It is my special project."

I thought of the fashion shops of Paris and London. "The market possibilities are enormous."

He nodded. "Would you like to see my office?"

"Yes, of course."

We moved on. Cathy walked a step or two behind us, consumed with her own daydreaming.

"Tell me," Justin said as we walked upstairs, "why does all this interest you?"

I was aware of his proximity. I turned back and glanced at all the workers. "My father was a coal miner." I searched his face for disgust and found nothing but astonishment.

"A coal miner?"

I nodded. "He and my mother died in a mineshaft. My brother survived a month after the accident but his lungs were irrevocably damaged by years of poisonous air."

"How old were you?"

"Too young, fortunately, to work in the mines," I smiled. "I don't even remember my family...but in a strange way, I am still bound to them. I keep thinking, that if they had not died, I would be down there...working alongside them."

"How did you—er—manage—?"

I laughed. "My Uncle took me in. He has a comfortable situation and I was fortunate to receive a good education."

"I sympathize with your tragedy..." His eyes hardened as he looked over his inheritance. "Incidents like those now belong in our past, gratefully forgotten."

Cathy's patience snapped. "We won't have time to see the office, Papa, for we are expected at Ashton Grove for luncheon."

Justin came outside to see us off. We were almost out of sight when I turned around and met his gaze. I wished I knew what he was thinking.

Ashton Grove, for a town house, boasted a remarkable resemblance to a small country manor. Surrounded by a solid iron fence, one could look past the perfectly manicured gardens to the eighteenth-century house.

Mr Ashton, dressed in a splendid purple coat, met us at the stairs. He wore a smug expression, his curly blonde hair bouncing with his sudden movement as he idly swung a pendulum chain attached to his breeches. "I dare say you ladies enjoyed your tour of Lester mill?"

"It was boring," Cathy confessed. "May I go in to Tabitha and Eliza?"

Brett patted her on the head in a brotherly fashion. "Of course— they're in the Drawing Room, waiting with an appetite that ill becomes them." He turned to me. "And what did you think of Justin's tour? Did he give you the twenty pence version or the twenty guinea version?"

"Twenty guinea, I imagine," I laughed.

"Is that so?" He offered his arm. "You must allow me then, Miss Woodville, to satisfy your appetite. We have cooked up a feast, you know."

"You mean your cook has."

His lower lip trembled. "I'm mortified that you have found me out! Governesses are good sleuths, I've been told."

The sound of porcelain and chatter floated from the Drawing Room. Brett opened the door to reveal a cozy party by the fire. Olivia and Vincent commandeered one rose-colored settee while Tabitha and Eliza sat on the other. Mr Spencer stood by the mantelpiece with his cup of tea while Cathy helped herself to a plate of sugared sweets.

Eliza rose to greet me, herding me into the private group. An odd sense of uneasiness overcame me when I caught Olivia observing us with open hostility. I glanced at Cathy to see if she knew her stepmother and Uncle would be here but she seemed as surprised as I did. She was delighted with her Uncle, of course, and went to sit beside him.

Olivia studied me with contempt. "Miss Woodville...you surprise me. You seem to have more days off than I recall my governess taking. How fortunate for you."

"I invited your governess for luncheon, Lady Braithfield," Brett apologized gallantly.

"Shall we begin luncheon?" Spencer suggested, to my relief.

Lunch passed uncomfortably slow. Olivia took every opportunity to make me feel ill at ease and accomplishing it in such style, she made everyone laugh. Cathy sat beside her adored Uncle and Vincent remained attentive to her, which vexed Olivia outrageously.

Why should they fight over him like starved alley cats? Undeniably a favorite of the *haute ton,* Vincent Braithfield used his looks and charm to seduce women. I could see why Madeline had chosen him for a lover. How had they managed to keep it a secret?

I studied the smooth, tanned face, looking for clues. His lips curled into a lazy grin. When he caught me watching him, an eyebrow rose in faint surprise and he ran his tongue along his lower lip, baiting me for a response.

I turned away, shocked. How could such a man behave so in company? I looked around but no one seemed to notice. His lack of propriety reminded me of Madeline's gypsy lover in London. Lucian possessed no qualms about seducing a woman beyond his class. Vincent Braithfield possessed no qualms about seducing his cousin's wife.

I recalled the look on Justin's face when he caught his wife staring at Vincent in the parlor on the day of his arrival. He was accessing her reaction, almost expecting her failure.

"He's a born rogue, isn't he?" Eliza whispered. "Half of England is in love with him...but of course he will have to marry a fortune for he is horribly reliant upon Justin and resents the condition, I believe."

"He doesn't look like he's starving," I said.

Eliza laughed. "You're quite right, Anne. I love your pique little remarks. Now indulge me...do you not find him attractive? Everyone's in love with him...Lillian quite desperately."

"Miss Lillian?"

"But he won't wed a half-wit, especially since she's lost Silverthorn."

"An estate entailed on the male line?"

Eliza nodded. "Yes, very bad business all that. Justin and Vincent squabbled incessantly about it—they are always at each other's throats for one thing or another. And of course it all started with Danielle."

"Cathy's mother?"

Eliza smiled at my hesitation. "I can see you want to know the story so I shall tell you, if you can endure my hushed whispers." She waved away Brett and continued, "Justin married Danielle when she was very young. She was a pretty thing, very much like Cathy lacking her father's spirit. Danielle resented falling with child so early...I don't believe she ever forgave Justin for making her pregnant and putting her through that birth..."

"But surely that is not his fault."

"No, of course...but Danielle and Justin became enemies from the moment she tried to kill her baby. Then, all of a sudden, there appeared to be reconciliation...and Brandon was the result. Things improved a little...until she died in that horrid riding accident."

"Riding accident?"

Eliza nodded solemnly. "She rode Philippe—madly, I'm told. But I'm getting ahead of myself...you see Danielle had fallen in love with Vincent. He'd come to Silverthorn and charmed Danielle into his arms. Everybody believed it to be a light flirtation but I knew better. The way she looked at him! I don't believe he was quite so sincere, though."

"No," I echoed.

"He simply wanted to annoy Justin."

"So he seduced his wife?"

Eliza smiled. "Oh yes, but I don't think Justin cared. Everybody knew their marriage was over...Danielle wouldn't even acknowledge her own daughter!"

"Poor Cathy bears many scars," I murmured.

"Danielle, poor thing, believed Vincent loved her. She inevitably found out the truth and went riding recklessly over the moor...well, they found her the next day...her neck was broken."

I shook my head. "So much tragedy surrounds Silverthorn...was it a great shock when Lord Thomas brought home his young wife?"

"Madeline," Eliza supplied. "Yes, indeed, it was a great shock. Justin had taken over the management of the mills when his Uncle disappeared abroad in his usual mad way."

"The Braithfield madness?"

She nodded.

"How severe was his condition?"

A frown settled on Eliza's find brow. "I don't know...they say it showed later in his life and there wasn't enough time to see how the madness progressed. He died so suddenly."

"And his young wife followed him?"

Eliza was impressed. "Brett is right—you are a sleuth! But I doubt you'll find all of Silverthorn's skeletons."

"I will certainly try to air them out," I replied whimsically.

"I admire your courage but be warned—you may not like what you find."

The musical party broke up and Cathy was walking towards us. "The truth is all I want."

Eliza glanced at me candidly. "The truth could get you killed."

The next few days passed uneventfully.

Justin left for London, in the hope of securing a new piece of machinery. Mr Spencer left the same day, taking with him the last of his sister's guests.

Only Vincent remained.

I confess I felt uneasy knowing he was in the house when Justin was away. He walked around, humoring everyone including the dour Mrs Simmons. The day after Justin departed, Olivia and he went riding together without a groom. Lillian saw them return late, flushed and disheveled.

She came to the schoolroom, her hair lank and unwashed, great shadowy circles under her eyes.

I put Laura down as Brandon asked "what's wrong, aunty Lil?"

Lillian looked at him sharply, obviously resenting the question. Cathy, sensing her discomfiture, herded the children to the other side of the room, leaving me alone with Miss Lillian.

"I ask you to keep your eyes and ears open while my cousin is away," Lillian whispered frantically. "Something is amiss here...I can *feel* it."

"What do you want me to look for?"

She gazed at me with large, brown eyes. "Don't be naive, Miss Woodville. It concerns Olivia and Vincent. Justin *must* be told the truth. He would believe it if you told him what you've seen."

"I've seen nothing, Miss Lillian."

"I *have*."

Acknowledging her funny mood, I simply nodded and managed to steer the conversation in a different direction.

Lady Braithfield's odd behavior over the next few days supported Miss Lillian's suspicions. Olivia, with Vincent every moment of the day, was feverishly merry and didn't seem to care about the scandal they created by their reckless behavior.

I thought about the conversation I had overhead on the night of the ball and how it all connected. There was no love between Justin and Olivia. She married him for money and discovered a genuine mill-owner instead of the usual bored aristocrat. She found Vincent's good looks and devil-may-care attitude irresistible. How far their relationship extended, we couldn't say.

I didn't want to get involved. Why should I be the one to inform Justin of his wife's indiscretion? Olivia and Vincent would deny it and we had no proof, apart from Miss Lillian's wild ravings.

I felt a sense of duty prevail upon me. I came here for a purpose. Without my noting, Silverthorn was weaving an insidious web around me, drawing me into its secrets. I shouldn't care about dislodging any skeletons except those directly related to Madeline.

However, I dreaded the day when I would have to leave. I couldn't imagine ever returning to the Rectory.

Silverthorn changed everything.

Silverthorn became *me.*

Doctor Carstares came to visit.

I invited him into the schoolroom and ordered tea.

He looked at me warmly. "I'm afraid I can't stay but would you consent to walk with me for a moment?"

Cathy raised a brow in question. "I'll look after the children, Anne...you take as long as you want."

Out of her hearing, I said, "my charge is generous but I hope you understand that I do have duties to perform."

"Certainly, Miss Woodville, I will be brief."

We came to a stop along the corridor leading to the west wing, where the windows afforded a good view of the grounds below.

"Miss Woodville," Mr Carstares began, "I have come to ask you to be my wife. I do not have much to offer...but I offer what I have—along with my heart."

I stared at him dumbly.

"Please do not decide yet. I know it has come quite suddenly but I do believe I'm in love with you." He stepped a little closer, his green eyes sincere. "I would like to look after you, if you would give me the chance."

I cursed my stupid heart. Another proposal from a decent man...why did I hesitate? I glanced at the Doctor's humble face and saw only Justin with his dark, good looks and cynical eyes.

I shook my head to clear the vision. How could I think of a married man so? A married man, I reminded myself, far beyond my reach. I did not belong in Justin's world, nor did he belong in mine. Why couldn't I accept a man like Greg Carstares? I tried to picture myself as a Doctor's wife, living in a neat little cottage whilst Silverthorn rose magnificently out of the mist on the moors, forever beckoning me...

"Will you at least consider my proposal, Miss Woodville?"

"Yes, please allow me some time to consult my feelings on the matter."

The look of pure joy on his face made me feel guilty.

"In truth, I dared not hope I could be so lucky...which reminds me, I managed to locate the person you were looking for—a Mrs Gardner. She lives in the village under the name of her new husband Smith. Number twelve, Lockhart Street. I often visit her husband—he suffers from.... whatever is the matter, Miss Woodville?"

The scene below in the courtyard burned my eyes. Vincent and Olivia—in a lover's embrace.

Greg was clearly shaken. "Oh dear...is *that* Lady Braithfield?"

"Yes...but perhaps we misunderstand and there is an explanation..." I was thinking of Justin and how the scandal could hurt him and the family.

"Your forbearance is admirable," Greg replied. "We *shouldn't* speak of this until we have all the facts—is Lord Braithfield out of town?"

I nodded. "I know it may seem strange...but I am aware the Braithfields display affection quite openly...it may not be what it appears to be."

The lovers disappeared. The private courtyard, only seen from the west wing and along this corridor, seemed an ideal place for an assignation. Lillian must have seen them too.

I could only think of one thing.

How would Justin take the news?

I decided to keep Greg Carstares' proposal a secret.

Cathy gave me a curious look, wanting to know and yet knowing me well enough not to press for information. However, Lillian mentioned she had seen me with the Doctor in the corridor.

She studied me acutely, her large brown eyes suddenly alert. "You...and the Doctor...yes, it fits quite well, doesn't it? I wondered at his frequent visits. "

"She may marry him," Cathy piped in, braving my look of displeasure.

Lillian glanced at me. "Really? How interesting..."

"What are you talking about?" Brandon pulled my hand. "Who are you going to marry, Anne?"

I was about to reply when Lillian snapped, "be quiet, little hybrid, this is talk for *adults* not children. Go and play over there!"

We were accustomed to Lillian's rapid mood changes. Poor Brandon received her ill temper this time. As I looked at the child, I realized what she'd called him: little hybrid. Could she know the parentage of the child?

I had no doubt now that Vincent knew Brandon was his. He spent little or no time with the child but on the occasions he did, he proudly ruffled the boy's hair, reserving a cool smile for Justin.

One thing was clear: Vincent Braithfield came to Silverthorn to create a scandal. He resented his cousin and his inheritance and remained here to inflict pain by seducing his cousin's second wife. He never gave poor Lillian half a glance and as a result, Lillian's friendship with Olivia quickly evaporated. Perhaps that was her motive for looking for faults in Olivia's relationship with Vincent.

The truth couldn't be denied—I had seen the ultimate proof.

Had Madeline entangled herself with this Vincent? I opened the book I had found in town and ran my finger over the words: *To Madeline, in remembrance, Love Vince.* In remembrance of what—their love affair? She'd written of him in her letters as attentive and charming but now I wondered if Vincent had turned unfriendly towards her.

Could Vincent be Madeline's murderer?

I managed to convince the household that I traveled into town to procure a book on history for Cathy's next lesson. Mrs Simmons barely blinked when I requested the carriage. I believe she thought I went to see the Doctor.

The only person I found difficult to deceive was Cathy.

I was now so totally engrossed in my role as Anne the governess I almost forgot Laura Morgan, Madeline's plain cousin. Perhaps because now, for once, I was free of her shadow. I reveled in my life at Silverthorn and couldn't imagine living elsewhere. However, I couldn't stay Cathy's governess forever. And how could I stay when the strength of my feelings for Justin grew beyond my control? I felt almost pained at the inevitable reconciliation, which must follow his turbulent marriage to Olivia.

I forced myself to enjoy the scenery. I wondered how Lady Beatrice fared in her seaside villa...

The coach came to an abrupt halt. I couldn't suppress a nervous excitement as I alighted and climbed up the three steps to the door of number twelve. Perhaps I would find some of the answers to my questions here.

I knocked.

A moment later, a black-haired woman in her early thirties appeared, a red plaid shawl wrapped around her plain muslin dress. Her liquid black eyes studied me curiously. "Who are ye look'ng for, Miss?"

"Doctor Carstares told me I could find Mrs Gardner here."

Her brows shot up in alarm. "What do ye want with her if she's here?"

"My name is Laura Morgan...I am here to find out what happened to my cousin Madeline, the late Lady Braithfield."

The barrier crumbled instantly. "Ye'd better come in, Miss Morgan."

She drew me inside a cozy parlor and asked me to wait while she made tea. She returned a moment later and settled the rattling tray on a small circular table. "Milady spoke of ye often...that's why I sent you her bracelet."

"Before we proceed, Mrs Gardner, I must beg of you not to mention our conversation to a single soul. The very thing could ruin me...you see, I have a post at Silverthorn—or at least Anne Woodville does."

Mrs Gardner put an extra cube of sugar in her tea. "I'll keep me silence, Miss, ye needn't worry."

I sipped my tea, unsure of how much to relay to this stranger. "I received a letter from Madeline before she died."

"Do ye think she was murdered?"

"Yes. She said 'they' were going to kill her. Do you know whom she meant? The circumstances of her death are very odd...I know she would never willingly put an end to her life—no matter how desperate. I came here to search for the truth."

Mrs Gardner studied me closely. "Ye do realize you're in a lot of danger if ye start poking 'round, don't ye? They covered it all up very nicely—suicide was the verdict. But I knew milady could never take her life...she had too much spirit in her."

"Did you notice anything strange happening before her death?"

She consulted her memory. "One day milady looked quite pale...that was before the ball. She didn't seem herself as I pinned her up her hair...she had such lovely hair...milady always loved parties and I thought it strange she wasn't excited about this one. She didn't even ask me how she looked and she always asked me how she looked.

As she left the room, I bade her farewell and she looked at me rather odd. She walked back to her dresser and opened her jewelry casket. 'Twas there she took out the bracelet and said, 'Viv, if anything happens to me, I want you to send this to Laura. Promise me.' So I promised and that was the last time I saw her." She frowned. "I thought it odd too...but I remember her whispering under her breath 'it's the only thing I can call mine.' So I never questioned it. Miss Lillian never asked about the bracelet so I didn't mention it."

"And nothing else happened that day? You must remember *something*," I appealed.

"Well, there's just one more thing, Miss. I don't understand it but she did mutter 'there's nothing worse when a grape turns sour'...I never saw her again. Lost me job too after she died...so I got meself a husband."

I prepared to go. "Thank-you for your help and please—"

"I know. I'll not mention ye to a soul."

"Oh...one more question. What did Lady Madeline think of Lord Justin?"

I watched Mrs Gardner very carefully. She leaned against the door and murmured, "well, it was hard for milady at first. Master Justin wasn't happy when milord returned with his new, young bride. When milady had that accident...and the child came early, Master Justin was the first to question it. But milord accepted the child and we all thought Master Justin didn't like being cheated out of his inheritance. After awhile, they all got used to milady an' seemed to accept her, except Master Justin. Because of this, I always felt milady had a fancy for him."

They were not lovers. I breathed a heavy sigh of relief.

"And Mr Vincent Braithfield? What did Lady Madeline think of him?"

Mrs Gardner smiled. "He loved her, of course, as they all did. I hear he's come back to Silverthorn?"

I questioned the surprise in her voice. "Why should it be odd for him to visit his family?"

"You mean all that time ye've been there, ye haven't heard about Master Justin's first wife? She fell in love with Master Vincent but it turned out badly...Master Vincent's eyes turned ye lady cousin...and the poor thing killed herself over it."

I had arranged to meet the coachman in front of the grocer and donning my hat and gloves, moved speedily in that direction. All the while, I experienced a sharp fear of discovery.

It was ridiculous—no one could possibly *know* my business with Mrs Gardner.

I looked around to see nobody of any significance.

Nevertheless, I knew I was being watched.

CHAPTER FOURTEEN

I met Vincent as the carriage came to a stop in front of the house. He caught my hand, forcing me to accept his assistance as I alighted.

"Why, if it isn't the little *governess.* What mission are you on today?"

I hastily withdrew my hand. "I have purchased a history book for Miss Cathy's lessons, Mr Braithfield. Surely it cannot interest you."

He attempted to reach for the book but I slid past him into the house.

He followed me, surprised by my desire to escape him. "*Many* things interest me...to prove it to you I must visit the schoolroom."

"Yes, I'm sure Brandon will enjoy your attention."

A faint uncertainty crept into his blue eyes. "Of course, Brandon is a dear boy...why should you think he is especially close to me and not Cathy?"

He was testing me. "Miss Cathy is capable of entertaining herself, sir, but Brandon is young. I merely suggested he might enjoy your attention."

"Your opinions are rather pert, Miss Woodville. I can see why Justin hired you for the job," he leaned closer to whisper in my ear, "has he visited your bed yet? Tell me, is he a satisfying lover?"

"Vincent!"

We both turned to a furious Olivia. It was a brief moment but one which condemned her.

They were lovers.

I looked from one to the other, repulsed. I took my cue and left, eager to escape. As I climbed the stairs, I wondered if others had noticed Olivia's outburst. Mrs Simmons? The servants? Cathy? No, she would not think ill of her adored Uncle.

As much as I hated the situation, I could not allow myself to get involved. My face was still flushed from Vincent's barbed insinuations. Yes, he had come to Silverthorn to annoy Justin. Yes, he was Madeline's lover at the time of her death. Could he be the grape she spoke of turning sour?

Cathy's piercing scream pushed these idle thoughts from my mind. I ran as fast as my legs would carry me, an acrid scent choking my senses.

Smoke engulfed the hallway.

A faint shadow came out of the smoke. It was Cathy. "I don't know what h—happened but Brandon...he's still in there—"

"In where?"

"The schoolroom. It's on fire."

I dropped the book and removed my coat.

Cathy frowned. "Where are you going?"

"To get Brandon. Go downstairs and call for help. Tell them to bring water. Quick!"

The door to the schoolroom was locked. I could now understand Cathy's desperation. She would have plunged into the burning furnace to save her brother without a thought. I tried not to listen to Brandon's cries of terror inside the room as I fiddled with the lock.

It was jammed.

"Brandon!" I pounded against the door. "I'm coming!" I looked around in desperation and found a thin, alabaster stand. I knocked the vase off and tested its weight. Using the best of my puny strength, I battered the door several times. However, the pounding chipped at the stand more than the door.

In sheer failure, I plummeted to the floor, my fingers raw and bleeding.

"Anne! It's too hot...too hot..."

Brandon. I had to try again. I could not fail.

To my delight, a small piece of the lock cracked and the door opened a fraction. Just enough for me to see the flames and Brandon's watery eyes. He smiled at me.

"Stand back from the door!"

Hurling away the stand, I stepped back and kicked the half-broken lock as hard as I could. I felt something pull in my leg as I did it but the door budged enough for Brandon to squeeze through to safety.

The last thing I remembered was laying him upon the carpet, inspecting his wounds.

The face hovering above me was familiar.

"You're awake!" Doctor Carstares announced, his hand on my forehead.

I closed my eyes. "My leg—"

"Is perfectly intact," another voice answered and my heart pounded. Justin slowly came into my view, his lips half twisting into a smile. "You were very brave—how do you feel?"

"Much better," I lied.

"His lordship has been good enough to wait upon you these hours, Anne," Greg explained softly. "You have a fracture on your hip bone but that should not prevent—" he blushed.

I groaned inwardly. I could see Justin raising a brow at the familiarity. "I believe some congratulations are in order?"

His half-amused voice goaded my emphatic reply: "Oh, no! It's not what you think—"

"Don't be so shy, darling," Greg reached for my hand. "I have asked his lordship and he has given his consent. There's no need to conceal our happy state."

"Hide? But what—?"

Justin didn't let me finish. He glanced at the two of us. "I must leave the happy couple. Miss Woodville, I will speak with you later."

My sudden engagement to Doctor Carstares caused a sensation throughout the household.

Mrs Simmons was very attentive; Lillian surprised; Cathy stunned; Brandon sad; Laura mute and I hadn't seen Vincent or Olivia.

I hated to be confined to my bed. Cathy dutifully reported on Brandon's progress. A special Doctor came down from London to care for his burns and I hoped his wounds healed quickly.

As I hadn't seen Justin since I awoke, I asked Cathy about him.

She avoided my eyes. "What is it? What's happened?"

Cathy could never resist some form of gossip. "Papa threw out Uncle Vince. He was very angry last night—I've never seen him so angry." She glanced at me. "It was over Olivia of course—he and Olivia were—"

"Yes, I know."

"You knew? I thought Aunt Lillian was the only one who knew. She never liked Olivia. Papa wouldn't have believed Aunt Lillian but Doctor Carstares said it was true. He said that when he was proposing to you he saw Uncle Vincent and Olivia in the courtyard...I didn't think Uncle Vince could be so—"

"But what about your mother, Cathy?" I asked, feeling this was a good opportunity to broach the subject.

She shrugged. "They were lovers too. But he lost interest when Aunt Madeline arrived. I know my mother was very angry with my Uncle and rode out and killed herself. I didn't care then and I don't care now. She hated Brandon and I. She thought only of herself."

Yes, as Madeline did. Poor Laura was an orphan only, I believed, because of Madeline's foolish ways. She didn't deserve to be murdered but I felt certain she could have taken steps to prevent it. Had her affair with Vincent turned so sour he threatened her about it? Had she wronged him in some way? Had she taken another lover? Brett Ashton perhaps?

His face on the night of the ball...his strange, slurred words. He was in love with Madeline, was *still* in love with Madeline. He too believed Madeline had been murdered—why didn't he alert the authorities? Why all this secrecy?

I thought of Mrs Gardner's words: *They covered it all up very nicely—suicide was the verdict.*

Who covered it all up? They? The same 'they' Madeline wrote in her letters? Whom did she mean? The family?

Everything about the case of Madeline had been hushed to avoid a scandal.

A scandal was damaging to the family.

Well, I wouldn't give up so easily.

Before I fell asleep, I thought of Mrs Gardner whispering to me: *'ye do realize ye in a lot of danger if ye start poking 'round, don't ye?'*

Lillian came to see me.

"I've been looking over Brandon with Justin...such a cruel, cruel thing to happen...and look at you! How is your leg, Anne? It was very brave of you to save Brandon like that. We all think so."

She seemed normal and I relaxed. "I am happy to have saved him in time. Today is my last day of rest—I will see him tomorrow."

"Oh, no! Justin said you're to remain abed for three weeks."

"Three weeks! I'm not an invalid, Miss Lillian."

She glanced at me with her docile brown eyes. "*They* think I'm an invalid. *They* think I'm mad...they say I'm mad like father...but I'm not mad. Sometimes I let them think so. Would you call me mad, Anne?"

"I—I would say you're very...*unusual.* Not mad."

She smiled. "I like you, Anne. You lie with a sincere face. Of course, you think I'm mad...like the rest of them but at least you have a good heart. The others don't."

I didn't know to whom she referred to and certainly would not ask.

Lillian rubbed her hands by the fire. "You must have heard from Cathy that my cousin is no longer here...you should have told Justin sooner like I said. He's the laughing-stock of the town now. Olivia deserves a divorce...a public divorce—but she knows Justin will never permit it. He won't allow a stain on the Braithfield name. And now Vincent is gone..."

I remembered how she loved Vincent and felt sorry for her. "I'm sure you can do much better than your cousin, Miss Lillian."

She smiled faintly. "Yes, I can and I will. Vincent has always been very wild...it came as no surprise when he seduced Danielle. She was such a stupid thing...she didn't realize how very fortunate she was to have Justin. But I suppose she paid for her faults..."

"By dying alone on the moors?"

"No, by monitoring Vincent's attachment to my father's new bride. She was a beauty that one. But she thought too much of herself..."

She was talking about Madeline.

"How far did their—er—relationship progress?"

Lillian raised her brows. "It's rather obvious they were lovers, isn't it? She only married my father for his money." Her laugh turned cynical. "He wanted a son from her. But all she gave him was a daughter...a useless girl-child like me. I should have inherited Silverthorn but alas, I am not a male. Therefore, Justin must inherit. Unfortunate, isn't it?"

"Cathy told me your father left Silverthorn to Justin with a mountain of debts?"

"Yes, it is true. He spent the last of the money running around the world like a man in his cups."

"And Justin has worked very hard to raise the family's fortunes?" I whispered.

"Only to have another anchor drain the surplus in the form of Olivia," Lillian muttered. "She will *ruin* him. She will *ruin* us. And if she flies to Vincent, she will find no help from him. Justin has cut off his allowance. He is virtually penniless."

He should have done it long before, I thought.

"Lady Braithfield will reconsider her situation and reconcile with her husband," I said, "they are bound by the laws of the church. She is his wife, his lady."

"Yes, she is," Lillian echoed and stood up to go. "Unfortunately, she is."

I went to see Brandon the next day. I walked to his room and saw Justin sitting by his bedside, turning the lamp low.

I didn't want to interrupt but my presence was discovered. "Miss Woodville, you have recovered. No, please, come back. We must talk."

I turned around and sat on the opposite side of the bed. Brandon lay motionless, his face, chest and arms bandaged. "How is he?"

Justin shook his head. "It is my fault. I thought he was with Lillian or Cathy. I thought—"

I touched his hand. "It's not your fault. It is mine. If I hadn't gone to—"

He caught my hand. "Oh, Anne, it is neither our fault but an unfortunate accident."

I didn't want to let go of his hand. We looked at each other for a moment, both unwilling to let go.

"Anne—"

A very unwanted Greg Carstares entered and broke the spell.

Within an instant, Justin changed. He stood and greeted Greg, spoke casually of Brandon. He was suddenly aloof when he asked about the wedding.

"I thought next winter," Greg said, beaming at me.

I wanted to scream no but I couldn't humiliate Greg so ungraciously. He deserved a private hearing for my refusal—certainly not in front of his better, which would inevitably expose my feelings.

Laura Morgan, a penniless orphan, was in love with her employer.

A married man.

A peer of the realm.

The Lord of Silverthorn.

I don't remember the remainder of the conversation. Justin collected the book and made for the door where he met a subdued Olivia.

She stared at him for a long moment, her large blue eyes struggling to show some emotion. Perfectly lovely in her soft sage green gown, she murmured to our exclusion, "Justin, I wish to speak with you."

I watched Justin carefully, pretending to listen to Greg in the process.

He tensed. "Very well; we shall go to the study."

They left, leaving me with a feeling of acceptance. They would reconcile, as man and wife should. I should not feel disappointed. I mustn't forget my reason for being here.

"...Shall you want children, my dear? I think I should like it very much...and so would my mother."

"Mr Carstares, before another word is said, I must beg your forgiveness. I cannot marry you. I am not yet ready to marry—"

"I will gladly wait until you are," he smiled gently. "I know it is an important decision and one that requires great forbearance."

"You mistake me. It wouldn't be fair of me to accept you when I can't..."

"Can't?"

This was more difficult than my refusal of Edwin Brody. How does one put it? "I would like for us to be friends—very good friends."

Greg's green eyes narrowed in confusion. "But what will you do? You can't stay a governess forever...you must think of your future. I am offering you a comfortable home where you will not need to earn your living. Do you think in time you may learn to care for me?"

"Oh, I do *care* for you! But not in the way you want. I am certain your mother will expect you to marry for love—it isn't fair to accept anything less."

He considered. "I suppose you are right."

I caught his hand. "I hope we shall always be friends."

Cathy appeared at the doorway. She looked at the two of us and tried to hide a little smile. "Anne, there is someone here to see you. In the parlor."

"Who is it?"

"I don't know. Mrs Simmons sent me to tell you."

Immediately curious, I left Cathy with Greg and Brandon. She winked at me on my way out and I sadly shook my head. No matter how many wished it, I would not be marrying the good Doctor.

I reached the top of the staircase and stared down over the balcony. "Theresa!"

I rushed down, breaking my own rule for Cathy. Theresa spun around at the noise, her sunny smile cheering me as nothing else could.

"Oh Anne," her brown eyes twinkled mischievously. "How I have missed you!"

"And I you," I replied, accepting her embrace. I should it should amuse Cathy to meet my old governess. I had often told her about Theresa and the benefits of being friends with one's governess.

The hard months in Blackpool had taken its toll. Theresa explained that after many requests she was finally granted leave and thought she might visit me. Would they mind if she stayed with me here at Silverthorn?

I found Maitlan giving a lecture to poor Hetty about the correct way to dust. I interrupted with a cough and asked if his lordship was in the house.

"He's in his study, Miss Woodville. Not to be disturbed."

I inclined my head dutifully and when out of his eagle sight, headed for the study. I need not have worried. Justin was standing in the parlor, talking to Theresa.

Though I trusted Theresa implicitly, she belonged to my past and the fact could be dangerous.

"Miss Woodville, you look as if you've seen a ghost," Justin said and I could see his charm had worked on Theresa. "It was very rude of you to leave your friend standing unattended in the parlor. Why did you not take her upstairs?"

"I was about to, my lord, but I wanted to ask your permission first."

Justin smiled as he pressed my hand. "That's our Miss Woodville, always so circumspect. I trust you've taught her well, Miss Banks?"

Theresa beamed at me. "Anne was always my brightest student."

His dark eyes studied me with amusement. "She's managed to turn my daughter into an agreeable lady, show interest in her employer's textile mills, rescue my son from a burning schoolroom, and at the same time encourage the local doctor."

"Oh?" Theresa queried.

I felt uneasy being the topic of conversation between them. Already, Theresa's sharp brown eyes had noticed my reaction to the handsome Lord Braithfield. As soon as we reached the privacy of my room, she shook her head.

"He can't be Madeline's murderer...I really think Madeline over-dramatized that letter."

"Yes, I'm beginning to believe the same."

For the first time, I felt completely at ease with Theresa. Stripped of my Anne Woodville tag, I updated her on my investigation. She sat there in fascination—so much so she forgot to remove her gloves and coat.

"To be honest...I didn't think this was such a good idea," she began. "But you have really made the most of it. When may I meet the children?"

"Cathy will be here any moment. I left her with Doctor Carstares."

"The one whom everyone wants you to marry?"

I assured her he was only a friend. "But a lot more palatable than Edwin Brody," I finished.

We were both laughing about Edwin Brody when Cathy entered. She held herself very well as I introduced her to Miss Banks. However, her natural curiosity shone through.

"You're Anne's old governess? I thought you'd be old!"

"Not all governesses are old," Theresa smiled.

"You see," I explained to Theresa, "I've told Cathy the benefits of being friends with a governess. Now she can see the fruits."

Cathy sat down next to Theresa. "I hated all governesses until Anne arrived. I *always* made them leave. But Anne is different...I don't want her ever to leave. She's part of Silverthorn now."

I caught Theresa's look. It said 'what have you done now?' I played my role too well—I'd managed to win friends and respect, friends and respect I could lose if someone discovered my identity.

I dared not think of the outcome.

We were invited to dinner.

Theresa glanced at me blankly when the invitation was extended to include her. "How is it you've managed to land such an incredible post? You have wonderful charges, a sympathetic employer—"

"A pretentious butler, a domineering housekeeper and you haven't met Lady Braithfield yet."

"Is this Olivia anything like Madeline?"

I summarized the cool beauty and should have known better for Theresa raised a brow in questioning. I changed the subject before I betrayed myself completely.

I was prepared to accept the inevitable reconciliation between Lord and Lady Braithfield and therefore her presence in her usual seat at the table came as no surprise. Dressed in a low-cut gown of ruby red, she smiled bitterly as we entered, clearly annoyed by our being invited to the table. She barely gave Theresa a glance in introduction.

Fortunately, Justin was an attentive host. He spoke warmly of the mills and his new piece of machinery.

Theresa and I were fascinated and would have asked more questions if Olivia hadn't been there, watching us with an air of haughty disregard.

Miss Lillian sat opposite us in a lovely gown of yellow. The color suited her dark coloring and accentuated the warmth in her brown eyes. She meant to press her independence from Olivia and establish her own person in society and therefore joined eagerly in our conversation.

As I spoke, I could feel Olivia's icy gaze upon me, taking measure. The feeling was unpleasant and ruined what might have been an enjoyable evening. I was relieved to get away.

"Lord Braithfield is charming," Theresa said to me later. "I am convinced Madeline is wrong. She wrote her suspicions to you for a reason. I wonder why?"

The question had often eluded me. "Madeline had a habit of omitting certain details...I must show you her portrait...it is how you would remember her."

Theresa's sharp eyes missed nothing. "Ah, lady of the manor? Well, wealth and prominence didn't work for her, did it? I can see your determination to see this through, Laura, but don't you think it may be a little dangerous? What if you uncovered the real killer? Or what if he found you first?"

"It is rather like a jig-saw puzzle and I only have pieces," I explained. "I know Madeline was terrified when she last wrote me...of what or from whom I do not know. Her position became insecure on the death of her husband...unless she was with child—"

"You've considered the possibility?"

I nodded. "If she announced she was pregnant after Lord Thomas's death, whom would it upset? Justin and Vincent. I *know* Justin didn't do it. He may have been unhappy about it—he *may* have realized what Madeline was really like...but Vincent? Perhaps she agreed to wed him after she'd born his child and passed it off as her late husband's? You remember what I told you about Mrs Gardner? How Madeline whispered on the night of her death 'there's nothing worse than a grape when it sours?' Perhaps she referred to Vincent? She reneged on the plan—for whatever reason—and he killed her for it."

"Is he the type to do such a thing?"

I thought over the last few weeks. If Vincent could blatantly seduce Danielle and Olivia, could it possible for him to commit murder? He wanted Silverthorn—Madeline gave him an opportunity to get it—if she secured it first. "Yes, it must be him. Madeline toyed with a dangerous man, to her detriment."

"Do you think she announced she was with child?"

"I think Cathy would have told me if she did."

"Ah, Miss Cathy. She was none to keen to come to dinner tonight. Could it be, I wonder, to avoid a certain step-mother?"

I shook my head sadly. "Cathy hasn't liked Olivia from the beginning—and now she has a valid reason to let her feelings show. It will be good, I suppose, if her father sends her to finishing school."

Theresa looked at me carefully. "And what about you, Laura? Will you stay on when Cathy goes?"

The thought of serving the Braithfields without Cathy was depressing. "I will for Laura's sake—if his lordship approves."

Theresa winked at me. "I don't believe you'd even need to ask. He admires you greatly—I can see it in his eyes."

Despite my attempt to avoid it, I blushed.

Theresa didn't laugh. "But do be sensible, my dear. He's a married man. Do you remember my sister Cassie?"

I struggled with my memory. "A little; she died unexpectedly."

"Yes, but I never told you the reason, did I? She secured a post at a country house called Bridgeton about the same time I began at Rohan House. It was a very comfortable post—two young children, a pleasant-natured mistress who spent most of her days in her room. Cassie controlled the management of the household and won the respect of all. I was proud of her at the time, but sadly, things were about to change.

She fell in love with the squire, you see. He was a handsome man, in his prime, and he took advantage of her. News of the affair soon reached the ears of the wife, who demanded he put it at an end. The squire had made no commitments to Cassie and as he'd married for money, had no choice but to dismiss her in disgrace.

She soon discovered she was with child. Realizing her desperate situation, she tried for another position...one that would support her through her pregnancy. But the lady of Bridgeton made it known in the county and none would hire Cassie. She had no money and unfortunately, her letter reached me too late. She took her own life because she didn't want to become a burden to society."

There was no point in trying to convince Theresa I wasn't attracted to Lord Justin. "Thank-you for the advice. I believe I shall follow my head, not my heart, as I have always done. As you pointed out, I haven't the liberty to endanger my respectability."

I thought of the way Justin had touched my hand as he looked at me over Brandon's bedside. He was trying to say something and I, foolish heart, had been encouraging him to say it! Yes, Theresa had come to visit at a crucial time.

"Think of why you came to Silverthorn…" Theresa yawned.

I lay awake awhile pondering upon those words. I thought over how my life had altered with that one letter of Madeline's…how it brought me to Silverthorn…how it ruined my chance of making a successful marriage. It would have been prudent to accept Mr Carstares. But I'd refused his hand because of Justin Braithfield.

Oh, why did things have to be so complicated? I'd won Cathy's friendship—she would feel betrayed if I left and I couldn't possibly explain my reasons for going. I couldn't desert her as I couldn't desert Brandon and Laura, fearing what would become of my three charges under Olivia's rule.

I would have to weigh things carefully before making a decision.

And, though I didn't want to admit it, I knew that decision would have to be made as soon as I discovered the truth about Madeline.

CHAPTER FIFTEEN

The rain kept us indoors for the next three days.

Justin granted me a few days leave in line with Theresa's unexpected visit. It was generous of him and I told him so, adding that Theresa well understood a governess's lot and I couldn't possibly neglect the children at this time.

Theresa was more than happy to help. She spent most of her time reading to Brandon and looking after Laura while I did lessons with Cathy. I also thanked her for engaging Doctor Carstares when he came to visit.

I believed her loyalty extended a little beyond for on the third visit of Mr Carstares, she kept him busy for more than two hours! We had relocated to Brandon's bedroom while repairs continued in the schoolroom. Brandon, Laura and Theresa remained on one side of the bedchamber while Cathy and I occupied the other.

There was a dividing wall between our two ends but I could see to the other side easily when I wished it. Theresa was still talking with the Doctor. He seemed completely at ease with her and she with him. Some of the surprise must have shown on my face for Cathy gave me a funny look.

"Well, *you* let him go, didn't you? Oh, I worry for you, Anne! You're too young to end life as a spinster. Don't you want to marry? I certainly do."

"Nothing but the deepest love could induce me to matrimony," I said.

Cathy considered. "You are right, of course. Governesses are always right. Do you think they'll marry?"

"Who?" I followed her gaze to Greg and Theresa. "No! Theresa is a dedicated teacher, she could never desert her post."

Cathy wasn't convinced. "Oh, I don't know...she needs to settle. I can sense her frustration. Like her, you need to marry too. You usually only receive one opportunity, you know. Especially—"

"Especially if I'm penniless?" I finished with a laugh. "You are correct of course. But for your knowledge I have received two proposals."

Cathy was intrigued. "Who was the other? Was he a dashing soldier? Or a studious shop-keeper?"

"I hate to disappoint you...but he was a plain Mr Brody, in line to inherit the Rectory from my Uncle. I didn't agree with the match."

"Is that why you had to look for a post?"

I nodded.

Cathy studied me pensively. "I'm sorry, Anne...I shouldn't have teased you—"

I smiled at her. "You don't have to explain."

"Yes, I do...it's...you see...we were all so surprised when you refused the Doctor. Papa especially. I think he was more surprised than any of us. And you know what he told me? He told me he wouldn't like to see you settled as the wife of a mere Doctor. He said you deserved much better."

I could feel the color rushing to my cheeks. "Who better than the doctor?"

Cathy shrugged. "Maybe he means Mr Ashton. He's rich and available—why not him? And he seems to like you well enough—he always admonishes you for not visiting him. I know he is like that with most women but if you *see* an opportunity—let him know how you feel—"

"You have a devious mind!"

Cathy grinned. "I may be only fifteen but I know how to win husbands."

"Well, don't win the wrong kind," I advised. "I wouldn't want to see you unhappy."

Unexpectedly, she hugged me. "You're so good to me...almost like a mother! I love you, Anne."

"I love you too, Cathy."

Theresa had been with us a week when she announced her engagement to Greg Carstares.

"I don't believe it."

Theresa smiled at me. "I hope you do for it you don't believe me, who else will? I've never been so happy, Laura. Why, he is the perfect gentleman—intelligent, well-respected, well-situated, what more can I ask?"

I studied her closely. "Do you love him?"

"Love? How many marriages do you know that are based on love? You've only to examine Lord and Lady Braithfield to speak for the general population. I believe Greg and I will come to value each other dearly—"

I still wasn't convinced. "Are you really sure? Will you be happy?"

Theresa touched my hand. "I can see what you're feeling. Oh, Laura...I'm so lucky! I never wanted to live out my life in service and this is my only opportunity. Don't you see? I may never receive another offer."

Yes, I could see the sense behind it...but to see my dear, beloved Theresa, my mentor, marry for convenience, made me feel uneasy. Could one so intelligent and practical do such a thing?

Yes, because it was a sensible course of action. I remembered how Uncle Clive's voice shook when I refused Edwin Brody. His reprimand rang in my ears, '*you foolish, headstrong girl. You will never receive another offer.*

The past appeared to haunt me afresh. I thought of the old schoolroom at Rohan House. Madeline was dead, Theresa was getting married, Elizabeth remained single and I served as a governess. How odd life is...back then I never would have believed Madeline could die so young, nor Theresa wed so quickly.

I watched her face in sleep, genuinely happy for her. She seized an opportunity I had refused.

I shouldn't feel envious. I had chosen a path in life—and now would have to live it.

I saw Justin the next day.

I decided to take a walk, leaving the children in Theresa's capable hands. She insisted I do so, to clear my mind of the events of the past, which had tortured me into the early hours of the morning.

The air was cool against my skin and I pulled my woolen wrap more securely around my shoulders. I walked down to the wrought-iron gates of Silverthorn and looked back at the magnificent castle-mansion. This is the place where I had first seen it and the impression lasted.

"Day-dreaming?"

I spun around at Justin's voice. Winter, Brandon's dog, hovered around him. At such an early hour, I assumed he would soon be heading off towards the mills.

"He misses Brandon," Justin leaned on one knee to pacify the impatient greyhound. "He was lying in my study this morning with such a forlorn face I decided some exercise would do him good."

"I can take him back to the stables, my lord. It will save calling a footman."

"Why don't we walk back together—unless you're going elsewhere?"

"No, I merely wanted to revisit my first glimpse of Silverthorn. It's lovely, isn't it? How does it feel to own such beauty?"

He glanced at me in an odd sort of way. "Wealth is not happiness, Anne. I have learned to live without both so I am fortunate. However, I envy my coachman, Thomas. He has a happy home-life, earns a neat living and is content. He lacks nothing nor is greedy for more. To me, that is complete."

His confession touched me. "You have a wonderful daughter," I said.

"Yes, thanks to you."

His blue eyes seemed to blaze into my soul. I turned away hastily. "I scarcely think I have made much of a difference...I have only been here a year."

"Is it a year? It feels like you have been at Silverthorn forever; I can't imagine the place without you."

"And yet I must leave soon...Cathy will be going to finishing school."

He paused, his dark hair tousled in the cool breeze. "I don't want you to leave, Anne. You're a part of us now. I want you to stay on...Brandon and Laura will need you."

"Does Lady Braithfield share your sentiments?"

The mention of her name froze his smile. "You needn't be afraid of my wife. She has abused her privileges."

"You will have my decision soon," I promised.

We commenced walking.

"I hear your friend Miss Banks is to marry Carstares...is this true?"

I laughed. "Yes, they are engaged."

"How do you feel about the matter?"

"I think they will be very happy."

"I didn't ask about them but about you."

"I am very happy for them."

"Are you?"

I frowned. "Yes! Why should you not believe me?"

"Cathy told me you refused another suit—a Mr Brody. A governess who breaks hearts as easily as she mends them?"

"I am hardly a *femme fatale*, my lord."

He turned to me with a smile. "Oh, but you are, Miss Woodville."

I assumed he referred to Greg's over-attentiveness. "Mr Carstares was merely in want of a wife...and Mr Brody, well, there were no hearts broken in the matter, I can assure you."

His lips twisted into a half-grin. "I'm glad to hear it."

We were nearing the stables. "I'll take Winter now...your coach awaits, my lord."

He laughed. "You know you are the first governess to be unafraid of me? I'm certain all the others believed I was some kind of monster. What do you think, Anne? Am I a monster?"

I couldn't decide whether he was sincere or teasing so, I said the truth: "No, you are no monster. For a man to accept—"

The smile vanished from his face. "Honor and discipline is all that matters." He handed me the lead. "Take him back to the stables, Miss Woodville."

I walked Brandon's dog back to the stables. What had I said wrong? It was my reference to Brandon that had changed him. Or did he believe I spoke of Olivia? Of course, Doctor Carstares would have told him I'd seen Vincent and Olivia together.

I shouldn't have reminded him of the scandal involving his cousin. As a professional governess, I should have said nothing about the affair.

Fool! Fool! Could I not manage to keep my mouth shut? I was still reprimanding myself when something impelled me to look up.

I saw Olivia in the window, watching me with an odd expression on her face.

I half expected her to come to Brandon's room. Fortunately, she didn't, and I spent a pleasant day with Theresa and the children.

Miss Lillian brought in Mr Carstares. When the two lovers greeted, she whispered to me, "why did you let him slip out of your fingers?"

"Because I'm governess-bred, Miss Lillian. I have many years of service ahead."

She seemed satisfied with this response and glancing across the room, asked after Brandon. I told her his skin was healing rapidly under his bandages and should, in time, return to its youthful vigor without much scarring.

"Aunt Lillian," Cathy interrupted, "you must convince Miss Banks to buy some wedding clothes."

Theresa's protests were waved aside. Miss Lillian and Cathy continued to badger her until she implored me with her eyes, "Laura, help me convince them."

I nearly choked. Fortunately, Cathy pounced upon the name. "Laura? Did you call Anne Laura?"

"Yes," Theresa amended, realizing her mistake. "Laura is Anne's second name...she often bade me call her Laura instead of Anne...and I suppose the name sticks at times."

Cathy considered this awhile, grinning broadly. "I think I'll try that for awhile. Aunt Lil...can you call me Emiline from time to time? It might be fun!"

"One is given a name; one should stick to it," Lillian said severely.

Cathy made a face. "Oh, you are no fun! What is your second name?" She thought for a while. "Marie! I shall all you Marie Lillian."

"Don't be ridiculous."

"I agree with Miss Lillian," Greg smiled. "A name is sacred. Once given, it should not be used in vain nor misrepresented."

The conversation flowed into other areas. I joined in for a time, in an effort to appear unaffected by Theresa's *faux pas*. When Laura started to cry, I had a valid reason to attend to her. Lillian decided to return to her Tower and Cathy, the one whom I worried about most for I knew her knack for perception, studied me curiously.

"Laura...yes, surprisingly, it suits. I hope you will consent to call me Emiline. Emiline sounds more...musical than plain Catherine. I would expect my mother to give me a plain name like Catherine."

"Catherine is a very sensible name," I said as I cuddled Laura. "What do you think, Laurie? Do you think we should call Cathy Emiline?"

Laura looked up at Cathy with large, green eyes. "A...Athy."

Cathy turned red in alarm. "Did she speak?"

Theresa and Greg stumbled over, shocked.

Laura hid her face against me. "You'll all frighten her," I whispered, unable to stop the smile of elation spreading across my face. She spoke!

"It's a miracle!" Greg murmured. "After all this time...I was beginning to worry. If the child started to talk too late, she may not have been able to formulate her words properly. Athy! That is marvelous, Laura! You mustn't be afraid to say it again. Athy will like it very much."

Cathy gave him a scowl. "My name is *Miss Catherine Braithfield*, not Athy. I refuse to be called Athy under any circumstances."

"It is all so wonderful," Theresa breathed. "I didn't believe you at first when you told me the child wouldn't speak. I don't think I ever saw such a beautiful, silent child. She reminds me—"

Fortunately, Theresa caught my warning and promptly closed her mouth.

"It reminds you...?" Cathy prompted.

Theresa waved her hand. "I can't quite think of whom...her mother must have been a great beauty."

Cathy's eyes lit up. "Oh, she was! Poor Aunt Madeline took her own life because she knew Papa would inherit Silverthorn and she would be a dependent on him. Aunt Lillian once thought Uncle Vince may have assisted her...but that's nonsense. Uncle Vince is not evil, no matter how naughty he is."

Before I could scold her for speaking out so openly, Theresa asked, "and do you think she was murdered, Cathy? Do you really believe she would have thrown herself off that Tower?"

Cathy shrugged. "I didn't know her that well...but I do know she loved to spend money and flaunt Silverthorn. When Papa refused to marry her I suppose could have terminated her own life..."

"Your father refused her?"

Cathy looked at me. "Of course he did. He could see she only wanted him for Silverthorn. She was so confident he'd accept her offer...for the children, she said. And I was very proud of Papa when he said no. After that, who could blame her for killing herself—if she wanted Silverthorn so desperately?"

"And leave a child in the process," I said, a little too bitterly. Yes, it was typical of Madeline to think only of herself. Why didn't she consider her daughter? Why didn't she heed my advice?

So, she planned to marry Justin. I could see Madeline planning her future with the confidence that came with her beauty. I had never known a man to refuse her before—why did Justin?

I couldn't suppress the feeling of elation that overcame me with the fact. However, it was soon replaced by the possibility that he could still be her killer. If she'd been with child...if she planned to pass the child off as her late husband's...Justin didn't lack intelligence...perhaps he knew of her affair with Vincent...and refused her because she carried another man's child.

My mind swam endlessly. I remembered the sharp, frantic strokes of Madeline's handwriting in her final letter...it was the same dramatic fear she displayed in London when she knew she carried the gypsy's child.

I was determined to remove it from my mind at present.

Greg soon departed and Cathy went to her room to dress for dinner. When we were alone, Theresa grabbed my arm. "I'm so sorry! Forgive me; I don't know what happened—"

I smiled at her. "Perhaps this marriage may not be one of convenience after all. You seem besotted with one another."

Theresa blushed. "I never knew such happiness! Oh, why can't everyone be as happy as I am? Oh, it's too good...after what happened to Cassie..."

"You deserve it. When do you plan to wed?"

Theresa bit her lip. "I have yet to meet *Mama*. If all goes as planned, we shall wed in a fortnight. I would like you to be my maid of honor. You were my brightest pupil...and now you are my dearest friend."

I hugged her. "And who will I be partnered with?"

"It shall only be a simple wedding...we both prefer it that way. I think Greg has in mind to ask a Mr Ashton. Do you know him?"

I laughed. "Oh, yes, very well. He is a dear fellow...I shouldn't mind to stand up with him."

Theresa searched my face. "A friend only?"

"A *friend* only. Please do not make any more out of it...I wouldn't wish to embarrass Mr Ashton."

Theresa grinned. "I promise there will be no embarrassment for either party."

Theresa and I went to Brandon's room. Since the fire, we conducted all our lessons here and ate our meals here too except for the occasions where we were invited to join Lord and Lady Braithfield's table.

Cathy was summoned to that table now and paused on her way to receive commendation on her dress.

"She's a lovely girl," Theresa said when she skipped away.

I smiled. "I found her rather different on my arrival. She had a fear of governesses, didn't she, Brandon?"

Brandon grinned. "I always liked you, Anne." A frown marred his perfect little face. "Anne...will I ever walk again? Doctor Carstares says I'm to stay in bed all day!"

I looked across to Theresa. "I don't know, darling. We'll have to wait until your burns have healed first. Think of all the books we can read!" Fortunately, I had brought one. "Here...I'll read this to you when you finish your dinner. Eat up, now."

A little cheer returned to his face. I felt my heart melt when Laura touched Brandon's bandages. "Branny...hurt."

Brandon chuckled. "I'll be all right, you just wait and see. I'll take Winter for a walk when I'm well and I'll take you if you like."

Laura's eyes lit up in expectation.

Our evening continued quietly until an hour later, Cathy stormed in, clearly distraught. I rose from the table. "What's the matter?"

She glanced at me with wide, frantic eyes. "They're fighting again...at the dinner table. I stayed awhile but it got worse. First, it was the menu. Olivia had filled it with all the foods Papa hates...he struggled to be calm in front of Aunt Lillian and I. And then I don't know what happened...they started screaming at each other. Olivia picked up her glass and threw it at Papa. Papa slammed down his knife and took Olivia from the room. He was very angry...I wonder what he'll do!"

"Where's Miss Lillian?"

Cathy shrugged. "I don't know...I left her at the table. She didn't seem very concerned about it...I know they fight all the time but I've never seen Papa *so* angry!"

"You needn't worry. My Aunt and Uncle used to argue at the dinner table sometimes...it is normal in marriages."

Cathy shook her head, unconvinced. "Not this one. Olivia married Papa for money. She
doesn't love him. She loves Uncle Vince and she ruined Papa! I *hate* her! She deliberately provoked him."

"If you read that far, my dear," Theresa said philosophically, "you would see they will reconcile their differences."

Cathy crossed her arms. "I don't care anyway...I can't wait to get away from here. I hate it. If it were not for you, Anne...I should go insane."

Conscious of Brandon hearing this uproar, I quickly changed the subject. Theresa and I had managed to bring a smile to his face and I didn't want him suffering any undue stress. Luckily, he didn't seem concerned with his sister's outburst. I knew that Olivia had come only once to see him since the accident.

Was it unfair of me to revel in the children's dislike of their stepmother?

I should have been more aware. Had I caused division in this household? I thought of Justin for a brief moment. Why did I have to fall in love with the unobtainable? Why could it not have been Greg? Or even the odious Mr Brody? Why? Why? Why?

I had to get away. I could not stay here with these feeling. Theresa was right—I had to remember Cassie.

I was in the schoolroom the following morning.

Workers were clearing the room in preparation for the next stage of repair. The fire had done more damage than I thought. I watched my teacher's chair being removed with a sense of mourning. I always grew attached to the most ridiculous things.

"I'll buy you a new one," Justin said behind me. "A better one. Mrs Clairmont, your predecessor, often complained about the stiffness of that chair. How is it that you like it?"

"My face betrays me," I smiled. "Yes, I did like that chair. I don't know why...stability, perhaps. It gave me a reason for being here."

He looked at me curiously for a brief moment before moving around the room, inspecting the new work with an uncustomary graveness. "You did a very brave thing, Anne...you saved Brandon's life."

I touched Cathy's burnt-out writing case. "I never apologized for ruining your statue, did I? If I had done such in my Uncle's house, he surely would have punished me for it."

"He sounds like a cruel man."

I smiled. "I would summarize him as a pompous, rigid clergyman whose vocation in life revolved around the local gentry, not his parishioners."

He laughed. "Do I detect an undercurrent of disapproval in your voice?"

It was my turn to laugh. "Yes! As you can imagine, he made my childhood extremely difficult."

"That is a great pity."

I am certain no governess engaged in a conversation like this with her employer. However, I felt perfectly at ease with Justin. He was nothing like the pretentious Rohan family and wore his title with an air of casual modesty I found refreshing.

To my surprise, Justin was still examining my face. "Tell me what you were thinking just now."

"Is that a command, my lord?"

He smiled. "Only this once."

"Very well," I breathed. "I was thinking how different you are to the gentry I have known."

"Thank God! I act in every way to *avoid* the general description. How do you see me, Miss Woodville?"

"A peer of the realm who isn't afraid to soil his hands with good, honest work."

A worker caught his attention then, suggesting where the fire may have started. Out of interest, I followed Justin to the fireplace where he stamped on a corner of the burnt rug.

"See how near this is put to the fire, milord?"

"Cousin!"

We all turned to a hysterical Lillian. She was standing in her nightgown, her brown hair loosened to her waist and her large eyes full of fright. Behind her, Mrs Simmons seemed unusually calm.

"She's gone."

Justin put a hand on her shoulder. "Who's gone, Lil?"

"Lady Braithfield was not in her room this morning, my lord," Mrs Simmons said quietly, glancing at me. "She is not to be found."

"She's gone to Vincent," Lillian whispered but everyone heard.

The expression on Justin's face was a combination of shock and guilt. He was thinking, as I was, about the public disagreement he had with his wife last night. Had she flown to her lover as a consequence?

A search began. Lady Braithfield often rode out without telling anyone and returned late at night. She did so, I remembered poignantly, when Justin was last away.

The entire household joined the search. I went back to Brandon's room and explained the situation to the children.

Cathy looked at me in surprise. "I can't believe she's run off with Uncle Vince! Poor Papa! How he hates scandals! Is he very angry?"

"Concerned," I replied, conscious of Theresa's gaze upon me. "They think Lady Braithfield rode out to the moors—"

"Just like Mama...." Cathy murmured. "Will they find Olivia's neck broken too?"

"Perhaps she went to Ashton Grove?" I suggested positively.

Cathy shrugged, flummoxed. "I suppose we'll soon find out, won't we?"

It was impossible to continue with studies so I resorted to telling a folk story Ruby had told me as a child—the story of Camelot, King Arthur and his knights.   I said the words almost motionlessly, my mind elsewhere.   Brandon seemed to follow it without difficulty.   Laura sat next to him on the bed, listening with rapture as Brandon translated in regular intervals.

"Is Genevieve like Cecily?" Brandon interrupted.

I had to think for a moment before I realized he meant the wicked Cecily of Silverthorn who pushed Eleanor from the Tower in order to wed her sister's fiancé.

Mrs Simmons's presence in the doorway saved me from a reply.   I followed her outside to the corridor.

"I fear...Miss Woodville...that her ladyship is nowhere to be found. This is a dreadful thing to occur...when I think of the children..."

"Yes, a scandal is never a pleasant affair."

Mrs Simmons looked at me sharply.   "I mean to put you on your guard, Miss Woodville.   I have seen...of late...how much his lordship admires you.   But I warn you—he will never leave his wife. He couldn't endure a public divorce...I have known him since a child," her eyes softened, "...he was always such a pleasant child...but more conscious of duty and honor than his cousin. Mr Vincent was always the bad egg."

As she walked away, I thought of Justin's own words, *duty and discipline is all that matters.* He was right, of course.   One could not be swayed by foolish desires—was his regard for me so transparent?   I didn't believe so.   Cathy was unusually perceptive, surely she would have noticed.

Noticed what?

The only thing confirming some regard on Lord Justin's part was the expression on his wife's face when she'd seen him and I return to the house together. An odd smile tugged at the corners of her mouth.

I wondered what she was thinking at the time.

Eliza Ashton came to see me.

"Is it true? Has she run away with Vincent?"

She had persuaded me to take a walk in the courtyard. "It appears so."

"Poor Olivia—what a fool to throw everything away for a heartless villain! She'll soon discover Vincent isn't always the charming lover and being outcast from society hurts. How is poor Justin coping?"

I shrugged. "I wouldn't know."

"Oh, I saw the way he looked at you at the ball.   There, you are blushing! I think you two would do very well together...but of course, he's married—"

"How is Mr Ashton?" I interrupted.

Eliza laughed.   "Oh, my dear, you are always so circumspect. Brett..." she sighed, "Well, Brett is Brett. He suffers from a broken heart."

"A broken heart?"

Eliza pursed her lips together as she plucked a leaf off a nearby shrub. "He's still in love with Madeline. Tabitha and I have endeavored to find him a suitable wife but he refuses to show any interest in this matter. I fear he will never marry."

"Was he so much in love with her?"

She smiled whimsically. "She was so lovely—every man in the county fell in love with her. Poor Brett must have taken her light flirtations as encouragement...and then, quite suddenly, she died. My poor brother never got over it."

I knew what must have happened. Should Justin refuse her offer, she decided to secure her own future—as the mistress of Ashton Grove. A poor achievement compared to Silverthorn, however, she didn't have a choice, did she?

"Will there be any attempt to recover Olivia, do you think?" Eliza went on. "I imagine so since the family cannot afford another scandal at its doors." She spun around with a smile. "Let's discuss something more pleasant...I heard a rumor that Doctor Carstares is engaged to your friend. Is it true?"

"If you're asking me, you mustn't know your brother is the designated best man."

"Is he? Naughty Brett...he's always so secretive. And are you the maid of honor?"

I nodded. "It will only be a simple ceremony...due to the suddenness of the event."

"I don't see why they should wait...they are grown adults. When my turn comes, *if it comes,* I shan't wait two years. I think I'd prefer to elope."

"And miss out on all those lovely wedding gifts?"

She laughed. "Some of them can be quite dreadful, you know. I gave Olivia a rather ugly vase...it could have been quite impressive if she knew how to arrange flowers correctly. Madeline knew how to arrange flowers—she was the perfect mistress of Silverthorn...but it seems her secret life murdered her in the end."

My heart started thumping. "Secret life?"

Eliza stretched her arms. "Let's sit over here...the sun gives me a headache."

Once we were seated and she had arranged her dress accordingly, she replied, "I don't know much about the whole thing...why are you so interested? Why, you're hanging on my every word!"

I was prepared for the question. "Cathy has stimulated my interest...in her special way."

Eliza understood perfectly. "Ah, of course...she has a penchant for mystery but, poor lass, she doesn't know the half of it...she still sees Lady Madeline as the beautiful, vivacious wife of her great-uncle. But, I wonder how many knew about the late Lady Braithfield's clandestine activities at night?"

"What activities?"

"I *do* know, and this is on strict confidence, that Madeline often visited a man at night...a man who frightened her greatly."

"A man?"

Eliza nodded. "One day we were picnicking. It was a lovely summer's day...the food and company excellent. The party, organized by the lovely Lady Braithfield, comprised of Miss Lillian, Tabitha and I, Brett, Justin, Vincent, Olivia and Spencer. It was later in the day when I noticed a little agitation on Madeline's face. She was usually so calm and in control...I remember thinking it odd at the time. I followed her gaze. A man approached up the embankment. She quickly slipped away from the party to meet him, anxious that the visitor shouldn't intrude. I couldn't see much of the man...except his dark coloring and that he was dressed...almost like a gypsy."

Lucian! His face swam before me...Lucian the gypsy.

"...The others didn't notice the brief interchange," Eliza murmured, "so I discounted it from my mind until Brett returned home from the spring ball a month later..."

I could feel the tension building as I paused, breathless, willing her to go on.

"He returned late...later than I expected. I waited up for him. When he came in, I knew something was wrong. He came into the drawing room and sat down beside the fire. The expression on his face was almost sad...and I suddenly felt like a protective mother more than a sister. I must have said the right words for he confided in me of his love for Madeline—which I'd already deduced...and his hope that she might one day agree to marry him. I couldn't have laughed—seeing the pain in his face—although it was obvious to everyone that she wanted Justin. However, I nodded along and then he told me he sensed something wasn't right at Silverthorn...and that it frightened Madeline."

"That's why he seemed so peculiar at the ball! I saw him, you know, studying Madeline's portrait...he looked angry and sad. And when I asked about her, he told me she was murdered."

Eliza nodded. "He must trust you...he's like a closed clam most of the time, tough and carefree on the outside, soft and vulnerable on the inside. That's why Madeline preyed upon him. She knew if she couldn't have Justin, she could have Brett. Perhaps that was why she spoke to Brett that night...she knew he loved her and would believe her..."

"What did she say?"

"She told Brett he didn't really know her...that she lived two lives. Then she told him of her desire to change but to do so, she must remove risks. She implied she planned to meet someone that night 'to clear the past', she said. Brett proposed to her again. She smiled and replied, 'you're a good man...maybe, maybe. I don't know. Come and see me tomorrow.' Despite Brett's pleas, she wouldn't elaborate and left him standing there. They found her body the next day. Brett was overwrought...you see—they had an appointment at eleven in the morning. It proves she was murdered."

"Why didn't he tell the authorities at the time?"

Eliza's eyes grew cold. "Bad timing, I suppose. They also found the gypsy's body that day...lying in a ditch not far from Silverthorn. He was shot through the head. When Brett found out he decided to keep silent...he didn't want to tarnish Madeline's name when it seemed obvious what had happened. The gypsy must have been blackmailing her...that was why he came to the picnic...probably wanted money. He must have visited Silverthorn regularly to extract money for his silence."

I thought of the handsome, enigmatic Lucian with his broad grin. I never believed he would return to blackmail Madeline. Perhaps he too had exhausted his options. He had the power to ruin Madeline...but why would he have killed her?

The questions tortured my mind. I looked into Eliza's eyes, hoping to discover the truth. "What happened that night?"

Eliza shrugged. "No one knows really. I think she intended to bury all her skeletons...and it went dreadfully wrong. Perhaps the gypsy—who knows? Who will ever know now that he is dead?"

CHAPTER SIXTEEN

I couldn't believe my discovery ended with the death of Lucian the gypsy.

After Eliza left, I went to my room to seek consolation from Theresa. She was examining a bridal gift she'd received from her mother-in-law-to-be. She pinned on the broach and asked my opinion. "It's…"

"Dreadful," Theresa laughed. "But she's a lovely lady. I do believe she's impressed with me."

"How could she not be?"

Theresa unpinned the broach and set it down. "The children are playing in Brandon's room unsupervised. Shall we go to them?" She paused by the door. "What's the matter? Did your extinguished guest not amuse you?"

"Oh, yes…Eliza. She's certainly no Elizabeth Rohan, I can assure you, but she has confided the secret of Madeline's death. I can't explain my disappointment. What did I expect?"

"What did she say?"

"She believes Madeline received unwanted visits around the time of the ball…from a gypsy."

Theresa drew in a quick breath. "Laura's father?"

I nodded. "They must have moved camp here and met. It explains the 'they' in Madeline's letter. She always referred to Lucian's crowd as 'they.'"

Theresa pursed her lips. "He found a quick way to lighten his pockets, no doubt. But don't expect any sympathy from me, dear Laura. Your cousin simply reaped what she'd sown…"

"It doesn't seem…*right.* I can't explain—"

"No, you can't. Come; let's go to the children. Forget about Madeline and live your own life."

I bit my lip. "You forget—I am Anne Woodville, not Laura Morgan."

"That's nothing to worry about. When Cathy goes to school, it will be the perfect time to change posts. Lord Braithfield will give you a good reference; you need not worry about work…what is it?"

"He has asked me to stay…"

Theresa shook her head firmly. "No, you cannot. I won't lose another friend to the lusts of men. He is a man of honor, Laura—he will not leave his wife. Go! Before it is too late. I'll meet you in Brandon's room."

I nodded, rummaging through my jewelry casket looking for the necklace Uncle Clive and Aunt Mary had given me. I always separated my jewelry to avoid entanglement—much to Madeline's amusement. However, everything was in disarray. I started to panic...searching deeper until I realized someone had been in my room.

My letters were missing.

I paused in front of a mirror on the way to Brandon's room.

I had been found out.

Did it show?

Who would steal my letters?

Endless questions plagued me. Had I moved them recently? No, they always remained at the bottom of my jewelry casket.

I was anxious to gage Cathy's reaction. I found her reading a book to Laura. She looked up when I entered but nothing registered on her face.

Lillian dozed in a chair by the fire, clearly disinterested in my distress. Theresa was the first to notice.

"Why Anne! Whatever is the matter?"

"My letters are missing," I announced, watching Cathy carefully.

She dropped the book in shock. "Who would steal *your* letters? You're only a governess!"

"Exactly," Lillian agreed. "Hardly interesting fodder. We seldom have thieves at Silverthorn...unless you've misplaced them on purpose?"

"Why would I do such a thing?"

Lillian shrugged. "I would—to create a sensation but then I'm mad, aren't I? None of you really understand me!" She stormed out of the room, slamming the door behind her.

"Oh dear," Cathy sighed, "I don't know why Papa doesn't put her in an asylum..."

"Cathy," I frowned.

She made a face. "I'm tired of her tantrums...but I shan't be here much longer—Papa has received confirmation of my place at Palmerston Chateau. I am to leave at the end of the month."

The announcement spelled the end of my sojourn at Silverthorn. In three week's time, Cathy would be going abroad and I would be returning to the Rectory.

I couldn't bear to think of it.

I went to speak to Justin about Cathy's acceptance.

He was in his study, cleanly shaven and dressed for dinner. He gestured to the pile of papers on his desk. "The mill is no longer safe to keep one's records. You remember my foreman, Mr Thompson?"

I nodded.

"He managed to save records from my office when a fire lit recently. He was in the building at the time—the damage was only minor, however, the incident convinces me to keep two sets of records. One here, one in my office at Lester mill. So you see I am in the process of duplicating."

I looked at the large pile. "How long will it take you to do it?"

He shrugged, resting his hands behind his head. "Who knows? Forever at this rate, I dare say. I can't trust anyone with the records—not even Thompson. When my Uncle gave me the mills to manage, I discovered his manager had been pilfering funds slowly over the years."

"Which explained why the mills were functioning so badly?"

He nodded. "It's taken quite some time to change the system. Now I am finally satisfied with my work."

I saw how much the mills meant to him. "Will you hire a man to manage one of the mills?"

He smiled faintly. "How well you read me, Miss Woodville. Yes...I've decided to give Thompson the management of Lester mill. The man has worked hard and deserves a share in the profits." He pushed the pile on his desk to a side. "And why have you come to see me? I dare not hope a chat before dinner?"

"I wish it were," I laughed, "but alas I have come on business."

He raised a brow. "Ah, business...perhaps I should engage you to assist in writing our records...but of course, you are Cathy's governess."

Was it an invitation or did he merely enjoy teasing me? "Cathy told me you've had word from Palmerston Chateau...is all settled?"

"Yes," Justin retrieved a letter from his desk drawer and handed it to me, "I have my reservations about Cathy going un-chaperoned. I wish there was a sensible young girl of your caliber hiding in the district. I fear Cathy is too much like her mother."

I lowered my lashes, searching for the right words. "Cathy has told me a little of her mother. She is determined she will not turn out the same but—"

"The blood is there."

"...The blood is there," I echoed, raising my eyes to meet his. I expected his to have hardened at the mention of his first wife but he simply grinned, that rare roguish grin that left me weak.

"When I first saw you at the Flying Eagle, I knew that you were the one...for Cathy. You have done a wondrous job...I will always be grateful. I only wish...no, it is better for you to leave—"

I searched his face, wanting to ease his torment. But how could I? There could be nothing between us—we were classes apart and divided by his marriage. Strengthened by the cool reality, I stood. "Brandon asked me yesterday when Lady Braithfield is returning—what shall I tell him?"

He looked at me, his eyes suddenly hard. "Oh, she'll return...when she discovers my cousin hasn't enough money to satisfy her desires. Tell Brandon whatever you believe he wants to hear. Good night, Miss Woodville."

"Good night, my lord."

The preparations for Theresa's wedding kept us occupied over the next few days.

Mrs Carstares insisted Theresa wear the family wedding gown so we went down to the Carstares cottage, prepared for the worst. Fortunately for Theresa, the cream lace dress suited her admirably and needed only a few minor adjustments.

Mrs Carstares also presented Theresa with her own wedding veil. She took it reverently from the box it had inhabited for the last thirty years and handed it to me.

I took the moth-eaten veil into Theresa. "Don't say anything to the poor old dear," she whispered, "she's half-blind, you know."

I still couldn't believe Theresa was getting married. Theresa Banks, the stalwart governess.

The Ashton family had kindly offered to provide the wedding feast. Theresa was still in shock when we arrived at Ashton Grove to discuss the details.

"This is hardly the reception one usually receives from the gentry. What do you think of it, Laura?"

"I am as amazed as you are. But your Doctor is well respected in the community and Mr Ashton has agreed to stand up with him..."

Theresa linked her arm with mine. "Let's not question it, shall we? Such attention certainly deserves to be enjoyed."

The Misses Ashton, Eliza and Tabitha, expected us in the Drawing Room.

"How I *love* weddings," Eliza sighed as Tabitha poured the tea. "When was the last...oh, yes, Justin and Olivia. That ended badly...will she be returning to Silverthorn? She'll soon discover that Vincent cannot afford to keep her...and Justin is too honorable to turn her away or divorce her...but of course, I shouldn't be discussing your employer, should I, Anne?"

I believe Eliza didn't require a response so I said nothing. She went on to discuss details for the feast. "Have you any family, Miss Banks?"

Theresa shook her head. "My sister died years ago. I have no one but Anne."

"Isn't it nice," Tabitha said to her sister, "that one can remain friends with one's governess for life? Remember our governess, Liz? We couldn't wait until she left!"

"I daresay Miss Cathy will miss you dreadfully," Eliza said to me. "Is she going to that school in France?"

"Yes...his lordship received confirmation of her place a week ago."

"Really? And what will you do?"

I shrugged. "I suppose I will start looking for a new post."

Eliza smiled sadly. "Your leaving will be a sad loss for Silverthorn...come with me for a moment. I would like to show you something."

I followed Eliza upstairs.

Curious, I said nothing until we entered a locked room.

"Is this Mr Ashton's room?" I asked in horror.

Eliza nodded. "Yes, but I want to show you something. We may not have another opportunity, you see."

"What is it?"

Eliza ignored me as she searched a drawer. At length she pulled out a silk-covered case. She opened it and after a few shakes, a key fell into her hand. "Now you will see."

The stiffness of the lock told me no one had entered the small chamber adjacent in a very long time.

Eliza lit a candle. "We are entering a tomb of sorts."

"Whose tomb?"

"The tomb of Lady Madeline."

Eliza drew me in, closing the door behind her. The single candle shed an eerie flickering light across the room.

I looked around. There were storage chests, ladies' gowns, accessories, magazines and books.

"Everything you see once belonged to Madeline," Eliza explained. "They auctioned it all off...and of course Brett bought every single item. He made this room into something of a shrine in remembrance of her."

My heart pounded. Madeline had suddenly turned into something of an enigma. She haunted us all with her early death. I walked around, touching, smelling, observing.

"They're lovely things, aren't they?" Eliza prompted, picking up a glove. "Look at the embroidery on this...it is exquisite."

I examined the glove. "Yes...it is."

Eliza peered into my face. "Are you all right? You look a little pale."

"No, I'm fine," I assured her, wondering what else I might discover in this room. There was nothing here that seemed to betray Madeline's former life—and her connection with me. Had she destroyed everything?

"You could almost call her Brett's fiancé," Eliza said in the dark. "She set her cap at Justin—but he wouldn't have her."

"Why? She was very beautiful."

"And very stupid. Oh, she knew how to play men. You only have to look at Brett to see that. But with Justin...I don't think he liked her from the very beginning. They were all suspicious of her...this young, beautiful, ill-bred wife of their mad Uncle. You couldn't blame them for thinking her an adventuress...and I suppose Justin proved right in the end—for her secret was exposed."

"The gypsy..."

"Yes...he was blackmailing Madeline for a reason. She mentioned to Brett she had made mistakes in the past...I think it may have something to do with Laura. I remember the way the gypsy looked at the child...and other times I caught Justin looking at the child with the same questioning expression. Laura must be the gypsy's brat...Madeline probably married old Lord Braithfield to cover up her unwanted condition and in the end, her gypsy lover murdered her."

Eliza summed it up perfectly. Madeline was an adventuress and paid the price for her unwise decisions in life.

I realized I should no longer be here. I'd come to Yorkshire for a reason and now I found the truth, I could go home.

The thought didn't entice me. I picked up another set of gloves. They looked odd sitting among the newer, fashionable pairs and I soon saw why. They were the gloves Aunt Mary had bought Madeline one Christmas. They were heavy...I put my hand inside and felt the rough edge of paper.

Eliza was moaning over the dresses. "I can't see why Brett won't let Tab and I wear them...what a waste! Well...he can't stop me trying one on, can he?"

I pulled out the small stack of bound letters and quickly flicked through them. There was one or two from Aunt Mary and one from Lady Beatrice and several from me. Evidently, Brett hadn't yet discovered their existence. I asked Eliza how often he looked through these things.

"Never! Or perhaps when he's in cups...but he never touches anything. He simply *looks.* This room is sacred to him."

Only the girls would discover the letters and being ladies of quality, they would never pick up an old, worn pair of gloves. I put the letters back.

It was the last page in the book of Madeline. I could see myself turning it, satisfied with the conclusion.

The day of Theresa's wedding arrived.

The ceremony was to be conducted in the town chapel. As Theresa didn't have any family to give her away, she asked Justin. Happy to be of service, he arranged one of his finest coaches to escort the bride into town.

A wedding was always a pleasant occasion, however, beneath Justin's smile I sensed his bitterness. Was he remembering his wedding to Olivia, a mere year ago? Had the wedding cheer softened his thoughts of her? Would there be a reconciliation if she returned?

Why did he have to be so honorable?

But that was why I loved him.

Yes! I was in love with a married man far above my station. I now understood how Cassie must have felt...and what prompted her to ignore convention and follow her heart.

I didn't need to fear the outcome of my condition for I would soon be leaving. I wondered what would happen if I did stay. How much longer could we remain as polite strangers? I knew the danger would intensify once Cathy went abroad.   Theresa had foreseen it...Mrs Simmons had put me on my guard...Olivia had sensed it...

"Laura! You are miles away!" Theresa complained. "Well, what do you think?"

I snapped out of my reverie and studied Theresa. She looked lovely in her cream and lace gown. Eliza gave her a bouquet of orange blossom as I made one final adjustment to her veil.

"Your Doctor will be enraptured," I smiled.

"Would you cease calling him my Doctor? Do I look like I need a Doctor?"

I hugged her. "Yes, you do."

I studied myself in the mirror beside Theresa. To compliment the bride, we had simply modified my blue gown and added a touch of cream lace to the hem and the neckline. I knew the dress became me well. Cathy's maid dressed our hair in the height of fashion and we were both pleased with the transformation from plain governess to women worth noticing.

Cathy bowled into the room. "Are you ready yet? The carriage is outside."

I sensed Theresa's agitation and linked her arm with mine. "All will be well, I promise."

Justin was waiting for us in the parlor. He looked very fine in a well-cut black suit—the only concession to his part in the wedding a small blue flower Cathy must have attached to his coat.

His gaze remained on me as we descended the stairs. What I read there left me breathless. How could I go on in life without him?

He smiled at me. "You almost outshine the bride, Miss Woodville."

I lowered my gaze to the floor, trying to suppress the telltale color rising in my face. The warmth in his voice left me feeling elated, something I should not feel.

When I didn't answer, he raised my chin up to face him. "Where's my courageous Miss Woodville?"

Theresa had passed us. I looked up into his handsome face, overwhelmed by my love for him. How could I hide it?

His dark eyes searched my face, reading the truth. "My darling girl!"

Before I knew it, I was in his arms and his lips were on mine...for one brief, glorious moment. I never wanted it to end, the rapture, the wonderful feeling I thought I would never experience.

It had to end. The sound of the carriage wheels reminded us of our duty.

"The coach is *waiting*," Cathy called from outside, breaking the spell. "Where's Aunt Lillian?

"Here," Lillian said from the top of the stairs. She'd elected to wear her favorite scarlet gown and by her face, I could see she didn't find attending the wedding of a governess and a doctor particularly pleasing.

We arrived at the chapel fashionably late.

Justin alighted first and extended his hand to me. I put my hand in his and so moved by the touch, lost my footing.

He caught me before I reached the ground, unwilling to let me go.

"Others will see," I panted.

He laughed. "Do you think I care what others think anymore?"

I didn't expect the church to be full. As soon as I reached the door, I remembered my nerves.

Mr Ashton came to collect me, his friendly, carefree grin lessening my torment. As we walked down the aisle, he whispered to me of his very great difficulty in finding the correct coat to wear and before I knew it, we stood before the altar and waited for the bride.

My heart swelled with pride. Theresa deserved the very best.

The ceremony was mercifully short. As the bells rang to confirm man and wife, Brett returned to my side.

"You do scrub up nicely, don't you?" he said, looking over my apparel. "Eliza always said you were pretty...but I never realized it until the spring ball. You shouldn't pin your hair back so severely, you know. Makes you look too governessy."

I laughed. "And am I not a governess, Mr Ashton?"

"You mightn't always be...shall we follow the bride and groom?"

"Yes, I think that is customary."

Brett shook his head. "I seem to have the unfortunate tendency to be misunderstood. I mean—dash it—will you marry me? Then you won't have to be a governess. You can be my wife. I wouldn't mind having you for my wife."

It was the strangest proposal I'd ever received. "Are you seriously in earnest?"

"I don't believe I look like an Ernest," he replied, "but I can be earnest sometimes. And today I'm very Ernest. Matrimony has never been my sort of thing...but you tempt me."

I searched the hall until my eyes connected with Justin's. He was watching Brett and I closely and didn't seem to be listening to the man talking to him.

"You can't be serious," I said to Brett. "I am a nobody. Why would you want to marry me?"

"For exactly that reason. I don't care for all these grand, pompous ladies. I only want a sensible girl who knows how to have a good time. Why don't you marry me, Anne? I promise I'll take you to Italy for a honeymoon. Would you like that? I know I would."

For a brief moment, I envisaged exactly that: a handsome villa by the warm Mediterranean waters...quaint, rustic foods...and Justin.

Why did his face have to spoil my future? I could have accepted Brett a year ago. I could have loved him a year ago—but not now. Justin would always be there for me and Madeline would always be there for Brett. Could we make each other happy on those grounds?

We sat down in a pew together. "I have a confession to make, Mr Ashton. I have been to your secret room...no, don't be angry with Eliza. I have known since the ball that you were and still <u>are</u> in love with Lady Madeline. I understand your pain but I don't think it would be fair to you or fair to me if we marry. You see—"

"You're in love with someone else," he sighed broken-heartedly. "Who is he?"

"I fear it is Lord Justin."

Brett nodded despondently. "He's a favorite with the ladies, always has been."

"You can see the hopelessness of my case. He is married...but I shan't stay at Silverthorn. I am going home when Cathy goes abroad."

Brett suddenly captured my hands. "You don't have to go home. We can still marry—now we know each other's secret. I am certain we could deal very well together."

He had a valid point and for one brief moment, I thought I could marry him. A future with Brett would be more pleasant than an uncertain future as a governess. But I knew it would not be fair to him. Especially when he lived so close to the man I truly loved.

Brett must have read my thoughts. "We can move away..."

I admired his enthusiasm. "I don't think it would work as much as I would like it to."

He sighed. "Oh dash it, we'll just be friends then. But if your lover fades with time, do come back to me. If you ever feel a need to run away from that horrid Uncle of yours—" he patted his chest, "come to Brett. I will look after you."

I kissed his cheek. "You are truly a gallant gentleman."

I will never forget that evening at Ashton Grove.

Eliza, proving her skills as an able hostess, arranged a splendid feast comprising of the finest dishes.

Mrs Carstares openly beamed due to the great honor bestowed on her son as the majority of guests belonged to that elite class.

Justin found me on the terrace. I sensed his presence before he said anything, anxious for a moment alone with him.

His hands came to rest on the balustrade. "The wedding went well—I believe some congratulations are in order?"

"Congratulations?"

"For the forth-coming nuptials between you and Mr Ashton."

"You are mistaken, my lord."

"Am I?"

I raised my face to his, struck by the intense look on his handsome face. I knew then I would never love another man—we understood each other. I don't know how long I stood there, staring up at him like a lovesick girl. For one crazy moment, I contemplated life as his mistress...

"Did Mr Ashton make you an offer?"

"Yes...and I refused."

"Why?"

I felt the color rush to my face. "I do not have to explain my reasons to you, my lord."

"Of course you don't," he replied softly, "but I want to know."

What could I say? Did he expect me to confess my love for a married man? I too had some pride. "Mr Ashton is in love with another woman..."

"Ah...Madeline. Are you certain she is the only reason?"

I would have denied it if I could have looked away. His hands settled on my shoulders, willing me to face him. "Tell me the truth, Anne—"

It was unfortunate that we should be seen at that moment. Eliza and Lillian froze like statues as they turned the corner and found us.

Justin extended his arm to me. "Miss Woodville, I believe my daughter is un-chaperoned in the hall—shall we see to it?"

I didn't trust myself to look at Eliza as we passed. "They'll make mischief," I warned Justin.

"Let them."

"It is my reputation that is at risk."

He paused. "Then I am grieved for your happiness is of primary concern to me."

I was still pondering over his words when we reached Cathy. We found her embracing Doctor Carstares' younger brother, a handsome boy of eighteen.

Having been caught out, the boy immediately deserted a breathless Cathy. "I'm sorry, Papa."

"Sorry isn't good enough—I see evidence of your mother in you and the trait is undesirable."

She studied him rebelliously. "Are you going to punish me?"

"Yes. Instead of Palmerston Chateau, you will be sent to Quinlin Convent."

Disbelief clouded Cathy's face. "Quinlin convent! But the nuns are so strict!" Swallowing uneasily, she appealed to me, "oh, Anne, do persuade him to change his mind...he can't sent me to Quinlin...I shall die!"

"You certainly won't die," I assured her, "and I believe your father is right. The convent is a much safer place for a young, un-chaperoned lady..."

"The words of a true governess," Cathy murmured bitterly. "You knew how much I wanted to go to Palmerston! How could you betray me?"

"Catherine!"

"Well, it's true, isn't it? I hate you both!"

She ran away and I started to go after her.

Justin caught my hand. "Leave her be. She needs to learn a lesson."

I felt betrayed. "Why didn't you tell me? I have worked so hard to gain her confidence...I had my own reservations about Palmerston...but it seemed to make her so happy—"

"Yes," he agreed coldly, "like the temporary happiness when given a new toy." He sighed. "Cathy hates to be likened to her mother. Danielle—" he said the name with some pain, "was but an indulgent child when I married her. I fear Palmerston will encourage the same selfish wildness in Cathy."

His face was half in the shadow. I felt drawn to him.

"Anne," he said softly, touching my face. "I—"

"There you are," Theresa poked her head around the corner, "Mr Carstares and I are leaving..." she glanced speculatively at Justin for a brief moment. "Are you coming to wish me well?"

"Yes..."

I followed her back into the Drawing Room, not trusting myself to look back at Justin.

Cathy was sick the next day.

She apologized to me in the morning, her eyes large and sorrowful. She realized nothing would now change her father's mind—she would go to the convent.

The morning passed quietly without Theresa. I missed her sorely. No more mid-night chats, no more secret confessions...I was once again on my own, playing a role I detested.

I took relief in knowing I would soon be leaving.

A shiver went up my spine as I remembered my stolen letters. I suspected Mrs Simmons first, however, she certainly would have exposed me to Lord Justin if she'd discovered my secret.

I must get away now...before they found out.

How could I leave the children? Did I not have a duty to care for Madeline's abandoned child?

It had been my resolve in the beginning to leave the moment I'd discovered the truth. I never imagined I would grow this attached to Silverthorn...and its inhabitants.

However, I must leave...and soon. "Brandon, do you know where the family vault is?"

He screwed up his face. "The vault? Why should you want to go there, Anne?"

I shrugged. "I don't know...I only realized I'd never seen it...and I should like to—just one time."

He seemed satisfied with my explanation. "You shouldn't go alone...but I will tell you how to get there."

I smiled at his childish directions. As the children went down for their afternoon nap, I snuck down to the parlor.

"Where are you going, Miss Woodville?" Mrs Simmons loomed behind me, her black eyes suspicious.

"The children are sleeping...I thought I'd go for a walk."

She nodded. "Very well, I shall look in on the children."

"Thank-you, Mrs Simmons."

The air was chilly outside. Once beyond the border of Silverthorn's southern garden, I looked back and wondered how different my life would have been if I had never came here.

I thought of all the faces of Silverthorn: Cathy, Brandon, Laura, Mrs Simmons, Olivia, Lillian, Justin...Madeline, Lucian, Danielle...Vincent...and the great house which seemed to play an important role in all of our lives.

I dared not think of the past...or of the future.

I thought only of Justin...and why I must leave this place.

The family vault, hidden in the middle of a circle of shrubs and trees, beckoned me through its rusty, iron gates. I found the centerpiece stone Brandon had mentioned, feeling chilled at the thought of what lay beneath. Madeline, with all her vibrant beauty, rested on the stony cold floor below.

Brandon had warned me about the trapdoor. "Cathy fell in one day...she was locked inside for two hours!"

Armed with a log, I slowly levered up the heavy, moss-covered stone lid, unprepared for the foul, stale air rushing up to consume me.

I almost dropped the lid and ran away.

Coward, I only had to do this once. Thinking of Madeline gave me courage. I stepped down to the third step, positioning the log to keep the lid open.

I took a deep breath and went down.

The cold and the damp chilled my soul. I glanced around at the numerous coffins and headstones, some of marble, some of stone and wished I'd remained at the house.

I should never have come alone.

People go mad in places like this. To set my mind at ease, I read some of the names on the headstones, pausing at the tomb of the late Lord Braithfield.

My heart skipped a beat. She was buried beside him, encased in a white marble tomb, worthy of an empress. The words carved on the front simply read: *Madeline, second wife of Thomas B, died 1878.*

I reached out and tentatively touched the stone, remembering our childhood together. Our lives seemed irrevocably entwined together and I remembered her as I'd first seen her that sunny morning...an orphaned child clutching a worn carpetbag, her tawny curls bobbing around her face.

After saying my farewells, I darted up the stairs...anxious to leave this gloomy place.

The dark shadow above should have warned me.

I was trapped.

I could not lift the fallen lid with my puny strength.

Utter despair engulfed me. It would be dark and no one knew I'd come here except Brandon. Oh, why hadn't I mentioned to Mrs Simmons the direction of my walk?

My foolishness pride had forbidden it.

In desperation, I tried again to push the stone lid open. I was so certain I'd placed the log securely...how could it have moved? Did it slip under the pressure?

I ran downstairs, looking for anything to aid my escape. I found nothing but the sympathetic echoes of the dead.

I was not going to cry. I shook my head and tried to think logically. Of course, they would miss me at Silverthorn. Mrs Simmons kept a check on my absences—certainly she would note the delay?

How long would she expect me to be gone? An hour at most...I quickly tallied up how long it had taken me to walk to the vault...a quarter of an hour...so I could not expect to be rescued for some time...and that depended on Mrs Simmons keeping a watch-clock.

She would look in on Brandon and Laura while they slept—perhaps once or twice. Expecting me to return within the hour, she might neglect to look again. There was a chance she may miss me altogether...

I consoled myself with knowing that eventually someone would come for me.

I simply had to wait.

An hour later, the cold started to creep up from below.

I clung to my woolen wrap, colder than I'd ever been before. I started to pace...hoping my movements would alleviate the condition. It worked for a little while...until the stagnant air began to infect my lungs.

It must be dark outside...and windy...I could still hear the wind. Oh, why had I been so stupid? Why didn't I heed Brandon's warning about the trap door?

The certainty of my placement of the log played upon my mind. It could have slipped...but did it? Or had somebody moved it on purpose?

The thought chilled my bones.

Someone had stolen my letters...someone˜*knew* I was Madeline's cousin.

I thought of Justin. He hated Madeline...surely, he would throw me out if he knew my real identity?

I detested my lies. I detested this web of deceit I had spun around people whom I really cared about. Had I jeopardized everything...for Madeline?

I sank to the floor beside her grave and wept bitterly. I wanted it all over...I didn't want to deceive any more...I wanted to return to the sensible, comfort of being plain and unloved Laura Morgan.

I couldn't feel my legs...it was so cold. I wanted to forget this nightmare...I wanted to forget everything. I wanted to return to the old days...where everything was uncomplicated and safe...

I didn't know how long I'd been trapped in that horrible vault until later.

I remembered hearing a faint noise...very faint. Then I was in Justin's arms. He shook me firmly, searching my face for any hint of life.

Did I smile? I can only recall looking into his eyes and knowing I was safe.

CHAPTER SEVENTEEN

"Anne...are you awake?"

I opened an eyelid and the room swam before me. I saw a face...peering into mine. "Cathy...?"

"It's me," she cried. "Will you ever forgive me?"

I closed my eyes and touched my forehead. "Where am I?"

Cathy looked puzzled. "At Silverthorn, of course. Don't you remember? You went to the vault and locked yourself in."

Oh yes. I *did* remember. "How did you find me?"

"I went looking for you...to apologize. Mrs Simmons said you went out for a walk...so I waited and when you didn't return, I thought it was odd. I went to Brandon's room and he told me you'd asked about the family crypt. He said he warned you about the trap door." She took my hand. "We were all so worried about you...especially Papa. I've never seen him so afraid."

Justin had come for me! He was afraid...of losing me.

I dared not assume too much...however, I still felt the elation through my very core, knowing I was valued by the one I loved.

Once my head settled, I found the courage to dress with Cathy's assistance.

A first, she was reluctant to help me. "What do you think you're doing? Papa says you're to rest...he was most emphatic about it."

"But I am perfectly recovered and—"

"Hungry?"

We both turned at the voice. Hidden behind the screen, I saw Justin standing at the doorway, that roguish smile tugging at the corners of his mouth.

"Papa!" Cathy gasped. "You shouldn't be here!"

"Well...can I interest you ladies? It is half eight and Lillian is ravished."

"We'll come," Cathy promised, shooing him away so she could help me dress.

As we walked down the grand staircase, I thought this would be the last time, I, as Anne Woodville the governess, dined with Lord Braithfield and his family.

The fact depressed me inconsolably. How could I leave...when my heart begged me to stay?

"Miss Woodville," Lillian stared at me across the table. "Whatever possessed you to visit the family vault?" She shuddered. "It is an awful place...poor Cathy was trapped there once you know..." she looked away, blinking back a sudden tear, "and my baby...is buried there..."

"I am certain, cousin," Justin interposed with a smile, "that Miss Woodville may promise you to never visit the family crypt again."

I raised my brows. "Do you think me a coward, my lord?"

Justin raised his glass, studying me peculiarly. "I believe you are a very brave woman. I know I wouldn't enjoy an afternoon locked in the family vault."

"Papa!" Cathy chastised. "How can you speak of it like that? Anne could have died!"

"I find this conversation extremely vexing over food," Lillian said, pushing aside her plate distastefully. "I think I shall retire to my room."

Before she reached Maitlan and the door, she turned around, a wildness in her usually calm brown eyes. "The next governess shall not be allowed to take meals with the family! It is against convention!"

She intended to frighten me out of my seat. When I did not move, she merely shrugged her shoulders and left.

"Oh dear," Cathy murmured later. "She's been so good lately too...what could have caused her to..."

"I don't know," Justin said under his breath. "But she has surrendered her privileges this evening."

I felt suddenly awkward. Lillian was right. I was a governess...I shouldn't be here.

I stood to go, thanking Justin for his hospitality. For a moment, he looked like he might ask me to stay. Before an opportunity arose, I smiled, "this is Cathy's last week. You should enjoy each other while you can."

I walked back to my room, forcing the tears from falling uselessly down my face. I would never be accepted here...Olivia would return one day and claim her position as Justin's wife and mistress of Silverthorn.

But I would not stay to see it.

I spent my final days preparing Cathy for life in a convent school.

When she refused to listen, I told her of my own upbringing at the Rectory (omitting location and other tell-tale factors), hoping this would encourage her to behave.

"Your Uncle's a veritable monster!" Cathy shivered. "I don't know how you managed...I promise I shan't cause Papa any more trouble...do you really think I will turn out like my mother?"

I shook my head firmly. "You are your own unique person. Remember, the choice is yours."

She hugged me fiercely. "I do love you, Anne! I shall miss you so much...but I'm sure we'll always be good friends."

"We certainly will," I assured her.

"Are you going to leave Papa then?"

How could I possibly explain? "My specialty is to teach young ladies like yourself."

"Must you really go?"

"Yes...I shall leave when you do. Now, do you think you're ready for the convent?"

I did not leave Silverthorn as planned.

Cathy departed on the Monday. Silverthorn was strangely empty without her.

I took my meals with the children. Justin insisted I join his table but I refused. Without Cathy's persistence and support, Mrs Simmons would not hesitate to remind me of my station. I knew she meant well and suddenly those glorious days of the ball, dinners and parties...ceased to exist.

Had they ever really existed? Had I imagined it?

Eliza came to see me.

Her brother must have told her of his proposal and she pleaded with me to reconsider. "Is it because of my showing you his shrine to Lady Madeline?"

"No," I said firmly. "I am very fond of Mr Ashton...but I cannot marry him. It is not because of Lady Madeline."

Eliza raised a brow in disbelief.

I decided to tell her the truth. "The last mistress of Silverthorn may be something of a legend here...but she is not to me. She was my cousin."

Eliza stared at me, speechless.

"Yes, it's true," I smiled.

"It can't be! You...and her...cousins..."

I nodded. "We grew up together in Uncle Clive's Rectory. She was always very wild and her beauty enabled her to become the toast of London—where she met Lord Braithfield and married him. I heard from her occasionally...until she sent me a last, desperate message..."

"A desperate message?"

I summarized my plan to find the truth.

"Who are you?" Eliza murmured. "Your real name is not Anne Woodville, is it?"

I shook my head sadly. "I wish I could be Anne Woodville." I laughed at her alarm. "Please do not class me with Madeline. I am entirely her opposite. She used to poke fun at my sensibilities—my real name is Laura Morgan."

"Laura...I think she mentioned a Laura once...it was in reference to Tabitha and her last suitor. She advised Tabitha to flirt. When she refused, I heard Madeline say, 'my, how you remind me of my prudish Laura.'" She looked at me afresh. "May I tell Brett who you really are? I am certain he would love to know."

We were in my private bedchamber but I felt an uncanny sensation that our conversation was overheard.

"You look pale," Eliza murmured. "Are you unwell?"

I went to my door and opened it slowly.

Down the hall, I saw the black skirts of Mrs Simmons swish down the corridor.

"Anne, will Cathy come back soon?"

"No, Brandon. Not for some time."

"But why? Why did Papa send her to France? Was she naughty?"

His bandages came off last week, showing new pink skin. I thought of Brandon running about with his inquisitive mind and felt wearied. I told him to finish his sums and we would talk about Cathy later.

Laura sat on the floor by the fire playing with her doll. It was the only thing Madeline left her...a doll. It was so reminiscent of Madeline...I felt strangely saddened by the thought.

How could I leave her child?

I supposed I could stay at Silverthorn. No one asked me to leave. But could I...knowing Olivia must return one day to reassume her position as mistress of the house?

By late afternoon, I felt the need for a solitary walk to ponder. I espied Hetty the housemaid in the hall and begged her to watch the children for the half hour. She seemed a little frightened and I assured her I would take the blame if Mrs Simmons found out.

She grinned. "Very well, Missus. I'll do it for ye. Out for a walk, are ye? Watch the nip, won't ye?"

Taking Hetty's advice, I seized my wrap and headed off in the direction of the stables. Once there, I greeted the groom and went to Philippe's stall.

I removed the sugar cubes from my pocket and offered them to the great stallion.

"I never expected Philippe to melt like butter in the hands of a governess."

Startled, I turned to face Justin. He stood beside the far stall in his usual day suit, his lips twisting pensively.

I swallowed uneasily, patting Philippe. "He's a magnificent creature."

"You're welcome to ride him as often as you like."

"You are very kind, my lord...I hope you do not think I am shirking my duties—"

"Not at all."

He came closer, his hand resting tentatively on the stallion's neck. "Philippe is very particular about who he likes...he's given Lillian the cold shoulder on many occasions and she is an accomplished horsewoman."

I remembered her complaint and laughed. "Yes, he doesn't like her, does he?"

"But he likes you. I watched you from the window in my study...I will not pretend I didn't come here for a purpose." He examined my face. "I want you to stay, Anne."

"But Cathy—"

"I am thinking of the other children...they need you."

"They need a mother," I said without thinking.

"Yes, a *mother.* I'm afraid my wife was a bad choice—she pretended to like children before we married and I could never understand why Cathy disliked her. I understand now."

What was this to do with me?

"Do you ever have any regrets in your life, Miss Woodville?"

"Regrets?"

"Yes, regrets."

"I don't know...I've never really thought about it before."

He smiled faintly. "You are too young to have regrets...too sensible, too perfect."

"You make me sound like a saint. Let me assure you, I am not a saint. Growing up in my Uncle's strict household only encouraged rebellion."

"The thought of you rebelling is tempting..."

"You are making fun of me."

He stepped closer, tilting my face up to him. "You should have married Brett, you know..."

I raised a brow. "Why?"

"He's a boy...he would suit you."

"I decided long ago I would marry only for love. I do not love Mr Ashton, my lord."

His dark eyes studied mine. "Do you believe true love exists?"

"I don't know..."

He grinned. "A sensible answer from a sensible woman. Unfortunately my previous wives lacked that quality—I only wish..."

"Wish, my lord?"

He reached out and touched my cheek. His fingers were warm against my skin and for a brief moment, I didn't care about right and wrong. I only wanted him.

He pulled me to him, enveloping me within his protective embrace. I laid my head against his shoulder, closing my eyes at the wonder of it. I raised my face and let him kiss me, my body longing to his touch. His mouth grew more demanding and I allowed myself to be swept away at the wonder of it.

If our passion surprised me, it surprised him too. "Anne..." he breathed against my ear. "This is wrong...wrong..."

"Don't let go," I begged, putting my hand on his chest. "Please don't let go."

He searched my face. "No...I cannot allow—"

I felt him pull away abruptly. He started down the opposite end of the stables and threw his arms down in frustration. "Oh, God," he muttered.

"What is it?"

He scarcely glanced at me. "It's Lillian. She saw us."

"Oh...what will you do?"

He shrugged. "Go to her and explain. I will not pretend...I followed you here."

"To make love to me?" I asked wryly, surprised at my own bashfulness.

He smiled. "Don't tempt me."

I felt my face flush at his burning stare.

"It is best if you return now...I will follow shortly." He shook his head. "I am ashamed of myself...for acting so rashly. It was wrong of me."

I didn't wait for him to continue. I didn't want to hear any more about convention or propriety. I could think on that later...I only wanted to savor the moment.

It must last my lifetime.

I was extremely inattentive to the children that night. I was reading a fairy story and Brandon complained several times of my repeating a sentence or two. In the end, he snatched the book off me and read it to Laura on his own. Laura snuggled beside him on the great bed. I watched them fall asleep, two virtual orphans together.

I removed the book and tucked them in properly, deigning to move Laura to her own bed. She insisted on sharing Brandon's room, as the dark frightened her. I knew her vulnerability appealed to Brandon's sense of bravado and he consented in his serious manner.

On my way out, I nearly collided with Mrs Simmons in the corridor.

Her black eyes widened a little and I wondered how much she knew. Had Lillian told her what she'd seen?

"Miss Woodville...his lordship requires you in his study."

"This late?"

"Yes, it is out of character..." she observed me closely. "I hope you are wise and avoid the sin of adultery."

She must know.

"It is not so totally unexpected," she added. "He is a man after all...and it has been some time since his wife left...I don't mean to pry, Miss Woodville, but I believe I have your best interests at heart. I've served his lordship all his life and I know he is good-natured. He would never do anything foolish but I believe he has a weakness where you are concerned. You will need to be strong."

I stared after her in disbelief. I'd always felt she hated me...yet could the fondness in her eyes be mistaken?

I was still pondering over her apparent change of heart when I reached Justin's study. I paused by the half-opened door, unsure why I had been summoned here at this unconventional hour.

He was sitting by the fire, a glass of port in his hand.

"Won't you come in, Laura?"

I must have frozen. I knew the moment would come—but I'd planned to tell him!

"Come in. Have a seat."

Shrugging off the coldness of his voice, I sat down and folded my hands. "I can explain—"

He stared at me, his lips drawn together in a taut line. "Explain? You...the cousin of that wanton!   You came here under false pretences...no doubt hoping for some game, never expecting such a grand accomplishment!   Well, you have not succeeded.   I have discovered who you really are."

"No!" I felt hot tears fall down my cheeks. "It's not what you think!"

He downed his glass before hastily pouring another. "I have read your letters...you concealed your relationship with that scheming bitch very cleverly. Do you understand what you have done? I *believed* in you...even loved you—"

"Please let me explain—"

"No. I won't allow you to contaminate us further with your deceit and your lies. I want you to leave this house at once and never return. Do you understand me?"

I ran from him, tears blinding my vision. I wouldn't stay another night.

Once I reached the haven of my room, I seized my travel bag from the wardrobe and threw it on the bed. I started pulling my clothes and belongings from every drawer, not caring how untidy I left it. Piling everything into the bag, I slammed the brass catches and hurried down the stairs.

The door was left open. They expected my instant dismissal.

I darted out in the cool night, determined never to return.

Somehow, I made it to town.

I paused outside an inn in utter despair.

"Are ye all right, missus?" a friendly voice said behind me.

I turned to an old, kindly cabbie. He looked at me compassionately. "Thrown out, are ye? Need a lift somewhere? Me master won't mind if ye climb aboard for awhile—"

"Frip! What the hell about you muttering about?"

The voice sounded familiar, too familiar.

It was Brett.

He blinked twice. "Confound it—is that you, Anne?"

I nodded miserably.

"Well, you don't look your best, do you?" he laughed, putting an arm around me. "Don't worry, Uncle Brett will look after you."

He helped me into the coach. I was relieved he didn't press me for an explanation. He simply joked returning home with me would cause a stir of local gossip.

"Here we are," he said triumphantly. "Shall we retire?"

I nodded mutely and accepted his hand. Once inside Ashton Grove's friendly parlor, I collapsed into a heap on the floor, the tears rushing down my face.

Brett picked me and put me in a chair by the fire in the darkened Drawing Room. "I usually like to sit here late at nights with a glass of wine. Would you care to join me?"

He handed me a glass. "There, now, it can't be that bad. Did you lose a glove?"

I tried to smile. "Thank-you for coming to my rescue. You remind me somewhat of a gallant knight."

He grinned. "I like to think so too."

"Do you think your sisters would mind terribly if—?"

"You stayed the night?" Brett finished. "Of course not! You've had a traumatic experience. Let's get a good night's rest and then you can tell me all about it in the morning—eh?"

"Thank-you," I whispered, warmed by his unquestioning confidence in me.

The wine must have helped me to sleep. I awoke in the morning to the shocking truth of my situation.

Ashton Grove! I lay abed for a full hour thinking of what I would say to Eliza and Tabitha. Would they turn me out once they discovered I'd been dismissed from Silverthorn?

I need not have worried.

Eliza snuck into my room, dressed in fresh printed muslin. "I didn't ask to come in for I thought you wouldn't let me. So, here I am...and I've brought up some hot chocolate."

She made me sip it before saying, "let me put your mind to rest. You may stay here as long as you want."

I thanked her but said I wouldn't take advantage of her family. "Unfortunately, Theresa is on her honeymoon otherwise I would not have presumed—"

Eliza laughed. "You are so politically correct about everything, dear Laura!"

"Lord Braithfield painted a very different picture of me..." I hid my face in my hands. "I never wanted it...to end like this. I am only grateful Cathy isn't here to witness my disgrace. I couldn't bear her turning against me too."

Eliza shook her head sadly. "Yes...I can imagine Justin would take it badly. He *despises* lies and deceit. What did you say in your defense?"

"He refused to listen to me." I shrugged indifferently. "I came to Silverthorn for a purpose...my purpose is now complete. I shall go home...and try to forget everything about it."

"Will you look for another post?"

"Eventually. I haven't any other choice, have I?"

"Yes, you do. You can marry Brett. He can sell the Grove...it's more than a possibility for if you were seen entering his coach last night..."

"How does he feel?"

"He wants to protect you from a scandal. Will you promise to re-consider his suit?"

I nodded slowly. "Yes, I promise."

Two days passed.

I wrote a letter to Theresa and Uncle Clive and Aunt Mary, preparing them for my imminent return to the Rectory. I intended to visit Lady Beatrice first. A spell by the sea might help me to forget this entire unpleasant experience.

I was busy packing in my room when Brett came to see me. He was not happy about my decision but eventually accepted it.

"I suppose," he said after careful reflection, "a brother is almost as good as a lover. Anne—I mean—Laura...you know Anne suits you better...did you pick Anne? How clever of you. My dear Laura, I shall miss your wry remarks...I can't believe Justin—"

"Please, I don't wish to discuss it again. It was wrong of me to assume a false identity...and I must accept full responsibility."

Brett looked at me speculatively. "Do you want to stop by the mill before you go? You should try to explain, you know. He might listen this time."

"How can I?"

"Eliza and I will take you. You will speak with Justin while we wait in the coach. Then we shall go to the station. Agreed?"

I hugged him. "How do you manage to arrange things so perfectly?"

He grimaced. "I am a brother born when there is distress. However, I will say that Justin is a dashed fool for throwing you out."

"Well, my business is complete. I only came here to find out what happened to Madeline. Now I know, I can go home."

"You are free to have anything of hers," Brett said suddenly. "I know she would've liked you to have her things."

"You are too generous—"

"Now, don't take too long will you? I am aware women lose track of the time when they look at dresses and things...but you wouldn't want to miss your train, would you?"

He concealed his surprise when I returned with only two items. One was the old, worn pair of gloves, hiding Madeline's private letters, and the other a small, tortoise-shell comb.

Eliza was waiting in the coach. She looked curiously at my chosen items. "I was so certain you'd select one or two of her gowns. They are so lovely."

"And why would a governess want to dress above her station?"

"Circumspect Laura," Brett tapped his cane on the roof of the coach.

I should never have made a visit to Lester mill alone.

As the coach came to a halt outside, I approached the entrance the more trepidation than I have ever felt in my life. I didn't know what to say...I didn't even know if Justin would agree to see me.

I only knew I had to try.

Fortunately, Mr Thompson recognized me and ushered me up the narrow, winding stairs leading to Lord Braithfield's office.

I did turn around.

"Is something the matter, Miss?" Mr Thompson touched my sleeve.

The echo of our steps betrayed us. I suddenly thought how ridiculous I must seem. Why had I come? What would it achieve?

Justin didn't look up as Mr Thompson introduced me but said simply, "close the door behind Miss Woodville, Thomas."

When Mr Thompson left, he shifted some papers on his desk. "I suppose you have come to collect the balance of your wages...take a seat; it won't take long."

"I haven't come about the money."

"No?" he raised a brow, examining me for the first time. "You will need it for your journey."

I looked down at my traveling clothes. "I have enough to cover my expenses. I simply came to tell you..."

"You came to tell me?"

I met his eyes. They were a glacial black. "I was wrong to apply for the position under a false name...but I knew you would reject me if I presented myself as Laura Morgan. I apologize for the embarrassment I've caused you and your family. I never intended to harm anyone and in the event of my business, I have grown genuinely fond of my charges."

"Ah...your business. I should have sensed the adventuress in you when I saw you the first time."

"Despite what you think, my intentions have remained the same during my time at Silverthorn. My purpose for coming here was to find out what happened to my cousin...Madeline sent me a note...a desperate note, as you would have read. I believed she was in danger."

"A mere consequence of her actions. You knew of her plan to ensnare my Uncle and foster a bastard on him. That fact alone condemns you."

I ignored his cryptic gaze designed to unnerve me. "Yes," I agreed, "it does condemn me. How can I explain? Madeline and I were thrown together as orphans. She was beautiful; I was plain. Our characters are as contrary as two people can be and yet we thought of each other as a sister. I never condoned her behavior; if you read the letters carefully you would see Anne Woodville is no different from Laura Morgan."

"And yet the name is so important." He rose from his chair and started to pace the room. "I cannot begin to tell you how Madeline changed our lives. She is impossible to forget."

It sounded like the voice of a lover. I swallowed uneasily. "You...loved her?"

"Loved her?" He turned to me in some surprise. "I *hated* her. I knew what she was the moment she arrived. My poor deranged Uncle didn't even question her when she gave birth two months premature. Triumphant her success, Madeline began her torment on all of us."

"Torment?"

"Yes, torment. She delighted in turning our Uncle against us. Poor Lillian was the first to suffer. Then she started on my first wife, Danielle." He paused to light a cigar. "Danielle and I were no longer on speaking terms. I had only just learned she carried Vincent's child. Unable to endure her deceit, she confessed everything. Her confession destroyed any hope of reconciliation between us, however, to avoid a scandal, I agreed to let her remain as my wife and give her unborn child my name. She accepted my bargain, knowing Vincent had already tired of her. We didn't see him again until Madeline arrived. He came to see the new bride."

"I know what happened. I found a book once belonging to Madeline with a private inscription. They became lovers?"

He nodded. "His open flirtations with Madeline drove Danielle to her death. I confronted him after the incident."

"What did he say?"

"He laughed. When I threatened to expose him, he merely shrugged and suggested I spend more time in town. We were in the library...Uncle came down, claiming Lillian had seen his wife with Vincent in the woods..."

"What happened?"

"Unable to calm his rage, Uncle retreated to his study and put a gun to his head. We found him the next morning."

"There was no inquest into his death?"

He smiled faintly. "We managed to convince the coroner it was an accident and as Uncle suffered from the madness in the family, the public accepted the verdict."

I imagined Madeline's last year—lived with a passionate recklessness so reminiscent of her. I now understood why she had not invited me to Silverthorn...she had no wish for a conscious. I was almost ashamed to ask how she took the news of her elderly husband's sudden death.

"Now free of all restraints, Madeline continued relentlessly. She wanted Silverthorn. As I stood to inherit my Uncle's estate and fortune, she asked me to marry her, saying that if I did not agree, she would announce her pregnancy and play the virtuous widow. She kept up the pretence until the spring ball, choosing as her costume a nun's habit. She wanted to convince the public of her goodness—to show me I could not win against her. She intended to denounce me at the ball by accusing me of murdering my Uncle—"

"How did you know?"

"I could see how her mind worked. My estimation of her character proved correct when, the day before the ball, a man came to see me—a gypsy—who claimed intimate connections with the present Lady Braithfield. He told me he was Laura's father and I assumed he'd been blackmailing Madeline for some time. Interestingly, he didn't ask me for money but seemed satisfied to tell me of his involvement with her. Armed with this information, I told Madeline at the ball to start packing. She stared at me for a long time, a strange smile on her face...that was the last I saw of her. They found her body the following morning...the gypsy's in a ditch not a mile away. He had a pistol with him. I concluded he shot himself after strangling Madeline."

"Is that how she died?"

He nodded. "We let the district believe she committed suicide and hid gypsy's death from his own people. They believe he ran away with a house guest to Australia."

"How did Vincent react when Madeline was found?"

"I little stunned, I daresay. Her loss represented his loss."

I absorbed this new information. "Do you think he was the father of her unborn child and hoped to marry her once she established the child as her late husband's heir?"

"Yes, he's always wanted Silverthorn. When that plan failed, he came back with the intention of seducing my wife...and he succeeded." He put his cigar out. "Are you now satisfied with the truth? Do you understand why I dismissed you? I was furious when Lillian exposed you as a fraud."

"Lillian?"

He nodded. "She came to me once, relating some tale how Miss Bank's called you 'Laura' by mistake. I didn't believe her, however, when she brought me your letters..."

"I would have reacted the same way...did you read all of them?"

"Not at first...but later I came to realize you were not the adventuress I believed you to be. Why were you so loyal to Madeline, Laura?"

My name on his lips sounded wonderful. "I suppose she represented the only family I had...besides my aunt and uncle. I—I hoped she would come to her senses."

He smiled faintly. "You were too good to her, my darling."

The words had slipped. I went to him in an unthinkable rush. His arms closed around me as his mouth settled on mine. I never believed such joy could be possible...I didn't want to leave him, now that I knew he loved me...

"I am so sorry, my darling, for thinking the worst of you...I should have known better." He held my face between his hands. "I wish...what is the use of wishing? I cannot do the honorable thing, Laura. I am married...however much I wish I were not."

"Do you love her?" I asked stupidly.

He turned away. "Once I thought I could...but I never really knew Olivia." He looked at me in painful regret. "I cannot offer you what you deserve...I should have never encouraged you. It was wrong of me and I apologize."

His words tore at my heart. "But if—"

He shook his head. "No, there is no way. A divorce would ruin my family...it if were for myself...but it is not. Leave my dearest, darling, Laura, and never return. Go, before we succumb into the temptation of sin...and where would that leave us? I love you with all my heart...that is why I am asking you to go now."

I removed my hand from his chest. "It's so difficult to do the honorable thing...how can I leave you when I love you so much—"

I was in his arms again. A wave of passion rose between us like a flame. I closed my eyes, unprepared to face the world without him.

He kissed my forehead, his dark eyes studying me with so much warmth and love. "You now know I am right. We cannot be trusted in each other's company, even for a moment—" He kissed me again. "Let it be the last...oh, God, how I wish I could make love to you!"

"Yes, do, do," I cried desperately.

He kissed my hands. "You are not thinking, my darling. I know you would regret it later. And I would not wish to drive a wedge between us. The memories are always sweeter if we hold to the principles. Give me some time...I can't promise anything." He raised my chin up to face him. "What will you do? Return to your aunt and uncle?"

"Yes...until I can secure another post."

He gave me some money, insisting I take it. He seemed a little angered by the fact Brett was accompanying me to the station.

"You should accept his proposal," he murmured. "Don't wait forever for me, Laura. If another offer becomes available to you, take it."

I searched his face. "How can I?"

It was the last thing I said to him. Mr Thompson knocked on the door and subsequently entered.

It was time for me to leave. I turned around, not trusting myself to look back.

I told Brett and Eliza I succeeded in clearing the misunderstanding.

I hoped Eliza didn't press me and tried to keep my expression solemn and pensive. However, nothing could stop the wonderful feeling inside.

He loved me!

The sensation was ephemeral, as I knew I must leave him.

He told me to expect nothing. I would have to prepare myself for the likely eventuality that I would never hear from him again.

I sat back and sighed. Anne Woodville was dead and I was no longer the timid Laura Morgan of the Rectory. I was Laura Morgan the experienced governess. I had no doubt in finding another post.

Flashes of Justin and Silverthorn appeared occasionally in the glass window. I couldn't stop a single tear from falling and reluctantly let it go. Ruby had always told me it was better to cry if one felt one must.

I must forget all that had occurred...and in time, God willing, Silverthorn would become but a faded picture in the recesses of my mind.

CHAPTER EIGHTEEN

I boarded the stagecoach at Victoria Station.

The road from London, worsened with the rain, didn't make a pleasant journey in the rickety old coach. I sat between a portly, middle-aged man, who snored the entire way, and an incurable optimist in the form of a young soldier's wife and her companion.

My final coach change couldn't come sooner. With the strain of the journey, my soaked bag seemed heavier than I remembered. I boarded the new coach, whipping a cloud of dust in my face.

Could things be any worse?

As we came into the village, I felt a wave of nostalgia pass over me. How different everything now seemed! My old battles paled into insignificance. I smiled, thinking of the Rohan family and how I used to value their good opinion.

As I alighted and walked to the Rectory, I had to think of the new occupants. Mr Edwin Brody now had a wife, the farmer's daughter, Tilly. Old Lord Rohan was dead and Adam had come into his fortune by marrying the heiress Josie.

I passed through the little iron gate into an untended and overgrown garden. How could Tilly allow it to become this way? She was fortunate, I supposed, that she did not have to answer to the Adam's mother, the previous Lady Rohan.

Exhausted, I knocked on the heavy door.

To my surprise, Ruby answered it. Without any hesitation, she swept me up in her arms, tears glistening in her dear eyes.

"Oh, my poor litt'e muffin! A poor sight I see." She examined me closely. "A wash n' scrub will do ye good...now," she stooped down to pick up my bag.

I stopped her. "Where is Jake?"

"Gone...they're all gone. I'm the only one left..."

That explained the poor upkeep of the Rectory.

"His lordship lost a lot of his money in gamb'ing to the despair of his mama and sister. He even cut into Miss Elizabeth's dowry...the dowager Lady Rohan is tak'ng it badly. Keeps to her rooms, she does."

I was dumbfounded. The regal Rohans—impoverished! "What of the new Lady Rohan? Has she appealed to her father?"

"Her father won't give Lord Rohan any more money and his lordship blames Lady Josie for the mishap. The poor wee thing's breed'ng again. Will fall any day now."

I was horrified Adam could treat his wife so harshly. However, I didn't feel a smidgen of pity for Elizabeth and the demise of her dowry. I imagined she would continue with her pretentious ways no matter how poverty stricken.

Ruby led me to my old room, chastising me for sending no word of my arrival.

"I wanted to surprise you," I said, quickly changing into a fresh gown of muslin and washing my face in a nearby basin. "Where's Aunt Mary? I can't wait another moment to see her."

Ruby avoided my gaze.

"What is it? Is she unwell?"

"Her cough has worsened...doctor says she's to keep to her bed."

"What of Uncle Clive?"

Ruby shook her head. "A myst'ry illness. He's losing his hair but it as crotchety as ever. Mr Brody says he's certain to die in the next few months. I'm sure his wish'ng it is help'ng him to his long-awaited meet'ng with God."

Aunt Mary was delighted to see me.

She laid her book aside and beckoned me to her. "My dear niece, how lovely to see you! When did you arrive?"

"Just now," I smiled, kissing her cheek. "Ruby tells me you are not well."

She smiled. "Do not fuss. But why are you here, m'dear?"

"My pupil has gone to a finishing school in France."

"Did you find out about Madeline?"

I gasped. "You mean—you knew?"

Aunt Mary nodded. "Not at first...but later I realized. I hope you freed Madeline's ghost so she can be put to rest."

"Yes, I have. She died of...complications."

"And what of her young daughter?"

"Lord Braithfield is providing for her as if she were his own. I wouldn't move her even if I could. She is happy there and has formed an attachment with Lord Braithfield's son. It is a better life than we could provide for Madeline's daughter."

"Yes...we certainly couldn't offer her a home..."

I asked why things were so bad.

Aunt Mary shrugged. "Yes, Lord Adam has almost ruined his family with his penchant for gambling...and we suffer along with him. Your Uncle is not well...I fear it shan't be long—" she glanced outside the window miserably. "What will I do if he dies? I am too old to go into service..."

"Mr Brody will certainly provide for you."

"I couldn't impose...he has a wife now and a family on the way..."

I ordered tea, promising to be back in a moment.

Ruby was waiting for me outside. "Mistress Brody wants to see ye...she's in the Draw'ng Room."

I nodded. "Could you make Aunt Mary some tea?"

Tilly Brody glanced at me speculatively when I entered. Though large with child, she was pretty with her golden hair, short nose and glass-green eyes. I wondered at Mr Brody's wisdom of choice when she began to speak in a farmer's drawl.

"Well, missy, you won't be expect'ng too much, will ye? Times are tough, y'know. We can't afford to keep you in food and rent."

"I am aware of my situation, Mistress Brody. Let me reassure you I shall only stay until I have secured another post."

In the distance, a baby squawked.

Tilly rose. "Ah, that's me youngin. I hope that lazy Ruby has warmed little Tommy's milk..."

I watched her go, feeling immense compassion for poor Ruby. Having served gentle folk her entire life, she was unprepared for the demands of a simple farmer's daughter.

I found Uncle Clive in the library. He seemed to have aged twenty years; his skin was drawn and pale and his hair loss phenomenal. He glanced up as I entered, adjusting his spectacles to sit evenly on his nose.

"Is that you, Laura? What do you do here?"

"I've come home, sir."

"Yes, yes, that is obvious, is it not? I will repeat my question. What do you do here?"

I was unprepared for his abrupt tone. "My assignment ended in Yorkshire...I have come home to look for another post."

"Why didn't you look for one up there?"

"I didn't have an opportunity—"

"The starved kitten returns," he sneered. "Can't you see, girl, that we've no funds to keep you? Perhaps if you'd done what you were told and married Brody...you always thought you were too clever. I knew you'd never amount to anything..."

"I will leave you, sir, since you are in such ill-spirits."

I closed the door firmly behind me, overwhelmed by a mixture of anger and depression. I should never have come back...

I retired to my room, fighting off a wave of unhappiness. My heart belonged in Yorkshire...at Silverthorn...where it would stay forevermore.

My arrival home caused quite something of a stir amongst our old acquaintances.

'Miss Laura's a traveled woman,' I overheard someone say in church, 'and has returned home to care for her aunt and uncle.'

Yes, it was true. Within a week I had secured a position as a paid companion to a very disagreeable lady named Mrs Fitzherbert. However, service to Mrs Fitzherbert provided me with a wage I could dispense to Ruby for my Aunt and Uncle's care. I trusted Ruby to see the money was properly distributed.

Mrs Fitzherbert, a wealthy widow with two married daughters, possessed a great deal of spare time. Over-indulgent in sweetmeats and chocolate puffs, she liked to believe she was as handsome as she was in her youth and constantly asked my opinion on her appearance. Obsessed with her looks, she didn't like to be surrounded by attractive young women so I was careful to avoid her displeasure by dressing in my drabbest clothes. I wore my hair in the severe 'governess' style Brett had often complained about.

I tried to forget Silverthorn...and Justin. I imagined Olivia's return from her long sojourn in France. I only wondered how she'd managed to stay so long with Vincent and his depleted funds.

Don't wait for me, Justin had said.

I must prepare for life without him. My new life revolved, for the moment, around Mrs Fitzherbert. I pictured her laughing at my stupidity and the experience made me even more determined to accept what must be.

What must be.

The words forewarned a life of emptiness. However, in time, if I was very good, I could perhaps meet with another Mr Brody...

The thought did not console me.

Three months had gone by since my arrival home.

I received a letter from Theresa. She was very happy in her new role as the Doctor's wife and confided she expected a child next winter. She also wrote of her handsome, young brother-in-law, pining the loss of Miss Catherine. *He is determined to wait for her*, she added, *though an imprudent match on both sides. I will try to encourage him elsewhere...*

She told me of her new acquaintances and briefly mentioned the Ashtons. I knew the part I dreaded most was next. *As you have confided the reasons for your abrupt departure from Silverthorn, I thought you'd be interested with the following: Lady Braithfield has not returned, nor can she be found. She was not, as we believed, with Vincent in France. At the moment, Lord Justin and his brother-in-law, Mr Weston, are conducting an investigation. They have been advised that it may take some months to discover the locality of Lady Braithfield.*

Olivia missing? I found this difficult to believe. Perhaps she did not care to be found...

It didn't make any sense. Why would she reject her brother? They seemed to share a special regard for each other—didn't she believe he would respect her wishes?

I had no wish to dwell on Olivia's motives. I was certain she would soon be found...and brought back to Silverthorn.

And I would go on with Mrs Fitzherbert.

Theresa said nothing about the children. I missed them dreadfully. Cathy had sent me a picture postcard from France, briefly detailing her existence at the convent. The postcard had been directed to Silverthorn and I wondered if she knew I was no longer there. I missed her sorely.

Mrs Fitzherbert asked about the postcard. "The maid foolishly put it with my mail," she attempted to lie, "and I couldn't help noticing the name of your friend."

"My ex-pupil, Miss Catherine Braithfield."

Mrs Fitzherbert raised her penciled brows in surprise. "Well, well, how were you so fortunate as to secure a position inside Silverthorn?"

"Do you know it, m'dam?"

Mrs Fitzherbert gave me her 'knowing' look. "I have never moved in *those* circles...but I do know of the house. A very grand place—" she gave me a long look, "not entirely the place I would have connected you with...but of course, wasn't your cousin fortunate enough to marry into the family? Died rather unexpectedly too, I hear?"

"Yes, she was young."

"And left a daughter?"

I nodded.

Mrs Fitzherbert eyed me shrewdly. "You are a very secretive person. You were recommended to me by your aunt...I would like to see your reference from Lord Braithfield."

"Oh, I forgot to ask him for one—"

"You stupid girl," Mrs Fitzherbert frowned. "A reference from Lord Braithfield would greatly increase your worth...it is a great pity I never met this Lord Justin—he could have done for one of my girls..."

I longed for an escape.

Later that day, Mrs Fitzherbert sent me on an errand to purchase some lengths of silk. She was always dreaming up a new creation to make her recapture the beauty she thought she once possessed.

It was a lovely day. Mrs Fitzherbert hated the outdoors so I seldom received an opportunity to go for a walk. Fresh air and exercise gave me an entirely new perspective and I began to recall my fondest memories.

"Is it you, Miss Morgan?"

I turned to a smiling Adam Rohan. He dressed as smartly as if he were strolling in London's Hyde Park and I wondered where the funds had come from for his new coat.

"Is it difficult to believe this is the little Laura from the Rectory," he grinned. "I hardly recognized you!"

"It has been a little over a year," I said.

"I've missed you, you know...I heard you were back...playing companion to some old dragon."

I laughed. "Yes, Mrs Fitzherbert has an unfortunate propensity to be constantly out of sorts."

"Why haven't I seen you in church accompanying this paragon of decorum?"

"Mrs Fitzherbert is greatly indisposed...which, alas, prevents me from attending."

"How unfortunate. I was hoping we'd meet again..."

I was about to ask after his family when I spotted Elizabeth Rohan on the opposite side of the road. Exquisitely dressed, she hurried over.

"Adam," she prodded, "the coach is waiting."

"Liz, have you forgotten Laura so soon?"

Elizabeth was hoping to avoid the renewal of my acquaintance. "We must not inopportune Miss Morgan in her business..."

Adam seemed reluctant to leave.

"...She does have to answer to Mrs Fitzherbert."

Adam nodded. "Yes, of course..." he raised my hand to his lips. "I hope we shall meet again soon, Miss Morgan."

I watched them go, wondering how I ever thought myself in love with a man like Adam Rohan. As an accomplished rake and dedicated gambler, he never failed to create new scandals on his seasonal visits home. Mrs Fitzherbert had mentioned two indiscretions.

I thought of us as children in the schoolroom at Rohan House. Elizabeth, Madeline and I...fate had dealt us different cards. Elizabeth—the loss of her dowry; Madeline—the loss of her life; and me...perhaps my loss was to answer to the likes of Mrs Fitzherbert.

I saw Adam Rohan several times during that period.

Limited funds prevented him returning to town and the company of his family didn't seem to satisfy him. I knew he was looking elsewhere for solace...and had set his sights on me.

Mrs Fitzherbert was quick to shoo him away. I supported her eagerness and soon Adam ceased calling.

We found out a month later that he was seeing a young girl named Simone in the village. And word quickly spread that another Rohan bastard was quickening in her belly.

I went to see Aunt Mary.

She seemed a little better. "How is Mrs Fitzherbert?"

I shuddered slightly as I poured the tea. "Disagreeable! Have you heard nothing of a new post?"

Aunt Mary looked at me softly. "You must try, my dear. Poor Mrs Fitzherbert is a widow..."

"Widow? She told me she was delighted with her husband's death."

"That may be so but..."

"You are too good," I kissed her cheek. "Have you heard from the dowager Lady Rohan?"

"Yes...she hopes Lord Adam will cease his wild ways. He has managed to dip into Miss Elizabeth's dowry again...the paltry sum left is now in the hands of a trustee."

"What of Josie's father?"

She shrugged. "Will not give his son-in-law another penny...which grieves the dowager Lady Rohan greatly. She blames poor Josie for their circumstance."

"That is unfair!"

"Oh yes," she agreed, "the poor child."

"How...is everything here?"

"Tilly bleeds what we have buying sugar and meat. It is only a matter of time...I've considered writing 'B'...when the time comes. Your poor uncle won't last long...dear Laura, don't take his words to heart. He...is cruel at times...but that is his way."

I'd never seen her admit to his faults publicly.

"Yes..." she continued, "the disease in his mind jumbles his thoughts...Doctor Pearson believes it won't be long..."

I didn't like to ask the question of months or weeks. Poor Aunt Mary...how would she survive without him and the Rectory? It had been her life and the threat of losing both at the same time unnaturally harsh. At least, I thought, she could rely upon Lady Beatrice when the time came.

Ruby took the tea away. She was deliberately trying to catch my Aunt's attention without looking directly at me. One look at Ruby seemed to remind Aunt Mary.

"Oh...how could I forget? A caller came for you yesterday."

I could feel my heart thumping. "Here?"

"Yes...Tilly received him. She said he was a gentleman. He asked after you...Tilly advised him you were staying with Mrs Fitzherbert. He requested the address...do you know who it is, Laura? He didn't leave a name...much to Tilly's annoyance."

I could imagine Tilly's overawed reception. Who could it be? I wanted it to be Justin, oh so desperately, but logic reasoned against it. Who else? Brett?

I suppose I would find out when I returned to Mrs Fitzherbert. I walked deliberately slow, trying to put my mind at ease. It couldn't be Justin...

The steps up to Mrs Fitzherbert's house beckoned me. I removed my gloves and hat when the footman opened the door.

I remember thinking the parlor unusually quiet before I heard Mrs Fitzherbert's shriek. I glanced at the footman, hoping for some information.

"You've returned, Miss. Madam requires you in the saloon."

"Thank-you, Alan."

My heart started beating wildly when I reached the saloon. I hid in the shadows for one moment...frightened to enter.

"Where is that girl?" I heard Mrs Fitzherbert say. "Probably loitering about...as she always does. You must excuse her, my lord."

I heard Mrs Fitzherbert shuffle towards the door and wanted to flee. However my feet would not move. I caught her eye. She glared at me with her finger crooked.

"Come here, girl, you have a visitor."

It was too late to escape. I walked into the room and met Justin's amused smile. Immediately weakened at the sight of him, I struggled to regain my composure.

"I must apologize for her delay, my lord," Mrs Fitzherbert gushed. "She is often rude and inconsiderate. Look at her now! Barely says a word in greeting to you...even though you have so *graciously* called while in the area with the reference she forgot to obtain from you."

I found my voice. "Reference?"

Justin nodded, handing me a concealed envelope. "You forgot to take it with you, Miss Morgan."

"You need make no excuses, my lord," Mrs Fitzherbert interrupted. "You have done the girl a great service in delivering it." She eyed me critically. "Well, girl, aren't you going to thank him for his effort? You are strangely tongue-tied...don't stand there gaping!"

"I—I am grateful, my lord," I inclined my head, trying to avoid his mocking eyes.

"Well, you have wasted enough of his lordship's precious time...you'd better see him out and thank him properly."

"Yes, Mrs Fitzherbert."

Once we were alone in the parlor, I asked him, "have you really come all this way to hand me a reference?"

"What makes you think I came rushing here to see you at all? I might have come for the hunting..."

"The area is not known for its hunting."

"Really? Its society then."

"Nor its society."

"You are very severe on me." He took my hand to his lips. "I believe Mrs Fitzherbert will be losing a patient and long-suffering employee."

Was he asking me to return?

"Yes, Laura," he pulled me into his arms. "I am not asking you to return as my mistress but as my wife."

"Y—your wife?" I stammered. "But surely that can't be..."

"Olivia is dead."

I searched his face for the truth. "How?"

He shrugged. "I have spent the past months searching for her. She never reached Vincent. We believe she drowned aboard the *Victorious Rose* when she capsized in the channel. There is no record of her being on board, however, she must have been traveling incognito since we have proof of her intentions to meet Vincent...she left a letter. Lillian found it. We can only assume, since Olivia never arrived at her destination, that she died in the channel."

"Then you are free...?"

"Yes...the circumstances of Olivia's death change nothing of my feelings for her. Our marriage dissolved almost as soon as it started. I never loved her...or my first wife...I love only you."

He kissed me and a giddy excitement overcame me, as I knew I could now be his wife. We would never be separated again.

"When I first saw you, I thought you would enter my life somehow..." he murmured against my forehead. "I love you, my dearest, darling Laura."

The words sounded wonderful...I didn't want him to leave, not even for a moment.

His gaze was passionately intense. "When can we meet?"

"I have to give notice to Mrs Fitzherbert," I bit my lip.

He took my arm. "Then we shall announce it to her now."

"Now?" I choked.

"Yes, now."

"And my aunt and uncle?"

"I will formerly ask your uncle for your hand this afternoon," he caressed my cheek, "don't worry, my love, I will not let him hurt you again...and when he leaves this earth, we shall care for your aunt."

I wondered how he knew so much. He must have seen the question in my eyes and smiled. "I have been speaking to the new Mrs Carstares for the past two months on a regular basis...I wanted to know everything about my future wife."

"What of Cathy? How will she take the news?"

He laughed. "She was the one to prompt me to divorce Olivia. I think she has always been aware of my feelings for you..."

I touched his face in wonder. "I love you so much, Justin...is it truly possible? You are able to marry me?"

He half picked me up. "Yes, my darling! We will be married as soon as I can obtain a license—a week, no more. We shall be married here in the church."

I smiled, thinking of Elizabeth Rohan and how sweet my revenge would be. "Do you mind, my lord, that the celebrant to marry us once proposed to me?"

He disengaged my arms from around his neck. "I think it best if you return to your room now, sweet enchantress. I will seek out Mrs Fitzherbert. I am certain she will behave differently towards you in the hours and days ahead."

I reluctantly let go of him. "I can't bear to be parted from you."

His eyes filled with passionate promise. "Soon, my love. I will take you to Paris for our honeymoon...then we shall journey home to Silverthorn."

Mrs Fitzherbert behaved differently from the minute she was informed of our impending engagement.

After a short spasm of shock mingled with utter disbelief, she congratulated me on my grand success. I could see the question in her eyes over the following days—why would Lord Justin Braithfield choose a penniless girl like me to be the next mistress of Silverthorn?

I was too caught up in the whirlwind before the wedding to notice. Mrs Fitzherbert took it upon herself to act as guardian and advised me on my wedding trousseau.

I was a little nervous when we arrived at the Rectory for dinner two days before the wedding. Uncle Clive had given Justin his permission to wed me, as I knew he would. However, he had not asked to see me.

I could see the surprise in his eyes as he greeted me. He never imagined I would one day become the wife of a distinguished gentleman like Lord Justin Braithfield.

Tilly was unable to speak during the entire night. Edwin, once over his initial astonishment, was delighted to have the honor to wed us on Sunday.

Aunt Mary cried. "I always knew you would be rewarded...you were always such a good girl."

I wondered if she had guessed the truth about Madeline.

I was married from the Rectory.

My wedding gown, a gift from Mrs Fitzherbert, far exceeded my expectations. A lovely silk creation, I knew I would look my best on the day. My hair was expertly arranged on top of my head, held in place with Mrs Fitzherbert's own diamond and sapphire tiara.

Lady Beatrice sent me a pair of gloves to wear, expressing her regret that she was unable to attend due to contracting a fever.

I set out on Uncle Clive's arm, feeling a small twinge of nervousness at my first sight of the crowded pews. My gaze rested briefly on the Rohan pew. Adam was there. He looked at me with a strange, sad little smile. Beside him, Elizabeth smiled sweetly, suddenly keen to remember our childhood acquaintance and she later introduced herself to my husband as an 'old friend.'

Justin was wonderful. I will never forget the expression in his eyes as we exchanged our vows.

"Can things possibly get any better?" I said to him as our carriage door closed.

He drew me beside him. "I shall ask you again tomorrow..."

CHAPTER TWENTY

I shall always remember our honeymoon in Paris.

Justin was a passionate and sensitive lover and our happiness was complete. We traveled down to Italy and to Monte Carlo...places I had only dreamed about.

My new status as Lady Braithfield came with all manner of delicacies...prestige, respect, jewels, expensive gowns and accessories, the ability to travel in luxury...and a generous allowance. I warned Justin about the consequences of spoiling.

"You deserve to be spoilt...the mills are profitable this year."

"I should like to help you run the mills."

I read the astonishment in his face.

"It will give me an occupation...I haven't been bred for the life of a lady, you know."

I think he loved me more in that moment. I didn't want to live in Silverthorn's shadow like Madeline, Danielle and Olivia. I wanted to travel and to work. I could never fill my days with arranging flowers and filling in menu cards.

I never wanted our honeymoon to end. I sent a letter to Cathy while we were in Italy, informing her of the events leading up to our wedding. I wanted her to believe I married her father for love. "Perhaps we should visit her at the convent?"

Justin was anxious to get back to Silverthorn and his mills. "She will come back at the end of the season, overjoyed to have you for a step-mother...as will Brandon and Laura." He looked at me whimsically. "We have quite a large family for being married only a month."

"Has Vincent shown any interest in his son?"

Justin shrugged. "He was surprised to see Spencer and I on his doorstep. Perhaps surprised isn't the right word. Shocked, more like. After we stated our business, he seemed a little more relaxed. He asked once after Brandon."

"Shall he ever claim him?"

"No. He takes great pride in knowing that *his* son will have a share in Silverthorn."

"What if we have a son?"

Justin kissed me. "It is the governess in you always thinking ahead. We shall decide when the time comes."

The talk of the imminent future unnerved me. I felt uncomfortable going back to Silverthorn as its mistress.

"I have sent notice of our arrival," Justin told me on the eve of our departure. "Mrs Simmons will prepare the servants. I think Lillian guessed the reason for my journeying into Kent. She will not be surprised to find me returning with you as my wife."

"Will she think it odd your marrying a penniless orphan?"

"Your hair will turn gray, my darling, if you don't cease this nonsense. I assure you, all will be well. Lillian is mad. She will accept you in time."

"And Mrs Simmons?"

"Mrs Simmons knows her duty. She will do as she is bid. Perhaps you would feel more comfortable hiring a maid of your own?"

I couldn't abide the thought of a maid running after me. "No," I said firmly. "I will enlist Hetty or Emy to help me. I'm afraid I'm too self-sufficient to have someone dress and groom me."

I was so different to Danielle and Olivia I think I shocked him. Underneath, I knew he loved me for that very reason...and I was determined to stay that way. I couldn't bear the thought of turning into an Elizabeth Rohan.

Our journey across the channel was smooth.

I thought of the terrible tragedy of the *Victorious Rose*, picturing Olivia's last days, recklessly leaving her husband to join her lover abroad.

Justin refused to speak of her. I knew he was anxious to forget the troubles in his past. Two unfortunate wives and poorly managed textile mills. He had been extremely successful in the latter which perhaps compensated for the unhappiness in his personal life. I wanted to understand the past to understand the future...but Justin wouldn't speak of it.

Ruby had advised me to 'let go of the past.' I remembered her help in dressing me before the wedding. Perhaps I would ask her to come to Silverthorn when Uncle Clive died.

I could not help feeling nervous the day we started out for Yorkshire. How would the servants react? They knew me as a governess. How would they treat me as mistress?

I didn't know anything about being a grand lady and felt a little inadequate. I thought of Olivia's penchant for entertaining and knew I'd be a dismal failure. I had not been bred to spend money and was naturally frugal.

I would need a hobby, I decided. I would continue to teach Brandon and Laura...I would help Justin in the mills...and I should like to encourage Silverthorn's bloodlines in horseflesh.

My imminent 'ventures' kept my mind occupied throughout the journey.

However, as soon as we reached the town, my anxiety returned. How would the Ashtons react to my becoming Justin's wife? How would Mr Spencer take the news of his brother-in-law marrying another woman only months after his sister's death?

For some unexplainable reason, Silverthorn beckoned me. I could not escape...as much as I wanted to.

I had to face my destiny.

The coach came to a halt.

Mrs Simmons was waiting in the parlor with Maitlan. She greeted me warmly and I believed genuinely.

I could not say the same for Maitlan. He stared at me in undisguised scorn and I wondered why Justin disregarded his rudeness. 'Maitlan has been in the family for years,' he explained to me. 'I cannot turn the old man out.'

"Would you like me to arrange a maid, my lady?" Mrs Simmons asked.

I blushed. "Oh no. I can manage. If I need help, I'll call for Hetty or Emy."

"They are house maids, my lady. You need a lady's maid."

I felt foolish.

Justin noticed my uneasiness and laughed. "Mrs Simmons is quite right, you know. I told you we should have brought one from Paris..."

Suddenly, I felt unprepared for my new life at Silverthorn.

"I shall show you to your room, my lady," Mrs Simmons said. "I had it prepared especially."

I left Justin in the hall and followed Mrs Simmons to the west wing. I wanted to ask why I must be installed in the oldest part of the house. I knew it was the fashion for lords and ladies to have their own bedchambers but my instincts rebelled against it. I wanted to be with Justin, in any room...

"Are you all right?" Mrs Simmons examined my face. "Perhaps you should sit down...see...the room is prepared."

I looked around at the beautiful, elegant arrangements, thinking I would prefer any other room but this one. Madeline had slept here...Olivia had slept here...

"Will you be requiring anything else, my lady?"

"No, thank-you, Mrs Simmons. I think I shall rest awhile...and then I should like to see the children. Will you wake me at four o'clock?"

"Very well, my lady."

Alone in my room, I felt like a prisoner.

Voices from the past echoed through my mind. I could almost see Olivia's mocking smile, taunting me for usurping her place.

I was careful to conceal my feelings to Justin. He would be angry...I knew he wanted to forget her as much as I did. But how could I when I was installed in her room?

It was the loveliest room I had ever seen and yet I couldn't relax in it. The priceless Louis XIV and XV furniture...ornately carved glass brushes and combs...unique vases and ornaments...

I imagined Madeline would have become easily accustomed to such luxury but I could not. I never desired such things, even though everybody expected me to use them as mistress of Silverthorn.

Mistress of Silverthorn!

I laughed at myself. I didn't want the fancy title...I only wanted to be Justin's wife. Why did we have to come back? Why couldn't we stay in Paris?

He knocked softly on my door as I was dressing for dinner. I wore one of the lovely gowns he had purchased for me in Paris. It was a beautiful crepe the color of the softest mauve.

"You shouldn't tempt me before dinner," he kissed me lightly on my neck. "Are you ready? I'm anxious to get this over with."

"And return to the bedroom?"

He pulled me to him. "Isn't it the custom for newlyweds?"

I wished I could feel as easy as he could.

"Happy?"

His arms enclosed me around me. "Very happy."

"You need something special with that dress."   He removed something from his pocket and linked it around my neck.

I breathed in wonder at the sparkling array of amethyst. "I hope it didn't cost too much..."

"Nothing. It's an heirloom...with the other family jewels. When I came into the inheritance, I didn't have much use for jewels so I gave them to Lillian for safekeeping. I only just retrieved them from her now."

"H—how did she take the news?"

"She's waiting to meet the new Lady Braithfield with the children. Shall we join them?"

Seeing the children again dispelled some of my fears.

I have never seen them so radiant. Brandon whispered he didn't like Mrs Simmons and could I be their governess as well as their new mother?

Their acceptance prepared me to face Lillian.

She smiled when we entered the Drawing Room and when an opportunity arose, asked to have a private word with me.

I expected the worst.

Her brown eyes studied me pensively. "Mrs Simmons showed me the letter to prepare us for your arrival. I now understand why Justin disappeared so mysteriously...but I never expected he would marry you."

I thanked her for her candor. "I hope we shall be good friends. Please do not think I married your cousin for money."

"I know you are not a fortune hunter. You are sensible. I can see why Justin values you..."

I warmed to her. "Justin tells me Vincent plans to visit in the near future...we saw him unexpectedly in Monte Carlo."

Lillian's face lit up.

I had given her new hope.

Justin returned to the mills the following day.

I felt the loss of his presence acutely. Everything had changed...our honeymoon couldn't remain forever.

I thought it lonely being lady of the house.

Madeline had always discussed the duties and requirements of great ladies. She understood their world because she wanted to be part of it.

I supposed everyone would find me a very different Lady Braithfield. To disguise my inadequacy, I spent the bulk of my time with the children, leaving the running of the household to Mrs Simmons.

"Why have you changed your name?" Brandon asked suddenly. "I like Anne better than Laura."

"So do I," I confessed.

"Are you really Aunt Madeline's cousin?"

"Yes. I came here in disguise to find out what happened to her."

"She died..." Brandon told me. "Like Mama and Olivia...you won't die, will you?"

I promised him I wouldn't—if I could help it.

Brandon smiled sunnily up at me before putting his podgy arms around my neck. "I love you, mama..."

"Well, if it isn't the governess turned mistress of the house..."

Vincent came into the room, a smug smile on his handsome face. I smiled in welcome. It was impossible to ignore his charm—he had an ability of weaving it around those less disposed to his character.

"I know you didn't expect me to take up your invitation so promptly..."

"Does Justin know you are here?"

"Where is the old boy? Working at the mill, I suppose. It was always his passion."

"What is your passion, Uncle Vince?" Brandon asked innocently.

Vincent grinned at the boy. "I am known to be an expert on sensitive creatures..."

Brandon's brow ruffled. "Like flowers?"

"Yes...similar to flowers. Some roses have sharp thorns, you know."

I turned away. Justin wouldn't be happy to have him here so early. How like him to arrive unannounced and premature? "Has Mrs Simmons directed you to a room?"

He smiled. "Yes. I am happily installed in the west wing...just down the hall from you. Cozy, don't you think?"

I could feel my cheeks burning and was relieved when Lillian arrived to take Vincent away. She appeared shocked by his visit but recovered quickly. I guess she was wondering, as I was, how Justin would take the news.

The afternoon passed quickly.

The Ashtons called with Theresa. I received them in the sun-lit courtyard, a little nervous over my new status.

To my relief, nothing had changed.

"I will never forgive you," Brett said, "for running off like that and then returning as Lady Braithfield. How did you manage it?"

I told them of the events leading up to Justin's arrival in my hometown. Theresa could not stop a few tears at the story and Eliza was equally sympathetic while Tabitha remained in awe. One didn't hear of a governess marrying into the quality every day.

Theresa entwined her arm with mine as I accompanied them to their carriage. "I feel a little ill with this child but I promise to return by the end of the week. I am anxious to spend the day alone with you." She examined me. "I've never seen you so radiant. You look beautiful."

"I never thought such happiness was possible..."

"Good. Nobody deserves it more than you, Laura." She kissed my cheek. "I shall return on Friday then."

I was anxious for them to leave as much as I enjoyed their company. I had to warn Justin about Vincent's arrival...

"Looking for me, cousin?"

Vincent joined me outside to wave off my visitors. "You know...you and I should get to know each other very well. We are connected in a bizarre sort of way."

"How exactly?"

"How quick you are to question me! It is the teacher in you, I suspect...how odd to think you are Madeline's cousin."

I felt my face flush. Our conversation in Monte Carlo only covered history and local gossip. "How do you know?"

He grinned. "Lillian. She is devoted to me."

"I hope you mean to act on your affection for her."

"Now who is being impertinent?"

I said nothing.

"Madeline and I were lovers...I believe I may have loved her for a time."

"Really?" I could disguise the sarcasm in my voice.

"Yes, really," he repeated. "I was as shocked as you by news of her death...especially in her delicate condition. I never believed in the verdict."

"Was Madeline with child? How do you know?"

"Because I was the father..."

"And you believe the gypsy murdered her?"

He nodded. "She planned to cut him loose. The vermin simply reached her first."

We walked a little further. "I came here to find out what had happened to her..." I began slowly. "I never believed for a moment I would belong permanently to Silverthorn."

"Yes...one can never expect these things. But I warn you, my dear new cousin, look to the past...you will see a pattern emerging."

I returned alone to the west wing.

As always, I felt a twinge of uneasiness as I walked down the deserted halls. There was something about the west wing that I found unfriendly...I imagined the ghost of Eleanor...pacing the abandoned corridors. I could almost feel her sad eyes watching me...warning me of danger.

Yes, I was afraid. Vincent's return unnerved me. Why was he here? I knew he wanted Silverthorn—always felt it should have passed to him. Perhaps that was why he had returned...Brandon's inheritance was now threatened with my arrival. What if I should give birth to a son?

I must tell Justin my fears. I would go to my room, dress for dinner, and wait for his return.

But I warn you, my dear cousin, look to the past...you will see a pattern emerging.

Vincent's words haunted me for the next hour. I locked the door to my room. I could not forget how he had seduced Danielle and Olivia. Would I be his next target?

The thought chilled me.

I sat on the edge of the bed, my nerves raw with fright. I heard every creak and moan. I fancied, for one heart-wrenching moment, footsteps pausing at my door...

Would he attack me so openly?

I heard a faint scratching sound on the connecting door and froze.

"Who is it?" I called out.

"Justin, who else?"

I went to open the door, feeling the relief flood my face.

"Why did you lock the door?"

I did not want to appear foolish. "I don't know...precaution, I suppose."

By his look, I could tell Mrs Simmons had told him of Vincent's arrival. He asked if I had spoken with him. I told him of my entire conversation with Vincent.

"He wouldn't have the slightest idea how to handle you..." Justin kissed me. "You are incorrigibly sharp-tongued."

"Yes, I scathed him once or twice. Why do you think he has come?"

"Not to seduce you, I hope, for he will be severely disappointed."

I wished I could remain in his arms forever...but Vincent's words kept taunting me. *Look to the past...you will see a pattern forming.* Suddenly, I felt uneasy. How much did I really know about my husband? Did I know him well enough to discount murder? He hated Madeline for disrupting his life...he publicly seemed to tolerate Danielle's affair Vincent but some suggested her 'riding accident' was no accident. And Olivia? She too stood in his way...

"Are you all right, darling?"

I forced a smile. "Yes...I've a slight headache."

He searched my eyes. "Is that all?"

I wanted to tell him how I felt...but I couldn't. Self-preservation prevailed upon me.

"You look pale," Justin murmured, "are you certain nothing is wrong?"

For a moment, I thought I could tell him my stupid fears. I wanted to hear his laugh of reassurance. "I—I think I will stay and rest...perhaps tomorrow I will feel better."

It was not completely a lie. I was feeling anxious. I hated this room...I hated the memory of Danielle and Olivia and most of all I hated my own doubts about my husband.

I needed time to collect my senses.

I didn't see Justin until the following morning.

I felt strangely uncomfortable without his presence next to me. The faces of the past three mistresses of Silverthorn came to haunt me. I recognized a faintly amused Madeline, a concerned Danielle and a mocking Olivia. I tried to push their images from my mind but they wouldn't go away.

I saw Madeline sitting in the chair by the hearth...dressed in her nun's habit the night of the ball...the night of her death. She appeared calm, her hands interlocked in front of her belly.

"Madeline?"

My puny voice barely echoed in the silence.

She frowned at me. "Beware of those closest to you..."

Before I could ask more questions, she vanished. I rushed to the connecting door. I didn't want to be alone...I didn't want the doubts.

My hand rested on the knob. I couldn't turn it as much as I wanted to. Madeline's warning rung in my ears, *beware of those closest to you.*

Could her warning hold some truth? The terrible question still attacked my mind when Justin appeared early in the morning beside my bed. He held my hand and inquired after my health. I replied that my sleepless night had worsened my headache.

"Then rest," he kissed my forehead, "and I shall see you later."

"Vincent?" I prompted.

"He will occupy himself in town today so you needn't worry."

I felt an overwhelming sense of relief as I watched him go. Without Vincent and Justin, I hoped to regain my usual composure. My doubts were unfounded and bordering on the ridiculous.

I reached for the bell beside me. I would send for Emy to help me dress...then I would have breakfast. One always felt better after food. Afterwards...I would visit Lillian and keep the afternoon free for Theresa and the children.

As Emy helped me dress, I tried to forget about Madeline...and her warning.

"Are ye all right, m'lady?" Emy peered into my face.

"Oh, yes," I smiled serenely. "I think I shall go for a walk...it always clears one's mind."

I left her to attend to my room, relieved to be alone. I knew I alone had to dispel these fanciful thoughts and feelings. I had imagined Madeline warning me in my idleness.

Content with the fact, I climbed the narrow, stone stairs up to Lillian's Tower. I tried the ancient latch, expecting it to be locked. To my surprise, it opened and I entered, calling Lillian's name softly. When she didn't answer, I thought I would wait awhile for her to return.

It had been some time since I'd last visited her in the Tower. I could almost feel the haunted, stale atmosphere and a small shiver ran down my spine. I studied the old tapestries of Eleanor and Cecily on the walls...reminding me of the dismal tale.

At least, some new decorations had cheered the room. I noted new hangings and drapes and a row of new pictures on the far wall. A flicker of light caught my eye and I looked back at the pictures. Something was oddly familiar...

I got up to have a look.

Madeline's portrait! It was flanked by Olivia's portrait and Danielle's likeness.

The three women who had tormented Justin's life...I knew he wouldn't permit them to be shown in the portrait gallery so Lillian had placed them here. I examined Danielle...she reminded me of Cathy with her pert, pretty face and golden hair. Beside her, Madeline seemed foreign and exotic with her tawny hair, green eyes and seductive smile. I drew my gaze away from her to view the cool, glacial beauty of Olivia, thinking my portrait would seem very dull compared with these three.

"How convenient of you to oblige me."

I turned at the voice of Lillian. She was standing quietly by the door, her hand resting on the knob. She looked peculiar...the warmth removed from her usually warm brown eyes.

She shut the door and moved stealthily towards me, following my gaze to the row of portraits...

I felt sickened. "I—It was y—you, wasn't it?"

Lillian crossed her arms. "Poor, simple Laura.... coming all this way to discover what happened to your cousin...you were not satisfied with the verdict of suicide—you had to come and find out for yourself. You were wise to leave when you did." She studied me thoughtfully. "Why did you return? Cecily hates you...she will kill you."

"Cecily?" I asked in a shaky voice.

Lillian cocked a brow, her lack of wit suddenly replaced with something sinister. "Oh, yes, I am Cecily. Haven't we met?"

My mind drummed, struggling to remember the story of the two sisters.

She shook her head. "You have an extremely short memory...I am disappointed in you. You, like they, think I am mad. But I am not mad. I am clever. They say 'poor mad Lillian'—she can't do anything.'"

"But Cecily can?"

She nodded. "You do understand. You have known me as Eleanor but Cecily is quite different. Cecily doesn't like you. Cecily was the one who stole your letters and showed them to Justin; driving you away...Cecily was the one who knew who you were for a long time...Madeline's little cousin. She didn't know at first, of course, until she watched you come to the west wing that night..."

I gasped. "You're the ghost!"

"A little haunting keeps away the suspicious. But you were determined to continue your search, weren't you? You made a few errors, which is not surprising for an amateur. You said you'd come from Cornwall but you told Cathy your home was in Devon at a Rectory. Your interest in your cousin was too transparent...your feelings gave you away. Then you foolishly surrounded yourself with that imbecile woman you call your 'governess' who called you by your real name. Do you remember? How relieved you looked when you thought nobody noticed the *faux paux*? You were too worried about Cathy to be concerned with me."

I met her eyes. "Why didn't you turn me in then?"

"Because I knew Justin would want more proof. Hence the letters."

"You knew he would dismiss me?"

She smiled. "I guessed his interest in you long before I found out who you really were...but I wasn't going to allow a little nobody governess ruin all my careful plans."

Suddenly, the pieces came together. I took a step backward, terrified and sickened by the awful truth. "T—there was no accident...was there...with Danielle?"

"No. I placed a piece of tin in her saddle...it all happened so naturally—no one might have known. You are the first to guess. She plagued Justin's life...I knew he wanted to kill her...but he is too honorable. I knew he'd never consider me romantically until all the women were removed from his life. He was destined to inherit Silverthorn with *me*...and it would have been that way if your meddling cousin hadn't succeeded in bagging my father."

"You killed her, didn't you?"

"I remember the day she arrived...she thought she was clever in fostering a bastard on my father...poor, simple-minded fool would never have guessed. He was blinded by her beauty and her charm...he wouldn't hear an ill word about her. Justin didn't like her...he guessed the truth about her. She tried to seduce him once...and failed. He told my father of it and called him an old blind fool when he refused to listen. My father wanted proof...the fact that Madeline gave birth prematurely to little Laura did not convince him."

"What did?" I asked, struggling to remain calm. Oh, where was Justin?

Lillian stared up at her portrait, a slow smile tugging at the corners of her mouth. "Madeline thought she could outwit me...she used to make fun of me and when she discovered my 'supposed' interest in Vincent, she was determined to seduce him in front of me.

I saw them together...I knew then I couldn't let this baggage sully Silverthorn any longer. My father was poorly...and she was nursing him. How easy it would be for her to slip a little extra laudanum into his medicine...but the opportunity never arose. I told him what I'd witnessed and the truth killed him.

Without him, Madeline struggled to retain her position. She wanted Silverthorn...and since Justin was to inherit, she thought she could ensnare him like she did Vincent and poor Brett Ashton. But Justin was immune to her calculated charm. She thought she would have time to win him over...after she took care of someone threatening to ruin her."

"Lucian the gypsy..."

Lillian was impressed. "The poor simple fellow only wanted money. She used to meet him up there—" she gestured up the stairs to the turret chamber. "She thought she had the right...to sneak into my private Tower without asking. She planned to move me to an asylum...so she could use the Tower for her own private adventures...she would have succeeded if Cecily hadn't come to my rescue."

"On the night of the ball?"

"A perfect time to commit murder...I followed her to the Tower and waited in the shadows. The gypsy arrived. When he demanded more money, she removed a pistol from her nun's habit and shot him. She thought to hide the weapon in my Tower...she was looking for a place when I stepped out of the shadows."

"Was she surprised to see you?"

"No. She thought I was harmless and tried to convince me she killed the gypsy in self-defense. But she couldn't fool Cecily, even with her tears. Cecily told her she would not succeed in winning Justin and Silverthorn. She smiled strangely in response and patted her belly, 'do you know what is growing in my belly, poor, mad Lillian? A son...he will be heir and I shall cheat you all out of it.' Satisfied with her cleverness, she tossed the pistol in an empty chest...come, I will show you the one."

I followed her numbly up the narrow, winding turret stairs. My heart beat furiously...I prayed Justin would find me in time. I had stumbled upon a monster...a clever, sinister woman who killed in the name of Cecily...

"Here..." Lillian led me into the small, darkened room. "Is this not a good place to hide a blood-stained weapon?"

I looked at the large, oak chest and nodded.

"After she hid the weapon, she glanced out of that window...perhaps feeling a little regret over her cruelty to Eleanor...but it was too late. Cecily pushed her out of the window and laughed when her head split on the road below. She laughed too when the coroner decided suicide...I should have won then for all my hard effort but Justin had to marry that ice beauty."

"Olivia?"

"Yes. I warned him from the start but he wouldn't listen. It wasn't difficult to destroy the marriage once Justin discovered what he'd married. A visit from Vincent, I knew, would accomplish the task. So I wrote him a letter, informing him of the wedding."

"You asked him to come?"

"It was all for Justin's benefit. I was the one to steal the key to the silver cabinet ruining Olivia's stupid ball. She was so fickle...even attempted to be friendly towards me for a time. However, I knew how to play her. Everyone saw Vincent and her together...therefore, it was easy to convince everyone of her flight to him. Fortunately, a ship sunk two days later. Once I learned of it, I simply wrote a note copying her childish scrawl confirming her plans to be with her lover. No one doubted the authenticity of the letter...not even Justin. I planned it so that he would never know."

I could feel the chill in my spine. I wanted her to stop...I wanted to shut out this evil.

There was a strange glint in her eyes as she continued: "...do you want to know where her body is? It is not lying at the bottom of the sea but in that chest...with Madeline's pistol. No one will find them. I shall probably put you there too..."

I struggled to find my voice. I knew I had to keep her talking...I needed more time...surely someone would come looking for me?

"I can see the terror in your eyes," Lillian began in a quiet voice, so deadly and foreign I hardly recognized it. "You should have obliged me by dying in that vault...yes, Cecily followed you there...she wasn't going to allow a governess to steal the man and the inheritance that rightfully belonged to her."

Lillian was watching me carefully, barring the stairwell should I try to escape. "I do like you, you know. You tried to be kind without being condescending—even in your triumphal return as Justin's wife. I enjoyed killing the others but with you...it is different. But Cecily must have her way. She cannot allow anybody to inherit but herself and her offspring..."

Suddenly, I fell against the wall, sickened with a dreadful thought. "Did you...start the fire in the schoolroom?"

Lillian raised a brow in surprise. "Of course I did! I thought a fire would look natural...pity you saved the boy. Cecily was angry with you...you are always trying to meddle...it is dangerous to meddle, you know..."

She began walking towards me. I felt trapped, weakened, utter numb. I could see the evil in her eyes...there was no use trying to reason.

Lillian!

No one would ever suspect her. I despaired. I would never be found.

She had a dagger in her hand.

I stepped backwards until I reached the landing where Madeline had fallen to her death. "Don't do this Cecily..." I begged, "I will help you. I am not like the others, like you said."

For one brief moment, I thought she might consider my plea.

But the sensation was soon replaced by ruthless desire.

I screamed.

Lillian laughed. "No one will hear you, you stupid imbecile. We are alone...and these walls are thick."

I glanced nervously at the chest. Would they find me? I thought of the gruesome remains lying in that chest and shuddered.

She was alarmingly close. The gleam in her eye intensified my terror. I stepped as far back as I could, looking around desperately for a weapon of some kind.

There was nothing but my own puny strength.

She lunged and I threw myself to one side, landing on the floor. Recovering quickly, enough to deflect her next attack, I screamed again, praying someone would hear.

Lillian laughed, her eyes glazed, as she chased me around the room.

I had to control my fear. "Why didn't you kill Cathy while you were at it?"

She didn't like my words. "I am fond of Cathy."

"If only she knew who you really were—she would spit on you!"

She caught the tail of my dress and spun me towards her. I shot out my hand, feeling the sharp edge of the blade. I had to get the dagger...

I rolled away from her attack, taking her with me. Her strength astonished me and I feared I could not continue to deflect her blows. In one crazed attempt, I scratched her face and retrieved the knife.

I threw it out the window.

Her hands settled like an iron band around my neck. I fell to my knees, struggling for breath. I saw Lillian's crazed face above me, twisted in sinister triumph...

A dull thud brought Lillian crashing to the floor.

I choked and spluttered, looking around for my savior.

Mrs Simmons peered into my eyes. "Are you all right?"

I looked down at Lillian and managed a little nod.

Mrs Simmons kept a wary eye on Lillian. "I was looking for you...the children were worried when you failed to arrive. Emy told me you went to visit Lillian in the Tower."

I could feel the tears burning my eyes. Dear Mrs Simmons! So astute with the affairs of the household...

"We'd best get your hand seen to," she said motherly. "Let me take a look."

"H—how did you know?"

She followed my gaze to the unconscious Lillian. "I have known for some time—of her dangerous tendencies. I have been monitoring her movements...I knew she was up to no good when my clothes started to go missing..."

"I—I thought I saw you once or twice..."

She nodded. "It was Lillian."

"Did you know about the murders?"

She frowned in confusion and was about to say something when Justin appeared. He took in the whole scene, with a mixture of fear and anger...until he saw me.

How could I ever have doubted him?

He rushed to my side and took me in his arms. "My darling...don't talk...it's all right now...I'm here now..."

EPILOGUE

An excavation of Lillian's Tower began the following day.

Greg came over to dress my hand while Theresa tried to lighten the situation. I knew the moment would come...and it was very soon. What would be in that oak chest?

Lillian had thrown away the key before she was taken away.

"When does Cathy return?" Theresa asked.

I shrugged, watching Brandon and Laura play in the corner. To think Lillian intended to kill the poor boy!

"She is the insane one of the family," Vincent replied charmingly, "just as I am the villain of the family. You see I am now acquitted of all crimes...in fact, I can scarcely believe this of Lillian...she always appeared so fragile."

"More the deadly for keeping the pretence," Theresa smiled. "At least, Madeline can now be put to rest."

"Lucky Mrs Simmons arrived when she did," Theresa went on, "I shouldn't like to imagine what might have happened...ah well...Miss Lillian should make a nice addition to the asylum...I believe his lordship has secured a permanent place for her there with extra protection."

I recalled the night before, how Justin and I came to understand one another. I told him all of my foolish fears and doubts—to which he patiently listened. We spoke of the past...of the three doomed mistresses...of Lillian...and the events leading up to her attempt to murder me.

I did not feel comfortable discussing Lillian. I had experienced her sinister hidden personality...and survived. I never wanted to think of her again.

They found Olivia at noon. Justin's face was very grim when he returned to me with the news. I examined him closely.

He must have seen the question in my eyes. "No, finding her doesn't change anything between us. I never loved her. I love only you, my prying little governess."

"Madeline wanted you..."

"Your cousin wanted Silverthorn—and I was her means to getting it."

That was the last time we spoke of Madeline...and the past.

Olivia was buried in the Weston family plot near the village church. Mr Spencer Weston decided not to have the murder of his sister tried in public.

Mrs Simmons and I are the best of friends. I can never thank her enough for saving my life. She doesn't like to be thanked—as she is a very private and professional woman. I know she will be a stalwart figure in the years ahead.

Cathy came home the following spring.
    Justin and I decided she should be told the truth about Lillian.
    "Is it really true? How could she have done all those vile things?"
    "She told me she wanted Silverthorn and your father."
    Cathy examined me in terror. "She tried to kill you..."
    "But I survived."
    "I'm glad!" She hugged me, "you are my dearest friend. Oh, it is good to be home! I shan't want to leave again...perhaps you can persuade Papa to let me stay? I know he will listen to you...especially as you are soon to provide the long-awaited heir. I wonder at Uncle Vincent...causing a scandal by claiming Brandon as his own son! I shall *have* to stay now...for little Laura needs a big sister."
    "She does," I smiled fondly at the girl I had grown to love.

Uncle Clive died in the spring.
    Aunt Mary went to live with Lady Beatrice and they both make the journey to Silverthorn every year. This year they had news to tell.
    "We have heard," Lady Beatrice began, "that the occupants of Rohan House have been evicted. It appears Lord Adam lost his inheritance to a game of cards. His mother has disowned him on hearing the news while his wife—Lady Rohan—left him to live with her father in town after his last bastard was born. Shocking business, isn't it?"
    I thought of poor, gentle Josie—the victim of Adam's debauchery.
    Aunt Mary squeezed my hand, giving a shameful look as Beatrice continued relentlessly: "but, my dear Lady Braithfield, there is more. Miss Elizabeth Rohan, having lost her dowry due to her brother's incessant gambling, is now forced into service to provide for herself and her mother—and her employer is none other than Mrs Fitzherbert!"

I often wonder at the gamble of life and how things came to be.
    If Madeline had never met crazed Lord Braithfield in London, my life might have turned out very differently. I thought she would be amused to know I owed my happy state to her wanton, adventurous spirit.
    My husband is wonderful...and my son, Conrad, has healed the wounds of the past. I can feel Madeline's smile upon us, unwilling to let go, which is why I cannot forget her.
    I never speak of Madeline to Justin...or her restless spirit.
    The book of the past is now closed.

We have the future to live for.

Made in the USA
Lexington, KY
03 February 2013